William Hepworth Dixon

# Robert Blake

Admiral and General at Sea

William Hepworth Dixon

**Robert Blake**
*Admiral and General at Sea*

ISBN/EAN: 9783337753795

Printed in Europe, USA, Canada, Australia, Japan

Cover: Foto ©Raphael Reischuk / pixelio.de

More available books at **www.hansebooks.com**

# ROBERT BLAKE

## ADMIRAL AND GENERAL AT SEA

BASED ON FAMILY AND STATE PAPERS

BY

## WILLIAM HEPWORTH DIXON

*A NEW EDITION*

*WITH TEN ILLUSTRATIONS IN PERMANENT
PHOTOGRAPHY*

LONDON
BICKERS AND SON, LEICESTER SQUARE
1885

TO

HIS EXCELLENCY

# SIR WILLIAM REID, K.C.B.,

GOVERNOR OF MALTA,

AND

AUTHOR OF "THE THEORY OF THE LAW OF STORMS,"

This History is inscribed.

# PREFACE.

I VERY willingly meet the flattering request—preferred by many correspondents unknown to me—for the issue of a cheap edition of 'Robert Blake.'  My unknown friends are pleased to think its wider perusal will do good: if so, the whole merit is due to the theme.  Blake is the very model of a British sailor—gentle, pious, resolute, and fearless.  My purpose in writing the book was to make known to a wider circle the simple virtue, the deep religious feeling, and the moderate views of a man whose supreme military and naval genius place him in the highest class of great captains.  Few readers have leisure for the perusal of manuscript state papers and family records, or even for a study of the brighter and more amusing procession of satires, eulogies, and proclamations of a past age. Few, therefore, have known anything of Blake beyond the vague and slender outline drawn by Clarendon and the royalist writers ; and the man who, next to Cromwell, was the foremost personage in England during the most troubled and glorious part of the seventeenth century, has been little more than a colossal name.

The defender of Lyme and Taunton—the chastiser of Rupert—the conqueror of Van Tromp, De Ruiter, and De Witt—the hero of Porto Ferino and Santa Cruz—the negociator with Italy—the liberator of Christian slaves—deserved to be better known. The detail of his life was as beautiful as the aggregate was glorious. Blake's ruling principle—like that of a man equally illustrious in our own day—was duty. When some of his captains wished to revolt against Cromwell, he replied, "It is not our business to mind State affairs, but to keep foreigners from fooling us." Blake disapproved of Cromwell's usurpation; but he was watching Tromp, then at the head of a powerful fleet, and any hesitation in the navy would have been disastrous to his country. His words became as famous in the navy of that time, as the device "England expects every man will do his duty" became in the days of our fathers.

One part of the naval career of Blake is of striking interest. He was the first man who broke through the old delusion that ships could not attack batteries. On three memorable occasions Blake attacked stone walls—at St. Mary's, at Porto Ferino, and at Santa Cruz—and each time with complete success. Contemporaries at first thought him mad, as contemporaries often think men of genius; and the enemies whom he destroyed behind their granite walls, consoled themselves with saying he was the devil. Even after his death, the wonder did not cease. Clarendon, a political opponent, says of him :—

"He was the first man that declined the old track, and made it manifest that the science might be attained in less time than was imagined; and despised those rules which had long been in practice, to keep his ship and his men out of danger, which had been held in former times a point of great ability and circumspection, as if the principal art requisite in the captain of a ship had been to be sure to come home safe again. He was the first man who brought the ships to contemn castles on shore, which had been thought ever very formidable, and were discovered by him only to make a noise, and to fright those who could rarely be hurt by them. He was the first that infused that proportion of courage into the seamen, by making them see by experience what mighty things they could do if they were resolved, and taught them to fight in fire as well as upon water : and though he hath been very well imitated and followed, he was the first that drew the copy of naval courage, and bold and resolute achievement."

There are officers who still think it madness to oppose ships to batteries, though steam has added wings to the man-of-war, enabling it to attack how and when it pleases, to retire from the range, to return at will, to shift the position, to defy winds and tides. There are still officers who think their chief business to lie in coming "home safe again." Blake was of another mind; Nelson was of another mind; Dundonald, I believe, is of another mind. Santa Cruz was Blake's

Cronstadt—one of the strongest fortresses of the seventeenth century: when Blake attacked it with his worn and rotting ships, it was strengthened by an enormous fleet—a fleet carrying nearly as many guns, and far more men, than his own. The Spaniards were as confident as the Muscovites in the impregnability of their fortress. Yet he entered the harbour, silenced the batteries, and burnt the fleet.

The royalist writers were overpowered by this brilliant feat of arms.

Bates, who speaks of the "unparalleled boldness" of the action, says :—"He found the harbour in shape of a crescent, defended by seven forts lying round it, and two castles placed at the points, with seventeen ships riding therein, their heads standing towards the mouth of the harbour, that they might fire with greater certainty upon those that offered to enter : nor could the Governor forbear to jeer and flout at the English. Blake, therefore, entering the mouth of the harbour with his frigates, thunders broadsides and small shot against the castles, till the soldiers flying from thence, he manned his boats with seamen and sent them in, who burnt and destroyed all the Spanish ships that were there."

Warwick says :—"Blake's rash and daring attempt proved very fortunate and glorious."

"Of all the desperate enterprises," says Heath, "that ever were made in the world against an enemy at sea, this of the noble Blake's is not inferior to any."

Clarendon speaks still more admiringly:—"The whole

action was so miraculous, that all men who knew the place concluded that no sober man, with what courage soever endued, would ever undertake it; and they could hardly persuade themselves to believe what they had done : whilst the Spaniards comforted themselves with the belief that they were devils, and not men, who had destroyed them in such a manner. So much a strong resolution of bold and courageous men can bring to pass, that no resistance and advantage of ground can disappoint them. And it can hardly be imagined how small loss the English sustained in this unparalleled action—not one ship being left behind, and the killed and wounded not exceeding two hundred men; when the slaughter on board the Spanish ships and on the shore was incredible."

Common men, of course, adhere to the common opinion : but uncommon men see that Blake was right, as well as successful, in attacking Santa Cruz. The most brilliant seaman of our generation—the true successor of Blake and Nelson—Lord Dundonald (who has done me the very great honour of revising the naval part of this narrative), has written some brief and pregnant notes on Blake's most celebrated actions. This was before the Russian war broke out, and long before the question of attacking Helsingfors and Cronstadt arose. With respect to Blake's attack on Santa Cruz, Lord Dundonald says, in a profound and characteristic passage :—" On the principle which I have never found to fail—that the more impracticable a task appears, the more easily it may be achieved, under judicious management—the attack on Santa Cruz was founded on a correct estimate of the probable result."

With this testimony of a man of genius, I commit my work to the reader; adding, that I have very carefully revised the new edition, in the hope of making it less unworthy of its illustrious subject, and of the favour with which it has been received by the public.

W. H. D.

# CONTENTS.

# LIST OF ILLUSTRATIONS.

# ROBERT BLAKE

# ROBERT BLAKE.

## CHAPTER I.

### 1599—1625.

### THE SCHOLAR.

In the early part of the seventeenth century the country lying between the South Channel and the river Severn was the most beautiful and important part of England. While Liverpool was still a swamp, and Manchester a straggling hamlet, when Leeds was a cluster of mud huts, and the romantic valley of the Calder a desolate gorge, the streets of Taunton, Exeter and Dunster resounded with arts and industry; and the merchant-ships of Bridgwater and Bristol were going out or coming in from the remotest corners of the globe. The fairest fields, the richest cities, the proudest strongholds lay in this region. The vales of Stroud, Honiton and Evesham are still unrivalled. When the vine grew in our latitudes it attained its highest perfection on the sunny slopes of Somerset and Devon; and a royal sybarite, whose taste at least has never been impugned, declared that in those days the south-west coast was the only part of England fit for the habitation of a gentleman.

The towns were in equal repute with the country.

Taunton was famous for its woollens while the Plantagenets were yet on the throne; in later times a band of industrious Flemings, flying from the persecutions of the Duke of Alva, brought their knowledge, enterprise and capital into the town, and under their teaching it soon obtained an equal reputation for serges. Parliament fostered these rising trades, and " Tauntons " were then as well known in the markets as are now Manchester cottons and Spitalfields silks. While the Yorkshire breeder of sheep was either too indolent or too ignorant to convert the wool of his native downs into an article of trade, the workmen of the western city obtained by the process wealth, cultivation and political power.

Bristol, inferior in population and maritime resources only to London, had long aspired to the honours of a western metropolis. Its history looked back to the remotest times. Its docks, its streets, its religious edifices, its gates and decaying fortifications, all bore testimony to its ancient grandeur. Only the city of London yielded a larger return to the royal exchequer. Commissions, commissioners and pursuivants levied money under many pretexts from its opulent traders, and the armies of Ireland and Scotland were frequently recruited among its hardy and adventurous population. From its situation as a point of departure for the west and south, it had gradually obtained a monopoly of Irish commerce. Its vessels visited the harbours of Portugal and Spain, whence they brought home the treasures of two worlds in exchange for the woollen cloths which constituted our sole manufacture. As its great houses increased in means, their enterprises took a bolder range. No longer satisfied to share their gains with the Iberian, they sought by new discoveries to win for their own port such advantages as Columbus had won for the Spaniard and Vasco de Gama for the Portuguese. Cabot had sailed from their river on his first adventure, and four of the five small vessels which composed his fleet were supplied by the Severn merchants. In voyages undertaken at their expense, he had added Newfoundland, Nova Scotia, and North America as far as the inlet of the Chesapeake, to the known regions of the world, and established a connexion with Hispaniola, Porto Rico and the coasts of Brazil, which was not abandoned even when the government, in virtue of a treaty to that end, gave up the rights of English discovery in those regions to the crown of Arragon and Castile. Inspired by these successes in the far west, they fitted out an expedition for the Arctic Ocean, and sent it forth to search for a new passage northward to China and Hindustan. These spirited men pursued their enterprise with admirable zeal; and only failed to rival the fame of more celebrated discoverers because nature had left them no outlet to find in that direction.

One of the most active of the Severn merchants in the latter part of the sixteenth century was Humphrey Blake of Plansfield and Bridgwater, father of the renowned Admiral. Humphrey's father, Robert Blake, the first of his family to step out of the narrow circle of a country life, removed at an early age from Tuxwell, the seat of his ancestors for several generations, to Bridgwater, where he hoped to share the abundant harvests of the Spanish trade. Where the family of this Robert Blake was first settled is unknown. Tradition gives it a home in Northumberland and derives the name from the river Aplacke in that county. The first of the Somersetshire Blakes whose name I have found, is Humphrey Blake who lived in the reign of Henry VIII., and held the estate of Tuxwell, in the parish of Bishop's Lydyard, in capite, by the payment of the fortieth part of the knight's fee. He had three sons, John, Thomas, and Robert; to the last of whom, when he died in 1558, he left the manor of Tuxwell. This Robert Blake was he who removed to Bridgwater, where he married Margaret Symonds, improved his scanty fortunes by commerce, and during a long life retained the respect and confidence of his fellow-citizens. He had the honour to serve as chief magistrate in his adopted town three times, in 1573, in 1579 and in 1587, as appears by inscriptions still preserved on panels in the Town-hall of Bridgwater. At his death, which occurred in October 1592, he bequeathed the large sum of 240*l.*, to relieve the poor and repair the causeways; setting an example of liberality to his townsmen and descendants which the latter at least piously followed. His son, Humphrey, succeeded to the estate and business. The property was not inconsiderable. He married a lady of good family and fortune; Sara Williams, widow of a gentleman named Smithers, and on her he settled at his marriage the lordship of Puriton together with divers lands and messuages in Puriton, Catcote, Bawdrippe, and Wollamington. Plansfield, which has always been described as the original seat of the Admiral's ancestors, was probably the dower of his mother. It had belonged to her family for generations; had been granted by Henry VII., to Sir John Williams after the Perkin Warbeck troubles, and had descended from him to Reginald Williams, John Williams and Sir Nicholas Williams, at whose death it reverted to the crown for lack of male issue; and it had been restored by Queen Elizabeth to Mabel, his widow. The Admiral's father was certainly the first of the Blakes who owned the manor of Plansfield. In the Heralds' Visitation of Somerset in 1523, he is styled Humphrey Blake of Plansfield, son of Robert Blake of Bridgwater.

Sara Williams, like Cromwell's mother, also a widow,

brought blood to the family. Robert, the Admiral, was her first son. He was born towards the end of August, 1598, and received the rite of baptism at the parish church of Bridgwater, on the 27th of September in that year. He was called Robert, in pious remembrance of his grandfather. Many children followed; in all twelve boys—Humphrey in 1600; William in 1603; George, who died in infancy, in 1604; George, the second of that name, in 1606; Samuel in 1608; Nicholas in 1609; Edward, who died in infancy, in 1611; Benjamin, who died in infancy, in 1612; Edward, the second of that name (he also died in infancy), in 1613; Benjamin, second of the same name, in 1614; John, who died in infancy, in 1617; and Alexander in 1619. The number of girls is not ascertainable, in consequence of irregularities in the registers; but the Admiral's will mentions two of his sisters—Bridget, who married Mr. Bowdich, of Chard, and another not referred to by her maiden name. The Heralds' Visitation speaks of a Mrs. Burrage as being one of Humphrey Blake's daughters; but this is probably a misspelling of Bowdich. The other sister mentioned in Blake's will married Thomas Smythes, of Cheapside, a celebrated goldsmith and banker.

After a lapse of two centuries and a half, it may still be possible to recover an idea, more or less faint, of the way in which the family lived in the west of England, and of the influences under which the Admiral passed the fifteen years of his childhood and early youth.

Bridgwater, on the river Parrett, stands in the centre of a rich plain, now sparkling with orchards and cornfields, but in the seventeenth century little more than a morass, bounded on one side by the Quantock hills, and on the other, at a less distance, by the wooded slopes of the Poldons. The valley, about three miles in width, includes several spots famous in English story. There the victorious armies of the King of Wessex had been arrested. There our own Alfred had found shelter from the Danes. There, in later times, Monmouth lost the battle of Sedgemoor. The town was built, as it is now, on both sides of the river; but at that time the eastern suburb, joined to the main body of the town by an ancient and solid stone bridge of three arches, was inhabited almost exclusively by the opulent traders and gentry. High Street, leading through the corn-market, —where there was a famous inn, the Swan, and a picturesque old market-cross,—was gay with shops; and, between the carrying trade and the shipping trade, the little town had an air of ceaseless bustle and business. Lying on the highway from Gloucester and Bristol to Taunton, Exeter and Plymouth, the western traffic all passed through the town. Pack-horses, laden with Yorkshire wool, tinkled their bells along its streets and over its old bridge night and day. Its port was crowded with vessels. Yet even then the town seemed to have passed its prime. Grass already grew in some of its streets, and many of its houses wore a dim and faded aspect. In former times it had been defended by a wall and gates; but nearly every trace of these defences had been swept away. The Castle, once a royal appanage, held by the Queens of England as a dower, kept watch and ward over the surrounding country; but, although an imposing structure in the feudal times, it had lost its former splendour. Rays of light from a distant past still lingered on its decaying turrets: in the Wars of the Roses it had often withstood siege and storm; and in spite of its decay, it could still boast the honours of a virgin fortress.

The first object to catch a stranger's eye as he now stands on the iron bridge, which has replaced the old stone edifice, is a row of chesnuts and poplars on the left bank of the stream. They grow in what was formerly Humphrey Blake's garden. The house in which the Admiral was born, in which he passed his youth, and in which, when at Bridgwater, he lived in the full blaze of his renown, still stands in what was formerly a part of St. Mary's Street; a house two stories high, built of blue lias stone, with walls of immense thickness, heavy stone stairs, oak wainscots, and decorated ceilings; a habitation of the Tudor days, and of unmistakeable importance in its time. The gardens, bounded by Durleigh brook, the river Parrett, and the highway, were about two acres in extent, mingling fruit-trees and flower-beds, scented plants and vegetables for the table. Though the house stood within a few steps of the church and the Corn Hill, it enjoyed a complete seclusion; and the windows looked out over a wide sweep of valley to the sunny slopes and summits of the Quantocks. In this secluded garden, by that old stone bridge, among the ships, native and foreign, lying at anchor in the river, and under the guns of the grim fortress, the ruddy-faced and curly-haired boy, Robert Blake, played and pondered, as was his habit, until the age of sixteen. From his father's garden he would daily witness the extraordinary flow of tide known as a Bore—a phenomenon only seen in the Ganges, the Severn, and two or three other streams; and the conversation of his father and of his father's friends must have helped to fix his mind on the sea and on maritime affairs.

When it is said that Humphrey Blake was a merchant trading with Spain, it is not meant that his days were spent in the routine of the desk and the exchange. The life of a trader was then a life of peril and adventure. He manned his own ships and sailed with his argosy.  Like later cruisers among the Pacific islands, his course and his destination was rarely known before he quitted port.  Failing in one harbour to dispose of his cargo, he spread his canvas in search of richer markets.  He saw strange lands and strange people; and he had to hold his own, not merely against the dues, fines, and exactions of legitimate powers, but against the still more formidable corsair.  Piracy was not, in the sixteenth century, the despicable calling it is now: in the opinion of that age, a pirate was but a soldier of fortune on another element.  France, Germany and Italy were overrun with mercenary heroes, eager to sell their swords in any cause where pay was sure and profligacy allowed.  Hundreds of distressed English gentlemen, when the civil wars left them stranded, took to the sea for bread.  In some parts of Europe the people of entire districts lived on plunder; persons now living can remember a time when the daring valour of the Greek and Biscayan freebooters was the theme of winter tales and popular ballads.  Nor were these unlicensed spoilers the worst enemies whom the peaceful merchant had to encounter at sea.  The Moors of Africa had erected piracy into a national system.  For ages the Salee rover had been a terror to the south of Europe; and the Tunisian and the Algerine, equal to him in skill, daring and fanaticism, had still finer ports and larger privateers.  No coast in Christendom was free from their incursions; but their favourite stations were the bays and harbours of Portugal and Spain, as in these ports they found it easy to attack and capture stragglers from the fleets of both worlds.  To the ordinary motives of the pirate, adventure and greed of gold, the Moor added the fiercer spurs of religious difference and hereditary hate.  Europeans, it may be justly said, had forced the Moors into piracy as a measure of defence.  Their expulsion from Granada in the fifteenth century roused in them the worst passions of human nature; and that band of armed priests, nestled behind the impregnable ramparts of Malta, and sworn to hold no truce with their race and faith,—a vow which they kept to the last letter, by piratical descents on the coasts of Africa, marking their path along the shore with burning villages, slaughtered peasants, and captive women and children, soon to be exposed by these Christian missionaries in the slave-markets of Venice, Seville and Genoa,—left them no policy but that of revenge and retaliation. In their undiscriminating rage, the followers of Mohammed waged war against the commerce of all civilised countries; when the opportunity offered, they seized both fleets and cargoes ; and, like the Knights of Malta, carried off their prisoners for sale to the bazaars of Tunis, Tripoli and Algiers.

For protection against these formidable enemies, the merchant had to trust to his own bold heart and steady hand. His vessel, however small, carried some means of defence. The crew were well armed. Aids to escape were kept in readiness. From the British Channel to the Straits of Gibraltar the course of the Severn adventurer lay through continual perils. Every rock and inlet along the coast had to be carefully examined before the little barque could venture on. The adventurer lived on deck, and he ate, drank and slept with his mind alert and his hand on his sword. At the return from a voyage, many were the tales of perilous encounter, chance-escape and valorous deed which he had to tell his friends and children on the dark winter nights :— and such stories were, no doubt, a part of the food on which the imagination of young Blake, silent and thoughtful from his childhood, was fed in the old mansion at Bridgwater.

The rudiments of a more regular education he obtained
at the grammar-school, then considered one of the best
foundations of its kind in England. This edifice has
long disappeared from the streets of Bridgwater; and
it has been replaced by another school of similar aims
and character, conducted in the house in which the
Admiral was born and in which he lived. At the
grammar-school he made some progress with his
Greek and Latin; something of navigation, ship-building and the routine of sea duties he probably learned
from his father or from his father's factors and servants.
His own taste however, his habit of mind and the bent
of his ambition, led to literature. He was the first of
his race who had shown any vocation to letters and
learning, and his father, proud of his talents and his
studies, resolved that he should have some chance of
rising to eminence. Nor was this early culture thrown
away. At sixteen he was already prepared for the
university, and at his earnest desire was sent to Oxford,
where he matriculated as a member of St. Alban's Hall
in Lent Term 1615, in company with Edward Reynolds,
who afterwards became bishop of Worcester, and John
Earl, subsequently bishop of Salisbury.

Little is known of Blake's college life. It is recorded
of him that he rose early, and was extremely assiduous
at his books, lectures and devotions; that he took great
delight in field-sports, particularly in fishing and shooting. If any credit is due to ancient gossip, which,
whether false or true, is traceable to his own age, and
is preserved to us as a contemporary scandal by a writer
who revered his name and was intimate with members
of the family,—his aquatic sports were sometimes irregular. "He would snare swans," says old Aubrey.
Most writers have rejected this report.

He had not been long at Oxford before his ambition

prompted him to try his strength against Robert Hegge and Robert Newlin in a contest for a scholarship then vacant at Christ Church. He soon found that a student without friends or influence had little chance of success in that aristocratic college. The failure of his first effort did not, however, cast him down:—he kept to his books and looked steadily towards the future. Nevertheless, willing to accept such friendly support as came in his way unsought, he removed from St. Alban's Hall, where he had found and felt himself a stranger, to Wadham College, at the request of his father's friend, Nicholas Wadham, a Somersetshire man, who had recently founded the noble edifice which bears his name. In this new college Blake remained several years; there he took the usual honours and completed his education:—and in the great dining-hall of Wadham, among the effigies of poets, divines and antiquaries, a portrait of the Admiral is still shown with pride as that of its most illustrious scholar.

During the years which he remained at Wadham College, waiting to establish himself in some permanent position in the University, the family prospects were gradually growing dark at Bridgwater. Humphrey Blake, his father, possessed the daring spirit of his class. The Severn adventurers gained money fast and lost it fast. With corsairs lying in every creek, it was easy to be rich to-day and poor to-morrow. Sometimes prosperous, sometimes nearly prostrate, Humphrey Blake had carried on his enterprises for many years, standing well with his fellow-merchants and honoured with the confidence of his fellow-citizens. He was twice elected to the chief magistracy of Bridgwater. But fortune turned more and more against him. Many of his ventures had failed. In some of these his losses had been severe. Much of his own and his wife's property was gone; and in the decline of life he found himself for the first time in serious trouble. Want of means chafed his ardent and ambitious mind; the more as his misfortunes had fallen on him when the energy of youth was passed, but not the cares of early manhood. He had married somewhat late in life; his family had increased rapidly; and at fifty-seven he found himself an old man with ten children, of whom the eldest, Robert, was only twenty, and the youngest, Alexander, was in the arms of his nurse. His troubles preyed on his spirits, and with the increasing darkness of his fortunes his health began to fail.

Robert, in his rooms at Wadham College, shared the family afflictions. He felt acutely the position in which his father stood, embarrassed with debts and surrounded with so many responsibilities; and the feeling gave a new and higher impulse to his desire to obtain a fellowship. A vacancy occurred at Merton, and he offered himself—not as in the earlier period of his college life, from a boyish ambition to achieve honours and place, but from a sacred wish to be useful to his brothers, and to relieve his father of the modest expense of his maintenance at Oxford. Alexander Fisher, John Earl, Edward Reynolds, his old comrades at St. Alban's Hall, and several other young men of parts and learning were in the lists. Had Blake's efforts been successful, the life of the renowned Admiral might have been passed in the seclusion of a college, among the books and studies he already loved so well, and in that case Taunton would in all human probability have remained in royalist hands, the battle of Naseby would not have been fought, Tromp would have remained unconquered, Spain unscathed, Tunis and Santa Cruz uncelebrated! How little did Sir Henry Savile, then warden of Merton College, dream that in rejecting Blake from his petty senate, he was turning back on the world one of those master-spirits who were to overthrow the government, humiliate his adored sovereign, and elevate England to the height of human grandeur! But so it was. Savile, a man of sense and acquirements, as witness his fine edition of St. Chrysostom, had an eccentric distaste for men of low stature, and chose his senators, as the Prussian king did his grenadiers, by their height. The young Somersetshire student, thickset, fair-complexioned, and only five feet six, fell below his standard of manly beauty. His influence was adverse, and Blake lost his election.

He remained five years at Oxford after this incident, and in good time took his degree of Master of Arts. There seems to be no ground for supposing that want of learning was the bar to his advancement in the University. He had read the best authors in Greek and Latin, and wrote the latter language sufficiently well for verse or epigram. Even in the busiest days of his public life, he made it a point of pride not to forget his old studies. When chasing the enemy or fiercely cruising before a foreign station, his grave humour—and never man had finer sense of sarcasm, or used that brilliant weapon with greater effect—loved to find expression for its scorn and merriment in the satires of Horace and Juvenal; thus in some degree relieving the stern fervour of Puritan piety with the easy graces of scholarship. His brother William, smitten also with love of letters, entered himself a student at Wadham, where, in 1624, he was already a Bachelor of Arts, and on the death of the antiquary, Camden, furnished a Latin epigraph to the book published by the University.

In the ninth year of his residence at Oxford, and in the twenty-seventh of his age, Robert Blake was called to his father's bedside. The old man had grown worse in health, and was no longer able to manage his affairs. At last his son abandoned the idea of a college life, gave up his rooms at Wadham, and took up his abode in the old house at Bridgwater. On the 19th of November Humphrey Blake died, leaving to his sons Robert and Humphrey, the care of his widow, and his family of young children.

The estate was encumbered with debts. Puriton, Catcote, Bawdrippe, and Wollamington had been conveyed away to trustees, for the mother's sole use during her life; the only property mentioned in the recital of the will, is the house and gardens in St. Mary's Street, Bridgwater, and these were bequeathed to Robert and Humphrey, and their heirs for ever, subject to the one condition that their mother, Sara, should have the use of them during her widowhood. To whatever family property remained, to all the lands, leases, debts, difficulties, and responsibilities which survived the broken merchant, Robert was heir.

Humphrey, William and George were of age or near it; Samuel was seventeen, Nicholas sixteen, Benjamin eleven, and Alexander six, at the time of their father's death. Not one of them, with the possible exception of William, was settled in life; and the four youngest had still to be in some measure educated as well as started in the world. The young girls had also to be supported out of the wreck. The first thing, then, was to ascertain the residue after paying all debts; and in order to clear off some of these claims, it may be that Plansfield was at this time sold. When the debts were paid, it would seem that property, exclusive of the house in St. Mary's Street, of about two hundred pounds a year remained. The means were slight, the responsibilities heavy; yet Robert accepted, and in due course achieved, the task of rearing, educating, and placing the whole of that numerous family. Humphrey lived with him, and followed his fortunes to the last, becoming in due time a public servant and a commissioner of naval prizes. William went to London, where he became a learned and successful man; he attracted the notice of scholars, was created a doctor of civil law by the University of Padua, and when he died, followed the example of his brother and grandfather in leaving a legacy to the poor of his native town. He also left a number of legacies to his brothers, nephews and nieces. George went to London, and became a goldsmith and banker of Cheapside. In after life he retired to Plymouth, where some of his children married and remained, though he himself subsequently settled at Minehead, on the Severn. One of his sons, Benjamin, had a taste for letters; and a copy of verses written by him on the death of his uncle, Dr. William Blake, is still extant. Samuel married early in life, and took to agriculture. A farm, consisting of a house and about one hundred and fifty acres of land, orchard, garden, meadows, and pasturage, at Pawlett, a village about four miles below Bridgwater, on the river Parrett, had been made over to him by his eldest brother. When the civil war broke out he joined his brother's company, and was one of the first martyrs of the good cause in the west of England. Nicholas engaged in the Spanish trade like his father and grandfather. He resided chiefly at Dunster and Minehead, successfully cultivated business, and acquired a moderate estate, which his descendants of Venne House still enjoy. Benjamin was at first a farmer; but he also turned soldier when the wars began; afterwards went to sea, served against Rupert and Tromp in his brother's fleet, took part in the expedition against Hispaniola under Penn and Venables, and was raised by the former, when he returned to Europe, to the rank of vice-admiral. Of Alexander it is only known that he lived till 1693, and was then buried in the church of Eaton Socon, in Bedfordshire, where there is a tablet erected to his memory.

During the nine years spent at Oxford, Blake's character was slowly but soundly developed. When he returned to his native town and again took up his residence in the family mansion, he was remarkable for that iron will, that grave humour, that free and dauntless spirit for which after-events found employment. Simple in his tastes and habits, there was a dignity and refinement in every line of his countenance which bespoke command. His manners, though austere for one so young, were relieved by a certain bluntness of address, while his peculiar sense of humour and great vehemence of passion rendered his conversation at once agreeable, emphatic, and picturesque. The abuses in Church and State afforded themes for satire; the profligacy which reigned at court, the moral laxity and doctrinal intolerance of so many religious professors excited his intense scorn, and in public and private places he inveighed against them with bitter sarcasm and solid argument. The weak worldliness of the prelates, the mean subservience of the Church to royal vices and follies, drove young Blake, as they drove thousands of the ardent and uncorrupted young men of that time, into Puritanism: the despicable pedantry, faithlessness and profligacy of the King, his favourites and his courtiers, insulting from their high station the moral sense of a virtuous, domestic and religious people, made him sigh for a republic like that of Pericles or of Scipio.

# CHAPTER II.

## 1625—1645.

### THE REVOLUTION.

For several years after his return from college, Blake's time was chiefly occupied with the care of his aged mother—who outlived her husband thirteen years, seeing her youngest son Alexander arrive at the age of manhood,—and in the education and settlement of his brothers and sisters. But he was a keen observer of public events, a politician by nature and early training; and as the action of the court became suspicious to good Protestants and menacing to the nation's civil liberties, he bent the force of his genius to create in his native county a party of resistance. Nor was the task difficult. Commercial habits and superior education had given a liberal bias to the men of that district; and whatever instinct of ancient and unreasoning loyalty still survived was rudely tried by the King's friends. Laud, appointed to the see of Bath and Wells shortly after Blake left Oxford, in two or three years, contrived by his zeal for episcopacy and royal right, his absence from the see, except as a persecutor of conscience, and his fierce denunciation of all classes and degrees of non-conformity, however slight—to rouse a stern spirit of opposition to the governing powers in Church and State. Possessed of the King's ear, Laud felt no scruple in turning the

executive arm against his spiritual opponents, and even
attempted to coerce the judges into instruments of epis-
copal vengeance.  On one occasion, when Lord Chief-
Justice Richardson returned to London from the
Somerset assizes, where he had heard and disposed of
cases in which the bishop took an interest, with a
moderation worthy of the bench in its better days, he
was attacked with so much fury at the Council-board,
that on retiring he remarked to his friends, he had been
almost choked with a pair of lawn sleeves.  Such a policy,
carried out in the vicinity of Bridgwater, and finding
its victims in men generally respected, gave force and
edge to Blake's keen invective.  The more famous proceedings of the same prelate, after his translation to
Canterbury, in bringing Prynne, Burton, Bastwick, and
other men more pious and learned than himself before
the Star-Chamber and Court of High Commission,—the
clipping of ears, the branding of temples, the slitting of
noses, the burning of tongues, the prisons, pillories, and
public scourgings to which he resorted for the maintenance of his Popish rites,—continued in the years
which followed that event to call forth his indignant
denunciation.  Nor was the spur of private resentment
long wanting.  Bishop Pierce, who after an interval
succeeded Laud in the see of Bath and Wells, resolved
to put down the famous Lectures, and suspended Mr.
Deverish, minister of Bridgwater, for preaching the
usual Lecture in his own church on market-day, and
using a short prayer.  Nor did this act satisfy the
prelate.  Humphrey Blake was the churchwarden; and
Pierce enjoined him to do penance for the crime of not
presenting Deverish for ecclesiastical censure.  Blake
could plead the usage of the church.  Since the days of
Queen Elizabeth these Lectures had been used by all
zealous and pious clergymen.  But Pierce was in-

exorable. A bold remonstrance against such prostitu-
tion of the powers exercised by the courts of conscience
was signed by many leading liberals of Somerset, and by
Robert Blake one of the first.

The remonstrants prayed the King to put an end to
religious persecution, and inveighed against the Popish
rites and ceremonies which Laud was trying to intro-
duce into the Church. Two Puritan divines, Deverish
and Norman, were the clerical leaders of the movement
party in Bridgwater; but their lay ally was its real
leader, and by his genius and activity the local influence
of the Stawells and Wyndhams, strong royalist families,
was overthrown, and a commanding position was
obtained for the new opinions.

The aspect of affairs at court was lowering. Charles
had not only married a French woman and a Papist—
causes of deep offence to a people jealous of foreign intrigues—but had entered into illegal and insulting
engagements with the wily minister who then directed
the policy of Versailles. As the price of Henrietta
Maria's hand, Richelieu had demanded that the young
Queen and her court should have a right to exercise
her religion—that the children issuing from the marriage should be under the control of their mother and
her advisers until the age of thirteen—and that for the
future all English Catholics should be allowed to perform
the services of their Church. These stipulations,
granted by Charles to gain the honour of an alliance
with the blood of St. Louis, were agreed to in a series of
secret articles; but their purport was soon known, and
the King's treason to the law of the land and the strong
Protestant instincts of the people alarmed and enraged
the country. Nor was the popular mistrust unjusti-
fied by events :—the children of this unhappy marriage
were so trained in early life as eventually to forsake the

religion of their country, and with that lapse to forfeit the splendid inheritance of their race. Seeing Popery enthroned at Whitehall, the people resented every inclination towards Rome in the clergy—whether that inclination showed itself in the lofty character of their spiritual pretensions, in the pomp and circumstance of their way of life, or in the boldness of their hostility to freedom of thought. On all these points Laud was obnoxious to the more ardent Reformers; and Charles himself was scarcely less hateful. His origin was bad. The disgust created by his father's claim to govern England—not by a semi-divine right of genius, like the first and last of the Tudor sovereigns, but by a divine right of birth—a disgust which outlived the poor pedant and weighed heavily on his son,—was not allayed by any act of manly sincerity or generous explanation. Questions of finance also arose to embarrass parties and embitter the contest about principles of government. Ireland and Scotland were even less tranquil than the supreme country, though from different causes. Beyond the Tweed, the religious question alone occupied the field of controversy. By law, Charles was not the head of the Church in Scotland, and his attempts—aided by his complaisant Archbishop of Canterbury—to bring its clergy under control, to rob them of their spiritual rights, to meddle with their church government, and to impose on their unwilling congregations his own ritual, perilled his secular power and alienated from his person the friends to whom he might otherwise have looked in the worst extremities of his fortune. In Ireland the elements of discontent were more numerous, but they nearly all had their origin in the religious disabilities imposed on the Catholic masses. When pressed for money, Charles had sold certain graces or indulgences to a body of men in the western counties of the island for 120,000*l.*, though well aware that the very word indulgence would have a startling and papistical sound in English ears. For this sum he consented to remove from the purchasers all penal laws enacted against their creed, to allow them a right to practise at the bar, and to exercise other functions at that time prohibited by statute. To the original infamy of this sale, Charles added the still deeper infamy of taking the money and refusing to fulfil the contract. When the poor dupes complained, he sent Strafford into Ireland with orders to repress discontent with a strong arm, to assimilate the Irish to the English Church, and finally to over-ride the ancient constitution and make the King's power absolute. Strafford succeeded in this task as only a man of genius can succeed. Attacking the Catholics in their opinions, their liberties and their properties, he frustrated every measure taken in their defence; and by harassing suits and galling disabilities, invented by an intelligence infinite in resources and carried out with a vigour which knew no pause and counted no obstacle, he achieved such a success with the higher classes and in the rich towns as intoxicated his royal master. The old nobles of the country were brought over, some by threats, some by cajolery, still more by fashion, policy, and personal ambition. But the Deputy's fierce and unscrupulous course of conversion fired the passions of the Irish people—and dread of his vigorous policy arrayed against him the whole liberal and constitutional party in England.

The armed revolt against Charles began in his native land. Harassed by Laud's agents, the Scotch Presbyterians took an oath and covenant to maintain their religious independence at all hazards; and when the King threatened them with the punishment due to rebels, instead of stealing back to their homes to escape

the royal wrath, they flew to arms, boldly crossed the
border into England, and offered to put the issues of
their quarrel to the ordeal of battle. The court raged
with passion and insulted pride. But its contortions
were as vain as they were undignified, for the reforming
House of Commons made the cause of the Scotch Covenanters their own, and the royalist policy received its
first sudden and serious check. Strafford was impeached.
Laud was lodged in the Tower. Finch the Lord-keeper
and Secretary Windebank were driven into exile. Concessions were obtained for the English people; and in
the northern kingdom Charles was stript of his most
coveted prerogative.

In the heat of his resentment against the Scots, the
King had summoned the two Houses to meet again
after a separation of many years; the step had created
an immense sensation in the country; and the most
active and liberal of the country gentlemen were
returned for nearly all the large towns. Blake went
up as member for Bridgwater. Vane, Hampden, Cromwell, Pym, and Elliot were returned to Westminster.
Their legislative labours were, however, of brief duration—this meeting of the House being that which is
known in history as the Short Parliament. Charles
wanted money to fight the Covenanters; but when
he asked for money in his usual peremptory manner,
the House replied with a long list of grievances, and
insisted that before any money-bills were laid on the
table, an inquiry should be made into the state of the
nation, especially in regard to the attempted innova-
tions in religion, interference with the rights of private
property, and invasion of the privileges of Parliament. Neither threats nor cajoleries could overcome
their resistance. After a vain trial of his strength on
the constitutional ground, Charles suddenly dissolved

the House in a fit of anger. Pym and Elliot were conspicuous during the brief session. But the great fighting-men were silent. Blake said not a word. Cromwell said not a word. Events, however, soon compelled Charles to issue writs for a new election; and before the year was out, the Long Parliament, fated to see and to survive so many governments, was sitting at Westminster. Of this famous assembly Blake was not a member until 1645, when he was returned for Taunton in the room of Sir William Portman, his seat for Bridgwater being occupied by Colonel Wyndham, governor of the castle, and a haughty opponent of the popular party.

The strife had not yet died away beyond the Tweed when it arose in the sister country. There, a long-cherished hatred of the Saxon race embittered the quarrel about lands and religions. Under the powerful rule of Strafford, the Celtic population had been made to feel its inferiority in a thousand galling forms; that statesman treating the country as a conquered province, subject to no law save the law of the sword, and capable of no rights but such as the prince might bestow and revoke at pleasure. Yet in spite of Stafford's cruelty and his own bad faith, the person and government of the King were popular among the light-hearted people : those papistical rites and doctrines which rendered him so suspicious in other parts of his dominions won for him the confidence and affection of his Irish subjects. In the King's name, and as they pretended with his approval, they flew to arms. Treachery of a confederate caused the failure of an attempt to seize Dublin Castle; but the insurrection spread into the remotest districts, and in one week from the outbreak, the open country and many of the chief towns in Longford, Leitrim, Cavan, Donegal, Derry, Monaghan, and other counties were possessed by the insurgents. The leaders declared by proclamation that their object in rising was to support the King against the popular members of the House of Commons, who had invaded the royal prerogative, intercepted the favours granted by the Crown to its subjects in Ireland, and designed to root out the Catholic faith from that part of the empire. The King's cause was adopted as their cause. Their fury was directed against the very men who had brought the great oppressor to the scaffold. In the drunkenness of unexpected success, their followers committed atrocities at which nature and history must shudder. The English settlers, whether of ancient or of modern standing, were cast into prison, their goods and lands seized and divided, their children torn from them, their women ravished before their eyes, and their whole body, the grace, the soul, the sustaining element of the country, was treated with every barbarity which hate could devise and victorious passion inflict. In this outburst of popular insanity, more than forty thousand Protestant settlers were butchered in cold blood.

Preparations were instantly made to check these atrocities. But who was to command the forces sent against the rebels? Those rebels openly declared that they had the King's sanction for what they had done:— a most unhappy declaration for the man in whose interests they professed to devastate and murder. The two Houses dared not entrust him with the means of repression. Charles himself felt how disastrous was the position made for him by his friends. He was compelled either to admit that the rising had taken place at his instigation, or to transfer to his new Parliament the general conduct of the war. He chose the latter evil, and in one day his enemies became masters of a fleet and an army. That day the contest between the two powers began. After he had ceded control over the forces necessary to suppress the rebellion, Charles, alarmed at his defencelessness, made efforts to get his creature, Sir John Pennington, appointed chief admiral in the Irish seas, a post of supreme importance at that moment. His requests were denied. Parliament had reason to suspect that officer of an intention to employ the force undır his command against the national movement; they refused therefore to accept the King's nomination, and sent the Earl of Warwick as their vice-admiral into those waters.

Soon after this event, Charles raised the royal standard at Nottingham, and called the gentry of England to his aid. The two parties now in presence of each other, arming to dispute possession of the realm, and determine the principles on which it should be governed, were as distinct in character as in cause. On the King's side, notwithstanding his personal meanness, a large majority of the men of old family was arrayed. Men of the highest birth and the gentlest nurture flew to the standard of their King. Brave by nature, and loyal from long habit, they were attached by ancient tradition or private interest to the forms of monarchy and episcopacy. But these loyal gentlemen, though hardy, heedless, and romantic, possessed no strong convictions, little of the sustained energy so needful in revolutions, and still less moral reputation. On the popular side were ranged a few men of the highest rank, separated from their peers by greater purity of life and by wider culture, together with the whole body of merchants, and the more sober, stern, and religious of the country gentlemen—the English Commons. A gay demeanour, a light heart, a passion for wine and women, marked the Cavalier. The Roundhead was distinguished by a grave aspect, an austere life, fiery enthusiasm, and fixed beliefs.

Between such opponents the contest could not have
been prolonged beyond a single summer, had they commenced it in equal numbers and with equal means. But
their condition as soldiers was as various as their
opinions. The royalists rode into the camp almost
ready for the field. Many of them had been long familiar
with the use of arms; and nearly all had been accustomed to a country life, to hunting, sporting, and the
exercises which best prepare men for the hardships of a
camp and the terrors of a battle-field. The rank and
file of the Roundhead forces consisted of students, small
farmers, and city tradesmen. To their hands, books and
implements of trade or husbandry were more familiar
than pikes and muskets. Devotion, courage, enthusiasm,
they could bring to the contest, but they had the art
and practice of war to learn from its very rudiments.

Charles quitted Nottingham for the west of England
at the head of six thousand men. Enthusiasm for his
cause in the opening days of the conflict was boundless.
At Shrewsbury his army had increased to nearly twenty
thousand. This sudden accession of strength induced
him to turn on London, the head-quarters of his most
active and powerful enemies, in the hope of crushing
them at a single blow; but he had scarcely quitted
his halting-place when the Earl of Essex was descried
hovering with a considerable force on his flank and
rear, ready to cut off stragglers, intercept supplies, and
enclose him between two fires, should he advance on
the capital. He was forced to retreat or to give battle,
and he chose the latter in confidence. Six thousand
men were left dead on the field of Edgehill: Essex
retired towards Coventry, and the King advanced his
head-quarters to Oxford, whence he sent out flying
squadrons of horse under Prince Rupert to spread terror
to the suburbs of London. For a few days the city was

distracted with reports, and the popular leaders showed a desire to treat; but unfortunately for the royal cause, while terms were being discussed under cover of an armistice, Ruthen, the Royalist General, assaulted Brentford. The cry of treachery was raised. The citizens flew to arms. The trained bands marched out of London and encamped before the captured town. By rapid marches Essex brought up his army from the midland counties; and instead of seizing Whitehall and the Tower, as he intended, Charles was compelled to throw himself beyond the Thames; flying like a fugitive across the bridge at Kingston toward Reading and Oxford, in the latter of which cities he resolved to pass the winter months, after fortifying with hasty works and strong garrisons all the more important places in the immediate vicinity.

Meanwhile Blake was on the alert in Somersetshire. Taking the King's hasty dissolution of the Short Parliament as a signal for action, he began, with the aid of his young and fiery brothers Samuel and Benjamin, to count his friends, to prepare arms and horses, to concoct watchwords, and to keep a keen eye on the movements of the King's partisans. His troop was one of the first in the field, and both the horse and foot played a conspicuous part in the first action of any importance in the west of England, when Sir John Horner routed the newly raised forces of the Marquis of Hertford at Wells. From that date he was in almost every action of importance in the western counties, fighting his way into military notice. He distinguished himself in the sharp encounter at Bodmin; and gained the confidence of his chief, Sir William Waller, by his conduct on the fiercely disputed field of Lansdown. Detached from the army to strengthen the garrison at Bristol, he missed the disastrous retreat at Roundway Down. Blake's attention

was not, however, confined to the war. His knowledge
of business, his activity, and his severe integrity pointed
him out for other employments, and he was made one of
the Committee for seizing and sequestrating the Estates
of Delinquents in Somerset :—a thankless office, the
duties of which he nevertheless discharged for several
years without giving rise to a single accusation of par-
tiality, or making for himself one personal enemy. But
the camp was his field of action ; his superiority to other
men about him lay in the marvellous fertility, energy,
and comprehensiveness of his military genius. Before
the field of action was as yet occupied by large armies,
he scoured the country with his intrepid dragoons,
rousing the spirit of his friends, carrying terror to the
hearths of his enemies, and levying contributions of
money and horses on such towns and hamlets as were
known to be disaffected to the national cause. In the
royalist camp Prince Rupert could alone be compared
with him as a partisan soldier ; and that brilliant cavalry
officer, fated to be foiled so often on land and sea by
Blake, first made the acquaintance of his redoubtable
enemy at the siege of Bristol.

Rupert's youth had passed like that of a hero of
romance. The son of a Bohemian king and an English
princess, he was connected in blood with half the
reigning families in Europe, and his long pedigree
stretched back through Charlemagne to Attila. Yet as
a boy he had known nothing of the grace of boyhood.
Storms raged round his cradle from his birth. In an
ante-chamber of the Hradschin he was one day snatched
up by his nurse while sleeping in the midst of flashing
fires and booming artillery ; Austrian and Bavarian
troops were thundering at the gates of Prague ; and in
the hurry of mortal fear the menial dropt her charge on
the floor, and there he was found by a chamberlain of

the palace, and flung into the last carriage that followed the unhappy court in its flight to Breslau. Army after army rose to avenge the dethronement of his mother, the famous Queen of Hearts, but they struggled in vain against the more prosperous fortunes of the southern Germans. Rupert and his brother Maurice wandered from court to court, but dread of the imperial arms silenced every sentiment of pity in the royal palaces of Europe; and Holland alone, in its pride of liberty and power, dared to offer an asylum to the unhappy fugitives. There Rupert passed his youth. A hard student at the University of Leyden, a hunter and hawker over the flat fields of the Zuyder Zee, the hero of many a courtly tournament, a volunteer at the siege of Rhynberg,—at the age of fifteen he was a man of the world, and a soldier who had won his spurs in actual service. A brief visit to England, where Laud proposed to make him a bishop, the Queen to marry him to a rich heiress, and the King, his uncle, to send him out as viceroy to Madagascar,—led to an insane enterprise of his own for the recovery of his father's family dominions on the Rhine. Defeated and taken prisoner, he passed three heavy years in the fortress of Linz, varied only by a love-affair with the young Countess of Kuffstein, whom he abandoned for ever the moment he obtained his freedom. His temper soured and his passions inflamed by adversity, he turned soldier of fortune, repaired to England, where his uncle's troubles opened a field for his military talents, and he was immediately made master of the royal horse. The Cavaliers were companions after his own heart. No sooner did he meet the easy, dashing, courteous gentle-men of England than he became their leader. Brave, active, impetuous, no foe could withstand the vigour of his onset or escape the celerity of his pursuit. Three months after his arrival his name was already a word of terror in the country. But if his daring spirit and indomitable activity made him a dangerous enemy,—it is also certain that his cold heart, his lust of money, his ruthless cruelty, his contempt of law, made him a still more fatal friend. In spite of his valour, his vigilance, and his success, history must describe the King's warlike nephew as the evil genius of his cause.

From his camp at Oxford, Charles ruled about a third of the territory of England. Wales and the border land adhered steadfastly to his banner; and his dashing master of the horse, after taking the important town of Cirencester by surprise, proposed to consolidate the royal power in the west by the capture of Bristol and the line of fortresses along the Severn. With his uncle's consent, he tried to win the town by treason, but the faithless citizens who would have made themselves his instruments and accomplices were betrayed to the authorities. Treachery failing, he advanced at the head of fourteen thousand foot and six thousand horse, and summoned Colonel Fiennes, the commander, to yield up the place to his King's officers. Though torn with factions, as were most towns at that time, Bristol was capable of a long, if not a permanent defence. Of regular troops within its walls, in cavalry and infantry, there were not less than two thousand men; many of the citizens were armed; the store of provisions was abundant and of excellent quality; shot and powder were plentiful; and a powerful park of brass ordnance was distributed among the forts and works. The lines, it is true, were incomplete. In many places the breastworks had not been carried to the proper elevation, and the ditch at some points required greater width and depth. But the castle within the town was a hold of some strength, and the minor forts along the line— one of the most important of which, Prior's Hill, was entrusted by Fiennes to Captain Blake—offered centres of support to the garrison. Had the chief command been in the hands of an able and resolute soldier, the city would probably not have fallen, and if so, not ingloriously.

On Sunday morning, July 23, Rupert and Maurice sat down before the walls, their force supported by a considerable train of artillery, and from their head-quarters at Clifton—a charming suburb even at that time—they summoned the garrison to surrender. This summons leading to no result, they spent a day and night in reconnoitring the position, exchanging a few shots with the outposts, and driving in foragers. Next day Fiennes issued an order that all citizens not actually engaged in the defence, should keep within doors, leaving the streets free for the soldiers. At the same time Rupert drew out his army in two lines, and marched them in order of battle within view of the forts, hoping to intimidate the citizens by his immense means of offence. But the display failing of effect, he fixed his positions, and began to erect batteries. In the afternoon Lord Grandison and a body of cavalry took possession of a rising ground, covered by a thick hedge, over-against Prior's Hill, where Blake was stationed with a small body of men; and the labourers threw up in haste a rude breastwork, on which, under cover of the darkness, they planted their field-pieces unseen. At midnight two cannon-shots from Grandison's position lighted the sky and broke the deep silence with their echoes. Blake quickly answered from Prior's Hill with a discharge of musketry and grape-shot. On the instant lights were seen moving in the beleaguering lines, and a nocturnal cannonade commenced, spread rapidly to adjacent parts, and lasted for about an hour. Next day preparations were made by the Royalists to storm the works; and when all was ready they advanced to the assault in six lines, the officers and soldiers wearing green boughs for recognition in the disorder of the expected sack. The men in the first line bore fagots on their backs; those in the second drove carts laden with earth to fill the ditch; the third line was armed with muskets; the fourth bore long pikes with wild-fire at the points; the fifth carried hand-grenades; the sixth was armed like the third with muskets. The charge was made with Rupert's usual intrepidity. Parts of the shallow ditch were filled—the works were scaled in several places at the same moment—and Cavalier and Roundhead met hand to hand in single encounters; but after a long and fierce struggle, the assailants were repulsed with loss at every point. While the infantry were storming, a squadron of the royal horse swept round the outer lines, and made an unexpected appearance before Frome Gate, with orders to cut down the sentries, and advance at a gallop on the rear of the garrison then engaged with the main body of the royal infantry. This attempt also failed. The guard at Frome Gate was on the alert, and a hot fire from behind their sheltered positions put the horsemen to rout. The fighting went on simultaneously at the forts. Two demi-cannon had been directed by Lord Grandison with some effect against the old walls at Prior's Hill; but Blake's vigorous fire kept the assailants at bay, and when night came down, and the combatants had time to count their losses, besides the usual casualties, Grandison had to deplore the death of his chief cannoneer; Blake, the mutilation of one of his three guns, and serious damage to his works.

The garrison of Prior's Hill had little breathing time. Before three o'clock in the morning, the grey dawn was streaked with bursting lights, and the sleep of the tired soldiers was broken by the cracking muskets of the Cornish division. Rupert was already awake in his tent; and on catching the first signal, he drew out his troops, and disposed some squadrons of horse under cover of the rising grounds,—ready to second the infantry in case of need, to check sallies, and enter the lines as soon as the foot had forced a way. His design was to break the curtain between Prior's Hill and the next position, a small redoubt, strengthened by two fortified houses; but finding his flank torn by Blake's steady fire, he sent Grandison with a body of picked men to storm the post, while he advanced with the main body against the intervening curtain:—the attack on Prior's Hill thus became the centre of operations for that day. Dividing his force, Grandison sent fifty musqueteers to alarm the line a little to the right of Blake's position, and fifty others to make a demonstration on the left. Within gunshot of Prior's Hill, the highway entered Bristol through the rude defences, the point of intersection being covered by a spur with a low breastwork, and barricaded by a gate of strong timbers. While the garrison at the Hill was distracted with the movements of the musqueteers, Colonel Lunsford, at the head of three hundred men, fell on the curtain,—but after a sharp struggle, was driven back with loss. Major Sandars was then sent forward with two hundred and fifty men to storm the spur, and bravely rushing through the fire from the works up to the gate, came to a pike and pistol contest with its defenders. Nine hand-grenades were thrown into the works. Captain Fawcett fastened a petard to the timbers of the gate, but the explosion only shattered a few bars, without opening a practicable breach. After an hour and a half lost in fighting a series of skirmishes, in which he saw Captain Howell and many of his most gallant commanders fall in vain, Grandison was convinced that so long as Prior's Hill remained in Blake's hands, the curtain could not be forced at that point; and he drew out his whole strength against the proved key of the position. Elated by success, the little garrison prepared to receive the foe. The Royalists, led by their impetuous and exasperated chief, pushed into the shallow ditch surrounding the fort again and again, but always to retire in confusion and with loss. Finding his ammunition about to fail, Blake ordered his men to hurl stones on the assailants below, while the best marksmen kept up a steady and destructive fire from the embrasures. Lunsford at one moment placed a ladder against the wall, and mounted as high as the palisades, but was then forced back. Lieutenant Ellis gained the line, but was instantly shot through the heart. Again the whole body advanced to an assault; again the little garrison repulsed them with slaughter. As the Royalists retired in confusion, Blake, feeling, with the untaught instinct of genius, that the decisive moment had come, lowered the drawbridge, and sallied at the head of his little troop. Rage and shame seized the royalist officers on seeing their troops turn from the fire of a mere handful of men; and mounting a horse that stood near, Grandison shouted to them to follow him. At the sound of his voice the fugitives rallied, and were led a third time to the assault. At the ditch they met the Roundheads, Blake in front; the struggle was renewed, pistol and pike, sword and musket. Grandison was shot in the leg and disabled. Colonel Owen advanced to take his place; he received the contents of a musket in his head. Hotly pressed in front, their leaders out of action, without plan or directing mind, the Royalists at last fell back in disorder to their old position. Having completely swept the line, and cleared the hill, so far as they came within range of his fire, Blake retired with his exhausted troops to their little fort.

At other points the fortunes of the day had been less favourable to the Roundheads. Between Brandon Hill and Windmill Fort, where the curtain was incomplete, and the defence weakest, Colonel Washington broke over with his regiment of horse; and the defenders falling back rapidly, he advanced at a brisk pace through the suburbs up to Frome Gate: but being unsupported by the prince, his ardour exposed his men to the risk of being enclosed and cut off. From the windows and roofs of houses a flanking fire galled and thinned his ranks; and some of his bravest officers fell at his side. Rupert hesitated to enter the broken line, and kept his troops waiting in a meadow at the foot of Brandon Hill, out of range from its guns. Had Fiennes made a vigorous movement at this time, he might have captured or cut to pieces the whole of Washington's regiment, seriously damaging the reputation of Rupert's redoubtable cavalry. But the governor's heart failed him as soon as the enemy appeared before Frome Gate. To the astonishment of the Cavaliers he made signs for a parley; and before midnight, he had already agreed to that surrender which blasted an honourable reputation, and brought his head within an inch of the block. Rupert undertook that the inhabitants should not be plundered, and that the garrison should depart without their arms. Blake's indignation was loudly and fiercely expressed. At first he could not believe that a man, who had evinced no want of courage in the House of Commons, could give up the second city in the empire after a few hours of not very serious fighting; and for his own part he refused to admit the terms of capitulation, and threatened to hold his little stronghold to the last man.  In the confusion of his preparation for departure on the morrow, Fiennes omitted to acquaint the commanders of Prior's Hill and Brandon Hill forts with the nature of the important act concluded with the prince ; and this negligence afterwards became a serious charge against him, as putting many valuable lives in peril.  When, therefore, at sunrise a body of Royalists appeared before the ditch to take possession of the little fort which they had vainly assailed the previous day, Blake replied to their summons with a volley of musketry.  On hearing that the commander at Prior's Hill refused to admit the articles of surrender, Rupert declared that he would hang him on the spot:—how different might have been his own career had he carried this threat into execution !  Twenty-four hours longer Blake held his post, and kept the Cavaliers at bay; but then learning, from persons on whom he could rely, the exact nature of the agreement with Fiennes, and that the Roundhead garrison was already on its march, he reluctantly quitted the position he had shown himself so well able to defend.  Fiennes was brought before a court-martial at St. Alban's, where he was tried for cowardice, convicted and sentenced to death,—but his life was spared by the lord general Essex.  Blake did not appear as a witness against him on the trial.

The loss of Bristol was one of a series of misfortunes. Ten days before the capitulation, Waller had been worsted at Roundway Down ; a fortnight before that disaster, the Fairfaxes had fought and lost a great battle on Adderton Moor, and were then shut up in Hull. Even Cromwell's genius had failed to keep down the Lincolnshire Royalists; Gainsborough was taken by their partisans ; Lincoln itself had to be abandoned. Hopton had encountered and dispersed the Roundheads at Stratton in Cornwall.  With the exception of London, the Associated Eastern Counties, and a few isolated towns, the whole country appeared to be reduced to obedience. Liberty appeared to be in its last throes, and one more decisive victory might have put an end to constitutions and parliaments in England for many years. With no fear of an enemy by the way, Charles passed from Oxford to Bristol, where he called a council to deliberate on the next movement. Rupert and the war-party advised the King to march on London and finish the war. But more timorous councils prevailed, and it was first resolved to reduce Gloucester, the only city of importance in the west of England still faithful to the national cause :—a fatal determination for the King, as it gave the Roundheads time to recover from the alarm of so many disasters. Rising to the height of the occasion, the London train-bands once more marched with Essex and his levies against the victorious Cavaliers. At their approach, Charles burnt his huts and raised the siege of Gloucester, and the battle of Newbury, though undecisive, restored in some degree the equality of the two powers.

Meantime Blake received new employments from the Parliament. He was named one of the Somerset Committee for Ways and Means, and appointed, as a reward for his exploits at Bristol, Lieut.-Colonel to Popham's regiment, one of the finest bodies of militia in the country. The corps was fifteen hundred strong, well equipped, and firmly attached to Roundhead principles. With a part of this force, in which his brother Samuel had command of a company, Blake made a dash into Bridgwater, with the hope of surprising its castle and securing that town for the good cause. Riding in by the old stone bridge on which he had so often played as a child, he stationed his men on the Corn-hill and market-place, and made the Swan Inn his head-quarters. But

Wyndham was alert. The guns of the castle, forty in number, were prepared for action; the royalist garrison was at least equal in strength to his own regiment; and swayed by the Luttrels, Trevelyans, and other county families, supported by a majority of the clergy, the townsmen themselves evinced no eagerness to throw off the Cavalier yoke. Without ordnance, field-stores, or other necessary supplies, Blake would not venture to sit down before the castle; so calling in his scouts and patrols, he gave marching orders for the south coast, where his regiment had been already destined for service in defence of Lyme. A melancholy incident marked the departure from his native town. Samuel, his younger brother, a gallant but imprudent officer, had left his quarters on a flying visit to his wife and children at Pawlett, four miles down the river. At the Shoulder of Mutton, a village ale-house still in existence, he heard that a captain of array and one of his followers were crossing the river at Combwich passage to beat up recruits for the King's service. This intelligence he ought to have carried at once to his brother, instead of which his zeal induced him to mount his horse and ride after the two officers. He came up with them at Streachill, a quarrel ensued, and he was killed in the fray, leaving behind him a widow and two young children. Blake was terribly shocked at this family disaster, but he bore it in the true spirit of a Roundhead. "When the news came to Bridgwater," says one who lived in his family and often heard the circumstance referred to, "the officers of the regiment were seen to cabal together in little companies, five or six at a place, and talk of it very seriously, none of them being forward to tell Colonel Blake what they were talking about. At last he asked one of them very earnestly, and the gentleman replied with some emotion, *Your brother Sam is killed,* explaining how it came to pass. The colonel, having heard him out, said, *Sam had no business there.* And, as if he took no further notice of it, turned from the Corn-hill or market-place into the Swan Inn, of chief note in that town, and shutting himself in a room gave way to the calls of nature and brotherly love, saying, *Died Abner as a fool dieth!*" The same writer adds : " But the sorrow of heroic minds, as it is more powerful than that of the general, so it is sooner spent ; and collecting his own great soul within itself, and remembering the duty and resignation to the Divine will, he was in a short time composed both in thought and look, and leaving the Swan room, conversed with his officers on the Corn-hill about their march to the south coast. After this gush of grief, he was never known to bewail his brother's untimely death, or let it dwell in his memory." But to the end of his career he never ceased to think with kindness and regret of poor Sam,—the only one of his brothers who resembled himself in contempt of obstacles ; and to the orphan children thus suddenly committed to his charge he became a father. The elder boy, Robert, evinced at an early age a longing for the sea; he entered the navy, and served with distinction in the fleets of his uncle; the younger, Samuel, showed a more pacific disposition. It was to the young seaman, Captain Robert Blake, that the Admiral bequeathed, as the true heir to his naval glories, the gold chain bestowed on him by Parliament for his eminent services to the Commonwealth.

After the fall of Bristol, the royal army, increased by new levies, separated into two grand divisions. Rupert and the King turned northward, Maurice went into the west with orders to reduce the few towns on the south-west coast still holding out for Parliament. Lord Carnarvon led the advanced guard of the western army, a powerful squadron of horse, and in a few weeks swept the country from the Severn to the sea. Dorchester struck without a blow. Weymouth, Corfe Castle and Portland Island fell into Cavalier hands; and these great losses were followed by the loss of Barnstaple, Dartmouth and Exeter. The natural strength of Plymouth set the land-forces at defiance; but with the exception of two or three insignificant places, like Poole and Lyme, it was the only position of influence still retained by the Roundheads in the west of England. Maurice, flushed with the glories of a triumphant march, tried an assault of Plymouth; but failing in the attempt, he left a detachment of his army to blockade the great fortress, and with a force of nearly twenty thousand men moved along the coast, intending to punish the petty garrisons of Lyme and Poole, on his way towards London.

Lyme was a little fishing town with nine hundred or a thousand inhabitants. Built in a narrow valley, at the dip between two hills, it was overlooked on three sides from the heights, and the cliffs commanded the whole inner line of the bay. Three narrow lanes, leading towards Charmouth, Axminster and Sidmouth, cut by a few irregular streets, formed the heart of the town. Generally the houses were built of soft stone and covered with thatch, the better sort having curious gables and balconies opening out pleasantly to the sea. The church, dedicated to St. Michael, stood on a rising ground on the left, but every part of the grave-yard, roof, and steeple was overlooked from the brow of Colway hill. As a port Lyme was of small importance, the water being shallow and the shore dangerous. Only vessels of the smallest tonnage could run in for shelter behind its ancient Cobb,—a low sea-wall built out four or five hundred yards from the town to break the tremendous force of the Atlantic waves,—yet as no other place of refuge offered itself for several leagues along that stormy coast, its roadstead sometimes swarmed with small vessels, the property of London merchants, and therefore good prize for Royalists. The town-defences consisted of a dry ditch, a few earth-works hastily thrown up, and three small batteries,—Davies' fort, standing a little above Church Cliffs on a high mound looking towards Uplyme, but which has since fallen into the sea—Gun Cliff, and the fort at Cobb Gate, the two latter being small batteries on the sea-shore, covering the bay, but useless against an enemy making his attack from the hills. Into this cluster of poor cottages Blake threw himself with part of Popham's regiment to protect the ships from marauding Cavaliers. Colonel Ceely, the civil governor of the town, had won distinction against the flying corps of Royalists; his brother-in-law, Harvey, a man of means, lent the assistance of his purse; and they were seconded by the zeal and devotion of Kerridge the mayor. Nor was Parliament unmindful of the town. A committee had been named to watch over its safety in conjunction with Poole and Plymouth. Money had been voted for arms, and powder had been sent from Plymouth. But the most sanguine member of the London committee never dreamt that Lyme would repulse the great army under Maurice, and that Blake's hold of this obscure and unfortified town would become one of the remarkable events of the war.

As the prince came down from the hills of Somerset, Blake counted his forces, and found the number did not exceed five hundred men. The town, though its spirit was good, afforded little aid, for its whole population fell short of a thousand souls; but with the assistance of the mayor and Governor Ceely, a body of volunteers, some of them from Charmouth and other neighbouring villages, was drilled for service. Earth-works, hastily thrown up, connected the points of the defence from Davies' fort, on the High Cliff, along the slopes beyond the town to Holme Bush fields, near that arm of the Cobb which connects the sea-wall with the shore. Two large houses, standing on opposite sides of the valley, about a mile from the line—Colway House, an ancient residence of the Cobham family, and Haye, a substantial farm, were occupied as outposts. Foraging parties were sent out in all directions, with orders to bring back fodder, cattle and other necessaries, for which receipts were duly given. Blake's comrades were still working at the rude defences when the glittering array of the royal army suddenly appeared above the brow of Uplyme Hill. The vast expanse of sea, the green slopes of that secluded valley, broken to the view by clumps of trees, orchards and corn-fields, and the white houses of the town, as they lay, serene and picturesque, in the morning sun, touched some chords of sentiment even in the grim bosom of civil war, and the Cavalier host rent the air with shouts of surprise and admiration. It was not until evening that Maurice descended into the valley, drove the outposts from Haye and Colway House, and summoned Blake and Ceely to surrender.

The extreme weakness of the place was well known to the Royalists; so that when the prince found his summons answered with a haughty defiance, he impetuously called his trumpeters to sound a general charge. The infantry hurled a shower of hand-grenades into the town, and in the disorder caused by their explosion, a squadron of horse rode down on the lines, expecting to carry them lance in hand at the first onset. But the tactics which had baffled the Royalists at Prior's Hill prevailed again at Lyme; after a fierce struggle between lance and musket, the horse, unable to force an entrance, drew off,

and retired up the valley. The foot then advanced in
deep columns to storm ; again and again they advanced ;
but always to fall back with loss of men and character
before an unwavering and deadly fire. Furious at this
sudden check to his career of arms, Maurice rode to the
scene of confusion, rallied the broken ranks, and gave
the word to charge once more ; but the men refused to
obey the word, until he wheeled round his cavalry and
drove them on by pistol-shots in the rear. It was all in
vain. Volleys of case-shot met them in front from an
enemy protected by cover from their fire ; and as their
ranks thinned, the line staggered, broke, and the men
turned and fled beyond hope of recal that day. The
prince then changed his plan ; convinced by the firmness of the first day's resistance, that, contemptible as
Lyme would appear to the King and his council, he
must either sit down to the labours of a regular siege,
or march away with his great army, leaving this vigilant
enemy in his rear and with the stain of discomfiture
on his hitherto victorious banner. Between these two
courses there was no choice ; so he took up his residence at Colway House, and threw up works on which
to plant his siege artillery. More than eight weeks
that fine army lay on the slopes over Lyme, baffled by
an enemy with only a handful of men, and mud-works
for ramparts. At Oxford, the affair was a marvel and
mystery. Every hour the Court expected to hear that
the " little vile fishing-town," as Clarendon contemp-
tuously calls it, had fallen, and that Maurice had
marched away to enterprises of greater moment ; but
every post brought word to the wondering council, that
Colonel Blake still held out, and that his defence was
rousing and rallying the dispersed adherents of Parliament in those parts. While the western division of the
Royalists was wasting its time and strength in an obscure

corner,—neither port, nor fortress, nor highway,—the most important towns and castles lay open to the Round-heads, and some of them actually fell into their hands. Lyme itself remained unshaken. Day after day, week after week, storm, stratagem, blockade, failed to subdue the little garrison. Maurice felt the humiliation of his position; unable to account to his uncle and his brother for the delay of its capture, he made a prodigal sacrifice of life to secure success. How often would the thought occur to him—if Rupert had only hung that Captain Blake at Bristol! In London the press was filled with the wonders of this remarkable defence; and Roundhead writers used it as a set-off against their own prolonged failures at Latham House. Yet the Cavaliers fought before the breastworks at Lyme with the most resolute gallantry, and some of the best blood in the west of England flowed into its trenches. After the siege was raised, and the Royalists had time to count up and compare their losses, they found to their surprise and horror that more men of gentle blood had died before Lyme, than had fallen in all the other sieges and skirmishes in the western counties since the opening of the war.

Within the town, all was activity, confidence, enthu-siasm. The volunteers from Uplyme, Charmouth, and the villages along the sea-coast, raised the effective force of the garrison to nearly a thousand men; many of them rude of speech, unused to arms, unbroken by discipline, but hardy, fearless, and devoted to the good cause. After a few days' service in that fierce school, under that steady command, they stood fire like veteran soldiers; and they brought into the camp a spirit of disinterestedness quite unusual in men of the sword. Under pressure of the defence, they served without pay, and lived on short commons; many of them had no

shirts or other linen, few wore shoes and stockings, and
still fewer could boast of a full suit of clothes. Yet no
murmur was ever heard:—each man felt some portion
of the greatness of the issue, and ordinary sufferings
seemed as nothing when borne in the name of freedom
and of God. Nor was this martial ardour confined to
the hardier sex; women not only tended the sick, and
waited on the wounded, but wrought at the ditch and
barricades, loaded the bandoliers with powder and shot,
and even learned to handle the musket with effect. One
heroine stood in the ranks during a furious attempt to
storm, and fired sixteen rounds of shot at the enemy's
columns.

Possessed of a regular siege-train, Maurice had a
great superiority in the more distant fighting. His
batteries, placed on the cliffs and slopes above the line
of defence, gradually silenced the little forts in the town.
Cobb Gate was destroyed by a battery erected at Holme
Bush, which battery also swept the bay, and prevented
the arrival of vessels, except under cover of night. A
powerful battery was erected on Colway Hill to act
against Davies' fort—the key of the defence,—but the
earth-walls on that side being hastily strengthened six
or eight feet, the cannon-shot spent its force on them in
vain. In the narrow streets and lanes of the town,
destruction went on slowly but certainly. Hand-
grenades were picked up in every yard; many houses
were soon rendered uninhabitable; those on the hill-
side near the road to Sidmouth were utterly destroyed;
the vessels in the harbour suffered much from the land
batteries; but not an inch of the line was lost by the
garrison. About seven at night on May 6th a grand
attack was made by surprise. Six days the Royalists
had been quiet in their tents, and the town-people had
been employed in securing their fishing-boats from the

rage of a tempest; the soldiers, a little off guard, were at supper—and the approach of the storming party—three separate columns, supported by musqueteers,—was concealed by a thick fog. Roused, however, by the enemy's signals, the Roundheads flew to arms, and met their assailants with valour and impetuosity superior to their own. Some companies of Royalists, fighting as if they had resolved to take the place that night, forced their way through the rude works, and pressed on with shouts towards the market square; but the defenders closed behind them, and cut off from their comrades, in the narrow alleys of an unknown town, the enemy in front, flank and rear, they perished almost to a man. The surprise having failed, the fog and darkness came in aid of the defence; and in less than an hour after the signal to storm the breastwork had been given, the Cavaliers were driven off from every part of the crescent, leaving behind them a heap of pikes, muskets, hand-grenades, and ladders. A hundred men lay dead in the trenches. By death, wounds and desertion, Maurice lost between four and five hundred men that night. Colonel Blewett, one of the best soldiers in the royal camp, fell, pierced with three balls, while gallantly leading his column across the works. The day he joined the camp before Lyme, the generals told him it was a mere breakfast matter, and that they would carry the town before they dined! Captain Pawlett and many other officers were left dead in the fields. Next morning, Maurice sent to beg the body of his friend Blewett, and Blake at once consented to restore it if his men were not disturbed while searching for the body, and picking up the spoil. He would not, he said, in such a case make conditions, but he would appeal to the prince's magnanimity to set at liberty Ceely's brother-in-law, Harvey, who had been seized when going about his affairs, and was then a prisoner in the camp. Blewett's corpse was found, washed and put into a new shroud and coffin; but Maurice refused to restore Harvey, and told the defenders they might keep the dead body if they pleased. Indignant at this reply, Blake had the coffin carried to the line opposite the entry on Holme Bush, where he signalled the heralds to come for it. "Have you," said he, scornfully, as the men approached, "have you any command to pay for the shroud and coffin?" They answered, "No." Curling his whiskers with his finger, he added with disdain:—"Nevertheless, take them: we are not so poor but that we can give them to you."

The news of this gallant repulse flew to Plymouth. Thence it was despatched to London, where it created the most lively joy. In the House of Commons it was read by Richard Rose, one of the burgesses for Lyme; and the House at once voted an aid of 300*l.*, and thanked the garrison and its chiefs in the warmest terms. Blake was urgent in his appeals to Parliament for succour. Provisions and ammunition were both failing; some of his most active partisans had fallen at his side in the daily encounters, and his little garrison was rapidly losing its strength by death, wounds and sickness. But to the Cavaliers he still presented the same resolute front. Late one night his scouts brought word that early next morning the enemy intended a surprise; against this plot he resolved to use counter-plot; therefore, when the assailants, moving with great caution, came to the works, they found them more deserted than they had dared to hope; the few men on guard fled before them into the town, and Cavaliers to the number of four hundred followed them into the net of close and intricate alleys where Blake had laid his ambush. Not a single man escaped. Cut off from their friends and enclosed in a ring of fire, poured on them from the cover of windows, doors and parapets, as well as from the soldiers in the streets, they struggled gallantly to gain some open space, but after a great part of their body had fallen in heaps, choking the way and rendering it still more difficult to advance or retreat, the rest laid down their arms and were made prisoners of war. A parley took place soon after this signal disaster, when Blake told one of the Royalist generals that he did not wish for advantage of position: the officer, then standing on the low breastwork, pointed out its weakness, and spoke with the confidence of an old soldier of its speedy capture. "Here," said the commander of the garrison characteristically, " you see how weak our works are ; they are not things wherein we trust ; therefore tell the prince that if he wishes to come into the town with his army to fight, we will pull down ten or twelve yards, so that he may come in with ten men abreast, and we will fight him." The Royalists replied that they would come into the town when they could do so to their own advantage :—which did not happen so long as Blake commanded.

The twenty-third of May found the civil and military governors anxiously counting up the store of bread and powder. A crisis was nigh ; in two weeks the last sack of flour would be consumed, and if no relief came in by sea the garrison would be starved out, and either forced to surrender or cut their way through the beleaguering hosts. But on that very evening they descried a sail rounding Portland Point ; and when morning dawned the fleet of the Earl of Warwick was seen in the offing, lying as near shore as the dangerous form of the coast would allow. He had brought by order of Parliament a small relief of provisions and some military stores. The sailors sent on land with these supplies were so shocked to see the naked and deplorable condition of the little garrison of whose prowess they had heard so much, that they immediately returned to the ships and spread the touching details of the story among their comrades. These noble fellows at once made a collection of all the articles they could spare; and many a man that day gave up his best shoes, his warmest shirt, and more than half his ration to the defenders of Lyme. They contributed from their scanty stores, thirty pair of boots, a hundred pair of shoes, a hundred and sixty pair of stockings, a heap of old clothes, a good round number of shirts, and a considerable quantity of bread and fish. Nor was this the largest part of their generous sacrifice:—they proposed to the commissariat to give up for the same purposes a fourth of their daily allowance of bread for the next four months, in all nine thousand pounds weight. While these arrangements were being made on board, the garrison was fighting bravely in the streets. Blake, at the head of a sallying party, was about to issue from the gate, when Captain Southern, sent by Maurice to make another effort to carry the town by assault before Warwick could throw reinforcements on shore, began the attack. The action was brief but terrific. Colonel Weir, Blake's most active and efficient officer, was shot in the abdomen; Captain Pyne, his gallant master of the horse, received a mortal wound; Blake himself was hurt in the foot, enough to make him lame for life. Sixty Cavalier corpses strewed the ground; among them was the corpse of Captain Southern, who for a freak had dressed himself in Lord Pawlett's armour —a man most hateful to the people of Lyme, and who was heavily mulcted for his share in these transactions for the express benefit of the town.

Few men had done so much for the defence as Captain

Pyne; and Blake ordered a solemn funeral to be performed in his honour. Unfortunately, the volleys fired over his grave informed the Cavaliers, who from Black Venne and Colway Hill could look down into the very churchyard, that some mournful act of the drama was in progress and the attention of the citizens drawn off from the defence; and when the people in their mourning attire were turning from the chancel where they had paid the last duties to their old companion in arms, a cry of attack was raised along the streets, and a cannonade, louder, fiercer, and more sustained than usual, commenced from all the batteries. After thundering at the works until noon, tearing away the earth-walls in several places, bursting through roofs and knocking down chimneys, the Cavaliers advanced with their scaling-ladders, hand-grenades, and long pikes, from Charmouth road, from Uplyme, and from the high grounds above Holme Bush. The Roundheads met the attacking parties with the fury of men suffering under a sense of outrage,—and that day blood flowed down the steep gutters, and the rivulet and the town-water were both dyed crimson. The Royalist gentlemen held their ground stoutly, but their ardour was no longer seconded by the common soldiers, and they were three times driven back with shame and loss to their entrenchments. Yet these repulses were dearly bought, and in the diary of the defence this day was marked as that on which the town suffered most severely in its garrison.

When all was still again, Blake went on board the fleet, and arranged with Warwick the details of an operation for the ensuing day. In pursuance of his scheme three hundred men were secretly landed from the ships; the fleet then weighed anchor and stood away eastward towards Charmouth, making feints of a design to throw men on shore at some favourable point.

Maurice, anxiously watching this movement from the heights, concluded that the Earl had taken part of the garrison on board with the intention of attacking him on his rear or flank; and under this impression he sent his cavalry, attended by a few hundred foot, along the brow of the cliffs, to wait on this suspicious movement, and if possible prevent a landing. By firing a few broadsides towards the cliffs, Warwick drew this force to the east of Seatown, seven or eight miles from Lyme, where he commenced a more steady cannonade, as if he designed to send a body of men towards Chideock Castle. The Royalists threw up a breastwork. Meanwhile, as Blake had foreseen, the Prince resolved to make a final attempt to carry the works. Three thousand men were chosen from the Cavalier ranks; they were arranged in three solid columns, and ordered to support and succeed each other in the attack. On the other side, by the accession of the three hundred seamen, Blake could now muster within his lines about twelve hundred men; and as Maurice's formidable cavalry was away among the hills beyond Seatown, the two forces approached nearer equality of numbers than they had been in any previous encounter; with the advantages for the defenders of concentration, narrow streets, houses, every one of which was a little fortress, and the works in advance, such as they were. At six in the evening, while there were still three hours of daylight, the first shots were exchanged, and until past eight the slope leading to Uplyme was like a battle-field, and the firing so swift and fierce as to give the town an appearance of being wrapt in flames. Some houses were set on fire and destroyed, others were battered down with shot; but the sight of burning thatch and falling rafters only served to inflame the courage of the people. A full third of the town was already in ruins, and even had he succeeded, Maurice would have

gained nothing at Lyme beyond glory and a heap of
stones. The first column fought gallantly for half an
hour; it retired, and the second column occupied its
post. By half-past seven this was also broken; and the
last column advanced with tremendous shouts on the
now almost exhausted garrison. Falling back a little, so
as to recover breath under the cross fire from the nearest
houses, the defenders made a vigorous stand, and in half
an hour the result was no longer doubtful. Blake then
gave his final orders. Advancing from all sides, as if
quickened with new life, his officers appeared on both
flanks of the enemy, while he pressed them steadily in
front. A little after eight o'clock the attacking column
was cut through, and the soldiers fled in disorder to their
entrenched quarters. Stragglers continued to fire their
pieces at intervals until night-fall; but the contest was
already over. That day cost King Charles five hundred
of his bravest followers.

Maurice had made his last effort, and it had failed.
Cannonades were repeated again and again, but the
day of hope for him was now past. Essex was moving
westward with a large army, and the Prince felt that his
position before Lyme was no longer tenable. As a
parting salute he fired into the town a quantity of red-
hot balls and bars of twisted lead. Poor Maurice! His
rage, though vain, was not unnatural: for his fortunes
and his military reputation were both broken on the
rocky beach at Lyme. The loss of the Cavaliers in men
amounted to two thousand:—more than had fallen in
the conquest of both the two western capitals, Exeter
and Bristol. Their loss in time, material, moral influence,
and military character were more considerable and more
irreparable.

# CHAPTER III.

## 1644—1649.

## TAUNTON.

THE long detention of the royal army in the valley
of Lyme, enabled Essex to march by slow stages from
London to Dorset, without meeting an enemy, and with
the advantage of being able to recruit his forces and
strengthen the interests of his party by the way.
Without great military talents, barren in conception as
he was slow in execution, Essex had yet the good fortune
to be everywhere popular. His name was a pledge of
order. A regiment of raw levies is seldom kept under
the curb of discipline, but the legions of Essex contrasted most favourably with Goring's crew and
Maurice's marauders. Many of those who had hitherto
been neutral in the quarrel, and comparatively indifferent to the issue, so that it should come speedily
and relieve their houses from pillage and their women
from insult, received Essex with open arms. Hundreds
flocked to his camp, anxious to serve under so chivalrous
a leader. Thus, while the Royalists were wasting their
strength to no purpose in an obscure corner of Dorsetshire, their enemies, recently broken, dispersed and dispirited almost beyond hope, were gaining in moral and
material power. Alarmed for his own safety, Maurice
had anxiously watched the movements of this new army;

and as soon as he heard of the dexterous turn which restored Weymouth to the Roundheads without the loss of a single man, he drew to his tents a great part of the Taunton garrison, and abandoning to the enemy all the trophies of his former march, fled away, with his reduced but still magnificent army, towards Exeter.

Essex, moving in the wake of Maurice, took the road towards Cornwall, in the hope of cutting off the western division of the grand army,—but leaving nearly all the important towns of Somerset and Devon in the King's hands, and separating his troops from their natural base of operations. His error was fatal. Every step westward led him deeper into an unknown country, with inhabitants either neutral or unfriendly, and in which all the strong places were possessed by Royalists. With the exception of Plymouth, still held in a state of blockade, all the great fortresses owned the King: Poole, Lyme, and Weymouth had been maintained or recovered by the national party, but between the seacoast and the head waters of the Severn, they had not a single town or castle of real military importance. The Cavaliers possessed Bath, Bristol, Exeter, Bridgwater, Langport, and Ilchester,—and they had powerful garrisons in such strongholds as Ninney Castle, Chideock House, Dunster Castle, Corfe Castle, Portland Island, Farley Castle, and the Scilly Islands. Essex, on his part, possessed no more of the country than his patrols covered with their muskets. Still he pressed on. Naturally brave, he could not see his enemy in full retreat without the wish to hang on his rear and compel him to hazard daily skirmishes. At Oxford his imprudence was soon understood, and Charles proposed to march into the west with all the forces at his disposal, place the Roundhead Earl between two fires, and compel him to fight a battle at a great disadvantage.

Affairs were in this position, when Blake, now master of his own movements, executed one of those bold and happy strokes which equal in importance the gain of a great battle. His idea was to break the formidable line of royal fortresses in the midst,—to cut off the supplies and interrupt the most direct communication between the Royalist camps,—to cover, at least for some days, the rear of Essex, now entangled in the Cornish hills, unable to force a battle or to retreat,—and, finally, to secure for himself and for the good cause a new and commanding centre of operations. These objects were all to be achieved by the capture of Taunton. A glance at any old map will show how that town was placed. It was surrounded by castles and garrisons. It stood on and controlled the great western highway. All letters, levies, stores and ammunition sent from Charles to Maurice, or from the generals and officers in the west to the King and to each other, had to pass through it. With the exception of cross-country roads, out of the way and almost impracticable for cavalry and artillery, no other route existed between Oxford, Bristol, and Exeter. But, besides its central position, Taunton was of singular importance to the Roundheads. The inhabitants— rich, brave, devoted, numerous—were for the most part well affected to their cause. The farmers, artisans and peasants of the neighbouring hamlets were mostly Puritans in religion. A large pile of arms seized in Roundhead houses by Sir William Portman, the borough member, was laid up in the old castle, together with ten thousand pounds in ready money, extorted from rich and poor of the same party. The Cavalier generals never imagined Taunton to be in danger. It was unwalled and surrounded at no great distance by strong fortresses and garrisons, Bridgwater and Langport, either of them within an hour's hard riding, Dunster and Ilchester

also within easy reach, and no enemy nearer than the
exhausted little troop at Lyme. But Blake, who had
friends in the place, was well informed of the state of
public feeling, of the exact strength of the garrison, of
the irresolute character of the military governor; and
notwithstanding the hazards of such an attempt with the
small force at his command, the prize being of supreme
importance in that stage of the war, he resolved to try
the effect of a sudden attack. His men were inured to
danger, and had never known defeat. His Taunton
friends assured him that he had nothing to fear from the
inhabitants, and that Colonel Reeves's garrison was
unequal to the defence of so large a town. Blake fore-
saw that his great difficulty would lie, not in seizing the
position, but in holding it afterwards against so many
enemies. Taunton was not like Lyme. No aid could
come to it by sea; on every side it was shut in by hills;
every road from it led to a royal stronghold. Yet once
master of the town, he did not despair of being able to
maintain himself long enough to give Essex time to
create a diversion in the west; and at the moment this
seemed sufficient. Joining his flying corps with the
regiment of Sir Robert Pye—afterwards governor of
Leicester, when Rupert stormed that unhappy town,—
he suddenly appeared before the gates of Taunton, summoned the garrison to surrender, and offered them
honourable terms. Startled at this unexpected appa-
rition, unaware of the exact strength of his assailants,
and not willing to throw himself on popular support,
Colonel Reeves asked for a parley, in which he agreed to
give up his post on condition of being allowed to march
away with his men to Bridgwater. As soon as the
Royalists had marched out in silence at the east gate of
the town, Blake and Pye entered with their respective
corps, amidst the peal of St. Mary's bells and the up-

roarious joy of the Puritan people. A demi-culverin, ten small pieces of ordnance, two tons of match, eight barrels of gunpowder, a considerable store of pikes, pistols, swords, and other arms, with a magazine of provisions, were found in the castle. A great quantity of household furniture—carried by force from the dwellings of suspected persons—was also found among the spoils of this bloodless victory, and was no doubt restored to its former owners. No accident occurred to dash the glory of his capture :—and when the news of it arrived in London, patriotic citizens lighted fires in honour of Colonel Blake, and Parliament hastened to appoint him governor of the town which he had so gallantly assailed and so unexpectedly won.

Blake took possession of Taunton on the eighth of July 1644; on the second of the same month Cromwell had defeated Rupert at Marston Moor. Intelligence of these events reached the court about the same time at Bath, whither Charles had moved to be nearer the scene of operations between Maurice and Essex. Two such disasters convinced the Royalist generals that to act with greater vigour or to see the west of England torn from their hands was their only choice. Exeter still held out for the Queen, a guest within its walls; all the active inland towns and garrisons, Taunton excepted, were with the King; and the Roundhead army under Essex had failed to establish for itself a decided superiority in the field. Under these circumstances it appeared to the royal generals that there was time—and only just time—to strike a blow such as would recover for them the whole west of England. A few rapid marches, undertaken with a clear purpose, had already brought the army from Oxford, across the Cotswold Hills, to Cirencester and Bath. Lord Hopton had been previously required to concentrate at Bristol a large body of troops, blindly devoted to the King, from the Welsh borders; and as this ever-increasing army continued its westward march, Blake, who had long seen that the object of the movement was to overwhelm the Earl of Essex, prepared to dispute its passage along the great highway, aware that the interruption of his line of march would compel the King either to throw himself on Taunton with his whole power or march through the hills over almost impassable roads. In either case a certain number of days must be lost to the Royalists, and during these precious days a man of military genius would have been able to reduce Exeter, or force Prince Maurice to fight a battle. Unhappily the Earl of Essex was not a Cromwell. Much discussion and some differences occurred in the royal camp as to the course to be pursued. The Cavalier gentry of Somerset and Devon burned with rage at the idea of one of the fairest towns in the two counties being held by rebels; the more ardent generals expressed indignation at what they called the insult offered to the royal army by Blake in throwing himself with a few adventurers into a position that every soldier knew to be untenable. They urged the King to advance from Bristol by the great highway and punish the rebel who had so shamefully foiled them at Lyme. But the very name of that obscure little town suggested the strongest reason for avoiding Taunton. Charles's object was an immediate concentration of his two armies on the borders of Cornwall, so that by a decisive victory over Essex he might be able to relieve Exeter and reduce Plymouth to obedience. If he attempted to force his way through Taunton, it was impossible for any one to tell how long he might be detained there, whilst the number of days to be lost in going over the Quantock Hills and round by north Devon to Exeter could be reckoned with the greatest certainty. The Royalists, therefore, leaving Blake for a time in undisputed possession of his prize, took the cross-country roads, and in due time arrived at Exeter. The King's plan succeeded. Joining Maurice at Liskeard, he found they had no need to risk a battle in order to conquer. Led by false statements into a country of which he knew nothing, Essex saw his army waste away by sickness, desertion and the enemy's fire, with no hope of action or of escape. Shut up in a narrow gorge by the sea-shore, land-locked on all sides, with a hostile population around him, provisions failing and a mutinous spirit spreading in the ranks, he at last determined to quit the command he could no longer hold, leaving his followers, many of whom had taken up arms expressly for his sake, to the clemency of an incensed sovereign. He embarked with a single attendant, secretly, and in the night:— next day the troops were without a leader, and nothing remained but to surrender at discretion. The army of the West was annihilated without a shot. This terrible calamity spread dismay throughout England: but nowhere was it so terrible as to the poor burgesses of Taunton. Of that great Roundhead army, not a single battalion kept the field to divide with them the attention of the victorious Royalists.

One man alone appeared undaunted by an event which laid the western counties at the King's feet. Blake not only prepared to defend his post against the foes who would soon be disengaged from other tasks and swarming round it in the hope of booty; he continued to carry fire and sword, levies and requisitions, into the enemy's quarters. Hanging, with a handful of intrepid men, on the left flank of the royal army, he had harassed their westward march, cut off their stragglers, intercepted their supplies; and by sudden and frequent visits to the weaker Royalist towns, had kept the district in such a state of alarm as, even after the flight of Essex, prevented Charles from settling the country in his own interest. His unfailing good fortune had raised the spirits of his followers to the height at which danger becomes a mere excitement; undaunted by the presence of two armies, unchecked by castles and fortified houses, their bold excursions were extended to the very gates of Exeter; and in the midst of rejoicings for the victory in Cornwall, ladies were suddenly alarmed by the appearance of a squadron of Roundhead horse under the walls of that city. From these sallies Blake and his officers seldom returned without bringing back arms, ammunition and prisoners. Nor was Taunton itself neglected. Though determined to keep as wide a space of country open round the town as vigour could clear and vigilance keep watch over, he did not overlook the fact that, isolated as he was from his Roundhead friends, it would be impossible to hold the open field much longer against the Cavalier forces occupying the western towns; such parts, therefore, of the ancient fortifications as admitted of hasty repair, were strengthened and restored.

Little time was allowed the garrison for preparation. Flushed with their successes in Cornwall, the returning Cavaliers swept the country from the gates of Plymouth to the suburbs of Taunton, without encountering a single hostile band. Charles himself, too elated to think of a single town in Somerset, was bent on a rapid and victorious march on London, whither he summoned all his subjects by common proclamation to attend him and compel the two Houses to make peace. But although the town was undisturbed by the grand army, parties of horse and foot from Exeter, Bridgwater, and Dunster

Castle,—Irish rebels, wild men from the Cornish mines, and yet more detested foreign mercenaries,—prowled about the beautiful hamlets near Taunton; not daring to approach too near the rude lines, or engage in an open assault, but committing acts of rapine and cruelty on unarmed persons met on the highways. Sir Francis Doddington, a brave but brutal soldier, at the head of a marauding party from Bridgwater Castle, made himself conspicuous by these outrages. One day he met a clergyman on the road a short distance from Taunton, to whom he shouted—"Who art thou for, priest?" The clergyman answered calmly—"For God and His Gospel." Doddington drew a pistol and shot him through the heart. While the Royalists were yet at Exeter, a council had been held to consider the loss of Taunton, and the interruption of the great highway. Many local magnates, indignant that the finest town between Bristol and Exeter should be held by rebels, urged the King to march in that direction; but the royal generals, anxious to gain time, resolved to proceed through Honiton and Chard towards London, leaving the task of reducing Taunton to Colonel Wyndham, governor of Bridgwater, and Blake's old rival in his native town. Wyndham was proud of his employment, hoping to triumph over a local as well as a public enemy. Suddenly appearing before the town with a small force drawn from Bridgwater, he wrote a letter to the burgesses in very menacing terms, threatening the town with fire and sword, if it were not immediately surrendered. Blake's answer was brief and emphatic:—"These are to let you know," he wrote, "that as we neither fear your menaces nor accept your proffers, we wish you for time to come to desist from all overtures of the like nature unto us, who are resolved to the last drop of our blood to maintain the quarrel we have undertaken; and I doubt not but the same God who hath hitherto protected us will bless us with an issue answerable to the justness of our cause ; however, to Him alone shall we stand or fall."— As his threats produced no effect, Wyndham sent a second trumpeter to his old neighbour and townsman, almost entreating him to accept terms of surrender ; for, as he urged, the town was unwalled—the place inconsiderable—and an attempt to defend it against the royal forces, now masters of the West, could only lead to an unnecessary waste of Christian blood.  Blake referred to his former answer as expressing all that he had to say in return :—and from that moment the siege may be considered as begun.

In some respects Taunton was a more defensible place than Lyme.  It lacked the vast advantage of a sea communication, but then it was not surrounded by heights commanding its streets and public buildings.  The nearest hills were far beyond the range of cannon.  The only rising ground for a mile or more was that on which the castle stood, near the centre of the town : consequently the enemy's powerful artillery inspired but little terror in the citizens.  The character of the country also favoured defensive operations, for the fields were small, the hedges thick and high, the roads narrow and circuitous.  In the opinion of one of the most eminent commanders of that age, every field was as good as a fortification,—every lane as defensible as a pass.  Only three entrances led into the town—the north road from Minehead and Dunster, crossing the river Tone under the castle-guns by means of an old wooden bridge—and the great highway, entering from Bridgwater and Bristol at East Reach, and passing out at the West Gate for Exeter and Plymouth.  The castle and the river covered the first ; a sort of stone blockhouse, honoured with the name of the New Castle, flanked West Gate.  East Gate had no other defence than a narrow passage closed up with a solid oak door. Walls there were none. On every side the town was open, except so far as garden walls, hedges, and outhouses might afford covering from an enemy. The town itself consisted then, as it does now, of three principal streets, corresponding with the three roads into and through it, East Street, North Street, and High Street, meeting in a triangular space near the castle gates. This open space was used as a market and a bull-ring. Part of it was covered with sheds and shambles; in the centre stood an ancient stone cross, and facing it were the low picturesque fronts of the Town-hall, and the famous Inn, then and long afterwards known as the White Hart. In the angle formed by the junction of East Street and North Street rose the high and graceful tower of St. Mary Magdalen. With one exception, all the streets were strait and winding. The houses were built of brick or stone, with peaked gables, tile roofs, and bow windows. The castle, a structure of the Saxon time, and a hold of importance during the wars of the Roses, was partly in ruins; but its position was good: the walls, gates, and old drawbridges remained, and a double moat, fed by a brook from the hamlet of Chedford, strengthened its outworks.

Blake completed his preparations. Strong barricades were thrown across the roads. Breastworks were raised at the gates; and at East Gate, where he believed that the principal fighting would take place, he planted some of his artillery, supplied by order of the House of Commons, and garrisoned the alms-houses on one side and the dwellings on the other with his best musqueteers. Still, when everything had been done that could be done, the situation struck the mind as hopeless. In the earlier periods of the war Taunton had changed hands as Royalists or Roundheads happened to be in greater force in the neighbourhood. Hopton had placed there a Royalist garrison. The men had fled at the approach of Waller, who left a body of troops to secure the place for Parliament. Hertford drove these Roundheads away, and left the government to his friends. Reeves in his turn had surrendered without a blow. Blake was the first man who had ever thought of holding the town against a superior force. The Cavaliers believed him mad. As they knew very well, he had no base of operations in his daring attempt, no flanks on which to lean for support, no source of supplies but the chances of an occasional forage, and no hope of relief until a new army could be created, drilled, disciplined, and led to victory. How terrible the present evil—how vague and distant the hope of aid from London!

On receiving Blake's brief answer, Wyndham made a demonstration in the meadows on the east of the town, hoping to intimidate the inhabitants and afford the Royalist citizens an opportunity of rising against the garrison. But a party issuing from East Gate, and falling unexpectedly on his line, obliged him to face about and defend himself, which he did at first with some firmness, though in the end he was forced to retire with loss from his awkward position. Unwilling, after this encounter, to risk an assault, his troops tore up the roads and barricaded them with fruit-trees, cut off communications with the distant Roundheads, and stopped the market-carts on their way into the town with produce. For several months this blockade continued; sometimes it was strict, at other times it was loose and ineffectual; altogether it produced no material change in the position of the two forces. Wyndham indeed had much to gain by delay. The entire district—Lyme, Poole, Weymouth, and Plymouth excepted—was occupied by his friends. He had Bridgwater and Ilchester to

fall back on in case of need, either to rest his men or to recruit his strength. The Roundhead towns were closely invested: though, being open to the sea, they were not in immediate peril. Yet they were too well guarded to send relief or create any diversion in favour of Taunton. Day by day Blake saw the stock of provisions dwindle. No effort was spared to bring in new supplies; every week or two a vigorous sally was made by part of the garrison, which for a moment broke the cordon, and enabled farmers and gardeners to carry in fresh garden stuff, corn and cattle; but hemmed round as he was by so many strongholds, it was impossible to enlarge the circle much or preserve it open long; and in spite of every effort to increase the store, with a most careful husbandry of means, the want of food soon became a serious question for the besieged. Hope of succour from without was for a time at least denied. Lord Goring, with a large army of Royalists, lay at Salisbury, ready to oppose the march of relief from Kent or Middlesex, and the parliamentary chiefs began to fear that Blake would ultimately be starved out of his commanding position, and forced to give up without a blow one of the finest towns in the west of England. But help came to him in the hour of need. A German officer, named Vandruske, passing with a body of horse on the flank of Goring's dissolute army, rode rapidly down the vales of Wiltshire, Dorsetshire and Somerset, and falling unexpectedly on Wyndham's line, cut through it and rode triumphantly into the town. In the panic thus created among the Royalists, Blake sallied out, attacked the beleaguering regiments, routed them at the first onset, and chased them in their flight to the gates of Bridgwater, in the castle of which town they found the first shelter from Vandruske's dragoons. The great roads being opened up by this action, Blake, attended by Vandruske's horsemen, made a circuit of the country, rousing his friends from the torpor of despair, and striking his exulting foes with a sense of the sudden vicissitudes of war. For a few days the action of the Royalists in those parts seemed paralysed. The garrisons retired behind their ramparts, leaving the open country at the energetic Roundheads' mercy ; every town in Somerset and Devon was disturbed more or less by these excursions ; and Goring's force was suddenly ordered down to Weymouth, lest the siege of that place should be interrupted by them.

The spirits of the Roundheads rapidly revived. The Weymouth garrison, driven by surprise from the upper town and the forts, still held out in the lower town, and shortly after Goring's arrival with his full strength of horse, foot, dragoons and artillery, the place, to use the words of the Royalist writer, " was retaken by that contemptible number of rebels, who had been beaten into the lower town, and who were looked upon as prisoners at mercy." Baffled at Weymouth, Goring retired with ten thousand men and a large park of ordnance into Somerset, raising wonder and horror along his line of march. War had made the country familiar with the ordinary licence of the camp. Exactions of money—levies of corn, horses and men— arbitrary arrests — drum-head trials — and summary punishments, were every-day events. But Goring's army—known by the opprobrious name of Goring's crew —pillaged without legal forms, insulted women, and burnt the property they could not carry off. Houses and villages were deserted at their approach. Drunkenness and debauchery marked their course; shame, misery and desolation followed in their track. The less warlike of the population, women, children, old men and ministers of religion, fled before them as before a consuming fire ; and with such effects as they could snatch up in the hurry of departure from their homesteads, threw themselves into Taunton. Of the clergy who thus flew to Blake for protection against Goring's crew, was one who proved singularly useful during the long and trying defence :—Thomas Welman, vicar of Luppit near Honiton. Educated at Oxford, where he distinguished himself by his learning, piety and gentle manners, he married a Honiton lady, and settled in a quiet country hamlet to the work of his Christian ministry, among a people who soon became attached to him by ties of gratitude and love. The rapine, cruelty and profligacy of the Cavaliers roused his mild nature ; he fled from the pleasant place in which his lot had been cast ; and during the hottest period of the siege of Taunton, his pictures of the shame and ruin he had seen that beleaguering host commit in the valleys of Devonshire, served to inflame and sanctify the patriot ardour of the garrison and people.

As time wore on, every hour developed still more the importance of the blow struck by Blake at Taunton. It had prevented the concentration of the royal armies. It had thrown a new subject of discord into the King's council. It had created a thousand local jealousies, discontents, and suspicions. Lord Goring, general of the horse, quarrelled with Lord Hopton, master of the ordnance, about the command. Sir Richard Grenville, Sir John Berkeley, and other West-of-England men, loudly expressed their discontent at what they called the meanness which permitted such an enemy to remain master of Taunton ; and in a critical moment, Grenville refused to obey the orders of his superior officers. He had sworn to capture Taunton, and he refused to move until his oath had been redeemed. Meanwhile the New Model was perfected ; and under the Self-denying ordinance, the command in chief of the Roundhead army was transferred from Essex to Fairfax, with Cromwell for his general of the horse. Cromwell joined Sir William Waller; and the combined forces of the two generals making a feint as if they would fall on Goring, the outwitted Royalist drew off to Exeter, leaving the road open for Vandruske and his dragoons to regain the main body of Roundhead cavalry. These indications of a change of fortune called the Prince of Wales into the west, where he summoned the Commissioners for Somerset to Bristol, to advise with him in person on the state of that county. They complained bitterly of the riot and insolence of Goring's soldiers, and mourned in spirit over the obstinate defence and troublesome sallies of the Taunton garrison; which, they said, kept the country for thirty miles round in a state of alarm, and rendered it difficult to raise either men or money for the royal cause in Somerset. On all sides, it was urged that the most important operation for the western armies would be the reduction of that town. Messages were therefore sent to Goring, and at his request two of the prince's council, Lord Capel and Lord Colepepper, went to Wells to consult with him on the aspect of affairs; when after long consultations, Goring drew up in writing a plan of action. Leaving the greater part of his horse and two hundred foot on the borders of Wiltshire and Dorset to observe the motions of the enemy,— but so conveniently placed as to be able to retire towards his main body, should Cromwell or Waller advance in strength,—he proposed to move with his infantry and artillery, a few select squadrons of horse, and as many of the flying corps as could be drawn together on a sudden, into the vale of Taunton, and either capture the heroic town or burn it to ashes. Prince Charles adopted this plan. Orders were thereupon sent to Sir Richard

Grenville to appear in the trenches before Taunton with his regiments, consisting of eight hundred horse, two thousand two hundred foot, and a large body of pioneers, —orders which he obeyed with the utmost zeal. The Commissioners of Somerset were instructed to repair to the camp, and encourage by their presence the labours of the besiegers, as well as use their local influence with the citizens. Magazines of stores and ammunition were prepared; and in a few days Grenville had already occupied all the roads leading out of Taunton,—put an end to the free intercourse between town and country,— and drawn his line within a few hundred yards of the suburbs.

Since the defeat of Wyndham, that officer had been quiet at Bridgwater or Bristol; no enemy had been descried from the castle-turrets; no warlike clangour had been heard from the bells of St. Mary's church. But the fiery Grenville soon made his presence known to the inhabitants; with dogged valour he was fighting his way to the gate at East Reach, when a sudden movement by Waller forced Goring to turn his force eastward. In expectation of a pitched battle, the Cavalier commander ordered Grenville to quit his trenches, and repair with his whole force towards Shaftesbury. Grenville refused to obey these orders. The Prince of Wales interfered; but the obstinate knight answered that his men would not stir a yard, and that he himself had solemnly promised the Commissioners of Cornwall and Devon not to advance beyond Taunton until he could advance through it. At the same time, he declared his conviction that in a few days the place must fall under his assaults; and then he would joyfully push forward to the rendezvous of the royal army. Two or three skirmishes occurred between Goring and Waller, but without result. Goring again complained to the

Prince that without important reinforcements he dared not risk a battle; Grenville answered, that with six hundred more men he would undertake to deliver Taunton into the Prince's hands in six days. Perplexed by these quarrels, without the character and authority necessary to overrule both officers for the common good, the Prince of Wales called a council to determine the best course to pursue. Rupert was present and took a share in the debate. Taunton still held out:—Grenville would not quit the trenches even at the positive command of the King's son, his own future sovereign, until it fell:—Goring could not fight a decisive battle without the four thousand men then occupied in the siege. These were the fixed facts of the case. Rupert urged that a combined attempt should be made to expel Blake; arguing that the possession of Taunton by the Round-heads was the chief obstacle to the raising of men and money in a rich and populous county; that the siege employed one of the best of the royal armies; that in the event of its reduction, not only would Grenville's forces be released for other service, but volunteers would come in, and new levies could be made at pleasure. In this way it was possible to pacify the four western counties, raise an army for Goring to lead into Kent and Sussex, and another for the Prince of Wales to carry to his father's camp. The six days mentioned by Grenville was considered enough to effect the capture; and the least sanguine officer in the royal army professed to believe that the town could not hold out more than ten days or a fortnight against the combined armies of Goring and Grenville. The council, therefore, resolved to compel the rebel town to make immediate submission at any cost of men and material that might be found necessary for the purpose.

An immediate concentration of troops took place.

Wyndham repaired to the camp with his regiment. Sir John Berkeley made his appearance there. Sir Joseph Wagstaffe brought down from Wells the main body of Goring's foot, and the whole of his great park of artillery. The forces thus gathered before Taunton were of superior appointment and overwhelming number. The very day of their arrival, Grenville advanced his lines within musket-shot of the town, occupying the entire circuit of the suburbs; and then set out to inspect Wellington House, an outpost five miles distant, into which Blake had thrown a small garrison. From a window of this house he was marked by a musqueteer, and shot in the thigh; the wound was considered mortal, and he was immediately carried away by his servants to Exeter. Sir John Berkeley, who had served in the leaguer before Lyme, and was therefore supposed to know something of Blake's tactics, succeeded to the command. The six days passed, and the town was unconquered. Week followed week, but no one could tell with certainty how many days longer it would defy storm and stratagem. Some progress the besiegers undoubtedly made. The little garrison at Wellington House was overpowered, after an heroic resistance, by superior numbers, and in their rage the Cavaliers set fire to the house and destroyed it utterly. The investing lines were gradually drawn closer round the town; the suburbs, especially the suburb of East Reach, were pillaged and burnt. Many houses in the outer circuit of streets and lanes were battered down with the incessant play of cannon; and now and then for a few hours the Royalists occupied advanced positions within the shelter of ruined cottages and gardens. But the heart of the town remained inviolate. The castle, churchyard and market-place never once saw the enemy. Berkeley hoped to see a profound moral effect produced on the garrison

and inhabitants by the storm and conflagration of
Wellington House :—Blake better understood the moral
effect of such wanton barbarity, and as soon as he heard
of it, he ordered the joy-bells of St. Mary's to ring out
a merry peal! In the outer streets—especially in East
Street and just outside East Gate—there were daily
battles. Blake planted a few pieces of cannon at East
Gate, in front of which the street widens considerably
and the road falls about twenty feet : the houses, almost
reaching to each other across the narrow gateway,
served his men for ramparts; the doors, balconies, and
chimneys for embrasures. Every day the Cavaliers
stormed up the outer street. When cannon and musket
could be used no longer with effect, the pike and pistol
had to decide. Without regular walls, and with insuffi-
cient artillery, Blake had few advantages of position to
set off against the tremendous disparity of men; and
gallant and unyielding as the little garrison proved
itself, he saw its ranks grow thinner daily, as his brave
companions fell under the enemy's fire, while the prospect of relief still appeared distant and uncertain. But
what distressed both people and garrison beyond the
loss of their houses and gardens, the fatigue of nightly
watches, and the destruction of daily conflicts, was the
terrible scarcity of provisions. Bread was sold for
fourteen pence a pound, beer at eighteenpence a quart
—more than twenty times their market value! Other
articles of food were equally dear. The rations of the
soldiers were reduced to the lowest limit; and in spite
of public care and private charity, it is probable that
many of the poorer inhabitants died of starvation.
Berkeley was well aware that famine fought his battles
in the town; for, as in every other place where there
were men, there were adherents of both parties within
its gates; and in his despair of being able to win his

way pike in hand, he sent to invite the garrison to surrender to the King rather than die the lingering death of hunger. Blake replied to this request, that he had not yet eaten his boots, and that he should not dream of giving up the contest while he had so excellent a dinner to fall back on! Tradition says, that at this time only one animal, a hog, was left alive in the town —and that one more than half starved: in the afternoon, Blake, feeling that in their tragic state of mind a laugh would do the defenders as much good as a dinner, amused them by having this hog carried to all the posts · and whipped, so that its screams, heard in many places, might make the enemy suppose that fresh supplies had been obtained. But while assuming this defying attitude towards the Cavaliers, he wrote frequent and most urgent letters to London for relief. He assured the Houses that if succour did not speedily arrive, they must be put to the last straits for bread and powder. He said he had hitherto met with scorn every offer of a parley: he had still a barrel or two of powder ; and as for food, the garrison had resolved to eat their horses. But he begged the Houses to consider their distress ; and, in conclusion, he said he committed himself and his cause to God, in the confident hope that He would relieve them in His own good time. Parliament answered this appeal by an assurance that aid should soon be sent. Fairfax and Skippen received pressing orders to fly to the relief of the noble garrison. Meanwhile, house by house and street by street, the town was being burned, razed, and destroyed by cannon-shots. Hand-grenades, and fire-arrows, were thrown into it from every post. Not a day passed without a fire ; sometimes eight or ten houses were burning at the same moment ; and in the midst of all the fear, horror, and confusion incident to such disasters, Blake and his little garrison had to meet the storming parties of an enemy, brave, exasperated, and ten times their own strength. But every inch of ground was gallantly defended. A broad belt of ruined cottages and gardens was gradually formed between the besiegers and the besieged, and on the heaps of broken walls and burnt rafters the obstinate contest was renewed from day to day.

The rage of the Royalists at this prolonged resistance knew no bounds :—and in the pages of Clarendon their loud wail and gnashing of teeth are still almost audible. Blake could not be conquered, and the royal army could not march away, leaving an enemy so redoubtable, so popular, so full of resources in its rear. The Prince of Wales left Bristol for Bridgwater to be nearer the scene of action, and to encourage his officers and men by hopes of royal favour. At the castle of that town, Commissioners for the western counties waited on him; and after long consultations it was resolved to raise and arm an additional eight thousand men in those parts, and to bring the whole weight of Royalist power in the west to bear on Taunton, which, it was now considered certain, must, from want of bread and powder, fall within a month. These things were all arranged, says Clarendon, "so that in order to the taking that place and to the raising an army speedily, all things stood so fair that more could not be wished." Yet Taunton did not fall! And all this time that famous Model Army, fated to break and humble the proud chivalry of England in almost every encounter, was being slowly created and organised by the genius of Cromwell. At length this force, reformed and re-officered under clauses of the Self-denying ordinance, was fit to take the field. But opinions were divided as to the course to be followed. Cromwell wished to face towards Oxford, where the King lay entrenched, and fight a great battle there while the

Royalists of the west were occupied in Somerset; urging in defence of this plan, that as the King himself, the chief army of the Cavaliers, and the best part of their artillery lay there, one defeat would put an end to the war, and the reduction of a few towns and fortresses would then become a mere question of time and detail. On the other side it was urged that the issue of battle was uncertain, even should it be found possible to force the King to engage in open field; that Taunton was the key of the four western counties; that its fall after so glorious a defence would produce a great moral effect in the country; and that, moreover, its heroic garrison had a right to expect the first relief that could be despatched into those parts. The humane considerations overruled the military: and the word for Taunton being given, the soldiers started with a burst of enthusiasm which shortened the journey several days. For an entire week, says Sprigge, the army refused to take an hour's repose; and they were already among the Cavalier tents in Dorsetshire before the Cavalier generals had heard of their departure from the neighbourhood of London.

But at Blandford, two expresses, riding post-haste from Westminster, overtook the army on its march, bringing an unexpected and unwelcome order to turn round towards Oxford, sending on a mere relief-party to Taunton. The reason for this sudden change of purpose, was the receipt of intelligence that Charles had taken the field, at the pressing solicitation of Prince Rupert, and was then on his way to the north, leaving Oxford with only a small garrison, which the Roundheads in that city promised to attack and overpower if the new army would advance against it. Fairfax at once obeyed; first detaching four regiments under the command of Colonel Welden, with instructions to recruit his strength on the way—enlisting all volunteers and carrying down all the flying corps willing to join in the relief—and to send word by trusty messengers to apprise Blake of his approach, and concert with him the signals to be used in announcing his arrival. At Dorchester six companies of foot joined his party; every town through which he passed afforded volunteers; and the whole garrison of Lyme, now freed from the enemy, turned out to the assistance of their old commander. By forced marches, Welden crossed the Chard Hills into Somerset at the head of two thousand horse and three thousand foot, to encounter an army more than thrice his strength. Berkeley had notice of the approach of this party, and tried by a stratagem to induce Blake to make a premature sally, during which he had hopes of being able to cut him off and enter the town by surprise. From the watch-tower on St. Mary's steeple Blake received intelligence that a large body of cavalry was approaching the Cavalier lines from the Chard road, as if to attack them; personal observation, however, soon convinced him that these were Royalist soldiers, and surmising the real fact—that it was a feint to tempt him out of his impregnable position, he stood still, waiting the development of this curious manœuvre. As the clouds of dust cleared off, he could see masses of foot and cavalry moving forward, and as they drew near Berkeley's tent the Royalists faced round to engage them. For more than an hour the battle seemed to rage, when the attacking party wavered and fled. But the ruse had failed. Convinced at last that Blake would not accept the bait, Sir John recalled his flying squadrons, formed them in deep columns for assault, and rushed towards the ruins which separated the real combatants. Vast quantities of hand-grenades were thrown into the houses, and two long streets were that day consumed to ashes. Never had the Cavaliers fought more gallantly. Pike in hand, they cleared the out-works, passed the gate, and stormed the timber barricades in East Street. But the besieged fell back only to concentrate their strength and recruit their stock of powder. Resisting with passive courage until the enemy began to shew signs of weakness, Blake then gave the word for his reserves in the bull-ring to advance at a pike charge, while the musqueteers stationed in and behind the houses in East Street, opened up a sharper fire. After a tremendous struggle the streets were again cleared, and the Cavaliers driven back to their entrenchments, leaving behind them hundreds of their comrades, killed, wounded, and prisoners.

While the Cavaliers were suffering from the effects of this severe repulse, the boom of artillery was heard among the Blagdon Hills, in the direction of the road from Chard, by which Welden's party was known to be advancing. Blake counted the echoes carefully, and when the firing ceased, finding that altogether ten guns had been discharged, he knew by the signals previously arranged with the scouts, that the army of relief had left Chard and was come within ten miles of Taunton. Intelligence of succour being at hand spread in the town, reviving hope in the brave and rousing despair from its apathy. Blake made his dispositions to co-operate with the relief in an attack on the still superior forces of the enemy,—and his companions in toil and danger retired to rest that night with a conviction that the morrow's sun would go down on an altered aspect of things. High as their hearts beat for the contest, proud and calm as their leader looked, they could not forget that Berkeley's army was large enough to spare a division superior to that commanded by Welden to watch and check his movements, and yet maintain the siege. If they knew no fear, they had little cause to exult.

At length the morning dawned, Sunday morning

May 11th; the troops were mustering in the bull-ring and in the court of the castle, when news was brought that the Cavaliers were already in full retreat on the roads towards Ilchester and Bridgwater, having struck their tents in the night and abandoned their entrenchments before sunrise. Trusty scouts were sent off to watch Berkeley's movements; from the church-tower the long lines of the Cavaliers could be seen in full retreat; the patrols sent word to their commander that the camp was almost deserted; and that in their haste to get away, arms, ammunition and camp-furniture to a great value had been left behind. Assured by his various intelligence that the retreat was not a mere feint to draw him into a snare, Blake sounded his trumpet for a sortie, and passing through East Gate he fell on the stragglers and rear-guard, put them to rout, seized a pile of arms, cleared the orchards and meadows lying between the Chard and Bridgwater highways, and would have pursued the fugitives farther, had they not taken the precaution to make the roads in their rear impassable for cavalry by cutting down the trees and throwing them across.

Their retirement from the works after so long and fierce a siege produced a powerful reaction on the inhabitants, and the pious people flew to St. Mary's to return thanks for so unexpected a mercy. Welman took for his text the words of Malachi—" I am the Lord: I change not: therefore ye sons of Jacob are not consumed." And the fervid preacher exhorted them to continue their trust in the Lord of Hosts. He assured them that their cause was the cause of heaven, and that all the powers of earth could not prevail against it. The miraculous retreat of the royal army,—since, in the opinion of its own commanders, it was equal to twice the number of Roundheads then arrayed against it,—gave

point and meaning to the preacher's words; and just as
the congregation had risen to the height of enthusiasm,
several persons ran into the church gasping out—
Deliverance! Deliverance! A squadron of Welden's
horse had galloped unopposed to the very works at East
Gate and exchanged greetings with the defenders. The
people rose to their feet at these magic words; some
embraced their friends and children; others ran about
wildly in the extravagance of their joy; many rushed for
the doors, anxious to get ocular demonstration of this
good news. But Welman called to them in a loud voice
to pause, and having recovered silence in the sacred
edifice, he motioned them with a solemn gesture to kneel
down and join with him in giving thanks where thanks
were most due for so great a mercy. The main body of
Welden's corps arrived at four o'clock in the afternoon,
when the aspect of Taunton and its heroic defenders
filled the rough soldiers, inured as they were to sieges
and battles, with wonder and pity. More than a third
part of the houses had been burnt or battered down
with artillery,—and both garrison and inhabitants were
dying of hunger in the streets. Harassed as they were
by the march over hilly and broken roads, the relief
party refused to touch a morsel of the still remaining
provision; and after effecting the first object of their
visit, returned that very night towards Chard.

Parliament heard in due time of the relief of Taunton.
Bonfires were made in London in celebration of the
happy event. A day of general thanksgiving was
appointed. Letters of thanks were sent to Fairfax for
having despatched the relief corps: Welden and his
officers received their share of the nation's gratitude
for their successful expedition; and the governor,
garrison and people were all lauded in high terms for
their zeal, courage, and sacrifices in maintaining a town

without walls or other military defences, and already exhausted by a long siege and blockade, for fifty days against such overwhelming numbers. Two thousand pounds were voted to the soldiers, and five hundred pounds were sent to Blake, as a testimonial to his genius and devotion to the national cause. Orders for special collections of money were also voted: London taking the lead in this noble effort. To the inhabitants of the town and neighbourhood the 11th of May was ever afterwards a day sacred to happy memories, celebrated in anniversary sermons and in popular ballads. To the Roundhead party throughout the country, Taunton, even in the depths of its material desolation, was a watchword and an omen of eventual triumph.

But its sufferings were not yet ended. At the first movement of the new Model Army, the court called Goring's forces from the west; but finding Fairfax march towards Devon and Somerset instead of on Oxford, as they had expected, a new and bolder policy was adopted. Charles despatched Goring to the scene of his former licence, to cover the leaguer before Taunton and crush the new Model, whilst he himself, considering Oxford strong enough to resist assault, resolved to make a rapid march northward—join his forces with those of Rupert and Maurice, raise the siege of Chester, sorely pressed by the Roundheads, and if possible regain some of his lost ground in the great county of York. But this division of the central and western armies proved fatal to the King. Covetous of the glory of reducing Taunton, and burning to flush his libertine soul with the spoil of a city famous for the wealth of its citizens and the beauty of its women, Goring led back his division into Somerset, after making a terrible oath that he would reduce that haughty town or lay his bones in its trenches. Fairfax turned his flank in obedience to fresh orders from London, and, to the consternation of King and court, suddenly appeared under the walls of Oxford. This movement recalled the royal expedition from the north, and the two grand armies were once more and for the last time in presence.

Goring's crew overran Somerset. Rape, robbery and murder again became daily and nightly incidents. Falling on Colonel Welden with superior forces, he drove him into narrow passes in the hills, from which a more skilful general would have made it difficult, if not impossible, for him to retreat without serious loss. But Goring's orders were so given, that Colonel Thornhill and Sir William Courtney, whom he had sent by different routes to cut off the Roundheads at Petherton Bridge, not aware of the double nature of the expedition, fell on each other, and with such ardour, that both officers were hurt, one of them was made a prisoner, and many persons were killed on both sides before the blunder was discovered! While they were fighting with each other, Welden escaped into Taunton. Goring followed in his rear, and once more the unhappy town was invested on all sides. In London the alarm and rage were great. A deputation from the House of Commons went to the Committee of Militia to ask for five hundred mounted musqueteers. But zeal outran the request. Hants and other counties volunteered men for the service. The Royalists acted on the defensive; patrolling the country, checking sorties, and trusting to the effect of famine. Goring boasted in his letters to the Prince of Wales that he could take the place in less time now that Welden's party had added to the wants of the garrison. All depended on the strictness of his blockade. Blake knew this, and his only chance of an indefinite prolongation of the defence lay in being able, by frequent sallies, to break the lines and open up

temporary communications with the country. Nearly
every day foraging parties went out in search of corn
and fodder; sometimes these adventurers were cut off,
more frequently they escaped the vigilance of the
Cavalier patrols; but such as returned almost invariably
brought in prisoners or provisions. The spirit of the
garrison rose with every encounter. They had learned
to regard that mixed host of Irish, Cornish, and German
mercenaries, so brave in the ale-house and the farmyard,
with a contempt equal to their hate. The governor's
sarcastic humour fed this feeling. One day, by way of
insult, Goring sent a poor fellow into the town, dressed
in rags, with a tattered drum, to demand an exchange of
prisoners. Blake expressed a superb contempt for the
insult—not by hanging the poor drummer, or by harsher
treatment of his prisoners, as the Cavalier general would
have done under like circumstances, but by dressing the
man in a new suit of clothes, giving him a new drum,
and setting the prisoners free.

In the valleys, Welden's horse did excellent service:
—but the courage of the colonel sometimes led him into
unnecessary dangers. One day, making a sortie with
his cavalry, he was received so firmly by Goring that
his charge was broken, and his whole troop put in peril.
Blake, from his watch-tower, saw the danger; sounded
his trumpets for a sortie, formed two squadrons of his
veteran horse in the market-place, rode at their head
through East Reach, fell on the flank of the Cavaliers,
and threw the whole body into momentary confusion.
Welden seized the moment to disengage his men, and
draw them off towards the town. Blake brought up
the rear, disputing every inch of ground, and retiring in
perfect order, and with his face towards the enemy.
The example of these brilliant episodes incited persons
at a distance to acts of romantic daring. A party

from the garrison at Lyme undertook to force their way through the Cavalier camps, and carry a small supply of powder to their former chief,—a feat which they performed with the utmost gallantry and success. As a reward, Blake invited them to witness a grand sortie, which proved to be the most murderous conflict that had ever taken place before Taunton, four hundred Cavalier corpses being picked up in the trenches after the battle. This victory was of immense and immediate importance to the besieged, as Goring drew off his men to a greater distance, enlarging the Roundhead quarters five or six miles; and the Londoners, once more roused to activity by the glorious news from Somerset, formed an association for the especial purpose of sending relief to Taunton. Members of the Common Council, private merchants, traders and gentry commenced a subscription, and in a few days four thousand pounds were already raised. Parliament also promised speedy and effectual aid, and Colonel Massey distributed handbills in the taverns and workshops, calling on volunteers to join him in the expedition. Such was the alacrity of the patriotic citizens, that before Massey was prepared to march with the government aid, they had already equipped at their own expense a thousand horsemen.

While Goring was employed in the vale of Taunton, the Cavalier cause was decided on the field of Naseby. With that battle the war was almost at an end. Fairfax turned westward to raise the siege of Taunton, crush Goring's crew, and recover the great strongholds of Somerset and Devon for Parliament. On the second of July he met Massey at the head of three thousand new levies, specially designed for that service, at Blandford. Goring gave way to panic. Heedless of the oath which bound him never to quit the leaguer before Taunton, he burnt his tents and drew off to Langport, whither

Fairfax followed him, and routed his troops in two or three brief but destructive encounters. The march of the Roundheads through the West was brilliant and victorious. Bristol was carried by storm. Bridgwater, Langport and Ilchester, keys of the western counties, were also carried by storm. Finally, Taunton was freed from its enemies; and all the neighbouring towns, castles and strongholds,—Dunster Castle alone excepted, —were soon in friendly hands. The last act of the siege had lasted five weeks—the former more than seven; but reckoning from the date when Blake seized the town to the day of Goring's retreat, there was exactly a year as the duration of his marvellous and successful defence. One of the King's best armies had been occupied and destroyed by it. Some of the bravest of his captains had lost their reputation or their lives in its trenches. Grenville, Digby, Berkeley, Hopton, Wyndham, Goring, and many others had retired from it foiled and dishonoured. Major-general Digby, brother of the famous Sir Kenelm, received there a mortal wound, and the last attempt to blockade the town cost the lives of fourteen hundred Cavaliers.

The town itself presented a most deplorable aspect. For many miles round, the country, once a rich and cultivated garden, interspersed with orchards, nursery-grounds, and water meadows, was a dreary desert. The corn had been cut down green—fruit-trees destroyed in mere wantonness—barns and mills emptied of their contents—farm-houses ransacked and burnt—the peasants and farmers driven with insult and violence from their homesteads. The relieving army noticed with horror that between St. Nicholas and Taunton they marched for half a day without seeing a single human creature or one human habitation standing, in the most populous and wealthy district of provincial England! In the immediate suburbs of the devoted town the work of destruction had been done completely:—there all was black, grim, ugly ruin. The streets of the town proper had all suffered, more or less, up to the walls of the church on one side, and to those of the castle on another. A third of the entire number of houses in the town had either been burnt by means of wild-fire and red-hot balls, or battered down by the artillery. Blake had the proud satisfaction to feel that he had kept his ground; but towards the end of his year of hard fighting, he was master of little more than a heap of rubbish.

After the retirement of Goring, his first care was to diminish the number of mouths to be fed daily, by sending Welden's corps to the lord general's camp; his next care was to provide for a regular supply of fresh provisions from a distance, until the ravages of the fierce soldiery could be restored, and the lands so terribly wasted could be again brought into culture. Nor were the heroic sufferings of the people forgotten at head-quarters. The two Houses issued warrants for a general collection in behalf of the ruined citizens, and the money raised under their warrants was chiefly employed in rebuilding the burnt and battered houses. For several months Blake's genius and energy were devoted to the relief of the inevitable distress, in aiding each man to recover his former position, and in forwarding the interests of his party in Somerset.

One of Blake's negotiations during the autumn was with the celebrated club-men or peace-makers. These men, instigated by the royalist gentry, had risen in arms under pretence of self-protection from the marauders of both parties, though in reality they desired and intended to serve the King; Goring, however, whose disorderly followers were supposed to be glanced at in their declaration, issued a severe order against them from

Exeter, which greatly incensed many of those who had expressed themselves to the intriguers favourable to the royal cause. Blake saw as clearly as Goring the inconvenience of having a third party in the field, of uncertain good faith, without leaders and without flag, and he therefore tried to win them over to his own cause, and induce them to combine with the parliamentary forces. To this end he proposed a form of submission for them to sign and send to Fairfax, in which they were to thank God for having freed those parts of "the plundering and dissolute army, which consisted of many papists, Irish rebels, and outlandish commanders, officers and soldiers, whose common practice was to rob and destroy the inhabitants,"—to assert their fixed resolution to protect themselves from violence and rapacity, —to express their readiness to join with Fairfax for the purpose of putting a speedy end to the war,—and to offer to submit themselves to the laws, orders and commands of Parliament. But the club-men refused to subscribe such terms. "Our intentions," they replied, "are to go in a middle way; to preserve our persons and estates from violence and plunder; to join with neither; and not to oppose either side, until, by the answer to our petition, we see who are the enemies of that happy peace which we really desire." On his part, Fairfax refused to treat with this anomalous body; and his lieutenant-general soon afterwards gave them a terrible chastisement near Hambledon Hill.

Early in the following spring, Dunster Castle still holding out against the victorious Roundheads, Blake, no longer fearing for the safety of Taunton, took the field with his recruited corps, joined by volunteer parties from neighbouring garrisons, in the hope of carrying that fortress by storm. Built on the crest of a hill, of very difficult ascent for troops, and defended by a body of men resolute in their attachment to the royal cause, it had hitherto resisted every attack, and was generally thought impregnable to the military science of that age. It was indeed a virgin fortress, and is often spoken of in the old writers as the strongest castle in the west of England. Blake appeared under its walls about the middle of April; and the demand to surrender being answered by a stern defiance, he gave instant orders to his trumpeters to sound a charge. The battle was continued for some days; but as the progress towards victory was too slow for his Roundhead zeal, Blake secretly prepared a mine, which he sprung at a favourable moment, throwing huge masses of the solid masonry into mid air, and making wide rents in the walls, through which the assailants stormed with an impetuosity that nothing could resist. Sun-down saw the red cross of England floating from the highest tower of Dunster Castle.

Though elected by the burgesses to represent them in Parliament, instead of Sir William Portman, expelled for disloyalty to the House, Blake continued to reside at Taunton, and to busy himself with the pacific duties of his government. Unlike so many officers who had hitherto been his rivals in glory and public service, when the King's cause was lost, and the King himself was become a prisoner, he made no attempt to throw himself into the centre of intrigues or to use his great influence in the West for personal advancement. With a true Roundhead contempt for wealth, and for the dazzling prizes laid open to the ambition of genius in troubled times, he remained at his post, doing his duty, humbly and faithfully, at a distance from Westminster; while other men with less than half his claims, were asking and obtaining the highest honours and rewards from a grateful and lavish country. A sincere Republican, it was his wish to see the nation settled on the solid basis of a religious commonwealth; but though his principles were stern, his practical politics were moderate. That, at any period after the sword was drawn and blood had actually been shed in the quarrel, he would willingly have treated with the King, as King, is doubtful; but after Charles's refusal of the terms offered for his acceptance while he was still with the Scottish army, it is certain that Blake no longer entertained a thought of maintaining the monarchy in his person. The town of which he was representative and governor, he at its head, prayed the house never to make peace or receive proposals from the perjured sovereign, but to continue the war to an end, so as to obtain a firm and lasting settlement of religion and public quiet—pledging themselves to support Parliament in this course of action to the last drop of their blood. Yet his patriotic zeal did not blind him to the suggestions of justice and true policy. The proceedings of the army-chiefs after Charles fell into their hands gave him great annoyance. Like Algernon Sydney, the younger Vane, and other of the wiser or more moderate men, he wished to see the King deposed and banished. He deprecated even the appearance of illegality and violence; and when he found the party of which Cromwell was the inspiring genius bent on the King's trial and execution, he expressed his discontent with their proceedings, and under the influence of his humane convictions, declared openly that he would as freely venture his life to save the King as ever he had done to serve the Parliament.

The influence, moderation, and military genius of Blake rendered him an object of jealousy and suspicion to the friends of Cromwell. Before they dared to bring the King to trial, they took the precaution to lessen his power, by disbanding the principal part of those forces

which had performed so many prodigies of valour at
Lyme and Taunton. Care was taken to conceal from
public notice the real motives for this measure ; and the
order was accompanied by an expression of gratitude and
thanks from the House for his eminent services, and by
another donation of five hundred pounds. Still, it was
known to some and suspected by many, that these
flatteries masked suspicion. Blake obeyed the orders without a word of remonstrance. Others felt and resented the
intrigue and the slight, though he did not :—and it was
not long afterwards referred to by one of the most distinguished naval commanders of that age, as affording a
sort of excuse and justification of his own treachery to
the national cause. But the governor of Taunton had
no share in such feelings. He never attempted to conceal his thoughts from friend or foe—for he had no fear
and no ambition. He considered Cromwell violent and
unwise in his desire to put the King to death. But he
never professed to think the question of what should be
done with the faithless King other than one of detail.
In the idea of founding in England a great religious
commonwealth, he fully concurred. What else was left ?
He had seen monarchy produce few fruits save false-
hood, tyranny, and spiritual pride. He wished to try the
experiment of a democracy founded on religious principles. Yet, overriding his private theories and desires,
reigned in his heart the strong sense of patriotic devotion.
Covetous of glory, but free from the vices which too
often grow in the neighbourhood of that noble passion,
his thought by day, his dream by night, was how he could
be useful to his country, and to those great Protestant
and liberal principles for which she had sacrificed her
domestic peace, and poured out her best blood in torrents.
An opening for a glorious career soon offered itself at
sea :—and the appointment of Blake to the chief naval

command—whether it arose from Cromwell's desire to remove a powerful and incorruptible officer from the scene of his own intrigues, or from the general belief of the parliamentary chiefs that his executive genius, dauntless valour, and unvarying good fortune would be conspicuously displayed in his naval exploits,—was a most important event, opening a new and brilliant era in the history of the British navy.

# CHAPTER IV.

### 1649—1650.

### NAVAL COMMAND.

In the earlier period of the Revolution the navy occupied a neutral attitude. The Earl of Warwick acted as lord admiral under the commission issued by Parliament in its own and the King's name jointly; but, with the exception of a loose blockade of Ireland, varied by skirmishes of no political or naval importance, the fleet had done little in those eventful times except ride in the English Channel, watch the movements in foreign ports, and guard our shores against the arrival of arms, levies, and munitions of war from France and Holland. Public opinion in the coast towns had placed nearly all those important stations in the hands of Parliament from the outset. In the famous sieges, storms, and blockades which make the historical romance of the civil war, there is scarcely one in which the fleet took a prominent part. On the whole this was a happy circumstance. Standing apart from the scene of strife, the seamen were less swayed by violent and bitter passions than their less fortunate brethren in camp and city. Not that they were indifferent to the quarrel. High church and divine right were as unpopular in the navy as in the army. But, mixing less frequently and fiercely in the actual conflict, naval men were less blinded by passion, and took a clearer and more moderate view of the course of events than generals and soldiers. As time wore on, and the nicer shades of opinion came out in stronger relief, some differences in religion assisted in dividing still more clearly the two great arms of the public force. The army became Independent—the navy remained Presbyterian ; and these words involve two entire systems of ideas and of policy.

When Warwick surrendered his command under a clause of the Self-denying ordinance, the affairs of the Admiralty were put in commission, and he was rewarded for his services by a seat at the new Navy Board, a post which he retained four years, notwithstanding the many changes which occurred in the other members. Admiral Batten succeeded to the command vacated by the Earl ; and so long as the King kept the field, this able officer discharged the duties of his station to the perfect satisfaction of Parliament. On occasion of the Queen running into Bridlington, a small port on the east coast of Yorkshire, with arms, money and stores from Holland, to support the failing cause of her husband, he followed the Dutch ship into port, and, to the horror of the Royalists, compelled her majesty to fly from her lodgings in the night and take shelter in a place protected from the fury of his guns. He made foreigners, as well as Cavaliers, respect the red cross of England—distinguished himself in the blockade of Ireland, and captured a Swedish fleet that refused to lower its topsails in token of his supremacy in the narrow seas. For his good services he received the nation's thanks on more than one occasion.

But Batten was no republican at heart. He served his country because his country paid his wages. He was equally willing to serve the King. Like Penn and other seamen he was on neither side. But the time was at hand when neutrality was impossible. Every branch of the public force was compelled to choose a part: and as the army grew more and more outrageous in its pretensions, murmurs began to arise in the fleet in regard to the conduct of those on shore. Flushed with its recent victory, the nation seemed as if about to divide against itself. The sudden rise and successful career of the Independents was a cause of fierce and deeply-seated jealousies in the navy; and the series of events, which led to the purchase of the captive King from the Scotch army, his unceremonious arrest by the soldiers at Holdenby, and his subsequent imprisonment at Carisbrook Castle, gave rise to dangerous explosions of discontent in the Downs. Charles was surprised and seized on the 4th of June; and, eight days after this event, the Earl of Warwick found it necessary to write to Batten, urging him to sleepless watchfulness, lest the men should be seduced from their duty, and the vessels under his command be surprised into some act of disobedience. He took care to remind the Admiral that Parliament had raised the seamen's wages above the rates paid in former times; and he expressed a hope that his old comrades would remain faithful to the Nation. As the mutinous spirit increased rather than abated, Batten himself fell under suspicion of fomenting an evil spirit in his men. He was therefore called to London. Colonel Rainsborough, an Independent, and one of the army faction, was put down as vice-admiral. But this new commander was unequal to the work, the mutinous spirit of the navy was fomented by the royalist intriguers of Kent, and Rainsborough no sooner arrived at his post than he was seized and displaced by the officers under his command. The mutineers declared for King, Parliament and Covenant, and sent a message to the Earl of Warwick, offering to obey his orders if he would come on board, and subscribe to the terms of their declaration. Unprovided with means to punish this act of usurpation, the Houses reluctantly concurred in the nomination of Warwick; and the Lord Mayor and Aldermen of London, whose commerce and supplies were threatened by the revolters, earnestly begged for the sake of peace that Batten might be restored to his command. Even these concessions were unavailing. The rebellious ships hoisted the royal colours, stood over for Calais in hopes of finding the Prince of Wales in that town, and failing that, made for Holland.

This important defection raised once more the drooping hopes of the Cavaliers. Prince Charles received Batten with open arms, though he had fired on his royal mother a few years before at Bridlington,— and conferred on him the honours of knighthood. Under the erroneous impression that the whole fleet would follow Sir William Batten's example, the Prince of Wales and his brother James, Duke of York, went on board the revolted ships and sailed towards the Downs, where Warwick was then lying, having already joined his forces in the river with the fleet from Portsmouth, making altogether nineteen ships and three ketches, a force about equal in men and guns to that under the two princes. On heaving in sight of the Roundhead squadron, Charles sent a messenger commanding the Earl to lower his standard and repair to the royal presence; orders which he of course firmly but respectfully declined to obey. The temper of his men was good, and Parliament being assured that they would fight with alacrity against the revolted ships, a formal resolution was passed authorising and requiring him to attack and capture them in spite of their having royal commanders on board. The two divisions of the fleet watched each other for several months without coming to an engagement. Both sides wanted energy, promptitude and well-defined purpose; and among the Cavaliers were loud and fierce dissensions. The common sailors again mutinied against their officers: Batten, Gordon, and Lord Willoughby quitted the service in disgust; and the better sort of seamen, deserting from the Prince's ships, daily returned to their former stations. Some of the repentant crews contrived to carry back their vessels; and it was soon apparent that under weak and purposeless leaders the debauched, quarrelsome and insubordinate seamen at Helvoetsluys were not strong enough to cause real alarm to their country. Nor in all probability would they have ever again required the attention of a great fleet, had not a new commander appeared, whose iron will and contempt of law gave him vast advantages over captains who contended in the names of liberty and civilisation.

Long before the battle of Naseby put an end to the war on a grand scale, Prince Rupert, distrustful of the issue, had tried to secure some part of the spoil which passed through his hands for his own future use; but one or two vessels which he freighted with plunder fell into the hands of Parliament. After the fall of Bristol and his disgrace with his uncle, the adventurer and his brother Maurice were ordered to quit the country. At first Rupert retired to Holland. From that state he went to France, where the romantic Queen Regent received him as a knight of chivalry might have been received in olden times by the Queen of Beauty. She offered him any post in her service which he would himself select. He asked for a troop of horse and a regiment of foot. He was made a Field-marshal, and placed at the head of all the English then serving in the French army:—not an inconsiderable body, as the Cavaliers who fled to the Continent nearly all turned soldiers of fortune. Under

Gassion and Rauzau he served in the Low Countries not
without distinction.  The defection of Batten and the
arrival of the revolted fleet in Holland threw a fresh
lure in the way of his ambition, and called him once
more to the side of his royal relatives.

The affairs of the Stuarts were at the lowest ebb.
The exiles starving in their retreat—the Marquis of
Ormonde unable to stand against the Roundheads and
clamouring loudly for succour in Ireland—ships without
stores and ammunition—officers without a plan—men
mutinous, disorganised and without pay :—such was the
state of affairs when Rupert returned to his cousins and
proposed to take the supreme command at sea.  On
being allowed his own terms, he pledged himself to
restore discipline, to supply the more pressing wants of
the royal court, to carry assistance to the lord-lieutenant
of Ireland, and to harass the trade of London and the
naval power of Parliament.  In return he asked to be
invested with the same powers at sea which he had
formerly enjoyed on land ; that is, to be free from every
sort of control.  The Prince of Wales, poor, wasteful
and  inexperienced,  consented.  From  that  moment
Rupert became a corsair in the very worst sense of the
word.  One of his largest ships he sold to the Dutch, and
with the money obtained for it he bought stores, powder
and shot.  Once out at sea, he threw off every restraint.
With him every ship that he could take was an enemy—
every argosy a prize.  No flag afforded protection against
his predatory warfare.  Not only were the merchants of
England  spoiled  of  their  goods ;  French,  Spanish,
Swedish ships were alike attacked, captured and sold by
this pirate.  On these robberies the court of the exiles
depended for daily bread.  If Charles found a merchant
willing to risk the discount of a bill, he drew on Rupert
for the amount, and sent a frigate out to inform him of

the date and sum of the transaction. When Rupert's sailors murmured at the long arrear of their pay, the freebooter bade them go out and catch a ship for themselves, the first that should heave in sight. In this manner, states with which England was at peace, powers which the young princes were trying to enlist in their father's cause, were insulted and robbed without regard to consequences near or remote. No country suffered more from the marauder than that very Holland from which he sailed, and which still afforded protection to his own parents and to the sons of his sovereign!

Against such a commander and such a system the Council of State saw how vain it was to oppose the Earl of Warwick and the naval officers of his school. While the Earl lay in the narrow seas with a powerful fleet, the Prince sallied from Helvoetsluys with two ships and captured as many prizes as enabled him to fit out the remainder of his vessels. When all was ready, he passed down the Channel to his destination on the Munster coast. His men showed a disposition to go over to their countrymen; but he excited a change in his own favour by audaciously bearing down on the hostile fleet and opening through its line of guard a passage to the south. To such boldness, energy and rapidity of action, it became necessary for Parliament to oppose qualities similar in kind. But with the exception of Blake, there was perhaps no man in England, having any knowledge, however slight, of sea affairs, equal to the Prince in personal courage, fertility of resource and brilliancy of execution. Blake was therefore called from his pacific government at Taunton to assume the chief command at sea, in conjunction with Colonel Deane and Colonel Popham— the latter a brother of his old friend and fellow-soldier of the same name—under the title, invented for the occasion, of Generals and Admirals at Sea, or as they came afterwards to be usually styled—Generals of the Fleet.

The tasks which the three Generals took upon themselves were at once varied and onerous. When they went on board, the navy was in a condition like that in which Cromwell had found the old army. Abuses existed everywhere. The Admiralty offices, the dockyards, the ports and naval stations, the ships, were alike corrupt; and many of the corruptions were of long standing and flagrant character. To provide the Generals with full powers to examine and correct abuses they were also appointed Commissioners of the Navy, with seats at the Admiralty Board. The mandates under which they acted required them to employ all available means to achieve these three ends:—1. To completely re-organise the naval power, so as to rid that great arm of the public service of all doubtful and disloyal elements; 2. To disperse, capture or destroy the revolted ships, and drive the Princes, Rupert and Maurice, from the high seas; 3. To co-operate with the Land Forces in a new and more efficient attempt, then in course of preparation by Cromwell, to put down the Irish rebels.

The new system began with a change of flag. From the accession of the Stuarts the Union Jack had streamed from the topmasts of every vessel engaged in the service of the state; but the King's removal having dissolved the necessary legal connection of the two countries, all ships at sea in actual service were henceforth ordered to carry only the red cross on a white ground. When the new Commissioners came to examine the details of the actual state of the navy, they found the disorder greater than had been feared. Few of the vessels were sea-worthy. The dock-yards were ill-managed. Stores and arms were systematically stolen. The wages of the sailors were not regularly paid; and when vessels came into port the poor men had usually to wait some weeks before they could obtain their money. No proper care was taken of the rations. Often the biscuit was mouldy, the beer sour, the meat rank. The system of forced impressment was bitterly complained of; while in the neglect to provide hospitals for the wounded and asylums for the infirm, the dictates of sound policy and the calls of humanity had been equally spurned. In all these matters Blake became a reformer the day he became an admiral. His letters, still preserved in the Admiralty papers, show how minute and constant was his care for the comfort and welfare of his men: in these documents his kindness of heart seems even more conspicuous than his naval genius. Fearless himself, he was remarkably tender of the lives, the health, and even the comforts of others. He would at any time weaken the force under his command in order to send a frigate home with a few wounded men, if he found they could not be treated with sufficient care on board in the midst of daily-renewed battles. The minutest details engaged his attention when the comfort of his men was concerned, even in the crisis of a great campaign. No wonder that he was adored! An instance of his popularity occurred soon after his nomination to the command at sea. The watermen of the Thames had by ancient usage a right to priority of impressment for the service; but the usage, like many other usages, had been waived with the full consent of all parties; the dangers and disorders of the service having few attractions for men possessing other means. But no sooner was the new system understood than the overseers of the watermen petitioned Blake to restore their old privilege; first, because the watermen on the river were well-affected to the Commonwealth, secondly, because they were the proper raw material out of which to make expert seamen, and thirdly, because the priority was an ancient right of their order.

The first measures adopted by the new commanders in fitting out the fleet gave evidence of the energy and character about to become the distinguishing marks of the service. They went down and purged each ship of the idle, the vicious and the disaffected; good and true men were alone retained, and it was to fill the places of the discharged sailors that the watermen of the Thames put in their claim. The ablest captains of the service were sought out and employed, without regard to age, interest or personal consideration. No incompetent noble or honourable person was allowed to occupy the place of a better seaman. Merit alone found favour. Penn, Jordan, Ascue, Stayner and Lawson, the most famous captains of the Commonwealth, were appointed to important commands. Although Blake was but one of three Commissioners, there is reason to believe that he took the lead in their deliberations; and that the general features of the campaign, which had to be adapted to the particular character of the enemy to be encountered, and the other exigences of the service, were the work of his brain. The naval forces were thus disposed:—Deane was stationed with a squadron in the Downs, having instructions to cruise between Portsmouth and Dover and keep the trade of the narrow seas free from interruption; Popham, with a second squadron, was to lie off Plymouth sound, check the depredations of the Scilly pirates, and guard the southern entrance to the Channel; Sir George Ascue, with a third squadron, was to cruise in and near the bay of Dublin, prevent the Irish rebels from communicating with their English partisans, and keep St. George's Channel open. Blake reserved to himself the task of chasing, fighting and destroying the pirate fleet under Prince Rupert.

Before going on board the flag-ship, he took care to supply himself with jacks, standards and studding sails for giving chace.

On the eighteenth of April (1649) at the age of fifty, Blake set his foot on deck for the first time as a commander, and from that moment to the hour of his death no man in England contested with him for the first place as a sailor. Envy, jealousy and hatred dogged the steps of every other officer in the service, but while the common sailors regarded him with an enthusiasm bordering on idolatry, the veteran admirals of Spain, Portugal and the United Provinces, against whom he fought in so many brilliant and destructive battles, considered him the perfect model of a foe. The country gentlemen of England, though they abhorred his political principles and affected to contemn his religious opinions, allowed that his course of action was frank and noble; and even the coarse and malignant writers of the Restoration spared his memory the mountains of abuse which they heaped on men like Vane, Hampden and Sydney.

After cruising for some time in the narrow seas, doing much damage to commerce, Rupert attacked and captured the Robert frigate; and the blockade of Kinsale having been raised by orders from London, he and his brother made for that harbour with the intention of co-operating with the Marquis of Ormonde, and establishing for themselves a convenient station whence they might sally out on their marauding expeditions and shelter their prizes from the pursuit of Blake. The town and castle of Kinsale being in the hands of Irish rebels who still made some show of loyalty to the King, Rupert had no difficulty in disposing of his stores and merchandise, the fruits of his formidable industry. His best ships were kept at sea in search of unarmed traders, and the harbour of Kinsale was soon filled with prizes of all nations. Lately without a shilling in his coffers, the royal buccaneer was now rich. The most daring spirits in the south of Ireland flew to the standard of a man who had set up this profitable system; and neither men, money nor stores were wanting to equip the captured vessels for the pirate service. The seceded fleet became for the second time a formidable power, and the daring outlaws began to plough the deep with all the confidence of prowess and success. Thus affairs in Ireland took what appeared to the court so happy a turn that even the cautious Marquis of Ormonde sent over to Holland and invited the exiles to that part of their dominions. He assured them that with the assistance of the squadron at Kinsale, the greater part of Ireland would soon be brought into obedience, — when large armies could be raised,—the Scots cajoled or coerced into a league,—and a vast material power could be suddenly hurled from those shores against England. The exiled court leaped with joy at any prospect of renewing the war. But Charles was poor and his credit low. He wanted money for an outfit—Rupert coolly and characteristically sent out a frigate, caught a Dutch trader, sold her for ten thousand pounds, and despatched the money to his cousin at the Hague.

As soon as the arrangements for his new model were got into a state of progress, Blake, his pennons flying from the masts of the Triumph, passed down the Channel with the fourth division to check the growing disorders at Kinsale. Nor was it long before the Cavaliers had reason to know that a new system had begun with the new general. Their fleet, returning from a cruise, encountered a storm, and the frigate Charles, separated from the other vessels, got involved in a dense fog, which prevented a good look-out being kept. Before the captain was aware of the enemy's presence he was assailed

by the Constant Warwick and the Leopard, part of
Blake's squadron, and after a sharp action was compelled
to surrender. Pushing forward this success, Blake
followed the returning fleet to their pirate hold and shut
them up safely within it,—as Ascue in an earlier part of
the summer had endeavoured to do without success.
The arrival of this new force at Kinsale disconcerted
the vast plans of the Cavaliers. Charles did not dare
to sail for the Irish coast; Rupert could no longer send
out his ships; and the sources of supply being cut off by
the blockade, his funds rapidly grew less. Though he
had more than half the island at his back, his prospects
were gloomy. His fleet was locked up. He could only
escape from his perilous position by cutting through the
guard-ships; and even if he got away from Kinsale and
from the enemy, he knew of no harbour in which he
could seek refuge from pursuit or carry on the sale of
his prizes. This posture of affairs was the more vexa-
tious, as the fine weather being come, and his fleet
careened and ready for a summer voyage, he had raised
an extraordinary levy of men. Instead of sweeping the
coasts and rivers of their mercantile marine, as he had
hoped, he was forced to act on the defensive, and erect
batteries on the shore to prevent the enemy's fire-ships
coming into harbour and burning his fleet. Worst of all,
his men began to murmur and desert. Blake offered them
lower pay and none of that license which they enjoyed at
Kinsale; yet his influence was already such in the navy,
that they went over to him at every convenient opportunity. Rupert, mad with rage, one day seized ten of
his men, on the plea that he suspected them of a desire
to escape, and strung them up at the yard-arm. Harassed
by these causes of discontent and impatient of a prolonged inactivity, he would have risked an engagement
with his wary adversary; but in a case of so much

moment, he listened to the counsel of his more experienced naval officers, who told him it would be rushing
on destruction to attack Blake in his present position,
until they had prepared some fire-ships, and crowded
their decks with an overpowering body of soldiers and
marines.    The town of Kinsale being open to the
country, Rupert went overland to the various port-towns
on the coast still possessed by the royalists, to engage as
many men as could be prevailed on to accept high pay
and hard service; but when he returned to Kinsale with
these recruits, the courage of his captains had been so
much cowed they still voted in the council of war that
it was unwise to hazard a trial of strength with such an
enemy, and that consequently the only course was to
secure their ships in the harbour until foul weather,
(which had already, even in the early summer, more than
once driven the hostile fleet to Milford Haven,) should
compel Blake to quit his station and either return to
Bristol Channel or the Downs.    Infinitely chagrined
at this turn of opinion, Rupert, compelled by the failure
of his funds, disbanded his new levies, dismantled the
useless barques, keeping only the flag-ships and four
frigates to wait on them, ready for active service.

One of Blake's letters to the House of Commons will
suggest the perils of the service even in the best month
of summer:

"MR. SPEAKER,—The high value which the honourable house hath been pleased to put upon our honest
endeavours, signified unto us by yours of the 5th instant,
we receive with all humble acknowledgment, desiring
from ourselves that the fruit of all may be to render us
more able and prosperous in their service, by making us
more lowly in the sight of God.  And as we have learned
from our Great Master, when we have done all we can,

to confess ourselves unprofitable servants unto God : so, for all the good he hath, or shall be pleased to do by us, his unworthiest instruments, it shall be sufficient unto us to be accounted but faithful servants unto men for the Lord's sake. Of this honour we shall ever be ambitious, but shall desire, next unto God, to owe it rather unto the prayers than thanks of men : as having more need of one than any right to the other. Being thus resolved, however, it hath or shall please God to exercise us with varieties of providence we shall not doubt through his blessing of good success and a happy conclusion in the end.

We have now been thirteen days absent from Kinsale, from whence we were forced by extremity of weather, and driven hither where we now are with eight ships—viz. Triumph, Charles, Leopard, Lion, Garland, Hercules, John, and Elizabeth. We shall, God willing, with the first opportunity, endeavour to get Kinsale Bay again and pursue our former resolution, if we shall find them there, or otherwise to follow them whithersoever they shall go.

In the meantime we have despatched away directions to Vice-Admiral Moulton - and others, advising them to put themselves into the strongest posture they may to defend themselves and oppose the enemy in case he should be gone out and nearer the Channel. We shall neglect no opportunity of doing our duty and discharging that great trust which the Parliament hath been pleased to repose in us, which may make it appear how much we are

" Your most faithful and humble Servants,

" ROBERT BLAKE,

" RIC. DEANE."

" From aboard the Triumph, in Milford Haven,
" June 13, 1649."

Meanwhile the approach of the victorious Roundheads by land, storming their way from Dublin southward, under the command of Cromwell, warned Rupert that, in spite of his batteries and castles, his hold was growing insecure. As dangers thickened around him, his mind became a prey to jealousy and distrust. He accused the governor of Cork of a desire to betray him to the enemy. He shot an ensign and all his company on suspecting them of an intention to afford a passage to Blake through the line of guard-ships. In his nervous agitation he conceived doubts of the fidelity of the Cavalier governor of Kinsale castle, and actually took that fortress by surprise as a precaution against an imaginary act of bad faith. As the winter neared and the strong winds of the north-east set in, Blake was forced to ride out at a greater distance from the mouth of the harbour; it being an extremely dangerous lee-shore, and without safe anchorage at any point. As the weather broke up Rupert prepared for the long-expected day of escape. But at the last moment he was unable to man the greater part of his ships, and he reluctantly left several of these behind a prey to the enemy. The castle he gave up to the Marquis of Ormonde, then retreating towards Cork before the parliamentary army. When he came to reckon up his effective force, he found that his whole fleet consisted of only seven sail of all rates. With this force, aided by the elements, he had the good fortune to escape from Kinsale. Continual storms had rendered it impossible for Blake to keep his fleet together off that terrible coast: many of his ships had been driven to the nearest ports for shelter; and towards the end of October, a violent gale having still further weakened the blockading squadron, and scattered the few remaining vessels widely about the offing, Rupert and Maurice seized an opportunity to steal away unobserved, and when once out at sea, they spread their sails direct for Portugal.

His naval duties at Kinsale ended by the flight of the two princes, Blake repaired to Ross. Cromwell was negotiating the surrender of that important town under the threat of such an assault as had already overwhelmed Tredah and Wexford with sudden ruin. Fate had not yet fixed the destinies of Blake. At the request of Cromwell, he became a Commissioner for the arrangement of Irish Affairs. His colleagues were, Deane, who had joined him at an early period on the Irish coast, Sir William Fenton and Lord Berghill. Cromwell wished him to take a command on shore, and wrote to the House of Commons on the subject. Men of his character were needed in Ireland, and the House of Commons offered him the rank of Major-General, and proposed to raise a regiment for him. But it left him his choice and he chose to remain at sea. He was called away from his duties as a Commissioner to go in chase of his old and formidable adversaries. With their characteristic impartiality, the Corsair princes, when they escaped from the Irish Seas, levied black mail on all nations. In standing across for the Continent, Maurice encountered a Malaga trader, which struck at his first summons, and was of course seized; shortly afterwards Rupert met with two English merchant-men, bound from London to San Lucar in Spain, and after a desperate struggle mastered and manned them for further service. While scudding along the shore towards the Tagus, in which river the King of Portugal, in his horror of Puritans and patriots, had given him a promise of protection against his pursuers, a vessel from Brazil, freighted for Lisbon with the property of Portuguese traders, stood across his line of sail, when he instantly gave chase, overtook, captured and condemned her as a prize, on the absurd plea that she had not struck her colours to him at the first summons. Though other nations suffered from these outrageous piracies, the chief losses, of course, fell on the mercantile men of England; and as the Council of State received from the London and Bristol traders most urgent complaints of the insecurity of the narrow seas, they took on the 4th of December the unusual resolution to fit out a winter fleet, and they invited Blake to assume the command and go in pursuit of the pestilent marauders.

By the middle of January, 1650, a small force, consisting of five ships, the Tiger, John, Tenth Whelp, Signet, and Constant Warwick, carrying altogether one hundred and fourteen guns, was ready for sea; and as soon as he could obtain his instructions, Blake went on board the Tiger. These instructions directed him " to pursue, seize, surprise, scatter, fight with and destroy" the ships of the revolted fleet, and to suppress pirates and protect lawful traders in the exercise of their calling. If any foreign prince or power joined with or assisted the corsair princes, he was required not to spare the revolters on that account; and in case the foreign power assisted the revolters by force of arms, he was to fight with them, and by God's help destroy them. He was to prevent any injury to the foreign prisoners who might fall into his hands; and to send them at his convenience to England, there to await the decision of Parliament. If any vessel or vessels belonging to the revolted fleet should be sold by their commander to a foreign power, or the subject of a foreign power, he was directed to demand, attack, capture or destroy them wherever found, as a part of the English navy which the revolters had no right to sell. These were the details. As to general principles, he was instructed that time out of mind the lordship of the seas had belonged to England. This ancient right he was directed to maintain; to cause the ships of all nations to strike their flags in his presence; and in case of refusal to seize and send them in as prisoners, unless they should offer such obedience and reparation as he might judge sufficient. It was submitted to his prudence, however, not to proceed so far in these demands as to force hostilities with any superior fleet, until the particular object of his voyage had been accomplished. But he was to keep for future use a strict account of any flag that refused to acknowledge his dominion of the sea. Towards foreign powers at peace with England he was directed to avoid every cause of offence and to renew ancient leagues of trade and friendship with them, unless such States should join with and protect the revolters; in which case he was instructed to assail the said powers, to destroy their fleets, and to capture their merchant-vessels, and send them as prizes into the most convenient English ports. Lastly, as events could not be foreseen, and the means of communication with London would be slow and uncertain, he was invested with a wide discretionary power in the disposal of his fleet. The final clause contained the essential spirit of his instructions—" You are to order and dispose of the said fleet and the ships under your command *as may be most advantageous for the public,* and for obtaining the ends for which the fleet is set forth; *making it your special care* in discharge of that great trust committed to you, *that the* COMMONWEALTH *receive no detriment.*"

To the five ships first equipped for this service eight others were added in the spring, four men-of-war—Resolution, St. Andrew, Phœnix, and Satisfaction—and four merchant-men—Hercules, America, Great Lewis, and Merchant—under the command of Admiral Popham, who also carried out additional instructions to his colleague.

In the meantime Rupert had sailed into the Tagus and received a cordial and flattering welcome from John of Braganza, King of Portugal, who assured him that he would protect him in that river against all his enemies. A friendly salute from the forts welcomed the fugitives with royal honours. The first night the princes anchored in Weyrs Bay, near the river mouth; next day they stood higher up the stream, fixing their station at San Katherina, until Rupert should find leisure to present himself at court in due form. His reception was enough to turn a steadier brain than his; King John sent some of his proudest nobles to attend the fugitive Prince from Belleisle to the palace, where he confirmed in person and in the warmest manner the promises of protection which he had previously made through his envoy. The fleet then anchored under the guns of Belleisle, and the officers sold the goods taken in their prizes to the Portuguese merchants; which done, they sailed to Lisbon, where they employed the seamen during the winter months in careening, victualling, and fitting out their prizes as men-of-war. At the approach of spring, Rupert, tired of court festivities, went on board and dropped down the river to Belleisle, with the intention of renewing, under more favourable auspices, the profitable piracies of the former year; but before he could get clear of the Tagus, Blake was at its mouth with his little fleet of five ships; and not daring to attempt a passage by force against such a commander, Rupert anchored under the guns of the fort. Blake now sent an officer to ask the King's permission to attack the revolted ships at their anchorage. John haughtily refused. Blake affected not to comprehend the King's answer, and ordered his boats to cross the bar. A few shots from Belim Castle stopped them. At the first discharge Blake sent a boat to inquire the reason for this show of hostility against a friendly power, there being no war at that time between Portugal and England?  The officer replied that he had received no orders to allow any other ships to pass.  With great moderation, Blake sent his complaint to Lisbon: and some prominent members of the Council, alarmed at the false position in which their King's rash promise to the revolters had placed the country, urged him to make concessions to the powerful Commonwealth even at the last moment, rather than incur the hazards of a naval war.  John's own fears inclined him to listen to these councils, so that, instead of a haughty reply, he sent one of his courtiers to compliment the new Admiral, and to beg that, for the sake of peace, he would not attempt to enter the river unless foul weather should force him to seek a shelter for his ships.  To these civilities he added a supply of provisions.  In return, Blake declared that he was anxious not to violate a friendly river.  But he reminded the King that he was there as the minister and representative of a powerful nation: that the fugitive princes possessed no country, nor even a single port of their own into which they could send their captures for legal condemnation, and were therefore incapable of being treated as a neutral power; that the ships then in their possession were a part of the English navy, which had been armed, equipped and furnished by Parliament in their own ports, and manned by their own servants; that, moreover, the two princes had acted as pirates and sea-robbers, and by adding the captured ships to their fleet, were growing into a power likely to prove dangerous to the lawful commerce of all nations; finally, that having no place in the world which they could pretend to call their own, they were unable to appeal to the law of nations, or ask the protection of any prince in their revolt and piracy, without thereby creating a cause

of war between that prince and the Commonwealth of
England.

To this clear statement of the question the King could
only oppose his personal feelings and his rash promise.
The royal Council was divided in opinion: the Conde de
Miro, an expert and sagacious minister, spoke the sentiments of the more prudent, and his views were shared
by all the traders and merchants interested in the commerce and colonies of the country. But the Queen,
ardent, prodigal, and fascinated, warmly espoused the
cause of her brilliant guest; and two violent factions
arose in the court and city, of which the rallying cries
were "peace" and "war" with England. The weather
growing foul, Blake entered the river with his fleet and
anchored in Weyrs Bay, whence he unceasingly pressed
the King and Council for leave to fall on the revolters;
but weeks passed on and he could obtain no satisfactory
reply to his requests. Duplicity and delay characterised
all the proceedings of the court. The Brazil fleet, then
fitting out for the summer voyage, was almost ready
to sail; and it became apparent to Blake that the
Portuguese were trying by their civilities and councils
to gain time until this fleet was despatched and out of
danger. Rupert himself was mystified. He complained
that his enemy was allowed to come up the river to S
Katherina, only two miles from his own station. His
sailors deserted to Blake in spite of every severity; and
one of his largest ships, the Swallow, of thirty-six guns,
was in the very act of escaping when the plot was discovered and defeated. Alarmed at these symptoms of
revolt in his crews, and doubtful whether the Queen
would be able to prevail against the Miro party in the
Council, he secretly prepared to defend himself; and if
his worst fears should be realised, to force a passage
through the English squadron or perish in the attempt.

His preparations did not escape the vigilance of the court, and they created a suspicion in high quarters that, urged by hatred and despair, he was about to commit some act of wanton hostility against his protectors. Fear in some, contempt in others, were thus raised. But the more factious and alarmed the city grew, the safer Rupert felt himself. As a ready means of sowing dissensions in Lisbon, he courted the priests and the populace. Though a Protestant, he did his best to rouse the passions of the Portuguese Catholics against his adopted country. He urged the priests to preach a crusade against England, not only as a point of conscience, but also as a means of increasing their own worldly influence. These men willingly gave their aid and countenance: they harangued against patriots and protested against the shame of a Christian nation treating with rebels, until the Lisbon people were so incensed that the King could hardly pass down the streets of his capital without hearing the exclamations of their rage and fanaticism. To gain over the mob to his interest, Rupert went among them, gave them money and soft speeches, and made a pretence of placing himself and his cause under their protection. These artifices succeeded so far as to compel the Miro party to be extremely wary, and to postpone a final arrangement of the question.

Not content with the success of this appeal to the basest passions, the fugitive armed an assassin against the life of his formidable enemy. The only plea ever put forth by his partisans in excuse for this attempt at private murder was a false report to the effect that some persons from the English fleet went on shore at Belleisle to attack a hunting-party, including Rupert, Maurice, and several other Cavaliers, in which, however, they pretend that the Roundheads got the worst of it, and were glad to retreat; the real truth being that the men were sent on shore in the ordinary way to obtain fresh-water, and while getting it were assailed by Rupert's party, who killed one of their number, dangerously wounded three others, and made five prisoners. Towards evening of the day on which this incident had occurred, a bombshell, placed in a double-headed barrel, with a lock in the middle so contrived that on being opened it would give fire to a quick-match and cause the whole to explode, was sent by Rupert to Blake's flag-ship, in a Portuguese boat, manned by a trusty sailor and two negroes, the former dressed as a Portuguese tradesman. The men sent on this murderous errand were instructed to say they were oil merchants come with a present for the seamen. But when the boat arrived at the ship's stern, they found the ports there closed, and while they were rowing round to the transom-port, some of the crew observed and recognised the Englishman as one of Rupert's men whom they had frequently met on shore at Belleisle; and before any mischief could be done he was arrested and the device of which he was to have been the executioner discovered.

Having missed his aim, and doubtful of the King's resolution, with failing provisions and wavering men on board, Rupert engaged the governor of the castle to connive at his passage, and prepared to fall down the stream with the first favourable wind. But Blake had friends on board the Prince's ships, and being informed of this design, he towed his vessels in a dead calm to the mouth of the river, which movement compelled Rupert to fall back to his old position. Months were spent in these blockades and negotiations without result. Blake, now strengthened by the arrival of Popham's squadron, represented to the King that his port had been dishonoured, that innocent blood had been shed; and he demanded in more urgent terms permission to right himself. Instead of complying with this request, the monarch at last threw off the mask, put some of the English merchants under arrest, and pronounced for the cause of the two princes. This change, while it simplified the state of affairs and left Blake to act as he thought proper, added the whole weight of the Portuguese navy to the force of the revolters. Blake's answer, however, was swift and sure. The Brazil fleet of nine sail coming out of the Tagus, he seized them without ceremony, removed the officers and crew, put trusty men in their places, and thus at a stroke raised his own effective strength from thirteen to twenty-two sail. At the same time he threatened to seize the American fleets on their return, if the revolters were not immediately compelled to quit the Tagus. The English Admiral had been so modest in his demeanour, so moderate in his demands, the King was astounded at what he called the temerity of these acts of self-defence ; and in the first outburst of his rage he gave orders to arm the coasts and fit out his fleets for service. Miro was disgraced. The friends of peace were discountenanced. A squadron of thirteen men-of-war was equipped; and, under the command of Vara John, was ordered to join the force under Rupert. Even then, they did not consider it prudent to attack the English, who continued to cruise at the river mouth, interrupting all commerce by sea, and threatening to intercept the richly-freighted vessels known to be coming home from the Brazils.

Autumn was deeply advanced. The fleet had been in those unfriendly waters seven months, and although provisions and stores had been supplied by Popham's squadron and by other means, the ships were sea-worn, the stores well nigh exhausted, the men suffering from the effects of long confinement and severe duties. Rupert trusted to the storms of winter, and the court of

Portugal believed it would be impossible for the English to stay on that bleak and hostile coast. But Vane, one of the greatest naval administrators ever born, was indefatigable at home in preparing the materials of war. In spite of the elements Blake remained in the Portuguese waters to encounter one of the Brazil fleets, consisting of twenty-three sail, just as they were about to enter the Tagus, when a brief but fierce engagement ended in the loss of the Portuguese flag-ship, which went down during the cannonade, and three other ships, which were set on fire and consumed; and the capture of the vice-admiral and eleven large ships, all laden with the most precious cargoes. Only seven of the smallest barques escaped; they got away, and slipped into the river while the contest was at its height. When the king heard of his great disaster, he went on board Rupert's flag-ship, and ordered him to attack the English with the combined fleets and recover his lost treasures. Rubert was willing, but the winds kept no terms with the royal thirst for revenge, and the Portuguese pennons floated idly in the river, while the victorious English repaired their losses and counted their magnificent gains by the late engagement. At last, however, a fair wind sprang up, and with provisions already on board for fourteen days—ample time as the courtiers thought to capture or destroy the blockading squadron, Rupert dropped down the river, at the same time hoisting signals for Vara John to follow and join him below Belim with all his disposable force. But the Portguese commander either could not or would not raise his anchor for several hours, and the revolters were already up with the English squadron before their Portuguese allies had got under sail. Want of concert prevailed throughout. The ships were scattered over a wide expanse of sea, and neither party was able to afford assistance to the other. While moving about the harbour in a thick fog, the Prince suddenly discovered the admiral, with Blake's pennons floating at the main-top, riding within pistol-shot of his stern; and with that fearlessness which concealed so many faults, he gave orders to tack round quickly and run alongside the flag-ship, without firing a single shot or raising the least shout till they were near enough to spring on board. The men of the admiral caught a glimpse of the sus-picious craft through the thick atmosphere, and as she passed in silence under their lee, poured into her a broadside that shattered her fore-topmast. Blake con-tinued his course, the fog slipped in, and the two ships were instantly out of sight. Rupert's fleet was too far to leeward to give chase or render assistance. Their outfit being exhausted, the allies returned to their for-mer station at Belleisle, mutually accusing each other of incapacity. Vara John was deposed from his command, and judged unworthy ever to be again employed in his country's service. Blake and Popham, after des-patching all their prizes to England, returned to block up still more closely the mouth of the Tagus.

A second descent of the combined fleets was equally unsuccessful. Without risking a general engagement, which he had no desire to risk, Blake remained master at sea. Rupert had seen no more service on this new element than himself; but it is curious that the veteran admirals of Portugal should have been foiled in all their attempts to force Blake either to quit his position or fight a battle. At length the loss of so many vessels, and the continual outcries of his subjects, induced King John to sue for peace on reasonable terms. As neces-sary preliminaries to a peace, Miro was restored to favour, and it was intimated to the fugitive princes with many feigned regrets that the crown of Portugal could no longer protect them against the might of England.

Rupert received a hint that as Blake was at sea in search of the dispersed fleets of Brazil, some of which had stopped short at the Azores, while others had run for safety into Spanish ports, he might get clear away with his ships. If the princes did not depart, they were given to understand that on Blake's return he would be allowed to attack them at their moorings. Rupert therefore again unfurled his corsair banner, slipped his cables, and under a friendly salute, the last he ever heard in Portugal, he dropped down the river in search of new adventures.

As soon as the princes had quitted Belleisle, Don John despatched an envoy to London to sue for peace and friendship with the English Commonwealth. His former pride was remembered against his present humility, and the Council of State made hard conditions. But the envoy granted all the preliminaries demanded. He agreed that the English merchants who had been under arrest should be set at liberty; that they should have all their losses made good to them; that the King of Portugal should defray a considerable part of the war expenses already incurred. When the envoy presumed to dispute some dates and details, the haughty Council commanded him to quit the country. However galling to his pride, Don John was obliged to submit. He sent a nobleman of high rank, the Conde de Camera, as extraordinary ambassador, to deprecate the anger of Parliament. The Conde assented to every proposal made to him by the Council:—but delays again arose through the change from the Parliamentary to the Protectoral form of government, and it was not until January, 1653 that the treaty of peace, trade, and friendship was finally ratified between the two powers. So long as he lived, Don John gave England little trouble.

At the close of the dispute with the court of Lisbon,

the owners of the nine ships seized and detained by
Blake at the mouth of the Tagus were allowed to present a statement of their grievance to the judges of the
Court of Admiralty.  Blake's conduct in the matter was
minutely investigated; Admiral Popham was called on
to give evidence as to the facts : and after a full inquiry
the judges decided that the General-at-Sea had acted in
the spirit of his instructions.  But they acknowledged
the private losses which the owners might have suffered
by the forcible detention of their ships, and decided that
the same compensation should be awarded to them for
the service, as in cases where ships had been hired by
the State.

# CHAPTER V.

## 1650—1651.

### CAVALIER-CORSAIRS.

RUPERT had not invented the corsair system. That honour belonged to George Carteret, governor of Guernsey. While the King was still at Oxford, and when Blake was vigorously defending Lyme, Carteret despairing of the royal cause on land, ordered a model galley to be built for him by the expert artizans of St. Maloes. She was fitted with twelve pair of oars and with large sails, so as to go against wind and tide. She carried one brass cannon and two swivels, and was manned by thirty-six desperate ruffians. She cruised in the narrow seas, and her captures were armed and converted into war-ships. Carteret became master of a fleet. He soon made himself terrible to the London merchants. Warwick, sent to reduce the islands to obedience, returned without crushing the freebooters, and their enterprises took a wider sweep. For a while Carteret was master of the narrow seas. Charles then gave him the commission of a Vice-Admiral in the Channel, and the royalist rover filled his coffers and strengthened himself in his hold, Mont Orgueil Castle, against the Roundhead forces. A career like that of Sir George Carteret, combining danger, enterprise and success, had an irresistible charm for Rupert; and it is demonstrable that from the period of his first offer to go on board the revolted fleet, he proposed to live by plunder. His intention was to establish one or more strongholds, from which he flattered himself that he should be able to interrupt at his will the rich commerce of the narrow seas. His first idea was to make his lairs, as many of the old northern jarls and vikings had done before him, in the Channel Islands, and particularly in the formidable groups of rocks lying off the Land's-end, the Isles of Scilly. Nature herself might have formed these islands for a pirate hold. Dangerous sunken rocks, an extremely intricate channel, and a sea unrivalled for swell and violence, prevented the approach of frigates or other armed vessels towards the centre of the group ; and, as the ruins still visible show, art had come efficiently in aid of nature. At every point where it seemed possible to effect a landing, stood block-houses and batteries connected with each other by lines and breast-works of the most formidable character. On St. Mary's Island, even at that time the wealthiest and most populous of the group, these field-works were bound together by castles of great strength and commanding position : Old Town Castle, a strong pile in the days of Leland ; Star Castle, with its ditch and ramparts, built by Sir John Godolphin in Elizabeth's reign ; and the Giant's Castle, standing on the crest of a bold and rugged cliff. Some of the islets were extremely fertile ; corn grew in abundance on many of them, and they were all well stocked with rabbits, cranes, swans, herons, and sea-fowl. Into this convenient hold Rupert poured men, money and warlike stores. To ensure his force against the risk of capture by sudden assault,—for the Dutch were anxious to possess so convenient a port, and their famous Admiral, Tromp, had been seen hovering about under suspicious circumstances,—he gave the command, civil and military, to the gallant Sir John Grenville, nephew of Sir Richard Grenville, Blake's old antagonist at Taunton.   The islanders, children of the sun and sea, willingly joined in the attempt to convert their home into an important magazine and naval station.   And to render the extraordinary combination of natural and artificial defences perfect, two thousand picked men were landed as a garrison, aided by a multitude of Cavalier gentry, whose private fortunes had been wasted in the war.

When cruising in the South Channel, before the approach of Blake's squadron had driven him to Kinsale, Rupert had carried the fruits of his terrible industry into this pirate hold.   The store-houses on these rocks were filled with the captured merchandise of all nations; but the chief articles stored up were silks, corn, wine, oil, timber, and the precious metals.   While in Ireland, apparently engaged in the work of co-operating with the Marquis of Ormonde in the royal cause, he had been occupied with the task of strengthening this position. On the 3rd of March he sent to Sir John Grenville from that country as much corn, salt, iron and steel as the ships could stow.   His project of starting as a corsair on a large scale was not disguised.   In April he wrote to Grenville on the subject nearest his heart :—" You will receive," he says, " if these ships come safe, such provisions as we can spare here, and also some men, which I was feign to send out of my own regiment.   They are all armed, and have some [arms] to spare.   The officers have formerly served his Majesty.   You may trust them. I doubt not ere long to see Scilly a second Venice.   It will be for our security and benefit; for if the worst come to the worst, it is but going to Scilly with this fleet, where, after a little while, we may get the King a good subsistence; and, I believe, we shall make a shift to live in spite of all factions."

The exiled family and their chief adherents seem to have entertained no scruples about this system of free-booting. On hearing of a new capture, Charles writes from the Hague to his cousin: "Having already disbursed for the fleet a considerable part of those moneys which we intended for own support and maintenance, and being now totally destitute of means to pay the debts of our dear brother, the Duke of York, and our own, and to provide for the subsistence of ourselves and family, we are no ways able to discharge the debts contracted at Helvoetsluys for the fleet; and we intend, therefore, to provide for the satisfaction thereof out of the proceeds of the goods in the ship lately taken, if it prove good prize."—Charles drew on the corsair prince as on a bank; and when Rupert could no longer meet the demand made on him by his royal cousins out of the stolen property at hand, he had recourse to the goods and chattels laid up for future use in his stronghold at Scilly. Prog, a merchant, who had discounted a bill of 5000*l.* drawn by Charles on Rupert, arrived at Kinsale to ask for his money; but being dissatisfied with the prizes offered to him in liquidation of his claim, the prince gave him 533*l.* in gold and silver, and an order on Sir John Grenville, at Scilly, for 10,909 lbs. weight of Ardasse silk, as an equivalent for the remaining 4467*l.* In this way the business of the exiled court was done. Men who had formerly been colonels of regiments became captains of frigates; those who could find no vessel to command, repaired to Scilly, Jersey, or Guernsey, to share in the defence or join predatory parties as volunteers; so that when St. Mary's Island fell at last into Blake's hands, he found as many colonels and captains in the forts and castles as would have sufficed to officer a large army. The court busied itself daily with these piracies. Instead of concerning itself with the affairs of nations, with the intrigues at Madrid, London and Versailles, the royal Council became engrossed with price-lists, trade speculations, and rates of exchange. Gossip from Amsterdam was received with more eagerness than gossip from Paris. The gravity with which the old states-men of the Stuarts discussed the market value of hides, sugar, silk, and timber, was excessively ludicrous. Claren-don, Cottington, and the most reputable members of the party sanctioned this course of life,—accepting from neces-sity that which the Bohemian Princes had adopted from love of adventure and lawlessness of spirit. Nor was Charles averse to share the disgrace as well as the profit. Carteret, his deputy-governor of Jersey and Guernsey, fitted out a fleet of ten light and fast-sailing frigates, each carrying eight or ten guns, for the purposes of piracy, with his consent, if not by his orders,—and this gallant freebooter brought in and sold numerous prizes in the ports of Jersey, while Charles himself was present on the island.

In one of his letters to Charles, Prince Rupert gives some account of his lawless adventures during his flight from Kinsale:—"Some forty leagues from shore," he says, "it happened that in the night, by a mistake of a light, all our fleet [five vessels] except Sir John Mennes's [ship] lost me. Two days after we made early in the morning seven ships to windward. We gave chase to them, and they to us, which proved to be our fleet: Marshall being come in with a prize, and my brother having taken another, made up the seven. At night, being moonlight, we made two great ships and a small vessel, which we immediately chased. In the morning the Black Lady, the Black Knight, the Scott, and the Mary overtook them. The small ketch bore up right before the wind, and the Black Knight gave chase, but in vain. The other two being proved English, did not alter their course. Our small ships fell to work, which lasted from seven in the morning until ten, about which time their admiral's main-top-sail-yard and main-sail were shot by the board, which stopped her way until my ship came up, to which she struck without a shot of ours: after which the other yielded also. These prizes being considerable, and being fearful of some disaster, having near three hundred prize-men aboard us, it was generally thought fit to secure and sell them with the first convenience to do, which no place was thought more convenient nor safe than Lisbon." The goods captured in these vessels he sold to the Portuguese merchants for 30,000*l.*; the vessels themselves he fitted out as men-of-war. Blake's vigilance and activity never allowed him to return to the Channel Islands; but it cost the country much blood and much treasure before they were reduced to obedience.

When the news arrived in England that Rupert had quitted Belleisle on a new piratical expedition, the Council of State hastened the preparation of another fleet to go in pursuit of him. The Fairfax, then on the stocks at Deptford, was rapidly finished. Penn was called in haste from St. George's Channel, the war being almost at an end in Ireland, and was appointed Vice-admiral of the Straits. The new fleet for the south consisted of eight of the best and fleetest sailers in the navy, commanded by some of the most eminent captains of the age. The flag-ship, Fairfax, Vice-admiral Penn, carried 52 guns and 250 men; the Centurion, Captain, afterwards the famous Admiral Sir John Lawson; the Adventure, Captain Andrew Ball; the Foresight, Captain, afterwards Admiral Howett; the Pelican, Captain, afterwards Admiral Sir Joseph Jordan; the Assurance, Captain Benjamin Blake, younger brother of the Admiral; and the Nonsuch, Captain Mildmay, were all frigates of 36 guns and 150 men each. The other vessel, the Star, Captain Sandars, carried 22 guns and 80 men. On the heels of this squadron, a fourth fleet, consisting of the Triumph, Tiger, Angel, Bonadventure, Trades-increase, Lion, and Hopeful Luke,—carrying in the whole 1226 men and 270 guns—was sent out under the command of Vice-admiral Hall, for the special purpose of acting as convoy for the protection of English merchants in the waters of Southern Europe. By these squadrons new and enlarged powers were carried out to Blake. Hitherto he had been required to forward all his prizes to England for condemnation and sale; he was now desired to deal with his prizes as he thought best for the service, sending them home or selling them in foreign ports, and using the money so obtained to revictual and refit his ships as occasion might seem to him to require. His commission was renewed for an indefinite term; and all the naval power of England in those seas, with the single exception of Hall's convoy squadron, was placed at his absolute disposal. This mighty and irresponsible power was wielded by Blake with a wisdom, energy, and success which received unqualified admiration in England, and extorted applause from the most rancorous of our enemies abroad. He had no instructions to control his movements. Translated out of the mere forms of office, the language of the Council of State to their great Commander was briefly this:—Uphold the interests and the honour of England; pursue, capture, or destroy its revolted fleet; protect its trade and its citizens abroad; overawe its rivals and false friends; harass and humble its avowed enemies! In the execution of his task he was bound by no forms of law. The Commonwealth knew that the rulers of the continent were not its friends; for although war had not been declared in words, the courts of France, Spain, Holland, Tuscany, and Portugal, had all favoured the royal fugitives, or pronounced their hatred and disdain of the English people and their Parliament by acts of hostility. The old ties of amity, the old treaties of commerce which bound England to the nations of Europe, were all broken and abrogated by recent events ; and not knowing when or from what quarter a blow might be struck at its peace and honour, it behoved the man who went abroad as the representative of his country, to treat with the suspected powers boldly, proudly, energetically, with words of peace on his lips, but with his hand always on the hilt of his sword.

After their expulsion from the Tagus, the crews of the revolted fleet were beginning a new life. As adversity gathered round him, Rupert grew reckless. Even a semblance of legality no longer seemed to him needful. " Misfortune being now no novelty to us," says the manuscript memoir found among his papers, " we plough the sea for a subsistence ; and being destitute of a port, we take the confines of the Mediterranean Sea for our harbour: poverty and despair being companions, and revenge our guide." In this spirit the Royalists sailed from Lisbon. Coasting the shores of Andalusia, they fell in with the Malaga fleet during a dark night, and any sail being now regarded as good prize, they fired into them, and captured two ships. Under cover of night the others escaped, followed by the Second Charles which vessel, missing the signal for retreat, parted company, and was for several days given up as lost. Rupert stood in for Malaga, intending to enter that roadstead by night and surprise the ships lying out of port. With this design the frigate Henry was sent forward with instructions to take up, as if by accident, a position between the vessels and the mole, so that when the Prince fell on them in the night it might prevent them from retreating

into the harbour. But some of the Henry's men deserted
when the frigate anchored off the mole; and as these
deserters informed the Spaniards of the intended night
attack, a signal from the batteries warned the ships of
their danger, and they stood safely in while it was yet
broad day. Finding his plan defeated, Rupert adopted
a friendly tone towards the citizens. Not able to drive
him away by force, they in their turn tried to soothe his
disappointment by the empty honours of a royal salute.
As nothing could be got by staying there, the fleet sailed
for Veles-Malaga, higher up the coast, where they had
heard that some English merchant-ships were lying in
security under the protection of a friendly power. On
hearing of the appearance of the Bohemian corsair on
the coasts of Andalusia, the governor of Veles-Malaga
despatched a courier to Madrid for instructions how to
act should the Prince make any hostile demonstration in
his district; but on the plea that this messenger had not
returned when Rupert arrived, he refused to interfere,
and six English ships were fired and burnt by him under
the guns of the Spanish batteries!

Blake was out at sea, waiting the arrival of a supply
of stores sent by the Council of State, when intelligence
of this atrocity, committed in a friendly port, reached
him. Having already serious causes of complaint against
the Spanish court, he wasted no time in communicating
with the English Admiralty. Leaving orders for Admiral Penn to cruise about the mouth of the Guadalquiver,
and watch the line of coast between Cadiz and Gibraltar
he at once turned his bows towards the rocky entrance
of the Mediterranean, and passed the Straits with all his
fleet, being the first English Admiral who had ventured
into those remote and celebrated waters since the time of
the Crusades. The chase again became close and exciting.
Rupert had sailed from Malaga, no one knew whither.

At Motril and at Capo de Gata, Blake could pick up
only vague and contradictory rumours. At Capo Palos,
near Carthagena, the revolted ships had last been seen in
the midst of a tremendous squall; when, fortunately for
their personal safety, the two princes separated from
their companions and ran out to sea. As the storm
abated, they descried a Leghorn trader, and the corsair
instinct being strong within them, gave chase, following
her to the Barbary shore, where she was at last overtaken
and captured. The remainder of the revolted ships ran
into Carthagena for shelter; and as soon as the foul
weather cleared a little, the English fleet was seen riding
before the harbour, cutting off every hope of escape.
Blake sent a messenger to inform the governor of the
town that enemies to the Commonwealth of England had
taken refuge in that port; that he, as Admiral, carried
instructions from Parliament to pursue and destroy them;
and that, the two nations being then at peace, he hoped
to be allowed to execute his orders without interference.
The answer to these demands was not satisfactory. The
governor pretended he could see no difference between
one Englishman and another; he said he had nothing to
do with their private quarrels; and he concluded by
stating his determination to protect every one flying to
his harbour who was not a declared enemy of his royal
master. Spain had not yet learned to comprehend
the genius of the young Republic. While professing
herself ready to acknowledge the new order of things,
she maintained a haughty and suspicious reserve of her
real sentiments. Willing enough to see England on
doubtful terms with her own enemies, the Dutch and
Portuguese—not much offended, in consequence of the
late King's behaviour towards the Infanta, at the disasters of the royal house, the court of Madrid, nevertheless, assumed a right to suspend judgment on the course

of events—to hold out a hand to either party as it might suit its pleasure or policy—and when occasion served to treat both Roundheads and Royalists with indifference and disdain. Nor was this proud caprice the only thing which Blake found written in his book of wrongs. Early in the year Anthony Ascham had been sent by the Council of State as their ambassador to Madrid. A suitable residence not being ready for him when he arrived, he repaired to an hotel with his servants and Baptista Riva his interpreter. Clarendon and Cottington were then in Madrid prosecuting a hopeless suit in favour of their master; and on hearing that Ascham was on the road from Cadiz, where he had received hospitality from the people, the two lords protested in bitter and indignant terms to Don Louis de Haro against his reception at court; and even hinted that, in their opinion, it would not be safe for him to appear in Madrid. Whether the Royalist lords were guilty of more than a wicked suggestion to their servants is a point involved in mystery; what is quite certain is the fact that Henry Progress, one of their personal attendants, and five other needy Cavaliers, went to Ascham's hotel the day after his arrival, and finding him alone with Riva at dinner, rushed in upon the two men, crying—Welcome, gallants! welcome! In a moment they both fell on the floor pierced with many wounds. This atrocious deed, done in broad day, on the sacred person of an ambassador, in the centre of a great city, and under the eye of the court, raised a storm of indignation not only in Spain and England but all over Europe. Clarendon and Cottington were suspected of being privy to the murder; and Don Louis gave them to understand that if the enraged populace of London should retaliate on his ambassador there, the King would hold them responsible for the shedding of innocent blood. A special agent was sent to deprecate

the wrath of Parliament, and a great parade was made
of prosecuting the assassins. But Progress, the man
whose confession was of greatest consequence, was kept
secreted in the Venetian embassy; the other scoundrels,
though murderers could not lawfully plead privilege of
sanctuary, were allowed to remain in a church to which
they ran reeking with blood; and after some time the
priests organised a scheme for their escape, which they
all effected except Sparks, who was taken in the act and
executed. These events made it absolutely necessary for
Blake to show a strong hand at Carthagena. Disdaining
to notice the governor's pretended ignorance of the state
of things in England, he bore down on the revolters,
mastered the Roebuck, set fire to another ship, and drove
the remainder on shore utterly disabled. The guns,
tackle, furniture, stores and ammunition were saved by
the crews, and after some negotiation these were delivered up by the Spaniards to the Admiral's agent.
With the exception of the Reformation and the Swallow,
the two vessels in which the princes sailed, and the Marmaduke, their recent prize, the whole of the revolted fleet
was now captured and destroyed; and that corsair
power, only a few days ago an object of terror to the
pacific traders of all nations, was reduced to so mere a
wreck that it seemed impossible for it ever again to
become an element in the European waters.

Not to leave a remnant behind him, Blake endeavoured to gain some intelligence of Rupert; and, put on
a false scent, either by design or otherwise, he steered
for Majorca, expecting to find him lurking about the
ports of that island. But the two brothers, feeling that
the game was nearly up,—for three vessels would be
unable to attack merchant convoys with certain success,
and from the position of royal corsairs making war on a
grand scale against all flags and fleets, they had now

become petty plunderers of unarmed vessels,—stood across for Toulon, where they had reason to expect a friendly reception from the omnipotent Cardinal Richelieu, that statesman being for the moment on bad terms with the Commonwealth. A sudden storm, however, separated the Reformation from its two fellows; Maurice rode, with his prize, into the great road of Toulon, where he was quietly allowed to sell her cargo; Rupert was driven by bad weather to the east, as far as Sicily, in which island he was compelled to remain part of the winter, entirely uncertain as to his brother's fate. At length, however, he reached Toulon, whither he was quickly followed by the English squadron. Blake instantly sent into the town to protest against the honours and succours granted in a friendly port to fugitives from justice and enemies to the English Parliament. This remonstrance producing no effect, the Admiral declared that he should consider the permitted sale in that port of a cargo of English goods, piratically seized, as an hostile act; and that unless Chevalier Paul, the French Admiral then commanding in the road, undertook to drive the corsairs from his harbour and restore their plunder to its lawful owners, he should hold himself free to make reprisals on the commerce of France. The Chevalier tried to avoid the necessity for such destructive measures, by hastening the departure of his dangerous guests. With his assistance they refitted and prepared for sea, when seizing a favourable opportunity, they escaped from the roadstead, and passed through the Balearic Islands.

Penn was left to destroy the pirates; he chased them from port to port, without falling in with them. Broken in spirits and in fortune, they made their way to the West Indies, where they lived by plundering the commerce of Spain and England; and were now and then heard of in

Europe for several years after through the tale of some
hapless merchant returning from the New World beg-
gared by their depredations. At length the two brothers
parted company in a tropical storm. Maurice was never
heard of again : but Rupert lived to invent pinchbeck,
and to enjoy the amenities of the Restoration.

Nothing is more curious in the history of those times
than the way in which Blake exercised the tremendous
powers entrusted to him by the Council of State. Men
of office and ancient routine were startled by his bold
and open policy, so far removed from the old turns and
tricks of diplomacy. His logic was brief and simple : in
face of any event he asked himself but one question—Is
this for the honour and interest of England ? Whatever
the answer, that settled the question. If it appeared to
him clear that the thing ought to be done, it was done.
There was no looking right or left, backward or forward,
to antecedents or consequences. Portugal and Spain
had refused either to do justice or to give him formal
permission to execute justice for himself; caring little
for their offended majesty and pride, he had taken the
matter into his own hands, and had taught them that the
young Commonwealth of England would not be cheated,
like an old and decrepit monarchy, with lying laws and
treacherous formalities. France had now roused his ire,
and powerful as that country was under the great Cardinal's sway, it soon felt the inconvenience of the reprisals
which he never threatened in vain. Months before the
affair of the Marmaduke at Toulon, there had been some
slight bickering between the two navies. James, Duke
of York, had issued from the Hague a number of blank
commissions to be filled up by his agents with the names
of persons able and willing to fit out privateers and
harass the coasts and commerce of England, all goods
taken by them being declared beforehand lawful prey.

Under the sanction of these commissions, men who cared nothing for Roundheads or Cavaliers, Republics or Monarchies, chartered fleet sailers, and manning them powerfully, roved about the narrow seas in search of plunder. Some of their prizes had been carried into Brest and Havre; and speedy justice not being obtained for this wrong from the Court of Versailles, Parliament in its turn had issued letters of marque against French vessels. Except in a single case, where he found a French man-of-war lying in wait for English merchants, Blake had hitherto scrupulously avoided every appearance of an intention to carry out his free instructions; but after the authorities at Toulon had openly received the revolters, he felt himself bound to retaliate on every occasion that should offer itself. On his voyage homeward, he captured four French prizes,—one of them a fine frigate of forty guns, the combat with which reads like an episode in an ancient romance. Meeting the Frenchman in the Straits, Blake signalled for the captain to come on board his flag-ship; and he, considering the visit one of friendship and ceremony, there being no declared war between the two nations, readily answered the invitation. The Admiral, when he entered his cabin, told him he was a prisoner; and asked him if he would give up his sword. Astounded at such a demand, the Frenchman boldly answered—No! Blake felt that an unfair advantage had been gained as the captain probably knew nothing of the Toulon affair or of the English threat of reprisals; and scorning to make a brave officer the victim of a mistake, he told him he might go back to his ship, if he wished, and fight it out as long as he was able. The captain thanked him for his handsome offer and retired. After two hours' hard fighting he struck his flag, and being brought once more on board the flag-ship, like a true French knight he made a low bow, kissed his sword affectionately and delivered it to his conqueror.

After an absence of twenty months, during which he had completely dispersed and destroyed the revolters, rebuked the pride of Portugal, read a significant lesson to Spain and France, freed the southern and great midland seas from privateers, and left a salutary dread of the young Commonwealth on the shores of Barbary and among the naval powers of Italy, Blake returned to England. For the first time during centuries the fleets of Venice and Genoa had found themselves in the immediate neighbourhood of an English power; and though the name of Blake had not yet grown into the word of terror it became in those distant parts a few years later, the rights and the honour of Englishmen began to be respected from the date of his first memorable cruise in the Mediterranean. Applause and more substantial rewards awaited him at home. The Council of State made him a Warden of the Cinque Ports. Parliament recorded its special thanks in his favour and voted him a donation of a thousand pounds. The whole country rang with the renown of a man who had revived the traditional glories of the English navy and exercised so perilous a power with unequalled wisdom, resolution and success.

Blake had little time allowed him for repose. Though the strength of the corsair Prince had been broken, the hold which he had built for himself at Scilly, not only held out against the power of Parliament, but the desperate men whom he had thrown into it continued to harass peaceful traders. The reduction of this group of rocks, together with the islands of Guernsey and Jersey, firmly held by the brave and enterprising Carteret, was the naval work laid out by the Council for the year 1651. Fears were entertained of Dutch interference; Van

Tromp, the oldest seaman of the naval Republic, was at sea with a mighty fleet and suspicious instructions. Parliament suspected him of a design against the islands, for which the depredations of the corsairs would have supplied some sort of excuse, and they sent ambassadors to the States General to demand explanations. At the same time they prepared to reduce the islands and scatter the pirates, and to remove all pretext for the intervention of Van Tromp. The former colleagues were again named Generals of the Fleet; and in April Blake and Ascue threatened St. Mary's, the largest of the Scilly group and the residence of the governor. On receiving the usual summons to surrender, Sir John Grenville replied in the tone of a man prepared to impose rather than submit to conditions. He said he was willing to enter into a treaty; but he spoke of having a large force at his disposal, not only sufficient to maintain the islands, but to restore the exile to the throne of his fathers. Despising this bombast, Blake selected eight hundred men, under the command of Captain Morris, to land at the back of Tresco, an island lying against St. Mary's, and of all the Scilly group the next to it in size and military importance. A garrison of nearly a thousand men, posted behind a line of breastworks, opposed this attempt; but the Roundheads threw themselves into the water, waded to shore, and as soon as the first company could form, advanced pike in hand to assault the entrenched positions. The cavaliers fought gallantly, disputing the ground with pike and pistol after their field-artillery had failed. But having obtained a lodgment in the outset, Morris held his conquest stoutly, and when night put an end to the contest the garrison withdrew to their boats and passed over to St. Mary's, leaving Blake in possession of their works, arms, and some prisoners. At daybreak the Roundheads pushed forward, passed the ridges of high ground, and came down the south slopes of the island, when one of the most picturesque and striking scenes in Europe burst on their sight. In front, girt with rugged rocks and green islets, rose the wealthy and populous island of St. Mary's, crowned with ramparts and castles. Below lay the narrow roadstead, shut in by innumerable rocks and points of land like a beautiful alpine lake, in which the pirate pinnaces and caravals were moored. As the light of morning fell on green meadow and rugged peak, on busy town and shining water, the beauty of the scene appealed to the sternest heart. Little time, however, had the Roundheads to spend in admiring wonder. Their chief soon fixed on a jutting point of ground, somewhat in advance of the regular lines for a battery, which, when finished, would sweep St. Mary's harbour and roadstead, and prevent the arrival of relief from Jersey or the harbours of Normandy. Erected almost as soon as it was planned, this battery became a source of deep annoyance to the garrison. Grenville's position was indeed growing critical. Besides the population, itself larger than the natural means of supply, more than sixteen hundred men were crowded together on the little islet ; and as all chance of free communication with their friends on the Continent was for the moment cut off, the Cavaliers saw themselves reduced either to submit to a blockade, certain to end in their destruction, or by a bold and combined effort to dislodge the enemy from Tresco, and again open the passage of the main roadstead. The latter, however, seemed a desperate adventure. Blake had landed a considerable force at Tresco and encamped them, as the remains of lines and mud-huts still show, on a low neck of land facing the harbour ; and nothing less than a battle and decisive victory could have enabled the Cavaliers to regain the position they had so hastily abandoned. Meanwhile, seeing that his batteries produced little or no effect on the castles at that distance, Blake adopted a bold and unexpected resolution. He brought his frigates through the intricate and dangerous channels, planted them in the roadstead under the castle guns, and prepared to fight a regular battle of artillery between land and sea. This feat has been achieved so often in later times, that it is not easy now to estimate the daring which it then implied. Up to that day it had been considered a fundamental maxim in marine warfare that a ship could not attack a castle or other strong fortification with any hope of success. Blake was the first to perceive and demonstrate the fallacy of this maxim; and the experiment, afterwards repeated by him in the more brilliant attacks on Porto Ferino and Santa Cruz, was first tried at the siege of St. Mary's. With great labour he got some of his lighter frigates through the rocks and shoals of that intricate channel, and moored them in the road, —when a furious cannonade began from the castle, still more fiercely answered by broadsides, and raged until dark. Daybreak saw this contest of cannon recommenced: but the battle was decided in favour of the frigates. A practicable breach being made in the castle wall, the command for an assault was given by Blake, when Grenville, very much changed in his opinion as to the impregnable strength of the pirate hold, sent to beg a parley, which ended in an engagement on his part to surrender the islands, garrisons, stores, arms, ammunition, standards, and all other implements and materials of war, on condition that the lives of the officers, soldiers, and volunteers should be spared; the common soldiers and sailors being allowed to enter the nation's service, and the gentlemen sent to London to await the final decision of Parliament in their favour. These terms were thought by many to be too favourable to the Royalists,—and that fallen party began to look up to Blake as the most friendly or the most lenient of their conquerors. To prevent the garrison from giving cause of alarm, he sent part of the men into Ireland and the rest to Scotland, to be there incorporated with the armies of the Common-wealth. Sir John Grenville and the corsair gentlemen taken with him, arms in hand, were put on board Sir George Ascue's squadron and carried into Plymouth sound. Acting in the spirit of Blake's articles, Parlia-ment treated Sir John Grenville with extreme leniency. He was even permitted to enjoy his forfeited family estates without molestation. For some years his turbulent soul, rebuked by a cause equally strong and magnanimous, remained quiet; but after the death of Cromwell he again appeared on the stage and played a conspicuous part in the drama of the Resto-ration.

The Scilly Islands cleared of their lawless occupants, Blake turned his attention to Jersey and Guernsey, the only remaining strongholds of the corsair power. Carteret commanded as deputy for Lord Jermyn. Carteret, a gallant officer, who had served in the royal navy while the navy was yet called royal, and had received and refused the appointment of Vice-Admi-ral under the Earl of Warwick, was one of the ablest generals and stanchest Cavaliers whom Blake had to encounter by land or sea; and his prolonged defence of these islands, especially that of Jersey, which he con-ducted in person, though in the end it was unsuccessful, covered his name with glory—and after the restoration of the Stuarts, when he became co-proprietor of an American province, Charles insisted on calling it New Jersey, in honour of his famous exploit. The sphere of duty which devolved on him at Jersey was exactly suited to his capacities. Daring as Rupert himself, but cautious as he was brave, his piratical adventures were conducted with forethought, gallantry and success. For more than two years his name had been a terror to the London merchants, and the council-board at Westminster was kept in a flutter of fear and rage by the letters which arrived almost weekly with accounts of the discomfiture and loss suffered by vessels carrying the national flag at the hands of this terrible freebooter. Whitelocke's journal throws jets of light on the scene of these disasters, while Blake was chasing Rupert in the south of Europe. For instance :—On Feb. 21, 1650, " letters that several merchantmen have been taken on the western coast by Jersey pirates; " Feb. 26, " letters that two Dutchmen laded with salt came to anchor within half a league of Dartmouth Castle, and that presently two Jersey pirates came up with them, cut their cables and carried them away." The gunners in the castle fired on the bold marauders, but without effect. Success made them still more daring, and the complaints laid before the Council became more frequent and more vehement. March 1, " letters of Jersey pirates very bold on the western coast; " March 6, " letters of several ships taken by the Jersey pirates ; " Mar. 15, " of the want of frigates on the western seas to keep in the Jersey pirates ; " March 17, " of the Jersey pirates taking several merchant-ships, and none of the Parliament frigates to help them ; " March 19, " letters of the piracies committed by those of Jersey." A few of the more respectable inhabitants of Jersey had firmly resented the loss of character brought upon their island by these piracies. La Cloche, an eloquent divine, denounced the thief from the pulpit ; declared that Jersey had become a nest of pirates, a second Dunkirk, and proposed an appeal to the king against the acts of his disreputable friends. Carteret

threw the preacher into gaol, and would have hung him had he found a decent pretext.

Even after the appearance of Blake and Ascue off the Scilly Islands, Carteret, still confident in his own resources and secure in a fortress which since the days of Rollo had never been assailed with success, continued his destructive warfare on commerce. He had, indeed, no choice. Upwards of four thousand men, the remains of veteran. armies and sea-roving adventurers, thronged the two little islands. He was bound to feed them, and it was desirable to keep the more daring spirits employed at sea. Of Jersey itself he had no fears. Its position was strong by nature, and had been rendered yet stronger by art. Storms rarely cease in that part of the English Channel. Sunken rocks, lying near the surface, not only render the navigation extremely dangerous for large vessels, even with good pilots, but cause violent currents, cross currents, and cataracts at every ebb and flow of tide. Nature itself seemed to have fashioned the coast of Jersey, rocky, steep, and broken, as the ramparts of a vast and impregnable fortress. Skilful engineers had added Elizabeth Castle, Mount Orgueil and Cornet Castle to the natural defences. Elizabeth Castle, built on a bold and isolated rock in St. Aubin's Bay, facing St. Heliers, the chief town in Jersey, and about a mile from the mainland, was at that time considered one of the strongest military positions in the world. This fortress, the key of his defensive operations, Sir George Carteret commanded in person. Mount Orgueil he entrusted to Sir Philip Carteret : and Cornet Castle, in Guernsey, to Colonel Burgess. While the sea was yet open to the marauders, they sent pressing entreaties to Lord Jermyn and to the royal exiles for immediate succour :—and in this position the Cavaliers awaited the Roundhead squadron.

While the expedition against these islands was fitting out at Plymouth under his personal directions, Blake employed a few stolen moments in visiting the naval stations on the coast, in strengthening weak points, in re-distributing the naval force, in stimulating the energy of his colleagues and in rectifying legions of abuses. His flag-ship, the Victory, flew about the Channel. One day its bright pennon was streaming in the Downs, the next day it was found at Spithead or in Plymouth Sound. Where work was to be done, apathy aroused, energy increased, there was the Victory and its indomitable Admiral. The tardy routine of the Navy Commission was the high rock against which his resistless will rolled with the least effect. Week after week he urged this body to proceed with greater rapidity and resolution. The Scilly Isles reduced, these officials saw no reason for maintaining a force at the Land's End; but Blake told them it was necessary to keep several powerful vessels at that point; to send a frigate to watch the Isle of Man and check the Irish marauders who continued to infest St. George's Channel; and to station a regular garrison on St. Mary's Island. When he quitted the Scilly Islands for Plymouth, he left a favourite officer, Colonel Bennett, in command of the Commonwealth forces there; and while the Scotch army remained in England he kept up a regular correspondence with him, considering that station as one of very great importance. Much of this correspondence is now lost; but the following brief note, relating to land as well as to sea events, has escaped the common doom.

"Plymouth, August 26th, 1651.

"Yesterday I wrote unto the Com^r of the Militia, which I believe you have partaken of,—How that according to the intelligence I have received the enemy was possessed of Worcester. By the pacquet this morning, I am informed that the enemy bended his course towards that place, but to prevent him coming there was a considerable force put into it. He is at a stand, knowing not where to go, and his forces mutinous in respect of their tedious marches. It hath pleased God to take out of this life my partner, Col. Popham, who died of a fever in the Downs, by reason whereof I believe my stay will not be long here. I have no more at present but to renew my desire that an eye may be had upon the disaffected."

In the depôts and dockyards the abuses against which he had to struggle were of the most formidable kind. Many of the ships were not sea-worthy. The stores, provisions and warlike materials were very deficient; and the seamen's wages were often in arrear. Blake compelled the authorities in London to listen to complaints; and from the extracts of letters written by various captains of vessels which he submitted to their consideration, it is still possible to gather some idea of the extreme poverty of means with which he had to perform his wondrous exploits. An example or two will suffice for this purpose: Captain Pearce, he says, writing from Londonderry on the 27th of August of this year, "complains that the fleets on that coast generally stand in great need of victuals, desires speedy supplies thereof, otherwise must greatly suffer; goes to half allowance, drinks water; hath but seven days' provisions, most of it stinks; butter and cheese not edible." Captain Vessey, of the Truelove, writing from Liverpool in the same month, complains, he says, that "the frigate wants all manner of stores; stands in great need of trimming; is very leaky; when she bears up hath a foot of water above the ceiling; hath been out nineteen months; her men in great need of pay to provide clothes for winter." This was very much the state of the fleet throughout.    A letter written by Blake to the Commissioners at their office on Tower Hill, from Plymouth on the 28th of August, proves his minute attention to every thing connected with the welfare of his men, and exhibits one of the abuses—the plan of paying all the seamen's wages in London—which for a long time resisted all the influence brought to bear on it by the reformer.—" Gentlemen," this letter runs, " there hath been this summer divers mariners prest in this and other western ports into the States' ships ; and, in respect their habitations are so far distant from London, many of them have, upon the going in of the ships they served in, been discharged here; and one Mr. Edward Pattison of this town, out of charity hath paid them their tickets, they being poor people and not able to look after it alone.    This man acquaints me that for some tickets, notwithstanding he hath been without his money a good while, he is in danger to lose it through delay.    I know not what the reason is, but I believe what he did was merely to relieve and ease the poor men.    I therefore make it my desire to you that you will give orders for the payment of such tickets as he hath or shall present unto you, they agreeing both in entries and discharges with the muster-books, and thereby Mr. Pattison not put to unnecessary attendance.    Therein you will not only oblige him but also your affectionate friend, Robert Blake."

The rectification of abuses, and the political uncertainties which arose for a moment through the Scotch invasion of England, detained the fleet at Plymouth several months.    Meanwhile Carteret maintained his reputation as a daring and successful cruiser.    Undaunted by the fall of Sir John Grenville at Scilly, he swept the sea from Land's End to Portland Reach, and the Council had still the mortification to receive the letters which

Whitelocke has briefly reported:—April 17, 1651, "letters of the Jersey pirates taking two barques laden in sight of Portland;" April 21, "of more prizes taken by the Jersey pirates, and of Captain Bennett's fighting two of them four hours;" July 14, "that five English vessels were taken by boats from Jersey, carrying four or five guns a piece;" July 18, "letters of two prizes taken by a Jersey frigate of eight guns, twenty-four oars and eighty men, and that there were twelve of those frigates belonging to Jersey;" August 7, "letters of much damage done by the Jersey pirates;" September 27, "letters of the Jersey pirates doing much mischief on the western coast."

By the middle of October the English fleet was almost ready for sea. Blake hoisted his flag in the Happy Entrance, a forty-four gun-ship, Captain John Coppin. The battle of Worcester had put an end to embarrassments on land, and left the powers that ruled in Westminster time to think of such matters as national honour and the security of trade. Taking Colonel Haynes and his regiment on board, together with two other regiments of foot, and four troops of horse, Blake sailed from Plymouth sound; and on the 20th of October, after suffering from a terrible storm, which scattered and slightly damaged many of his ships, he obtained a precarious anchorage in St. Ouen's Bay on the west side of Jersey. The sea broke furiously on the rocky shore, and a heavy rain added to the difficulty of making observations. But the officers of the Happy Entrance could see that the coast was alive with defenders, horse and foot, men active, courageous and well-disciplined.

After a brief rest, Blake ordered his boats to be lowered at three in the morning, but the waves broke too grandly in their front to permit a landing. When day dawned, a second attempt was made, but without success.   Carteret had only to look on and see his enemy baffled by the elements.   The boats put off, filled with armed marines, dismounted troopers and their horses, bodies of infantry with their pikes and matchlocks; but the sea rose before them like a vast rampart, and one or two boats which ventured into the raging surf, were overset in an instant.   Blake resolved to try the effect of a cannonade.   The ships being got into position, the cannoneers began to play, and their fire was quickly answered from several little forts and redoubts in the bay, as well as from twenty-four brass field-pieces attached to the militia service.   In the fury of the moment some of the frigates ran close enough for the men on board to use their muskets, and many Cavaliers rushed into the water in the eagerness of their zeal; but as a cannonade of four hours' duration, in which the Roundhead gunners spared neither powder nor shot, produced no apparent effect on the garrison, the fleet drew off to a more sheltered position in St. Brelard's Bay, about a league distant, where the Admiral made a new disposition of his power.

One squadron was sent back to St. Ouen's Bay; another was ordered to take up a strong position in St. Aubin's Bay, over against St. Heliers, and ready to act against Elizabeth Castle.   Other ships were commanded to cruise off the coast of St. Clements, threatening every hour to make a descent; and a further division was sent to Grouville Bay, on the extreme east of the island, to operate against Mount Orgueil Castle.   These movements perplexed the defenders, and Carteret was obliged to detach a part of his forces to wait on and watch each squadron.   Blake himself remained in the Happy Entrance at anchor in St. Brelard's Bay, and the chief force of the Royalists encamped on the rising grounds, ready to resist the Roundheads should they attempt to land.

A little after midnight, though a thin rain was still falling, the moon broke out for a few minutes, and by her pale light Carteret saw that a large body of foot was being lowered from the ships into flat-bottomed boats brought from Plymouth for that service,—in all ten battalions of four thousand men. A brisk fire was opened on them from two small batteries erected in favourable positions on the shore, and mounted with excellent ordnance. The Happy Entrance replied with her broadsides, and other of the Roundhead ships joined in the cannonade. But either in consequence of the discovery of their intention, or because the tremendous swell of the sea prevented the necessary measures being taken, the attempt to land that night was abandoned. When the battalions returned to their ships, new orders were given out. A squadron of nineteen sail was left in St. Brelard's Bay to occupy the attention of the camp, while Blake, with the remaining body, returned to his former position in St. Ouen's Bay, where he had found more sea-room, and had now resolved to effect his purpose of throwing Colonel Haynes and his troops on shore. Sir George Carteret left the dragoons and his own company of fusiliers, supported by four companies of militia, to watch the nineteen ships and frigates, and started with the infantry on a harassing night-march along the beach; keeping the fleet in view as well as he could in the uncertain light of early morning. Blake's policy was to wear out the men by constant marches, alarms and cannonades. Every moment some of the fleet-guns thundered at the shore, or at the exposed column; and many times during the long march Carteret had to halt and bring his artillery into position and return the fire. Nor could he gain a single moment's repose for his harassed comrades during the day. Instead of pulling up his fleet in the centre of the bay,

as was expected, Blake held on his course, making for
Letac, the extreme northern point of land, and thither
Carteret was compelled to follow him.  But as soon as
the ships were all come up in front of that headland, the
captains were signalled to tack about and return to the
southern point, La Frouque, five or six miles distant.

Carteret could no longer keep his men together.  They
had been under arms three days and two nights, during
which time rain had fallen without intermission; they
had made several marches and counter-marches over bad
roads and broken ground; and they had stood the fierce
though intermittent fire from the enemy's ships.  At
sunset he allowed them to depart for the neighbouring
villages in search of refreshment and repose; he himself,
with a few dragoons, alone remaining on the beach, along
which, however, he had all the camp-fires lighted.  The
weather changed in the night.  The rain ceased, the
wind died away, and the swell of the sea abated; but
not a star was visible, no moon arose to tell the tale
of preparation; for years, the pitchy darkness of the
sky that night was recollected as an omen of disaster.
The fires along the shore appeared to warn the Admiral
that his endeavour to throw Haynes' regiment on
shore at that point would be attended with other difficulties than a threatening sea and a rocky coast on a
dark night.  Yet nothing could check his ardour.  So
long familiar with success, he despised obstacles; and
towards the close of the civil war even the Roundhead
soldiers had learned to feel that contempt for Cavalier
prowess, which at an earlier period the Cavaliers had
affected to feel for the valour of tailors and serving-men.
At eleven o'clock at night, the boats were again lowered,
and by a desperate and gallant effort were run ashore.
Holding their arms above their heads, the men leapt
into the surf, many of them up to the neck in water, and

pushed for land. While struggling to obtain firm footing, and to free themselves from the returning surges, Carteret's horse rode down furiously with the hope of forcing them back into the sea; but, forming his men in the dark midnight, Haynes led them to the charge, and, after a conflict of half-an-hour, he drove the Cavalier horse from the field, and pursued them inland more than a mile.

Early next morning, Haynes marched against a fort near his halting-place, but found it abandoned. Several pieces of cannon and some colours fell into his hands, but no enemy appeared to dispute his advance. During that day and the next day other forts and military positions were taken without a blow; and in three days the whole island, with the exception of Mount Orgueil and Elizabeth Castle, had surrendered. Finding it useless to contend in the open field with his dispirited troops against the victorious Roundheads, Carteret withdrew his entire force into Mount Orgueil and the Castle, which last place he had a reasonable prospect of maintaining against every assault. Money, guns, ammunition, stores, and provisions for eight months had been carefully piled up there in anticipation of the siege which now threatened it. Cut off from the mainland and surrounded by rocks and seas, commanding the island though not commanded by it, Elizabeth Castle was considered an impregnable fortress. The nearest point of land on which a fort could be raised against it was more than three-fourths of a mile distant, and the sunken rocks lay so near the surface all round, that a frigate or man-of-war could not approach it within several furlongs. With plenty of men and an occasional supply of provisions from France, Carteret hoped to hold this rock until a change of fortune came to his royal master; and into this fortress the chiefs of the

Cavalier gentry, the clergy of the island, and a picked garrison retired at the approach of the Roundheads. Haynes and his victorious troops took possession of St. Heliers.

Having already battered down a strong fort at St. Mary's Island, Blake believed he could also damage Elizabeth Castle from his fleet; and therefore sending Colonel Haynes to invest Mount Orgueil by land, he himself carried his frigates into St. Aubin's Bay, and planting them as near the fortifications as the pilot could find sea-room, he opened a tremendous fire on its old walls. The garrison answered with a loud cannonade. But at the very outset of this furious attack, an accidental shot from the Happy Entrance produced a disastrous moral effect on the defenders. A cannon-ball struck the little church on the rock, splintered the stones and killed several persons; at which Lady Carteret was so alarmed that she earnestly entreated her husband to make terms with the Admiral before the island was blown to pieces. The commander was himself firm; but so many persons, male and female, pestered him with their fears, that he was forced to send away his best boats with them that very night to France. Neither Lady Carteret nor the ladies and gentlemen who accompanied her in her hasty flight could have been of much use in the defence. But seeing these persons going on board under cover of the dark night, a part of the regular garrison, equally desirous of saving their lives, made an attempt to get off; and all who were taken in the act of trying to escape were hanged as deserters. Still further to dispirit the defenders, Mount Orgueil surrendered after a fortnight's siege:—Sir Philip Carteret obtaining from Blake the promise of an amnesty and act of oblivion for himself and his comrades in arms, a promise which was in due time confirmed to them

by Parliament. Twenty brass and iron guns, as many
barrels of powder, a thousand stand of arms, and two
months' provisions for seventy men, were the spoils of
the victors. The land forces were then moved to a hill
near St. Heliers and opposite the Castle. But the
ordinary field-artillery was useless at so vast a range,
and Blake had to send to Plymouth for mortars
of greater calibre. From these mortars a succession
of missiles were thrown into the castle; many of the
houses were knocked down and multitudes were killed
by the exploding grenades; but, without one word of
encouragement from his master, one message of hope
from Lord Jermyn, Carteret gallantly held his little
rock for two whole months, though at a terrific sacrifice of human life. At last a magazine of stores was
blown up and eighty officers and men were buried in
the ruins. This crowning calamity induced him to
hoist a white flag, and after a parley, to surrender on
condition of being taken, with such officers as chose
to go, and landed safely at St. Maloes, on the coast of
Normandy. The garrison had been reduced to three
hundred and eighty men. A great park of artillery, and
stores of powder, shot, bread, beer, beef, salt, wine and
brandy, were found in the remaining magazines. After
these signal successes, Cornet Castle, in Guernsey, surrendered without a blow,—and the English seas were
at last cleared of every enemy to the Commonwealth of
England.

For this important service Blake received the special
thanks of Parliament, as did also Colonel Haynes. A
public thanksgiving was ordered for these victories and
for the conquest of Limerick, which city had been
taken about the same time. The election of members
for the Council of State being about to take place,
Blake was nominated by Parliament, in a full House,

one of that supreme body.  His hands were already
full.  He was a Commissioner for sequestrating the
Estates of Somerset Delinquents—a Commissioner for
purging the Ministry of improper persons — a Commissioner of the Navy and Admiralty—a member of the
House of Commons—and a member of the Council of
State.  And now, as if these offices implied no cares
and duties, he was appointed, in the probable event of
a fierce and sanguinary war with Holland, sole General-
at-Sea for the ensuing year.

But this accumulation of offices and honours did not
prevent the great seaman from looking with care and
courtesy to the interest of his humblest companions in
glory.  His letters at this as at every other time exhibit
his characteristic kindness of heart, showing the utmost
readiness to hear complaints and to rectify grievances.
One of his earliest suggestions to the Navy-Commis-
sioners, after the reduction of the Channel Islands left
them at leisure to think of abuses at home, was a
strong recommendation for them to adopt the plan of
paying the seamen's wages in the port in which they
were discharged, and as soon as they came on shore ; so
as neither to give them the trouble of walking to
London nor keep them waiting several days at Portsmouth or Plymouth, in idleness, at great expense, and
at a distance from all the salutary influences of family
and home.  His regard for minor and individual cases
of distress was illustrated by numerous special appli-
cations to the Commissioners.  Every sufferer found a
zealous advocate in his Admiral.  And although abuses
of many kinds continued to prevail at the Admiralty
Office and in the dock-yards, defying every effort of
the courageous reformer, there is reason to suppose
that when Blake pleaded the cause of his own seamen,
he generally obtained justice for the applicants.

# CHAPTER VI.

### THE DUTCH WAR.

A CHERISHED dream of the English Republicans had been the idea of forming the United Provinces of Holland and the new insular Commonwealth into one mighty Protestant state. The Dutch were the greatest naval power in the world. The sea seemed to be their native element,—and their fleets of war and commerce were known in every port, from the farthest east to the remotest west. Their colonial empire was only inferior in extent to that of Spain; while their wealth, energy, and valour, gave promise of an indefinite expansion. England possessed a larger home territory, better harbours, and a finer geographical position. Its population was more numerous; its maritime resources were scarcely inferior; and its land forces, after putting down the proudest chivalry of Europe, were no longer to be compared with the mercenary troops of Italy and the Empire. A confederation of the two Commonwealths would, therefore, have produced a vast and powerful Republic, capable, should the need arise, of resisting all the crowns of the Continent. Such a confederation would have been able to dictate peace to powers like France and Spain. It would have secured the ascendancy of Protestant ideas and a liberal policy in the north and west of Europe; and would have furnished a ground from which knowledge and free institutions might have contended against the ignorance, bigotry and despotism which in modern times have found their strongholds in the east and south. But this splendid conception was opposed by commercial jealousies and dynastic interests. William, second Prince of Orange of that name, had married in the days of Stuart rule, a daughter of Charles I.; so that in addition to his princely antipathy to commonwealths, he was urged to thwart the idea of such an alliance by the powerful motive of a possible succession for his wife and children to the English throne. He was popular with the lower classes of his countrymen; and so long as he lived, the two Protestant states remained on bad terms. He refused to extend to the Parliament's agents the ordinary protection of the Dutch laws. Dorislaus, its first envoy, was murdered at the Hague by followers of Montrose. Strickland, who succeeded to the perilous office, suffered daily insults in the public streets. Yet no redress could be obtained. Recent prosperity, a career of victory unrelieved by check, had raised the pride of Holland to the highest. Within a few years the renowned Admirals of the Republic had humbled the power of Spain, punished the insolence of Dunkirk, compelled the Prince of Salee and the Deys of Tunis and Algiers to sue for peace, and made the Sultan of Fez and Morocco tremble on his distant throne. After such successes, nothing seemed to them beyond the reach of their ambition; and many of their people, led by the Orange party, were anxious for a rupture with England at the moment of its supposed exhaustion, believing that in a few weeks they could wrest from it the vain but fiercely disputed right to be considered mistress of the narrow seas.

But the Prince of Orange died somewhat suddenly,

leaving the heir to his honours and passions yet unborn; and the democratic party, comprising nearly all that was liberal and enlightened in Holland, seized the opportunity to abolish the office of Stadtholder and restore the pure form of republican government. Their success encouraged the English leaders to believe that even if their idea of a confederation could not be realised, a close alliance, offensive and defensive, might be formed between the two states. Oliver St. John was sent over as ambassador to the States-General to propose a treaty of trade and friendship. His reception was at first cordial and flattering; but the negotiations went on slowly and uncertainly. After a long consideration of the English proposals, their High Mightinesses offered a counter project. Debates, interviews, and written explanations multiplied; time wore on; and at length St. John found that his leave of absence had expired. His pride was hurt at these delays. The exile court was still at the Hague; and in addition to his ill-success with the States-General, he was subject to frequent outrages from the Cavaliers. The Dutch, on their side, were angry with Parliament for having fixed a day for his return, fancying it intended as a sarcasm or a menace. Probably the true cause of the delay was a desire on the part of Holland not to commit herself to the new Commonwealth until the result of the Scotch invasion should be seen:—St. John answered their complaints in haughty language, and took his leave, war between the two countries already raging in his heart.

As soon as the battle of Worcester had put an end to doubt as to the stability of the new Commonwealth, Dutch statesmen saw their mistake. In turn the States-General sent envoys to assuage the wrath of Parliament, and endeavour to resume the negotiations at the point where they had been broken. But new causes of offence were in the way, and the terms once rejected could no longer be obtained. Some English merchants, in consequence of complaints made to the Council of State of their losses by Dutch privateers, had received letters of marque against the ships of that nation; and in a short time more than eighty prizes had been secured in the ports of our east coast. A more serious obstacle to negotiation had arisen in the Navigation Act. The Dutch were a nation of traders. Their whale, cod, and herring fisheries occupied a great number of vessels; but the largest and best part of their commercial navy was employed in the carrying trade. Amsterdam and Rotterdam were the exchanges of Europe; and the ship-owners of these wealthy ports made their fortunes by transporting the produce of art and nature from one country to another. Under the Stuarts, England had neglected this important branch of naval industry; but the Navigation Act, in declaring that no goods, the produce of Asia, Africa, or America, should be imported into England except in vessels either belonging to subjects of the Commonwealth, or to the countries from which the goods were imported, put an end, so far as these islands, with all their colonies, connexions and dependencies were concerned, to that lucrative and fruitful branch of Dutch enterprise. The first prayer of the new ambassador, therefore, was that this severe law should be repealed, or if not repealed at once, that its action should be suspended during the progress of negotiation. But while urging this point in the name of peace, they were careful to hint before the Council of State that they were then fitting out a powerful fleet for the protection of their trade. Parliament took the hint as a menace, and replied by ordering its captains to exact all those honours to the red cross which had been claimed by England in the narrow seas from the Saxon times. The order raised new troubles. Commodore Young, falling in with a Dutch fleet returning from Genoa, sent to request the Admiral of the convoy to lower his flag; the latter refused to comply with a demand so unexpected; and Young poured a broadside into the ships. A sharp action ensued, and the Dutchman was obliged to strike. To revenge the insult to their colours, the States-General fitted out a fleet of forty-two sail and placed it under the command of their renowned Admiral, Tromp, with instructions to use his discretion as to when and how far he would insist on the point of supremacy; but he was positively required to repel on all occasions, and at all hazards, attacks on the traders of the Republic, and to support the dignity of its flag. Tromp's genius was well suited to the execution of these vague and menacing orders.

War had not yet been declared, and the ambassadors were still in London talking of peace, when Admiral Tromp suddenly appeared in the Downs. Bourne, stationed with a squadron of the fleet near Dover, despatched a messenger with the intelligence to Blake, who was then cruising in the James off Rye, in the usual manner of the summer guard. Suspecting evil designs, Blake instantly gave his orders, and in a few hours his whole force was under sail for the Straits. Next morning he saw for the first time his celebrated enemy lying in Dover roadstead; when he came within ten or twelve miles of the nearest ships, Tromp weighed anchor and stood out to sea, but without either lowering his flag or offering any explanation of this act of defiance. Blake fired a signal-gun to call attention to the omission. No answer was returned. To a second and a third shot Tromp replied derisively by a single gun, still keeping his course, the Dutch flag flying proudly at mast-head. Over against Calais road, it was observed by the English

fleet that Tromp fell in with a ketch coming full speed
from Holland, the captain of which evidently brought important orders, for Tromp veered round and made towards
Blake, his own flag-ship, the Brederode, being in the
van.  The English officers were mystified by these movements.  In spite of the presence of the Dutch ambassadors in London, Blake felt a strong impression that
Tromp had received instructions to offer battle, and he
lay-to and got his squadron into as good fighting posture
as he found possible on so short a notice.  The Dutch
had a vastly superior force.  Tromp counted forty-two
men-of-war and frigates.  Blake counted fifteen.  He
had sent orders for Bourne to join him with his squadron
of eight ships; but these were not yet in sight, and
possibly would not arrive in time for the engagement.
The disproportion of vessels did not, however, indicate
the true disproportion of force.  As a rule the English
ships were larger than those of Holland, carrying more
guns and a greater body of men; but, on the other hand,
the Dutch ships were manned by veteran seamen, while
the great body of men on board the English fleet were
raw soldiers sent from the camp and unaccustomed to
the new service.

When the two fleets came within musket-range, Blake,
affecting not to notice the enemy's menacing attitude,
shot out from his main body and advanced towards the
Brederode to speak with its commander about the refusal
of honours formerly paid to the English flag.  Tromp
sent a broadside into the James and stopped her short.
Blake and several of his officers were in the cabin when
this salute burst on them, smashing the glass, and
damaging the stern.  He lifted his eyes from his papers,
and coolly observed—" Well, it is not very civil in Van
Tromp to take my flag-ship for a brothel, and break my
windows!"  As he spoke, another broadside rolled from

the decks of the Bredcrode. Curling his black whiskers round his fingers, as he always did in anger, he called his gunners to return the fire, and in a short time the battle became general.

The English admirals then in service had not hitherto seen maritime warfare on a grand scale, like Tromp and the officers who had served under his orders in the great contest with Spain; and only one of them, Vice-admiral Penn, had received a regular naval education. When the Council of State appointed Blake to the sole command against Holland, they gave him two blank commissions, that he might select his own vice and rear-admirals for the ensuing year; and in conjunction with Cromwell, he had named Penn and Bourne to these important stations. Penn went on board the Triumph, sixty-eight guns, taking young Robert Blake, son of the Admiral's dead brother Samuel, as his lieutenant; Bourne raised his flag on board the St. Andrew, of sixty guns. But not expecting to be assailed while the Dutch envoys were still soliciting peace in London, Penn had got leave of absence from his ship, and was on a visit to his family; so that Blake had to contend with vastly inferior power against the greatest nautical genius of the age, without having at his side a single person of practical knowledge as a seaman.

At four o'clock the contest began with a succession of broadsides. On the part of Blake at least, no line appears to have been formed; fleet met fleet and ship grappled ship as they chanced to fall in each other's way. From the first onset, the James, a fifty-gun ship, carrying 260 men, bore the brunt of the action. The recollection of Lyme and Taunton, of Scilly and Carthagena, fierce as the fire was, faded before the terrific work. More than seventy cannon-balls were lodged in his hull; his masts were blown away; and his rigging was torn into strings by the tremendous gunnery of the Dutch. His master, one of the mates, and several other officers fell, dead or wounded, at his side. For four hours the shot of the enemy flew about and around him without intermission. Six men were killed, thirty-five were desperately wounded, and many more were hurt; but his crew maintained the unequal contest with a bravery and resolution after his own heart. As night came down, their energies were roused anew by the thunder of Bourne's cannon bursting in the enemy's rear. The sound of artillery, booming along the waters, had reached the rear-guard, consisting of the St. Andrew and seven other ships, and Bourne immediately crowded sail and stood out to sea in hope of sharing in the battle. He arrived in the crisis of the engagement, and his 300 additional guns sufficed to turn the scale of victory. Unable or unwilling to engage this new enemy, Tromp retired from the scene about nine o'clock with the fast-fading light, leaving his intended surprise and destruction of the English fleet at best a drawn battle. Blake was too much disabled to follow, his mizen-mast being shot away, his sails, cordage and spars all torn and broken. He came to an anchor about four miles off the Ness, and spent the night in repairs and preparations for the morrow. When day dawned the Dutch were not in sight. Far as his eye could reach, the Channel showed no trace of an enemy :—and the Commonwealth was once more lord of the narrow seas. During the fight two Dutch ships had been boarded and taken. One of them was so much damaged it was feared she would go down in the night, and after rifling her holds and cabins the crew turned her adrift. The other, a ship of thirty guns, was brought in safely and manned for immediate service. Young Robert Blake distinguished himself greatly. In the absence of Vice-admiral Penn, he commanded the

Triumph, and evinced such skill and courage, that on Penn's removal to the James, he was appointed captain of that important vessel. With the one exception of the flag-ship, the fleet had not suffered materially. Only nine men were reported as slain in all the other ships. Of the Dutch, two hundred and fifty were taken prisoners, and nearly as many more were said to be killed.

The encounter of two powerful fleets in the midst of peace, without declaration of war or other previous formality to prepare men's minds, produced an extraordinary sensation in the two countries. In London, the mob rose, and would have burnt the house of the Dutch ambassadors at Chelsea, had not the government sent down a troop of horse. These ambassadors made strenuous efforts to explain the causes of the rencounter. They declared that Tromp was not the first to begin. They accounted for his appearance in the Downs by alleging stress of weather. They said he was about to lower his flag when Blake began to fire; they expressed deep regret for what had occurred; and urged, with apparent earnestness, that violent counsels should give place to renewed attempts at negotiation. Tromp also pretended that he had not violated the peace; that from first to last he had merely stood on his defence. He declared that had he chosen to make use of his immense superiority of force, he could have destroyed the English fleet. People received the declaration with contempt. At last the ambassadors offered to disavow and disgrace their great Admiral; but the more they pressed their point, the sterner and more exacting Parliament became. England, it replied, had suffered insult and wrong; its duty was therefore to obtain reparation for the past, security for the future. Every day, as war came nearer, the States-General seemed more resolved to adhere to a pacific policy. As a final effort they sent over their grand pensionary, Pauw, a man whose character and office were thought likely to give unusual weight to his overtures; the demands of Parliament rose at every turn, and after a fruitless attempt to negotiate, this eminent ambassador gave up the vain effort to reconcile the two powers, and took his leave.

Blake remained master of the Channel. All reserve being thrown away, in consequence of the late engagement, he exerted his power to harass the enemy's trade, and to fit out the vessels which had fallen into his hands for immediate service. His cruisers brought prizes into port almost daily during the latter part of May and June. He captured ten merchant-men at one swoop. One day he received intelligence that a Dutch fleet of twenty-six traders, convoyed by three men-of-war, was coming up Channel;—they were all captured, traders and convoy, and the latter were immediately manned and fitted for service. In less than a month, to the surprise and ecstacy of the Londoners, he had sent into the river more than forty rich prizes captured in open sea from their powerful and vigilant enemy. The Dutch merchants were compelled to abandon the Straits. Their argosies from the South of Europe and from the Eastern and Western Indies had to run for safety into French ports and send their cargoes overland at an immense loss, or to make the long and dangerous voyage round by the North of Scotland. This brilliant success inspired the Council of State with new life. Orders were given to strengthen Dover pier. Forty sail were added by one vote to the fleet. At Blake's suggestion six additional fire-ships were prepared. The seamen's wages were raised; and the Vice-admirals of all the maritime stations from Norfolk to Hampshire were requested to summon together all mariners between the ages of fifteen and twenty, young, ardent, docile, and engage them in the

State's service. Knowing the vast resources and inflexible spirit of the people with whom they were about to enter into conflict, the Council of State, Blake being a member, and in all matters connected with the navy its chief authority, resolved that the entire fleet should be raised to 250 sail and 14 fire-ships. The divisions were to be commanded and located as follows:—30 sail were to go forthwith to the west Channel, ply between Brest and Scilly, and keep the sea open towards the south; 20 sail were to go northward, disturb the Dutch fisheries and capture their Baltic traders; 30 sail were to ride in the Straits; and the remaining 170 sail and the fire-ships were to keep together under Blake's immediate orders to oppose and fight the enemy. These magnificent ideas were never realised in full:—but at the end of one month from the fight off Dover the energetic Admiral could count with patriotic pride no less than 105 vessels, carrying 3961 guns, under his flag. He was not, however, equally strong in men. His constant cry was—seamen, soldiers! And the Commissioners of the Navy were engaged day and night in devising means to supply him with this essential element of maritime power. Two regiments of foot were taken on board bodily, and from that time marines became a necessary part of the equipment of our men-of-war.

Meanwhile the Dutch preparations for the campaign were made on the grandest scale. The dockyards of the Texel, the Maas, and the Zuyder Zee resounded with the note of coming strife. Sixty men-of-war, larger in size and more perfect in equipment than had ever yet been seen in those northern seas, were commenced. Convoys not too far away were called back; merchant-men of heavy tonnage were pressed into the service; the ablest seamen found in their ports, irrespective of age or nationality, were lured into the service by offers of high wages and the hope of plunder; and in a few weeks their renowned Admiral, ripe in age, honours and experience, saw himself at the head of 120 sail—a power more than sufficient in the opinion of every patriotic Dutchman to sweep the English navy from the face of the earth.

The swift and unexpected opening of the war had placed the mercantile marine of both nations, especially in the North Sea, at the mercy of privateers and cruising squadrons. At that period few English vessels ventured to the south of Europe; the distance checked the enterprises of the timid, and the more substantial peril of Algerine pirates and Salee rovers prevented the brave from seeking fortune in waters where the might of England was little known and still less feared. In the opinion of these African marauders, Holland was the only naval power of Europe. More than once she had chastised their insolence with stern severity; and, as her traders ploughed the southern waters in comparative safety, the spices of the Levant, the silks of Italy and the wines of Portugal, were chiefly brought to England in Dutch bottoms. Baltic commerce, on the contrary, was chiefly carried in our own ships; and at that very moment an unusual fleet of vessels were in the North and Baltic Seas, Parliament, in anticipation of war, having sent out several traders to purchase hemp, tar, and ship-stores for them in Sweden, Denmark, and Pomerania. These stores were now become of vast importance. The dockyards were bare; not a frigate in the fleet was decently supplied; and in the face of a contest which must occupy months and might extend to years, it was necessary to send a strong squadron to the north to collect these ships and convoy them safely home with their precious cargoes. Other reasons compelled Blake's attention to the squadron of the north. Ever since the atrocious action at Amboyna, which wrested the Spice Islands from our hands, the fleets of Holland had generally returned from either east or west by the long route of the Orkneys, so as to avoid bringing their freights within view of Dover Castle. One of these rich argosies was now known to be on the homeward voyage, and the Council of State was anxious that it should be harassed, and if possible cut off. Again, unable or unwilling to make use of the noble fisheries that nature has lavished on our coasts, the English of the sixteenth and seventeenth centuries had allowed their more enterprising neighbours to reap the harvest almost unquestioned. A fisherman's life suited the Dutchman's coarse and laborious habits. The hulks or busses engaged in this trade, averaging from three hundred to five hundred tons burden, were each manned by about a dozen persons; usually the master with his wife and children, and about six or eight others, men and women. On board these herring-boats, children were able to earn their own bread from the age of four or five. The life was rude at best—the wages were always scanty. But the people had learned to live on stormy and sterile seas, to flourish on mud-banks and sandy plains. More than once our ancestors had tried to establish rival fisheries, but never with a chance of profit. With an old Saxon chivalry, still found in some portion of the lower classes, they refused to allow the women to divide their coarse toils or share their daily perils; nor had they yet learned to look without horror on infant labour. Free from these scruples, the Frisian found in his baser nature a commercial advantage against which it was ruinous to compete. The Dutch family, huddled in a corner of the buss, found a part of its coarse food in the waters on which it exercised its craft. The English fisherman, who left his wife and children at home, had to support them out of the profits of his spoil.  Thus the whole trade fell into Dutch hands; and at the opening of the war between the two countries the boats engaged in it were counted by thousands.  Could the Dutch make good their claim to fish among the Northern Islands?  This was an open question.  They did fish in those waters.  But while the fact was allowed, the right was denied; and on taking the supreme direction of the war, Blake was anxious to give practical effect to the denials of his government.  While the squadron was preparing for sea, information came to hand that the spring fleet of these herring-busses, consisting of more than six hundred sail, convoyed by twelve men-of-war, was on its way home laden with fish.  His first idea was to send Sir George Ascue to the North, and stay in person to oppose Admiral Tromp; but as that great genius of strategy lay still in the Texel, making no sign of an intention to put to sea, he changed his plan, and resolved to go in person to the North.  Sending swift messengers to the Baltic, to desire all the merchant-vessels, private and public, ready to return home, then in and about the Sound, to rendezvous at Elsinore, and there await his arrival,—he went down to Dover, installed Ascue as his lieutenant in the Channel, with orders to keep a sharp eye on Tromp's movements, and set sail in the Resolution for the North, attended by a magnificent array of sixty ships.

On the 21st of June, Blake fired his parting salute in Dover road.  On the 9th of July letters reached the Council of State announcing that a gallant fleet, supposed to be General Blake's, had passed in sight of Dunbar.  Two days later, despatches left Westminster in hot haste, by mounted couriers, to inform him that a sudden change had occurred in the enemy's dispositions,—that as soon as he was known to have passed the Frith of Forth the

Dutch Admiral had quitted his lair,—that he was then riding with 102 men-of-war and ten fire-ships in the Downs,—that the whole coast was alarmed for its safety, none knowing where a blow would first be struck,—and that so far from Ascue being able to afford them any protection, he had himself been compelled to run under the guns of Dover Castle. The couriers rode day and night with urgent letters of recal; but before these came into the Admiral's hands, one of the three great objects of Blake's expedition had been accomplished. Meeting the great herring-fleet off Bockness, his advanced guard of twenty sail fell furiously on the men-of-war, and after a gallant contest, prolonged by the obstinate valour of the Dutch against superior numbers for three hours, sunk three of the twelve and took the other nine. All the herring-busses, six hundred in number, fell into his power with their crews and freights. But as these boats belonged to poor families, whose entire capital and means of life they constituted, he took from them, on a rough computation, every tenth herring as a royalty, and then warning the men never to fish again in the creeks and islands belonging to the Commonwealth of England without first obtaining from the Council of State a formal permission, he sent them home with all their boats and the remainder of their cargo untouched. This act of clemency called down severe censures on Blake in certain quarters. Many condemned such generosity to an enemy as Quixotic. "If the fish," said the politicians, "were of no use to the fleet, he should have thrown them into the sea." The answer was, "That they were human food, and that thousands would suffer, none would gain, by their destruction." Even men like Ludlow blamed him for not keeping possession of the poor fellows' boats. A remnant of the Dutch boats escaped into the Sound, whither Blake followed them; but his entrance into those waters alarmed the Danes along the shore, and they flew to arms as if to repel an invader of their country. A letter from the English Admiral to the King of Denmark put an end to their fears, for he declared that he had entered the Sound in chase of an enemy to the Commonwealth, and would refrain from every act of hostility on his part. He required, however, that the Dutchmen should be compelled to quit the asylum which they had found in Danish harbours.

Kent was in arms to repel the invader. Seamen crowded on board Ascue's squadron with offers of service. The regular militia turned out. Between Deal and Sandown Castle a long double platform was erected, with cannon at intervals to sweep the shore should the Dutch attempt to land. But these warlike preparations, though they evinced the national spirit, did less to preserve the coast from outrage than those elements which have so often proved our best allies in the hour of danger. Calms kept the enemy bound in mid-channel until the country had recovered from its first alarm. When the wind returned, it blew from the land, and with such steady violence, that with all his skill Tromp was unable to get near enough for a passing broadside. To the south of his position, Ascue rode in perfect safety with his small squadron; and some fresh ships, preparing to join him just before the Dutchman's appearance in the Straits, were retained in the Thames by a counter order. Tromp, it is believed, had expected to intercept this reinforcement as it left the river, and then by a sudden onset to crush Ascue under overwhelming cannonades. Success at these two points would have left Blake with about fifty sail—for he had despatched eight of his best frigates to strengthen the Downs squadron—against a fleet flushed with victory and of thrice his power. But the weather having foiled him in these hopes, the wily

Dutchman returned with the strong gale then blowing to the Texel, where a vast fleet of merchants were impatiently waiting to set forth on their voyage under his protection. Convoying these vessels northward, he saw the Baltic traders through the Sound, the busses disperse to their fishing stations, and the Indiamen separate to pursue their several voyages out of all danger from English cruisers,—and then went in search of Blake's squadron, confident in his immense superiority of force, and not unwilling to put the fortunes of his country to the arbitration of a battle. Since his recent victory, Blake had suffered severely from storms, and his ships were scattered among the roadsteads of the Orkney Islands for repair; but on hearing that his great enemy had followed him into the North, he hastily prepared for an encounter.

Towards evening, on the 5th of August, the fleets came in sight of each other between Fair Isle and Fould, almost half-way from the Orkneys to the Shetland group. Smarting under a recollection of former wrongs, both confident of success, Tromp trusting to his naval genius and superior force, Blake in the Lord of Hosts and the valour of his men, they eagerly prepared for action. But the empire of the seas was decided in favour of a new claimant. Whilst preparations were being made in the Resolution to attack the Dutch fleet, the sky gradually assumed a dark and threatening aspect. The wind, which had been extremely variable for some days, suddenly settled itself north-north-west. In the excitement of the moment, these signs were not at first observed; but as the gale rose, and the sky continued to grow black and lurid, Blake signalled his ships to look out for the coming storm; and leave the enemy to shift for themselves, certain that there could be no engagement that day. At length it burst:—and the fiercest of mortal passions were stilled in a moment before the awful demonstration.  Fitful gleams of light, now and then caught through the storm and darkness, told the commanders that another power had undertaken to disperse and separate their fleets.  Many of the ships were soon unmanageable.   Rudders were wrested violently off; sails were torn and twisted into knots, and the waves went through and through them at every swell, throwing their white and seething foam into the very sky.  The darkness, danger, and distance from aid and shelter, filled the excitable imaginations of the sailors.  "The fleet," says the Dutch writer of Cornelius Tromp, "being as it were buried by the sea in the most horrible abysses, rose out of them only to be tossed up to the clouds; here the masts were beaten down into the sea, there the deck was overflowed with the prevailing waves; the tempest was so much mistress of the ships, they could be governed no longer, and on every side appeared all the dreadful forerunners of a dismal wreck."  The storm raged through the night without abatement; and when day came down on the rolling waters, instead of the imperial fleets which rode so proudly among the rocks and islands a few hours previous, anxious in their strength and majesty to put the freedom of the sea to an hour's arbitration,— a remnant of scattered, helpless and damaged ships were alone descried between land and sky.  The Dutch had suffered terribly.  More than one of their frigates had been dashed on the rocks, splintered into fragments, and every soul on board sent down into the foaming surge. Tromp picked up broken relics of three of his fire-ships: —their fate could not be doubted.  They had all gone down.  Most of his men-of-war and frigates were considerably damaged, and the greater part of his fleet was scattered beyond the possibility of recal.  Some of the ships found refuge in the harbours of the Shetland group,

others fled towards the Norwegian coast. After spending several days in the vain attempt to collect the damaged elements of his power, Tromp was obliged to run into Scheveling with a remnant of only forty-two sail, to his own infinite chagrin and the extreme astonishment of his countrymen at the failure of an enterprise so vast and costly. Blake had been fortunate enough to keep his fleet together under shelter of the mainland of the Shetland Islands, and although he had not escaped without serious injury to many ships, he was able to keep the sea, and hang with his whole body of sixty-two sail, fleet and prizes, on the rear of the disabled Dutch. Finding the enemy disinclined to put out again from their harbours, he ravaged and insulted their coasts from Wadden to Zealand, and then ran across to Yarmouth with his prizes and nine hundred prisoners.

In a few days his standard was again waving in the Downs from the masts of the Resolution. Ascue and De Ruiter had met and drawn a battle, but the spirit of the States-General seemed to rise with their unexpected want of success, and they prepared another large fleet for service in the Channel under command of the renowned admiral and statesman De Witt. Tromp had retired into private life. Clamorous at a reverse in one long accustomed to triumph over every foe, a Dutch mob insulted his age and misfortune ; and in a fit of disgust the veteran laid down his commission. De Ruiter, too, had been anxious to retire from the responsibilities of command. He pleaded his long services, his old age, his failing health ; but his countrymen would not listen to his complaints ; they expressed a boundless confidence in his genius, and urged him to lead them once more as of old to victory. When the new squadron was ready for sea, De Witt joined De Ruiter, and took the supreme command. To oppose this new danger, Blake

called in the force under Ascue from Plymouth; and
the two fleets—that of England, composed of sixty-
eight ships of various gunnage—that of Holland nearly
equal to it in number of ships and guns—were once
more in the same seas, and anxious to try their strength
against each other.

An episode delayed the battle. Blake was cruising in
the Channel at the beginning of September, expecting
every day to fall in with the Dutch admirals, when news
was brought to him that the Duke of Vendome, having
recently encountered and scattered the fleets of Admiral
the Count d' Oignon, was concentrating war-ships,
frigates, transports, men and military stores on the coast
of Calais and Dieppe, with the design of throwing relief
into Dunkirk, then hotly pressed by the Spanish forces
under Archduke Leopold. The defeat of d'Oignon had
left the sea open to the French; should Vendome throw
men and prisoners into the private town, it would probably not fall.

The course of events before Dunkirk gave the Council
of State much concern. As yet they had taken no part
in the war between Condé and Mazarin, though the interests of their commerce had led them to sympathise in
secret with the cause upheld by Spain. France leaned,
as of old, to our enemies, the Dutch. Should Dunkirk be
preserved to Louis XIV., it was probable that at no distant day, it would be used by the admirals of Holland
as a basis of operations against towns on the coasts of
Essex and Norfolk. How were the English to secure its
fall? Only by arresting the relief squadron. But then
there had been no formal declaration of war between
France and England. Though the privateers of Brest
and Dunkirk continued their depredations on the merchant navy, and though many English cruisers bore
letters of marque against French ships, these disorders

had not seriously compromised either government with its neighbour, and a show of friendship was maintained between London and Versailles. Nor was there time for Blake to write a letter to his colleagues of the Council of State. The transports were on board, the ships under way, when his intelligence came to hand; and before a messenger could reach Whitehall, the French fleet would have been safely anchored under the batteries of Dunkirk. It was one of those cases in which he was allowed to act on the impulses of his genius. He believed it for the honour and interest of the Commonwealth, that Dunkirk should fall—and the question was submitted to a council of war, whether it would be possible to destroy, capture, or disperse the collected fleet? The council having advised, Blake stood away in the Resolution, followed by the Sovereign, and about twenty other ships. The Sovereign, then the largest as well as swiftest vessel in the navy—carrying eleven hundred men and eighty-eight guns, of which twenty were forty-four pounders—led the way, and was the first to engage the enemy. Its fire was terrible—the second broadside sinking one of the royal frigates—and its key-shot cutting off the main-masts of five others. As the frigate was going down, Blake bore into action with his pennons flying and trumpets sounding; and immediately singling out the Douadieu—commanded by one of the Knights of Malta—he ran alongside, and boarded her pike in hand. The rapidity of the attack, and the instantaneous advantages gained, disconcerted the French; some struck their colours—some fled—fiercely pursued by the Sovereign and the lighter vessels towards Dunkirk; and in a few hours the whole body of the French squadron, war-ships, fire-ships and transports, admirals, officers and men, were either gone down, or safely harboured under the guns of Dover Castle. Dunkirk immediately surrendered to the

Archduke Leopold : — and the seizure of Vendome's squadron remained, not only an illustration of the extraordinary powers exercised by Blake at sea, but a striking instance of bold conception and rapid execution.

These prizes safely harboured, the cruise in search of De Witt and De Ruiter recommenced. On the 28th of September, Penn, still on board the James, came in sight of the Dutchmen off the North Foreland; on seeing his signal, Blake, at that moment more than a league in advance of his main body, rode up to the vanguard and gave his brief but emphatic orders—" As soon as some more of our fleet comes up, bear in among them !" De Witt was taken unawares; his ships were in disorder ; a bad spirit prevailed among the men ; and De Ruiter urged him to avoid a battle. Pride made him deaf to his sage councillor, and he resolved to fight at a disadvantage, rather than exhibit to the world the spectacle of a Dutch admiral in retreat before the presumptuous islanders. His dispositions were made hastily and in confusion. De Ruiter was to lead the van, he himself the main body, De Wilde the rear. Evertz was stationed with a reserve to watch the action from a short distance, and pour out succours when they were most needed. At the last moment De Witt sent an advice-boat round to each of his ships to beg the captains to do their duty in their respective posts on that day. But his prayer was not heard. Apathy, intrigue, and discontent were on every deck. The Brederode, Tromp's old flag-ship, was in the fleet, but the officers and men refused to allow the new Admiral to come on board her ; and just before the action began, De Witt's standard was removed to a huge Indiaman. Resenting the disgrace of their favorite leader, several other ships disputed the new Admiral's orders, or obeyed them without the zeal which is essential to victory. Yet unwarned by these signs of disaffection—hoping that success would restore confidence and loyalty to his crews—De Witt laid his topsails to the masts and formed his fleet in line.

About four o'clock in the afternoon, the English being well up, a single order was given out from the Resolution—to hold back the fire till close in with the enemy,—and the flag-ship, followed by the James, the Sovereign, and the whole body of the vanguard, bore down on De Witt's line, which kept up an intermittent fire as it advanced. At this moment the Dutch tacked, and the two fleets came into collision. The crash of the first broadsides was terrific. The ships were close together, and an unusual quantity of shot struck home. For more than an hour the roar of artillery was incessant. After that its action slackened; there were occasional pauses in the storm; and the Dutch ships sheering off to a greater distance, the sulphurous atmosphere broke in many places, and the wind drifted it away in masses. But although the Dutch fell back, they fell back fighting, and with their faces to the enemy, and with obstinate valour they continued the battle until night-fall. De Witt had suffered most severely in men, Blake in masts and rigging. The most experienced admirals in both fleets were of opinion that De Witt could not have held out an hour longer without seeing his power broken and annihilated. De Ruiter had commanded his division with consummate skill and bravery. A great part of his own crew was swept away; his main-yard had fallen over to the left side; his main-sails, mizen-sails, and rigging were torn to shreds; his hull was seriously shattered; and he had received no less than four shots between wind and water. De Witt had atoned in a great measure for his rashness in fighting, by his courage and conduct during the action. Nevertheless, the Dutch were unmistakably worsted. Under the first shock of the onset, two of their ships went down. Two others had been boarded and taken; one of them, the rear-admiral, was the prize of Captain Mildmay of the Nonsuch. The two captains and all the crews were prisoners. Throughout the Dutch fleet the loss of life had been great. And to the infinite vexation of De Witt, about twenty of his captains, either disaffected to his person or unwilling to renew on the morrow so destructive an engagement, took advantage of the dark night to quit the main body with the ships under their command and make for Zealand, whither they carried the first news of the disaster.

All night Blake saw the lights burning in the enemy's ships, and assuming that they would fight again at daybreak, every hand on board the English fleet was employed in repairing sails, masts and cordage — in securing the prisoners—in helping and soothing the wounded sailors—and in the sad and pious duties connected with the burial of the dead. The grey light dawned on the sleepless crews still at their labours, and before sunrise the whole fleet was in motion bearing up towards the enemy. At first the Dutch seemed disposed to renew the bloody work of the previous day; but before the English van had got within range of cannon-shot, a change of opinion took place, and they made sail and stood up the Channel. De Witt had wished to fight. But Evertz and De Ruiter over-ruled his voice in the council of war, where it was resolved that an attempt should be made to collect the shattered and scattered remnants of their fleet; to gain one of their own ports and communicate with their masters; to repair, refit, and re-man their ships; and then await the commands of the States-General. Blake kept as close on their rear as the disabled state of his ships would allow; and having chased

them into the Göree, where the shallows yielded them
protection, he returned the insults offered to our coasts
by Tromp in the early part of summer.

Reports of the battle of the North Foreland were
read in London with boundless joy. It was the first
great naval action since the reign of Elizabeth; and
indeed there was room for honest exultation. The
prowess of England had now been arrayed against the
best seamen and the most famous admirals in the
world, and the English had come off victorious. At the
first trial of strength, they had proved themselves
equal to the acknowledged masters of maritime war.
Hitherto Tromp, Evertz, and De Ruiter had been
regarded by Europe as peerless, if not invincible, commanders. Yet an English land-officer, with only three
years' experience of the sea, had learned to contend with
these renowned admirals on equal terms; rough soldiers,
drafted from the camp, had, in the same period, ceased
to fear the veteran sailors who had swept the imperial
navies of Spain from the ocean. Blake was rising into
the first name in our naval history. His southern campaign, made while his genius was still unaided by experience, had placed him in general estimation by the
side of Drake and Frobisher. His drawn battle with
Tromp, his victory over De Ruiter and De Witt, raised
him into the highest rank of admirals.

Parliament shared the liberal enthusiasm of the people.
With a premature contempt of their powerful enemy,
they commanded Blake to dismiss a part of his fleet
to the merchant service from which it had been taken;
they allowed the fortifications erected between Deal
and Sandown to be destroyed; and they ordered the
guns planted on the line of breastworks to be removed
into the two castles. At Blake's most urgent request
they ordered thirty new frigates to be built; but in

their minds the victory was already won, for the moment
all was confidence and security. The Council of State
began a diligent study of the *Mare Clausum*, Selden's
learned book on the right of England to assert her
dominion in the narrow seas, and to exclude the Dutch
from any participation in the advantages of the northern
fisheries. They had the book translated into English;
and questions which had tested the learning of men like
Grotius and Selden were rapturously debated in taverns,
and triumphantly settled in the council. Vendome's
complaints were treated by the Council of State with
haughty indifference. They fancied their power was
fixed in the Channel for ever. They had not yet learned
to understand the genius of their enemy or the magnitude of his resources.

# CHAPTER VII.

### TROMP.

De Witt's return to Holland with a discomfited fleet was the signal for disorders in that country. His enemies of the Orange party charged him with rashness, cowardice and treason. The common sailors, turbulent and disobedient before the engagement, carried their dislike to the verge of mutiny after their defeat. On the flag-ship itself, De Witt's position was most disagreeable, even if his life were not in danger. Before going on board in the Texel he had been compelled by a decent regard for naval discipline to hang two of his seamen in Amsterdam, and at the execution he had been under the still more unfortunate necessity of shooting several citizens to prevent a rescue in the streets. In his day of power and of untried fortunes these acts of severity were borne in silent rage; but when he returned from sea with broken power and faded laurels, the popular passions swelled against him like the surges of their own stormy coast. In Flushing he was mobbed as soon as he landed; and his proud heart almost broke at the insult. In anger and disgust, he took to a sick bed. De Ruiter shared in some measure the unpopularity of his chief, and he also offered to resign his commission. The hour of alarm and general indignation—for the Dutch had so often triumphed over every enemy at sea, they could not understand their reverses, except on the principle of gross misconduct,—sent the inconsiderate people to the feet of their old commander. They now remembered, that if Tromp's success in the early part of the war had not been such as their impatience had expected, he had not suffered a signal defeat; if he had lost a powerful squadron, they had the consolation to feel that nature and not man had been the cause of its overthrow. When the failure of his rivals allowed them time to estimate his claims with less haste and less passion, they could not but see that his reputation as a sailor still towered above that of every other man in Holland; while, on the other hand, personal hatred and the memory of an ancient grudge fitted him in a peculiar manner for the chief command in a war against England.

At ten years old, Tromp was present in his father's ship at the famous battle fought against Spain under the walls of Gibraltar in 1607. Shortly after that event, he was captured by an English cruiser after a brisk engagement in which his father lost his life. Two years and a half he was compelled to serve in the menial capacity of cabin-boy on board the captor:—and thus the seeds of hatred to England and the English were sown in his proud and passionate heart. Once planted, this hatred grew with his growth. For a long time his life was passed on board fishing-boats and merchant-men; but his nautical genius was irresistible, and he fought his way through legions of obstacles to high command. At thirty he was confessedly the ablest navigator in Holland. More than twenty years he had commanded with success against Spain,—and had done more than any other individual to humble the pride and reduce the power of that extensive empire. The disastrous opening of the English war scarcely impeached his naval genius ; and the insult offered to his former success in stripping him of his great employments because nature had raised a destructive storm in the northern latitudes, appeared to the States-General gratuitous and unworthy as soon as they discovered that his future services were necessary to the Republic. The old Admiral's passion was soothed by compliments and royal offices. The King of Denmark, alarmed at the sudden growth of the English maritime power, made interest with the leading Dutch statesmen, with a view to promote a vigorous renewal of hostilities ; and at his special intercession Tromp was restored to his former post and his former honours, the most eminent of his rivals in naval ability and domestic influence, De Witt, De Ruiter, Evertz and Floritz, being appointed to serve under him as his Vice and Rear-Admirals. De Witt, too much mortified at his recent failure to have any wish to re-appear on the scene in an inferior place, excused himself from serving on the ground of ill-health ; De Ruiter therefore again went on board as second in command.

Other nations became interested in the quarrels of the two Republics. The war had barely commenced before the States-General sent ambassadors to Denmark, Poland and other powers in the north of Europe, to engage them in a common league against England. Frederick III., King of Denmark and Norway, listened to these proposals ; and though he did not as yet choose to commit himself by an open acknowledgment of his leanings, he sought by indirect and unexplained acts to forward the views of his powerful continental friends. Under pretence of securing them against Dutch cruisers, Frederick refused to allow the ships which Blake had ordered to rendezvous at Elsinore to pass the Sound :— an idle pretence, since the English were at that time masters at sea. As the hemp, tar and naval stores from the Baltic were urgently needed in the dockyards, Parliament wrote to King Frederick desiring him, as a friend and ally of the Commonwealth, to deliver up to their Admiral all the goods and ships then lying in his ports : and at the request of the Council of State, Blake detached Captain Ball with twenty men-of-war and frigates to add force to this reasonable request, and in the event of its receiving favourable attention to convoy the ships home in safety. After an absence of some weeks, Ball returned as he went out. Pressed to declare itself, the Court of Denmark vamped up a story about some old debts contracted by the late King of England on account of the German war, and claimed a right to detain the vessels until these debts were paid. The expected supply of stores was therefore not obtained,— and the Commonwealth had a new enemy to deal with in the north of Europe.

The term for which Blake had been commissioned to act as sole General and Admiral of the Fleet was near its close. He felt the weight of his great command, and he requested that two colleagues should be joined with him in the command as in the first years of his naval service. During his absence in the north he had seen the disadvantage of leaving the Downs to an inferior officer, however able ; and in the belief that such a division of the supreme command would be serviceable to the country, he set aside personal considerations and proposed to have two officers, enjoying the full confidence of the Council of State, associated with him in the new commission. Popham being dead, the choice of admirals fell on Colonel Deane, his former colleague, and General Monk. His own commission was renewed. Deane and Monk were then employed in suppressing the last remnants of the war in Scotland, and they could

not for some time to come take any active part in the
naval war.

Severe weather being set in and the Dutchmen busy
in their dockyards with the preparation of another vast
armament, Blake made the usual winter distribution of
the fleet. Besides the twenty ships sent to Elsinore
under Ball, Penn sailed with a similar squadron towards
the North to convoy a fleet of colliers from Newcastle
to London; a division of twelve ships was stationed in
Plymouth Sound; fifteen of the most damaged vessels
were ordered into the river for repair; and with the
remainder of his force, consisting of thirty-seven men-
of-war and frigates, the fire-ships and a few boys,—
Blake rode in the Channel, cruising from port to port,
between Essex and Hampshire, and expecting no enemy
to appear until the return of fine weather. In this he
was mistaken. Tromp's energy and influence had infused
an extraordinary degree of activity into the marine department, the harbours and dockyards of Holland. In
an incredibly short time the Dutch had fitted out and
manned a vast fleet; and as soon as the English squadrons
were dispersed for the winter stations, Tromp secretly
and unexpectedly left the Texel and appeared off the
Goodwin Sands with more than a hundred sail of the
line, frigates and fire-ships. His plan was bold and well
conceived. Throwing himself suddenly into the Downs
with this overwhelming force, he intended to close up
the Thames and cut off re-inforcements from Chatham
or the Lea, to fall on Blake's little squadron with his
mighty force, and crush or drive it down Channel
towards the Land's End, and then, with the entire coast
at his mercy, to dictate peace to the Commonwealth on
his own terms. At that time the thought of a winter
campaign filled men's minds with terror; but Tromp,
by a swift and daring blow, proposed to conclude the

war in a few days. Blake was scarcely aware of the
Dutch stirring in their ports before their ships were
seen from the out-look of the Triumph, to which vessel
he had removed his pennon. Late in November the two
fleets were in presence between Dover and Calais; and
the knowledge that Tromp was on board assured the
English Admiral that mischief was meant. A council of
war was called on board the Triumph. Blake described
the situation of the two countries at that moment,
glanced at the superior force of the enemy, at the distance of his own squadrons, and ended by declaring his
resolution to fight, if it were necessary, but on no
account to fall down the Channel, leaving the coast-
towns to be insulted, and perhaps destroyed by that
mighty and uncrippled armament. The captains accepted his decision, and returned to their several ships
to prepare for action. All that day the two admirals
watched each other's motions, the object being to gain
the weather-gage. The night came, cold and tempestuous, even for winter, and the ships were unable to
keep together. With the appearance of light the man-
œuvres of the previous day were renewed, the Triumph
and the Brederode dodging each other for several hours
in a slight and variable wind, their somewhat oblique
course inclining slowly towards the Ness. At three in
the afternoon the fleets were near each other off that
Essex headland. Tromp's patience was worn out, and
anxious to engage, he made a sudden effort to get alongside
the English Admiral at an advantage; but a rapid and
decisive movement carried the Triumph under his bow to
the weather-gage. In passing, the two ships exchanged
broadsides. Blake was closely followed in his dexterous
movement by the Garland, and missing the Triumph,
Tromp ran against her with such violence as in an
instant to break her bowsprit and ship's-head with the

weight of the crash. The Garland and the Bredcrode engaged, the English ship of forty-eight guns fighting with consummate bravery against its powerful enemy, until the Bonadventure, a trader of thirty guns, came to the rescue, and placed the Dutch Admiral himself in peril. Tromp encouraged his men by shouts and ges- tures to renewed efforts; he appealed to their love of country, their pride of race, their affection for himself. But all his exertions would have failed had not Evertz seen his exposed position, and brought his own ship to bear on the Bonadventure, thus placing the gallant little merchantman between the fire of two powerful admirals. The four ships were grappled together; but the English held out manfully against tremendous odds for more than an hour, when the contest was decided in favour of number of men and weight of metal. Out of two hun- dred men on board the Garland at the beginning of the action, the captain and sixty officers and men were killed, and a still greater number were severely wounded; the Bonadventure had suffered to an equal extent; and the survivors being no longer able to defend their decks, the Dutchmen boarded and captured both the vessels. The Triumph, the Vanguard and the Victory bore the chief brunt of the action. At one time these three vessels were engaged with twenty of the enemy; and although they suffered most severely in men, and were greatly damaged in their hulls, masts, and rigging, they came off safely from the desperate encounter. Night, which at that season of the year came down early, was already separating the fleets, when Blake heard for the first time of the unequal battle waged between the two Dutch Admirals and the Garland and Bonadventure; and not- withstanding the fatigue of his men, he gave orders to bear up to the Brederode, and endeavour to recover the captives. Other of the enemy's ships, however, crossed his line, and a more destructive conflict than had yet taken place ensued. Blake was surrounded by the Dutch ships. Three several times the Triumph was boarded in gallant style by the foe; each time the boarders were driven back to their boats with fearful slaughter. The flag-ship was reduced to a wreck. The foretopmast was shot away. The mainstay was gone. The sails and tackling were all in strings. The hull was shattered and pierced with hundreds of shots. The wonder was how she kept her head above water; and had not the Sapphire, a trader of thirty guns, and the Vanguard stood by him with unwavering steadiness and devotion, the English Admiral must have fallen before such overwhelming numbers. Thick fog and darkness put an end to the struggle. Under cover of night Blake drew off his ships, the Triumph being the last to retire from the scene of action, towards Dover roads. Tromp could not, or would not, follow. Next day the weather was thick with fog; the enemy was not in sight. The disabled vessels were ill prepared to brave the fury of the south-west winds; and, master of his own movements, Blake proposed to run into the Thames, and anchor in Lea-road to repair damages, ascertain the enemy's intentions, make some necessary alterations in the fleet, and wait the recal and concentration of his distant squadrons. The Dutch had not gained an easy victory. Their loss in men was great. One of their vessels had been blown into the air, every man on board perishing. Tromp's ship and De Ruiter's ship were both put out of service, and many others were seriously crippled. But their victory was unquestionable; for the moment they were again masters of the Channel.

There seem to have been three principal causes of this disaster—the first and last that England experienced under Blake's command—any one of them sufficient to account for it:—(1.) The overwhelming superiority of force on the part of Tromp. (2.) The extreme weakness to which some of Blake's vessels were reduced for want of men; and (3.) The cowardice or disaffection to the service, manifested at a critical moment of the battle by several captains in the English fleet. To the first of these causes Blake himself professed to attach only a secondary importance. Had all the thirty-seven ships behaved like the Garland, Sapphire, Vanguard, Bonadventure, Victory, and Triumph, the result would probably have been other than it was; and even his defeat, if the retirement of a squadron before a fleet three times its strength can be so called, was less galling to his proud nature than the idea of having officers under his command who at such a time could fail in duty to their country. In the letter which conveyed to the Council of State the first news of the reverse of fortune, he says:—" I am bound to let your honours know that there was much baseness of spirit, not among the merchant-men only, but in many of the State's ships. And therefore I make it my earnest request that your honours would be pleased to send down some gentlemen to take an impartial and strict examination of the deportment of several commanders, that you may know who are to be confided in and who are not. It will then be time to take into consideration the grounds of some other errors and defects, especially the discouragement and want of seamen. I shall be bold at present to name one—not the least,—which is, the great number of private men-of-war, especially out of the Thames. And I hope it will not be unseasonable for me, in behalf of myself, to desire your honours that you would think of giving me, your unworthy servant, a discharge from this employment as far too great for me, especially since your honours have added two such able gentlemen [Monk and Deane] for the undertaking of that charge;

so that I may spend the remainder of my days in private retirement, and in prayers to the Lord for blessings on you and on this nation."

But instead of receiving the acceptance of his offer to resign, Blake found that the misfortune which might have ruined another man had given him strength and influence in the country. The Council of State wrote by return of courier to express their unanimous thanks for his gallant conduct in the late action, and to assure him that all his proposals,—except the one which referred to his own retirement,—should be adopted. Never had he been so necessary to the country as at that moment, and his hints and requests were immediately carried into effect, so far as lay with the Council. Three of their own body, Colonel Walton, Mr. Chaloner, and Colonel Morley were sent down to inquire into the alleged misconduct of the officers, to report on the ineffective condition of the fleet, and, in case of need, to assist in a Council of War, to be called by the Admiral after their arrival. Messengers were sent to recal the convoys to the Downs. Orders were sent to Deane and Monk to hold themselves in readiness to go on board at twenty-four hours' notice, and assume the responsibilities of their rank. Cruisers and other vessels lying at Harwich and elsewhere on the near coasts were instructed to repair to the general rendezvous. A resolution was carried to raise the effective marine force to 30,000 men. More care was taken with the store magazines. The Navy Commissioners, long crippled by the perfidious policy of the Danish King, were empowered in this emergency to seize on hemp, tar and pitch, where-ever these important articles could be found. But not a whisper was heard against the Admiral, either in the Council or in the city. There was no attempt on the part of the Navy Commissioners to meddle with his plans or to abridge his authority. The Council of

State reposed an almost unbounded confidence in his genius and fidelity. Five days after the engagement off the Ness, they ordered—" That a letter be written to General Blake, to acquaint him with what the Council hath done for the giving him an addition of strength,— to let him know that (in regard the state of affairs is before him, and he hath a perfect understanding of them) *the Council do leave to him upon the place to do what he may for his own defence and the service of the Common-wealth.*" The next day they wrote again in the same spirit:—"The Council suggest objections to General Blake going with his fleet into Lea road, and recommend Harwich as a better position: *but still leave it to him to act according as his Council of War shall advise upon the place.*"

Curiously enough, the first disaster experienced by Blake at sea gave him power to effect reforms in the service and to root out abuses which had defied all his efforts in the day of his success. One great abuse was abolished that in his opinion lay at the source of the late defeat. To encourage merchants and others having vessels capable of armament to place them during the war at the disposal of Government, an Order of Council had hitherto allowed the masters of such vessels to command them after the change of service. Many persons thus came to occupy, as a private right, important offices in the navy who had no real attachment to the new order of things, and there was reason to suspect that some of the secret partisans of the Stuarts had crept into places of trust in this way for the express purpose of betraying the Commonwealth. These Royalists kept the exiled court well informed of the state of the navy, and the exiles in turn communicated the latest information to the States-General. Thus the Admiral had not only to fight his great and astute adversary, but to struggle against intrigues abroad and treason at home. Before Tromp sailed from the Texel, Charles Stuart had caused a secret memoir to be drawn up by Lord Clarendon and the Marquis of Ormonde—to be presented to M. Borrel, Dutch Ambassador in Paris—in which he proposed to the States-General a plan for creating divisions in the English fleet and consequent excitement and weakness in the country. He declared that he was aware that many captains in the Commonwealth navy were his own friends; and he offered to go on board the Dutch fleet as a private officer, seeking no command, except of such vessels as should desert to him from the English. De Witt, however, as a sincere Republican, refused to accept this doubtful aid; but a knowledge of the fact on which the proposal was based, that many of Blake's officers served under false colours, and were ripe for an act of treason, was of vast importance to Tromp in the arrangement of his bold and masterly campaign. Certain incidents in the late battle left no doubt that several captains had acted with direct or indirect reference to the enemy's design; and without being able to bring the crime of treason home to them, the Admiral took the occasion to insist on having a regulation adopted by the supreme Council, that in future captains and other officers should receive their appointments from the State.

As the inquiries of the three members, Walton, Morley and Chaloner proceeded, several officers were suspended, either for neglect of duty, lack of courage or other faults, against whom no suspicion of treachery or disaffection could arise. It was necessary to purge the fleet of its weak, as well as of its faithless, captains. No naval scrutiny was ever conducted with greater justice, openness and severity. The three members reported to the Admiral the results of their investigation in each case, and he delivered sentence of arrest or dismissal with a stern rigour, even when the law fell in its full weight on his own household and his own family. Francis Harvey, his secretary, was cashiered. Captains Young, Taylor, Saltonstill and others were put under arrest until the pleasure of the Council of State should be known. His brother Benjamin, to whom he was strongly attached as a brother and an officer, fell under suspicion of some neglect of duty; and however painful the exercise of power under such circumstances, he was instantly broken and sent on shore. This rigid measure of justice against his own flesh and blood silenced every complaint; and the service gained immeasurably in spirit, discipline and confidence.

While these reforms, recruitments and renovations were proceeding under Blake's immediate eye, Tromp rode up and down the Channel with a broom at his mast-head, a prosaic emblem of his right to sweep the narrow seas; and the States-General, more elated with their victory than their Admiral himself, put out a proclamation against our manufactures — sent intelligence of their great successes to foreign powers—and interdicted all correspondence and communication with the British Islands, pretending, as if they were already assured victors, to place them in a state of naval blockade. Ballads, by-words and scurrilous caricatures delighted the ears and eyes of the excited populace. The names of the vessels captured in the fight afforded Dutch wits a theme for abuse: they had carried off the "garland," they said, from the islanders; and there were squibs and jokes about the "bon-adventure" having realised the prophecy of its name in falling into their hands. But what concerned the Council of State more than these squibs and sarcasms, was a report that Tromp contemplated making a descent on the Isles of Jersey and Guernsey, and a very natural fear that the trading part of the community would suffer from the cruisers of their watchful and active enemy. These alarms hastened their preparations for the second winter campaign; and on the 8th of February Blake, still in the Triumph, sailed from Queensborough, at the head of sixty men-of-war and frigates, having Monk and Deane with twelve hundred soldiers from the camp on board. Penn was Vice-admiral, Lawson Rear-admiral. In the Straits the Portsmouth squadron of twenty sail came in, and with this addition to his effective strength, Blake resolved to seek the Dutch fleet and give battle. Tromp had gone southward to meet a large fleet of traders, ordered by the States-General to rendezvous at the Isle of Rhe, opposite Rochelle, and convoy them home; but intelligence had there reached him that the English were about to quit the Thames in his absence with sixty sail, and he intended to arrive at the river mouth in time to block it up, prevent their departure, and keep the Portsmouth squadron from effecting a junction with the main body. Blake had stolen a march on the Dutch Admiral, and when the latter turned Cape de la Hogue, he was surprised to find the English with a force equal to his own prepared to dispute the passage of a sea so lately swept by his potential broom. Confident, however, of victory, he accepted with joy the offer of a battle which fortune enabled him to decline without disadvantage had such been his pleasure.

Day was breaking on the morning of February 18, when the vanguard of the Dutch Admiral was descried from the mast-head of the Triumph. Blake dressed and went to the out-look. Nature could scarcely boast a grander spectacle than rose before him as the sun came forth, showing that heaving sea covered with ships, and lighting their sails and pennons with its pale radiance. The darkness of the weather had prevented recognition until the foremost ships were within a league of each other. The English Admirals were close together; the Triumph having Penn's ship, the Speaker, and Lawson's, the Fairfax, both within hail. But Monk was some miles astern in the Vanguard, and the main body of the fleet lay about a league and a half apart. Tromp saw his advantage. With the wind in his favour he might have carried his convoy to the Scheldt in safety, and returned at his leisure to give battle; but he chose to play a bolder game, and fancying the English vanguard of only twenty ships would prove unable to resist the weight of his attack, he sent his traders to windward, out of gun range, with orders to slacken sail and witness the engagement. Personal combined with public reasons to lend a thrilling interest to the coming battle. The two nations had now had time to collect their forces. Their largest ships were in array. The most popular admirals were on board the respective fleets: Blake, Deane, Penn and Lawson on the one side; Tromp, Evertz, De Ruiter, Swers, Floritz and De Wilde on the other. It was the first time Blake and Tromp had met on equal terms; and even the common seamen felt that the day had come to put their prowess to the test. At the outset, all advantages of position were with the Dutch. Their ships had the wind, and were close up together. When their extended line of fire opened on the English vanguard, it seemed almost impossible for about twenty ships to withstand the crash of such tremendous broadsides. As usual, the Triumph was the first to engage, and the Brederode, ever in the van, advanced to meet her, reserving fire till the two vessels were within musket-shot, and her charge could be delivered with the most deadly effect. With a strong breeze in his favour, Tromp shot by the Triumph, pouring a fearful broadside into her as he passed; and then, suddenly tacking round, fired a second time close under her lee, splintering masts and spars, tearing canvass and cordage, and strewing the deck with heaps of killed and wounded men. With this salute the Admirals parted company for the day, Penn dashing in between them with the Speaker and other vessels to cover Blake from some part of the circle of fire in which he lay exposed. The battle became general as the other divisions of the English fleet came up. On both sides the wreck was awful. In less than an hour from the first shot being launched from the guns of the Triumph, the sea was covered with spars, torn sails and broken planks. Almost every ship engaged in the action had even then had its cables cut asunder and its masts shot away. One moment an English crew were seen boarding a Dutch man-of-war, the next moment the boarders were driven back, and their own vessel was assailed in turn. Here there was a ship wrapt in flames; there one was going down with all her men on deck, their cries unheard or their terrors unheeded by friend or foe; elsewhere a fearful explosion sent decks and crews whirling into the black and lurid atmosphere. It is said in contemporary accounts, that the roar of the artillery could be heard along the shores of the Channel, from Boulogne on the one side to Portland on the other. About mid-day Monk came up with the white division, and from time to time other ships joined in the contest, thenceforward fought on nearly equal terms. De Ruiter justified his old renown. Early in the battle he had singled out and engaged with the Prosperous, a hired merchantman of forty guns, commanded by Captain Barker; but as the fire of the English ship was maintained with steadiness, he grew impatient with the distant fighting; and ordering a boarding-party to prepare for action, he ran his ship alongside the Prosperous, when his men gallantly leaped on her deck pistol and sword in hand. The close combat lasted a few seconds only.

Driving the assailants back to their ship, Barker threatened De Ruiter in his turn; but the brave old seaman, shouting in his fierce humour to the men, " Come, my lads, that was nothing—at them again ! " led them to a second and more furious assault. With his numbers reduced and his ship unmanageable, Barker was unable to resist the onset, and he and his crew were prisoners. At that instant Blake came up. The prize was instantly recovered, and De Ruiter himself almost surrounded by the English. Vice-admiral Evertz and Captains Swers and Kriuk hastened to relieve their countryman from his dangerous position, and the battle soon raged round this new centre with extraordinary violence. Penn's ship, the Speaker, was shattered by the guns, and condemned as no longer fit for service. When night put an end to the engagement of that first day, Penn was despatched to the Isle of Wight to bring up the guard-ships left at that station. Kriuk, in the Ostrich, fought like a true sailor, till his rigging and masts were shot away to the very hull, and his deck was covered with the dead bodies of his comrades. At last, he was boarded by the English. As the unfortunate vessel seemed to be sinking, and her officers and crew were nearly all killed or wounded, the English made a hasty plunder of her contents and left her to her fate. De Wilde offered his aid in an effort to bring her off; but a sudden calm came on, and not having a yard of sail left, the attempt to tow her away failed, and she was again abandoned. Next morning, Blake found her drifting about, the unburied corpses lying where they had fallen the previous day, and not a living soul on board. Captain Swers—afterwards the distinguished admiral of that name — was taken prisoner. Seeing his comrade, Captain De Port, roughly used by two English frigates, he flew to the rescue with his ship, and the four enemies were immediately locked together. De Port's ship was struck between wind and water and began to fill; he himself was severely wounded by the fall of a splinter; yet he continued to urge his men by shouts, and to flourish his hanger as he lay on his back in agony, until ship and crew went down together. Effective as the Dutch cannonade had hitherto been thought, it was no match for the destructive fire of the English frigates; and after a desperate struggle, in which the enemies proved themselves worthy of each other, Swers' ship also went down, himself and several of his officers and crew being taken on board the frigates and their lives preserved. Towards dusk, Blake felt himself strong enough to detach a number of his swiftest sailers with orders to gain the wind, and if possible prevent the escape of the vast fleet of traders which had been hovering on his flank all day; Tromp saw the movements of this squadron, and guessing its motive, fell back with a great part of his fleet, so as to cover the merchantmen. His retreat put an end to the first day's engagement; for on seeing their Admiral turn his face from the enemy, some of the Dutch captains hoisted sail· and fled away under cover of the gathering darkness.

Blake remained master of the scene of action, but his ships were too far damaged and his men too much exhausted to permit of an active night-chase. Heroic valour had characterised the officers and men on both sides. The Dutch had lost eight men-of-war, either taken by the enemy or destroyed. The Prosperous, the Oak, the Assistance, the Sampson, and several other English ships had been boarded and captured during some period of the day, though every vessel had been afterwards recovered. The Sampson was our only loss that day. Her brave commander, Captain Button, and nearly all his crew being slain, Blake took out of her the remaining officers and men, and allowed her to drift away. This excepted, no other ship in the English fleet had suffered so severely as the flag-ship, the Triumph. Her captain, Andrew Ball, fell that day covered with glory; Sparrow, the Admiral's new secretary, was shot down at his side; and nearly half the crew had been swept into eternity. Blake himself was wounded in the thigh, and the same ball which lamed him for the remainder of his life, tore away part of Deane's buff coat. The enemy's loss in men could not be ascertained; it was known to be very great by the entire clearance of more than one vessel; and the decks and guns of the captured ships were so spattered with blood, as to sicken and appal the most callous of the victors.

As soon as night came down, Blake's first care was to relieve the agonies of the wounded men by sending them on shore to the well-prepared hospitals, where persons of all ranks aided in promoting their comfort and recovery; collections of money, clothes and linen being made for them throughout the West, and the defects of the service supplied by the spontaneous enthusiasm of the people. His own wound, though not dangerous, demanded repose and careful treatment; but he listened to no friend who urged him to go on shore and seek for himself the relief which he took care to put in the way of his humbler comrades. The two fleets lay almost close together, with their lights streaming all night across the wintry sea. Until dawn next day, every effective hand on board the English fleet was employed in restoring sails, stopping leaks, cleaning guns, and repairing the waste of war. Everything was made ready to renew the contest with the return of light, for a dead calm had succeeded to the fresh breeze blowing when the battle began, and this calm continuing, it was impossible for the Dutch to avoid another battle.

As day broke a light wind sprang up, and Tromp, anxious to get his traders home in safety, disposed his fleet in the form of a crescent, the two hundred merchants in his centre, and crowding every inch of sail that he could spread, stood directly up Channel. Blake followed with his whole power; the breeze which favoured the flight also aiding the pursuit; yet it was twelve o'clock before the Triumph came within gunshot of the rearmost enemy, and nearly two before the main body came up with them off Dungeness. Compelled to fight against his will, Tromp ordered the merchants to make sail for the nearest Dutch port, keeping close under the French shore between Calais and Dunkirk for protection, and then turned like a panther on his pursuer. On both sides the battle was renewed with fury. De Ruiter gave fresh proofs of his skill and courage; but the fortune of war was still against him. After some hours of this second engagement his vessel became unmanageable, and would have fallen into Blake's hands had not Tromp seen his danger and sent Captain Duin to bring him out from the fight. With great difficulty he was extricated from his position and carried away. An hour or so later Tromp also began to fall slowly back towards Boulogne, still, however, contesting every wave, and the mingled rout and battle lasted until night again separated the hostile hosts.

Fortunately for the English fleet, though the air was bitterly cold, the sky was unusually clear for winter, so that the enemy's lights served them as signals, and enabled their ships to keep pretty close together and well up for the battle of the morrow. On the second day Blake had captured or destroyed five Dutch men-of-war. The advantages gained by the recent reforms came out clearly in face of the enemy:—the Admirals had not a single complaint to make as to the courage, steadiness and unity of purpose displayed by the inferior officers.

In the Dutch fleet, on the contrary, want of concert, party-bitterness and personal envy, combined to clog the genius of the great commander. At the close of the second day's engagement several captains sent word to the Brederode that they could resist no longer, pleading want of powder as an excuse, and Tromp was compelled to send these men away from the main body in the night so as to prevent treason and cowardice from spreading to the other ships. To conceal the true nature of this defection, he made a pretence of giving them instructions to take up a new position to windward of the traders, and begged them to make such a show of resistance as would keep the English frigates from coming too near. But his device failed of its own weakness. When daylight dawned, Blake saw at a glance that the fleet had been considerably reduced, and inferring that a squadron had been despatched in the night to cover the flight of the merchants, he sent off a division of fleet sailers, drawing little water, in pursuit of them, while he himself bore down once more with the main body on his reduced but still unconquered enemy. Tromp fought, as usual, with the most desperate courage: but he had now little hope, with his broken and divided power, of doing more than occupy Blake's attention until his richly laden merchants could run into the nearest port. Even this was doubtful. After the first shock of the third day's battle, he sent Captain Van Ness to the merchants, with orders for them to crowd sail and make for Calais road, as he found himself unable to promise them more than a few hours' protection. As the fight grew fiercer, he sent his Treasurer to urge them to press on faster, or the English frigates would soon be amongst them. But the wind was then blowing from the French coast, and notwithstanding his energetic attempts, Van Ness was unable to carry such a number of disorganised ships

sufficiently near land to be out of danger. More than
half the Dutch frigates and men-of-war had now been
taken, sunk or scattered; and considering it a species
of insanity in Tromp to continue the engagement until
they were all destroyed, the other captains, contrary to
their express orders, retreated on the flying traders.
Confusion then reached its height. Some of the English
frigates came up; and the merchants, in their alarm and
disorder, ran foul of each other, knocked themselves to
pieces or fell blindly into their enemy's power. Still
fighting with the retreating men-of-war, Blake arrived in
the midst of this wild scene late in the afternoon, and
finding several ships run against him, as if desirous of
being captured, it occurred to him that this was a device
of his wily adversary to stay the victorious pursuit, and
give time to rally some part of the discomfited fleet,—
and he issued strict and instant commands that every
war-ship still in a condition to follow and fight the
enemy should press on with all its force against the
main body, leaving the traders in their rear to be watched
and seized by the frigates already assigned to that
service, or driven into ports whence it would be easy to
recover them should the Dutch fleet be swept from the
Channel. Darkness alone put an end to the exciting
chase. Tromp ran in under the French shore, about four
miles from Calais, where he anchored the remnant of his
once mighty fleet—now reduced to less than half the
former number of masts, and these damaged in every
part. Blake consulted pilots and others well acquainted
with the coast, as to what Tromp could do in his new
position; and the general opinion of these men being
that the Dutch could not weather the coast of Artois,
as the wind and tide then lay, and would be compelled
to come out to sea in order to get home, he cast anchors
and sat down to repair his damages. The night was

unusually dark, with a high gale blowing, so that the enemy's lights could not be seen; and when day again dawned the sea was quite clear in that direction, Tromp having slipped away and tided towards Dunkirk, whence he got off into the harbours of Zealand. By twelve o'clock in the morning, Blake was ready to give chase, but no enemy being then visible; and seeing how useless it would be to follow the runaways into the flats and shallows of their own coast, he stood over towards England, and the gale still rising, carried his fleet and prizes into Stoake's Bay, in the Isle of Wight, whence he and his colleagues in command wrote to inform the House of their success.

Extremely false and exaggerated accounts of the great Battle of Portland were published in the two countries. Excepting the loss of their traders, the States-General tried to make the world believe that their fleet had done as much mischief as it had suffered:—but when Tromp was asked to sail against the enemy and recover his laurels, he frankly confessed that his best war-ships had been lost or destroyed. In their report to Parliament, the English commanders stated that their loss was confined to the Sampson, the vessel turned adrift during the first night of the engagement,—and that their gain from the enemy was seventeen or eighteen men of war, and a large fleet of merchant-ships, the precise number not being ascertainable at once, the prizes having been carried into different ports. Sixteen sail were brought into Dover. Altogether it is probable that more than fifty of these vessels fell into English hands. On both sides the loss of life was great. The Dutch captains, Balk, Van Zaanen, De Port, Spanhem, Regemorter, Fokkes, and Allart were slain: Swers, Schey, and Van Zeelst were taken prisoners. England had to mourn the deaths of three of her bravest captains — Ball,

Mildmay and Barker. Blake himself was severely wounded, as was also his gallant Rear-admiral Lawson. Few of the more distinguished persons on board escaped without a wound.

In London the first news of this battle was received with enthusiasm. At last the two nations had met on a fair field; the genius, strength and courage of the officers and men had been fairly tried; and the Commonwealth had gained a splendid victory. Special letters of thanks and congratulation were written to the three commanders. A day of general thanksgiving was appointed. Parliament began an immediate subscription in behalf of the wives and children of such as had fallen in the action: and a short time afterwards a public provision was made by the State itself for their support. Troops of horse escorted the prisoners from the various ports where they had been landed to London, and in every town through which these cavalcades passed on the journey, the people rang the joy-bells in celebration of the battle. As to Blake himself, less mindful of his own wound than he was of the hurts of his humblest companion, he remained in St. Helen's road and about the Solent for some weeks after the action, refitting his ships, taking in fresh stores, and preparing to chastise the Brest privateers, who still infested the seas and made spoil of English and other traders engaged in the commerce with Ireland. In April he received information that Tromp was making great efforts to equip another fleet, so that he was still unable or unwilling to go on shore. With a hundred sail he appeared before the Texel, where he found about seventy Dutch men-of-war and frigates; his vanguard fired into them as soon as he came within gunshot, when they hastily retreated, leaving fifty of their doggers behind as prizes. Tromp had gone out on convoy service; but no longer able or

willing to try the Channel passage, the Dutchman was obliged to go round the north of Scotland to meet the fleet of Spanish and Levantine merchants. He contrived by consummate seamanship to bring his ships home, though the wits of London and Westminster had their laugh at the expense of that top-gallant humour which had so lately threatened to brush the English navy from the seas in which he no longer dared to show his pennons. Leaving him for the present secure in his fortified and inaccessible ports, Blake sailed towards the North with a small squadron, while Monk and Deane returned with eighty sail into the Downs, where they witnessed and acquiesced in Cromwell's dispersion of the Long Parliament and in his assumption of supreme power.

The precise objects of this northern cruise have not been clearly stated. But as it had the effect of removing from the Downs and from the majority of his naval comrades a popular commander, known for his sincere attachment to the Commonwealth, at the very moment when Cromwell had resolved to venture on the rash, indecent and unlawful act of dispersing by brute force the representatives of the nation, it is not difficult to surmise by whose intrigues the Council of State had been induced to urge it.

On the famous 20th of April, 1653, Blake was cruizing with twenty ships between the Friths of Forth and Moray, when the troopers marched down to Westminster and cleared the House. Next day Cromwell dissolved the Council of State. On the 25th a council of officers in London declared for Cromwell, and the same afternoon brought despatches from Deane and Monk, with their adhesion and that of certain captains of their fleet to the number of thirty-three. Penn and the officers with him signed to the same effect. But neither the Admiral himself, his brother Benjamin, nor his nephew Robert, set their hands to these documents, so that the name of Blake does not occur in the papers which carried to the usurper an assurance that his violence would not be opposed by the navy.

That Blake was dissatisfied with a change that soon condemned Algernon Sydney to the privacy of Penshurst, consigned Sir Henry Vane to a prison, and drove many of the moderate men whose opinions he shared, into private life, there is no reason to doubt. To his friends and associates he made no secret of his resentment. Had he been in his place in the Council of State when Cromwell entered, there would probably have been a louder and more important protest against the act of usurpation than that made by the Lord-President Bradshawe. But he was far away, deeply engrossed with the duties of the service, when the deed of violence was done in Westminster; and before the intelligence reached him on his distant station, the change was an historical fact, formally accepted by the army and the fleet. From that moment Blake gave up politics. The gentry of Somersetshire returned him as their representative in the new Parliament; but he never appeared in the House except on the business of his department. The fears and intrigues of the usurper caused him to be excluded from the new Council of State. In a Parliament without power, even his fearless truth and uncompromising honesty could do little harm to the Lord-General's interests: while his very name on the rolls of the New Representative, lent a dignity to that assembly which Cromwell understood, and which his admirers still claim as a triumph for their hero. The case was different as regards the Council of State. Within that smaller and more powerful body, he might have proved a dangerous adviser and opponent so long as the great question of a settlement of the nation was still under discussion: it was, therefore, a necessary precaution, that, for a time at least, he should be excluded. Blake's opinions were known to be unfavourable to military rule, not only in England, but on the continent generally; and when the Dutch heard of a sudden revolution having been accomplished by the army in London, they at once leapt to the conclusion that their most redoubtable naval adversary would no longer carry on the war with his old vigour.

In these hopes they were deceived. Calling his captains together as soon as the messengers arrived at the fleet, he told them, that whatever might be their private opinions, he considered it to be his duty and their duty to act in their several posts, while out at sea, with good faith, and in such a way as would best conduce to the public peace and welfare. He spoke of the irregularities which had occurred in London; but he would not admit that in such a crisis, threatened as the country was on every side with foreign enemies, the fleet had any right to plunge the country into the horrors of civil war. When pressed by some of his captains to declare against the clique of army officers and their leader, he at once took up a position which he never afterwards abandoned. "No," he said, "it is not for us to mind affairs of State, but to keep foreigners from fooling us." Though he suspected Cromwell and abhorred military rule, he had manliness and patriotism enough not to deprive his country of such services as he could render, because it had allowed itself to submit to a power not of his choice. And fortunately this resolution was taken with his usual rapidity; for Tromp, Evertz, De Ruiter, and De Witt, under the impression that the fleets of England were divided from each other and rent by discords, sailed from the Göree with 120 ships, brought together and manned in haste, for Dover road, into which they drove a few stragglers, took two or three prizes, and began to fire on the town. The fleet then in the narrow seas was divided into three squadrons. Deane and Monk, with the red flag, in the Resolution, had under their immediate orders 38 sail, carrying 1440 guns and 6169 men; the white division, under Penn, consisted of 33 sail, with 1189 guns and 5085 men; Lawson commanded the blue, composed of 34 ships, having on board 1189 guns, and 5015 men; making a grand total of 105 ships, 3840 guns, and 16,269 men. The Dutch were about equal in guns and men, though they had a greater number of vessels. Blake, meanwhile, having learned by mounted couriers riding day and night that Tromp was again in the Channel, and had fired into Dover, spread his sails and poured impetuously down the north coast before a full breeze, burning to revenge that insult and re-establish his invaded supremacy in the narrow seas.

Early in the morning of June 2d, the two great fleets sighted each other about three leagues from the Gable. Lawson pressed in advance of his comrades, and charged through the enemy between eleven and twelve o'clock in the forenoon, separating De Ruiter's squadron from the rest of the Dutch fleet, and engaging it in a severe contest before the main body on either side could be brought to bear. In about an hour Tromp was at the elbow of his gallant comrade, and at three o'clock the cannonade was general. One of the first cannon-shots that swept the Resolution killed General Deane: Monk threw his cloak over the mangled corpse of his colleague, and shouted to the men to avenge his death. Tromp had that morning given out an extra quantity of liquor, and for some hours his Dutchmen fought with reckless and extraordinary courage; but when darkness put an end to a long day's engagement, he found himself not less damaged than the English.

All that night, while the hostile fleets, at gunshot distance from each other, were trying in haste and disorder to repair the havoc of the last few hours, Blake was riding with his division, under full sail and with streaming lights, for the scene of action, unaware of the day's events, the loss of his old friend Deane, and the doubtful position of the channel fleet. All night the officers and men in the Downs, dispirited at the death of their old general, watched and waited anxiously for the signals of the Sea King. The summer morning dawned early, but no trace of his coming could be descried on the horizon. Fortunately, Tromp was unaware that Blake was expected in the course of the day, believing him too far north to be recalled; and he spent the precious hours of the morning in a series of skilful movements intended to recover the weather-gage; but, owing to a sudden calm, he was unsuccessful in his attempt, and about noon the two fleets were again within range of the great guns. The battle was renewed, as if by mutual consent, at the point where it had ceased the night before: it was maintained with energy; but neither party could claim an advantage over the other until the expected squadron hove in sight. Early in the afternoon, high above the din of battle, and breaking through it as the thunder-clap cleaves through the roar of wind and rain in a storm, the explosions of his terrible artillery were heard by the anxious and excited seamen on the Dutchman's rear and flank; and the sound of carnage roused them like a sudden inspiration. Young Robert Blake was the first to engage the enemy; he broke through the Dutch line, and was received with tremendous cheers from the sailors of the English fleet, to whom he brought proof of their great commander's arrival on the scene of action. At four o'clock the battle ended and the rout began. Tromp fought with the energy of

despair; but nothing could stand against the impetuous
onset. The men of the Brederode, stung to madness
by the cries and reproaches of their Admiral, boarded
the Vice-admiral—the James—but were repulsed by
Penn's crew, who entered the Brederode with them,
gained possession of the quarter-deck, and would probably have captured the ship, had not Tromp, resolved
not to fall alive into English hands, thrown a light
into the powder-magazine, and caused an explosion which
sent the upper-deck and the gallant boarders who occupied it into mid air—the planks shivered into a thousand
splinters—the men horribly scorched and mutilated.
By a miracle Tromp himself was scarcely hurt; but a
report of his death spread through the fleet, and many
of his disheartened captains turned and fled. De
Ruiter and De Witt exerted themselves in vain. After
his marvellous escape, Tromp quitted the disabled
Brederode for a fast-sailing frigate, in which he flew
through the fleet to assure the sailors of his safety,
encouraging the brave, threatening the waverers, and
firing on the timid as they fled. But it was now too
late: the day was irrecoverably lost, and the brave old
sailor at last and with stern reluctance gave his sanction
to the order for retreat. As the flight became general,
a fresh gale sprung up to favour the pursuit. Allowing
the enemy no pause, the English admirals pressed hotly
on their rear, sunk many of their ships, captured several
others, and would have destroyed the entire armament
had they been favoured with two more hours of daylight.
But favoured by a dark night, Tromp sought shelter
in the road before Ostend, and the next day escaped
with the remnant of his fleet into Weilingen. Blake
and Monk had to report that among their captures they
counted 1350 Dutch prisoners, including six captains,
Verburg, Schellinger, Laurence, Duin, Fietersz, and

Westergo: eleven men-of-war, including a vice-admiral and two rear-admirals; two water-hoys and one fly-boat. The other ascertainable losses of the enemy included six men-of-war sunk, two blown up and one burnt. In the English fleet they counted 126 men slain and 236 wounded. Several of their ships had their bows shot away, and the masts and rigging of many others were shattered or destroyed.

Intelligence of this great defeat threw the United Provinces into a ferment. The mob rose in various towns, deposed the magistrates, and accused the government of incapacity and treason. The admirals offered to resign their commissions. Tromp told the Deputies of the States that it was impossible to fight the islanders any longer, unless their fleet could be reinforced by a great number of large ships; and De Ruiter boldly declared that he would go to sea no more with such a fleet as they then possessed. In the Assembly of the States, De Witt spoke the truth still more clearly out:—" Why," he said, " should I keep silence any longer? I am here before my sovereigns; I am free to speak :—and I must say that the English are at present masters both of us and of the seas." This was the opinion of the well-informed in both countries. The naval power of Holland was for the time completely broken, and the final battle of the war hazarded and lost two months later, was but an expiring effort made with crippled means and under circumstances of the greatest discouragement. The condition of the Dutch flag-ship was little worse than that of their navy throughout :—" The Brederode," says Tromp, in his report to the States-General, " has received several shots between wind and water; and though we have had her caulked as well as possible, she still leaks so fast, that last night, in spite of all our pumps, the water gained on us above five feet in height: till the present time we have contrived to keep her above water; but if after all we find our labour lost, we shall be obliged to run her ashore." Under these circumstances the States began to think of peace, and a vessel carrying a white flag was sent with an agent on board, who was instructed to go to London to prepare the way for two fresh ambassadors fully empowered to arrange the preliminaries of a treaty.

Though it kept the sea, the English fleet was in scarcely better condition than that of the enemy. After sending the wounded men on shore at Ipswich, where hospitals had been prepared for their reception, with strict orders that every care should be taken of their wounds, and every comfort afforded them during the progress of their recovery,—Blake pursued the flying enemy, keeping his great ships out at sea to avoid the shoals and sand-banks, but running his frigates close in land and scouring every bay and inlet. His objects were, to place the coast of Holland from the Zwin to the Texel in a state of blockade—to intercept and destroy the Dutch trade—to hinder the herring-busses and whaling-boats from going out on the usual summer voyage—and to keep the fleet closed up in the Texel and prevent its junction with that refitting in the Weilingen; and having determined on his plan, he collected such of his ships as appeared to be unable to remain at sea for some weeks to come, and sent them back to England with the prizes, himself remaining with the other portion of his fleet in the Dutch waters, capturing stray ships and holding the long chain of towns and ports between Ostend and the Ems in a state of perpetual alarm and irritation. His letters written at this time from before the Texel and the Vlie show with how wide a range of obstacles he had to contend, and add new elements to the admiration excited by his victorious career. Five days after the battle he writes to the Board of Admiralty :—

"GENTLEMEN,—Since ours of the 6th present, we are got between the Texel and the Vlie, where we shall endeavour to hinder any men-of-war coming out from thence to make a conjunction with the Dutch fleet now at the Weilingen, as well as hinder their fishing and merchandising trade so near as we can.

"The ships sent for England with the Dutch prizes, of which you had an account in our last, we do desire they may be refitted and sent unto us so soon as possibly you can, and that the Commissioners of the Navy may be sent unto, to give order for as much victuals and water to be put on board them as they can well stow, also that so many other ships with victuals and water as can be got ready in that time may come along with them, and for those victualling and water-ships now with us, we shall use our best endeavours to get it out as fast as we can, and dispose of it to each ship according to their necessity so far as it will go, and then send them back for recruits, whereby the charge of hiring more ships for that service may be saved; but as yet we have not had time.

"We do desire that two or three of the best-sailing frigates may be hastened to us with powder and shot, which is our great want.

"We have sent orders to all those ships and vessels in Yarmouth road to repair unto us with all expedition, and do desire that for the future no more ships-of-war or others may be sent thither, but that they repair into the Zwin, where we shall send to them and for them as the service requires.

"We would gladly know certainly what quantity of victuals there lies now ready at Hull, Yarmouth, and Harwich upon any occasion.

"It is supposed as soon as the enemy is in a capacity to show his head, he will endeavour to attempt somewhat upon our own coast; but we hope you will take care that he may be prevented, and if he shall come again and shoot into Dover pier, that you will not be much startled at it, though we assure you there shall be nothing wanting in us to hinder him in that or any thing else that may disturb the peace of this Commonwealth, so far as the Lord shall enable us.

"We do desire all diligence may be used to supply us with seamen, and that the first ships that come may bring as many with them as they can. We are," &c.

Next day he wrote again, complaining that the ships were in very bad condition and much in want of powder and shot. But supplies came in slowly. Want and sickness increased day by day. On the 12th he again wrote:

"The 11th present came many letters of yours to our hands, several of them, bearing date in May last, are duplicates of some we formerly received, and have already answered as to the material things therein. The same day also came Colonel Goffe, Major Bourne and Captain Hatsell, and seven ships-of-war, with eleven victuallers and water-ships in their company. What their lading particularly is we cannot as yet give you an account; but so soon as it comes to our hands, we shall communicate it unto you, which we hope will be by the next; only this we have in general, that there are 140 barrels of powder in the Samuel merchant, and 172 in the John and Katherine (besides a quantity of shot) over and above their proportion; also 700 soldiers, which might have been serviceable unto us had care been taken to have sent bedding and cloths along with them, according to your resolutions at Chatham in that particular, which we hoped would have been adhered to; for want whereof they are likely to occasion much sickness amongst us, instead of answering your expectations.

"As soon as we have disposed of the victuals now come to us, we shall send the ships that brought it back again with what speed we can, that they may be recruited and returned to us; and we hope you will use all diligence for the hastening back the ships we sent into the river as a convoy to the Dutch prizes; we having many ships here will be unfit for service before they get to us, let them make what haste they can. We sent the other day eleven ships and frigates to Harwich to wash and tallow, and then to complete three months victuals, as also to take in the ammunition remaining at Yarmouth for the fleet, and so to return with all speed.

"For those ships and frigates of Captain Badily's squadron, which we understand are in a capacity for service, wanting some men, we desire they may be supplied and hastened to us, the rather because we are informed there are eleven or twelve great frigates newly launched at Amsterdam, Enchuysen, and thereabouts, which carry fifty guns a piece, besides the ten men-of-war which came home with the French fleet. We understand some hammocks are come in a hoy to Harwich, for which we have sent, but hear not of the other necessaries of wood and candles, so often mentioned unto you, of which the fleet wants a proportion of six weeks to even with our present victualling. The 1000lbs. is now come in the John and Katherine, and John Poortmans intends to get it aboard to-day, which we hope will yet be serviceable: for the Cock and Brier which you mention are on their way towards us; the latter of them we conceive may be very useful in her station on the western coast, and therefore do not desire her here. We have desired Major Bourne to remain about Harwich and Yarmouth, the better to despatch to us the ships and frigates that are or shall be sent thither, and such other vessels with provisions as are necessary for the fleet; and also to maintain a constant and mutual correspondence between the Council of State and yourselves with us. The supply of ammunition you have made unto us, especially of shot, will not answer our present wants in that behalf, wherefore we desire the continuance of your care therein, that what further quantities can be suddenly provided may be sent unto us accordingly."

About a fortnight later he complained that his stores and provisions were all run short; the beer, he said, was sour, the bread bad, the butter rancid, the cheese rotten. The amount of sickness on board was very great; and in spite of the enemy's present weakness, and the immense advantage of holding them in close blockade, he expressed a fear that, unless relieved, he would be compelled by want and sickness to return to England. His own health was bad, the consequence of his neglected wound, but of that he said little. The close of his letter, in which he had described one of his captures, gave excellent reasons for maintaining the blockade:

"It hath pleased God this last week," it ran, "to deliver several merchant-ships of the enemy into our hands, which was thus: Upon the 19th present some of our frigates, appointed to ply to and again before the Vlie, met with eleven sail, which proved to be Dutch ships, some of them come from the West Indies; and being ships of force, they fought for some time, but at length committed themselves to sailing as their securest way; whereby five of them escaped, but four are taken, one sunk, and another burnt. In this encounter Captain Vessey, Commander of the Martin, was slain, whom we understand hath left a poor widow with a great charge of children, whose condition we leave to your consideration. Upon the 22nd some other of our frigates met about thirty sail more to the northward of the Vlie, which being ships of no force endeavoured wholly an escape ; but yet eleven of them were taken and some of the remainder scattered, and the rest got into port ; two of these came from Sweden laden with guns, all new, whereof two are brass, and most of them carrying a bullet from 24lbs. weight to twelve, as we are informed, which we hope will be as seasonable for us as for them, had they escaped ; there were no more amongst them had any guns but these two, the rest are richly laden for the most part ; they are not all come into the fleet as yet ; when they are, we shall send them in under the convoy of such ships as are least useful, also such sick and wounded men as are not fit to be kept on board ; upon whose arrival in Lea road, whither we shall order them, we do desire speedy directions may be given concerning them as may stand with the good of the service. We intend also (if the Lord will) to make a trip over with the whole fleet upon the English shore, to see them out of danger, and then to return with what speed we can, leaving in the meantime so many of the best frigates we have to lie between the Dogger Bank and the Riff, to intercept the enemy's ships of trade expected home. We earnestly desire you will hasten unto us as many clean ships as you can, apprehending more service might be done than now is, had we a considerable number of them ; also that you would send to Major Bourne that those ships now tallowing at Harwich may be expedited to us.

" We still continue before this place, sometimes at an anchor, at other times under sail."

One more extract from this correspondence will complete the dreary picture of this victorious fleet, and will bring down the story of the war to the point where Blake was compelled by illness to go on shore :

"Since our last, wherein we acquainted you with our resolutions to sail with the main body of the fleet for Sowle Bay, we have had blowing weather for the most part, whereby we were driven to leeward as far as Flamborough Head; but are now, through the goodness of God, come thus far on our way, and hope to get into the place of rendezvous this night, or to-morrow morning at furthest, where all diligence shall be used to accomplish the end of our coming thither; and therefore desire that what victualling ships and others can be sent from London within the time limited for our staying upon this coast, may be expedited to us, and we have written to Major Bourne in the like manner for such provisions as can be sent unto us from Yarmouth and Harwich. Our men fall sick very fast every day, having at present on board this ship upwards of eighty sick men, and some of them very dangerously, which we hear is generally through the whole fleet alike, proportionable to the number of men on board; so that we shall be constrained to send a considerable number unto Ipswich for their recovery; where there is room enough for them and good accommodation, as we understand by a letter from Dr. Whistler lately come to our hands, to whom we have written that special care might be taken of them, and suitable provision made for them, according to their conditions; and do desire a considerable number of seamen may be sent unto us with what expedition you can, or else it is apprehended we shall be very weakly manned, to do service answerable to what is expected from us.

"We have this morning sent away the Worcester frigate for Chatham, being very foul, and wanting a new foremast, which could not be supplied here. We should have ordered him to stay in Lea road to receive your directions, but that we apprehended much time would be lost that way, being appointed to make his repair unto the fleet with all expedition. The captain of her is a godly and valiant man, whom, with Captain Newbery, commander of the Entrance, we do especially recommend for two of the best frigates now a building, which if you shall approve of and appoint unto, we shall deliver them commissions upon notice given. We hope you do not forget to send us paper and canvass for cartridges, with a considerable quantity of old junk for wads, our necessity in this particular having been several times made known unto you. There are two honest captains more whom we desire to recommend unto you for removes into some of the new frigates now a building, with good strength, viz. Captain Bragg in the Marmaduke and Captain Hermon in the Welcome; they are already in ships of good force but slow sailers, and do apprehend they would do more and better service if better provided. We earnestly desire you will send down to us as much victuals as will complete us to the last of September, if you can, or else the quantity of butter, cheese, and bread that was lost in the Golliott hoy, of which we gave you an account already, being much in want thereof. We also desire you will hasten unto us what clean ships and frigates you can from London, for want whereof so much service cannot be done as otherwise might be."

Next morning the fleet put in, and Blake was carried on shore more dead than alive, leaving Monk, Penn and Lawson on board to carry out and complete his plan for the final reduction of Holland.

One more blow, and all was over. Taking advantage of the temporary absence of the blockading fleet, the Dutch squadrons of the Texel and Weilingen put to sea and effected a junction with each other on the south coast; but their shattered power was no longer capable of bearding their powerful enemy, and when the English admirals hove in sight at the close of the month, they endeavoured by flight to avoid another battle. Penn and Lawson won their brightest laurels in this final conflict with Tromp, Evertz and De Ruiter. The fighting began at dusk; but night soon parted the combatants. Next day a heavy gale and thick dirty weather prevented a renewal of the action. On the third day the last shot was fired. The aged and able Admiral of Holland received a musket-ball in his heart; and after his death the captains of his fleet fled away, the English for the first and only time in that war pursuing the fugitives without mercy, as the ruthless Monk had commanded them to give no quarter. They made no prisoners; they killed all who fell in their way; and after a few hours the contest became a massacre rather than a battle. The States-General, now thoroughly humbled, sent ambassadors to sue for peace; the negociations were carried on without further interruption; and early in the following spring a treaty was made in which they formally conceded to England the honours of the flag—agreed to banish the royalist exiles from Holland—gave the East India Company compensation for its losses—settled a sum of money on the heirs of their Amboyna victims—and made amends to the English traders who had suffered in the Baltic.

In modern times there had been no maritime war to compare with this Dutch war, either as to the genius of the combatants, the interests at stake, or the magnitude of the operations conducted. In less than two years the English Sea-General and his officers had, according to our own computations, captured or destroyed seventeen hundred Dutch ships; the Hollanders themselves admitted that they had lost more than eleven hundred vessels. Twenty months of naval war with

England cost the States-General more money than they had expended during the twenty years war so gloriously waged against Spain.

Honours and decorations awaited the successful admirals in England. The Council of State proposed that Parliament should order two gold chains, each of 300*l.* value, to be made and presented to the two surviving generals, Blake and Monk. Two other chains, valued at 100*l.* each, were given to Penn and Lawson. Four chains of 40*l.* each were presented to the four flag-officers. Rewards and promotions fell to the lot of many of the inferior officers. Penn was raised to the rank of Sea-General in the place of Deane. Lawson was made Vice-admiral. Captain Badily —who had recently fought and lost the battle of Porto Longone, the only event of any importance which had occurred in the Mediterranean during the Dutch war —was made Rear-admiral at the same time. A sum of 1040*l.* was voted for medals. Bonfires were lighted in all public places, and most conspicuously on Tower Hill. A day of general thanksgiving, as usual with the Roundheads after a great victory, was appointed. But all this time Blake lay at home in a dangerous fever, and only heard the public exultation at his success through the occasional echoes which, in spite of medical precautions, came to disturb the repose of a sick room.

# CHAPTER VIII.

## THE MEDITERRANEAN.

During the remainder of the summer months of 1653, it is at least probable that Blake lay sick at Knoll, a country-house attached to an estate which he had purchased about two miles from Bridgwater. Fever, of a slow but obstinate character, arising in the first instance from his neglected wound, combined with other ailments, including dropsy and scurvy, then common to all men leading a sea-faring life — to lay him for awhile completely prostrate. But a land diet, gentle exercise and his native air gradually produced a change for the better in his condition. Knoll was at all times a favourite retreat. When absent from his political and professional duties, it was his delight to run down to Bridgwater for a few days or weeks, and with his chosen books and one or two devout and abstemious friends to indulge in the luxuries of seclusion. He was by nature self-absorbed and taciturn. A long walk, during which he appeared to his simple neighbours to be lost in profound thought, as if working out in his own mind the details of one of his great battles, or busy with some abstruse point of Puritan theology, usually occupied his morning. If accompanied by one of his brothers or by some other intimate friend, he was still for the most part silent. Good-humoured always, and enjoying sarcasm when of a grave, high class, he yet never talked for the sake of hearing his own voice, or encouraged others so to employ their time and talents in his presence. Even his lively and rattling brother Humphrey, his almost constant companion when on shore, caught, from long habit, the great man's contemplative manner; and when his friends rallied him on the subject in after-years, he used to say that he had caught the trick of silence while walking by the Admiral's side in his long morning musings on Knoll hill. A plain dinner satisfied his wants. Religious conversation, reading and the details of business, generally filled up the evening until supper-time; after family prayers, always pronounced by the General himself, and a frugal supper, he would invariably call for his cup of sack and a dry crust of bread, and while he drank two or three horns of Canary, would smile and chat in his own dry manner with his friends and domestics, asking minute questions about their neighbours and acquaintance; or when scholars or clergymen shared his simple repast, affecting a droll anxiety, rich and pleasant in the conqueror of Tromp, to prove by the aptness and abundance of his quotations that, in becoming an admiral, he had not forfeited his claim to be considered a classic.

During the whole period of this recovery he was in constant communication with his colleagues the Sea-Generals and with the Navy Commissioners. When his commission expired, it was again renewed; and not an order of any consequence was given in that branch of the public service on which his opinion was not first taken. His brother Humphrey was named, with John Sparrow, Richard Hill, Robert Turpin and Richard Blackwall, a Commissioner for the condemnation and sale of prizes,—an extremely responsible and lucrative office. In October he entered the House for the first time since his election. The House was deeply moved; and the speaker, by command, returned him the thanks of the nation for his splendid services. In December an Act of Parliament named a new list of Lords Commissioners of the Admiralty, at the head of which his name appeared. A few weeks later, though still suffering from ill-health, and lamed for life by his late wound, he returned to active service, going on board the Swiftsure at Spithead, with the new Sea-General Penn, whose plain good sense and wide range of nautical information were of use to him in his high station.

The Dutch negociation was not proceeding so rapidly as could have been wished; the ambassadors, with the proverbial slowness of their nation, dallying with the English claims, he determined to bring them to the point at once by an active renewal of hostilities, no truce having been entered into by the two powers. He had also some accounts to settle with the Brest privateers, that port having lately grown into another Dunkirk. Spreading out his winter guard, he closed up the south entrance of the Channel, and spent most of his time in daily chase of such adventurous craft as dared to try the narrow seas in preference to the long voyage round the Orkney Islands, until the treaty with Holland was actually signed and ratified by the two governments. With this result he was extremely pleased. Though his highest renown had been gained in the Dutch war, that war had never met with his private approval. Holland, like England, was a Protestant State, and it galled him to think that the two guardians of free thought and reformed religion should be wasting each other's power, while Popish Spain looked haughtily on. A war against that empire was his passion by day, his dream by night; like a true Puritan, he suspected and bated the Spaniards as the real children of Anti-Christ; and could he have chosen, he would have waged none but anti-Popish and anti-piratical wars. When he went on board the Swiftsure, he carried in his pocket instructions from the Council of State to lie at the entrance of Brest harbour and prevent ingress or egress, until satisfaction was obtained for the injuries done to English commerce; but on consulting pilots and captains well acquainted with the coasts of Bretagne, he found that the strong westerly winds generally blowing there would render it extremely hazardous for vessels to attempt to ride near the shore. He therefore stationed a part of his squadron at convenient points, to watch and overawe the depredators, while the main body kept out at sea in search of the Hollanders.

The progress of the Dutch treaty had put an end to the necessity for a winter campaign. The colleagues returned to London; and Blake went down to Bridgwater in a new character, the formidable Sea-General being suddenly transformed into a commissioner for purging the churches of England, Puritan, Independent, Presbyterian, and all other, of ignorant, scandalous and inefficient pastors. From the cockpit of a man-of-war he passed into the chapter-houses of Somersetshire, carrying that stern and resolute spirit of reform into his new sphere of action which had already made him so conspicuous at the Navy Board.

For the moment, the active part of his professional career seemed about to close; and a new world of public duties was opening before him, when government, having its own reasons, public and private, for wishing to keep him and his comrades at a distance from London, commenced the outfit of a new expedition, which occupied the summer months of 1654. Cromwell kept the objects of his naval armament a mystery, though it is probable that Blake was in the secret. In May he left the fleet in the Downs and went up to London, where we find him dining with Cromwell. From this time until September, when the first squadron sailed, the dockyards were alive with preparation. Of course, it was soon noised abroad that the islanders were fitting out a new fleet; but the service on which it was to be employed—the commanders to whose skill and fidelity it would be entrusted—could only be surmised by friend or foe. France and Spain, constrained by the late issue of events to think with less scorn of the new Commonwealth, waited with anxiety the fall of the thunderbolt. The war which had long raged between these European powers, exhausting both countries without producing a decided preponderance in either, rendered the friendship of England, now mistress at sea, of the utmost importance. That the armament now preparing was intended to take a part in the contest was assumed on all sides:—but into which scale would the swords of the Sea-Generals be thrown? Causes of dissatisfaction, general and special, were not wanting with either country. Spain as the great Catholic power, was the natural enemy of Puritan England. Its commercial system was prohibitive, and therefore opposed to the interests of our merchants and manufacturers. Its arrogance offended our national pride. The favour it had shown to Prince Rupert and the revolted fleet during the doubtful fortunes of the Commonwealth, was neither forgotten nor forgiven. France, on its part, had afforded an asylum to the royal exiles, had allowed its subjects to attack the merchants of the Channel, had interdicted the importation of English silks and woollens, and without an open declaration of war, the private and national cruisers of the two states had long carried letters of marque against each other. Up to the close of the Dutch war, England had favoured the cause of Spain as against France. Agents of that state had been allowed to recruit their armies in Ireland, and the succours so raised had enabled them to reduce Gravelines and invest Dunkirk. At a critical moment Blake had captured the relief-guard under the Duke of Vendôme, and caused the loss of this stronghold. Either party, therefore, might be struck and both feared the blow. But the urgent inquiries of the two crowns as to the object of the new armament were evasively answered by Cromwell, and no one could tell in what quarter the storm would burst.

Meanwhile the work of equipment was carried on throughout the summer and autumn months. As the ships got ready for sea, and the plans of the government came to maturity, the fleet was divided into two grand divisions : the first, entrusted to Blake, consisted of the flag-ship St. George, carrying sixty guns and 350 men, and twenty-four sail of ships, carrying altogether 4100 men and 874 guns ; the second, placed under Penn, consisted of the flag-ship Swiftsure, and thirty-seven other ships, besides two ketches, one hoy, and one dogger-boat, the whole carrying 4410 seamen and 1114 guns. On board the latter squadron about 3000 soldiers were also placed, with General Venables at their head. Captain Robert Blake went out with his uncle ; Captain Benjamin Blake, restored to his former rank, commanded the Gloucester, of 54 guns, in Penn's division.

Towards the close of the year 1654 these mysterious armaments sailed from the Solent with sealed orders, the smaller squadron passing by Brest towards the south of Europe, the stronger bearing away into the Atlantic, as if bound for the Isle of Barbadoes ; leaving the minds of men, not only in England, but on the Continent, in a state of profound uncertainty as to their ultimate aims.

At first popular opinion inclined to believe that a great blow was to be struck at France ; and this belief was fostered by the arts of the wily cardinal then ruling the destinies of that country. Every day rumours were spread of an approaching rupture between the two powers, and a body of troops was sent down to Dieppe, as if to repel an expected invasion in that quarter. Public belief was mystified by Cromwell and Mazarine ; it was commonly reported that Blake, with his entire division, was about to enter the service of Spain, and the price at which this powerful aid had been purchased was actually named.  Many weeks elapsed before Europe learned the real nature of this armed demonstration.

The secret aim of the government was to deal a blow at the pride and power of Spain.  Though the expedition had other objects, this was its paramount purpose.  Envy of her colonial wealth, hatred of her religion, and impatience of her narrow views of commerce, combined with the recollection of ancient and unredressed wrongs of a political kind to give popularity to a war against Spain. Blake, with his flying squadron, was to watch the ports and rivers of that country, to intercept ships entering or leaving them, and, if possible, to cut off all communication between Madrid and the West Indian Islands ; while Penn and Venables, after raising a large additional force at Barbadoes and other English settlements in those seas, were to make an attempt on Hispaniola and San Juan, or, failing these, on the mainland of South America, between Oronoco and Porto Bello.  The conception of this double campaign was masterly ; Blake holding the mother country in a state of profound isolation, while Penn and Venables invaded and captured her distant colonies.  Had it been executed with vigour and precision, it is more than probable that England would have founded an empire in South America as well as in the North.

During the few weeks which must necessarily elapse before Blake's co-operation would be required in this service—no war being as yet declared against Spain, nor any intimation afforded that the West India squadron was directed against her possessions—he undertook to seek redress for minor and more miscellaneous wrongs. Our traders still suffered from the privateers of Brest and Toulon. The Duke of Guise threatened an invasion of Naples, which it was thought due to English interests to impede, and, if possible, prevent. Rovers from Salee, Tunis, Tripoli, and Algiers, then and long afterwards the pests of European commerce, had recently captured and sold into slavery several crews of our merchantmen. The Commonwealth had also cause of offence against the Grand Duke of Tuscany, who had supported the revolted fleet, and allowed Rupert to sell his prizes in the port of Leghorn. The Knights of Malta too, equally zealous against heretics and infidels, had piratically seized some English ships. All these wrongs, suffered during the troubles on land, he had a roving commission to inquire into, rectify and redress; his powers being to that end as vague and extensive as the work to be done was novel and undefinable.

Early in December, his squadron anchored in Cadiz road. He was received, not only by the Spanish authorities, but by captains and officers of all nations at that great emporium of trade, with extraordinary demonstrations of respect. The English residents crowded the beach, eager to catch a glimpse of their renowned countryman. A Dutch admiral, lying there with his fleet, lowered his flag in honour of the red cross. One of our tenders, parting from the fleet, fell in with a Brest admiral, on his way with seven ships-of-war to join the

Toulon fleet, fitting out to cover the operations of the Duke of Guise and check the movements of the English in the waters of Italy and France; but on learning that it belonged to the English squadron then at Cadiz, the Frenchman sent for the captain into his cabin, told him he was at liberty to return, invited him to drink Blake's health in a cup of Burgundy, and ordered a salute of five guns to be fired in his honour. The renown of Blake's exploits had gone before him to the warlike ports and towns of Barbary; and some Algerine cruisers, having a number of English captives on board, brought them as presents to appease his wrath. Every prince and people in the south who had insulted or outraged the Commonwealth learned to tremble at his approach. In his imagination the Grand Duke of Tuscany already heard the thunder of his cannon booming across the waters of Leghorn. The terrified Pope gave orders for a solemn procession, and the sacred Host was exposed for forty hours, to avert the threatening calamity from the dominions of the Church.

As peace had not yet been ratified between France and England, the Brest admiral, finding Blake's ships at the entrance of the Straits of Gibraltar, feared to attempt a passage in presence of so uncertain a friend, and fell back with his reinforcement to Lisbon. Meanwhile news reached Cadiz that the fleet of the Duke of Guise was still at Naples; and the English immediately weighed their anchors and passed the rock of Gibraltar under full sail, making their course directly for the southern limb of Italy. When they arrived at Naples, the Duke was gone; but whether into the Gulf of Venice, or that of Genoa, they could not learn from any trustworthy source. What appeared to be the best accounts described him as having sailed for Leghorn; and as soon as the fleet had taken in bread and water,

Blake quitted the Bay of Naples—where he had received every kindness from the people,—and followed in pursuit of his enemy along the Papal coast, not ill pleased at the idea of making Anti-Christ tremble in the midst of his altars and palaces. The alarm of the Holy City was extreme. Many of the rich citizens fled away from Rome. Some buried their wealth in secret places—others carried their effects, for greater safety, into the Umbrian Appenines. Trains of monks paraded the streets in penitential garb, and new works were hastily raised about the chapel of Loretto to preserve it from pillage. When the cause of all this ferment arrived with fourteen sail in sight of the towers of Leghorn, he sent his secretary on shore to desire instant redress from the Grand Duke for the owners of all vessels which had been seized and sold in his territories by Rupert and Maurice, fixing the money value of these various injuries at the sum of 60,000*l.* sterling. The Duke hesitated and protested; but on finding the Sea-General urgent and inflexible in his demand, he offered to pay down a part of the money, and to confer with his friend and ally, the sovereign Pontiff, about the residue. Blake replied, that the Pope had nothing to do with the matter, and that he expected the Grand Duke would at once pay down the entire sum. This peremptory message brought down thirty-five thousand Spanish pistoles and twenty-five thousand Italian, together with information that some of Rupert's piratical seizures had been disposed of in Roman ports. This information was peculiarly acceptable to Blake, who sent an officer to Rome with a demand for reparation. Doubts, equivocations, and refusals followed on the part of the newly-elected Pontiff, Alexander VII. But remonstrances and supplications were idle; the right was clear; the power to enforce it was at hand; and ultimately the Pope's fiscal was obliged to pay down to the heretics twenty thousand pistoles :—probably the only money ever brought from Roman coffers to enrich the public treasury of England.

Ever mindful of the religious interests of his countrymen, the Sea-General wrote a letter to the Grand Duke of Tuscany, urging him to permit the Protestants of England and other countries, whom pleasure or business might induce to settle in his dominions, full liberty to follow their own form of worship—a privilege not then formally conceded by any Catholic power in the South, though Jews, Greeks and Armenians, were all permitted the open exercise of their religion at that very time in Florence. No threat accompanied this request; but the imposing power of the Commonwealth and the marvellous successes of Gustavus Adolphus in Poland, roused the fears of even the least tolerant of the Italian princes, and the Duke rather deferred than denied the request of the bold heretic, alleging as his excuse for delay, the want of precedent for such a concession in any Catholic country. Blake contented the English residents in Florence and Leghorn by a promise that, on his return to England, he would urge the government to adopt measures for effecting their object. Other business now demanded his attention. French pirate cruisers, reported to be growing more and more formidable to our peaceful traders in and about the Balearic Islands, required a check; he therefore sent the Langport and three other frigates to ply between Capo Palos and Majorca. Intelligence also reached him to the effect that a general rendezvous of the Moslem fleets had been ordered by the Grand Seigneur at Tunis on an affair of great moment, probably with a view to an attack on Venice or some other Christian state. New orders likewise came to hand from London touching the

Spanish Silver Fleets, then slowly wending their way from the New World towards Cadiz, which made it absolutely necessary for him to despatch his affairs in the Mediterranean and sail with convenient haste for the western coast of Spain.

But sickness, foul weather and contrary winds detained the fleet near Leghorn. Two French vessels from the Levant, brought in as prizes, unfortunately communicated plague to their captors. Blake himself was struck down by this new and terrible disease, and for several weeks he was unable to hold a pen or even dictate a letter. The winter storms also put the fleet in daily peril. On the 19th of January, Blake wrote from Leghorn to the Commissioners in London:—" My last unto you was only a postscript of the 5th January—sent by the way of Antwerp—added to a duplicate of my former of the same, being then under sail bound for Trapani. Since which time it hath pleased God to exercise us with variety of wind and weather, and with divers mixed providences and strange dispensations never to be forgotten by us, especially in regard that He hath been pleased in them all to rouse His compassion to prevail against His threatenings, and His mercy to triumph over His judgment. The day we set sail we had a fair wind at N.E., with clear weather and great hopes of the continuance thereof, forasmuch as it had been a long time foul and stormy before, almost ever since we came into the road. The next day we had the wind at E. and E.S.E., sometimes at S.E. and S.S.E., but not much wind. We were then engaged among many islands ; a place of no small danger, especially for a fleet. At night, hauling up our sails, and it growing calm, we drove upon a sudden so near Capua, that if it had not pleased God to spring up a fresh gale in the very nick, the ship would have been in hazard, almost inevitable of perishing there.

The Worcester and Langport were in the same danger
with us, being nearer the shore than we, especially the
Langport, which was in much less than the ship's length
of it, being a steep and upright rocky place.  The (St.)
Andrew and some others were also in no small danger.
But it pleased God wonderfully and in great mercy to
bring us all off in safety without any loss but of an
anchor and cable of the Langport.  The next day retain-
ing still some hope of a favourable wind and weather
to carry us on our intended voyage, we kept plying and
turning to windward, and so continued till yesterday
morning, at what (which) time, there being no likelihood of obtaining our first intention, the wind S.S.E.,
blowing very hard and murky weather, we were forced
to bear up for this place; where, although not without
much danger in our way, by reason of a shoal and rock
lying under water upon which divers ships have been
wrecked, we arrived yesterday by a most merciful and
good hand of providence, leading us, as it were, by the
brink of destruction into safety: for which we, in our
gratitude, have great cause everlastingly to praise the
Lord and His wonderful goodness, and to rejoice in these
His salvations with fear and trembling.  So we doubt
not, when the papers shall come to your hands, your
hearts will likewise be filled with the thoughts of the
same and of His unspeakable love."

The first day of good weather the fleet left Leghorn
road for Tunis, intending to pay a flying visit to Tripoli
and Algiers, after arranging some open questions with
the Dey, to impress those formidable corsairs with a
salutary dread of English power.  On the 8th of February they anchored in Goletta road, having on the way
sent out a vessel to recal some frigates formerly left at
Trapani in Sicily; but even before his arrival on the
coast of Africa, Blake had learned that no gathering of

the Barbary powers was likely to take place. Nevertheless, there were accounts to settle with these pirates;
for years they had been in the habit of plundering
English vessels, and carrying English crews into the
interior as slaves. Some of their depredations were quite
recent; and it was suspected that many Christian captives lived in their city in all the suffering and degrada-
tion of slavery. War was their charter, its spoils their
revenue. The Dutch had tried more than once to make
peace with them, but they would not hear the word:
pirates by birth, education, and policy, they knew no
power but that of the sword, admitted no law but that of
necessity. The Dey of this warlike and lawless race
hearing that the strange people, whose flag had not
waved in those seas within memory of the oldest Mus-
sulman, intended to visit his port and demand reparation for the past, guarantees for the future, formed a
temporary camp of several thousand horse and foot, light-
ened his heavy ships, and drew them in shore under the
guns of his great castles of Goletta and Porto Ferino,
raised a new platform, strengthened by batteries along
the inner line of the bay, brought out from the arsenal
his largest guns, and then, with all the pride and confidence of a barbarian, he waited the enemy's approach.

Wisely considering that wherever the pirate powers
appeared in unusual force it would be for the honour
and interest of England to be near at hand, Blake, acting
on the false report of an intended gathering, had made a
somewhat hasty and unprepared appearance before the
walls of Tunis; he had come to fight or to make a passing observation, as the case might seem to require, rather
than to higgle about terms and conditions, to measure
words and concoct articles with the usual tediousness of
diplomacy. For such slow work his fleet was in no condition. The very sea in which he rode at large was

strange and hostile to him and to his country.  England had then no Malta, Corfu, and Gibraltar as the bases of naval operations in the Mediterranean; on the contrary, Blake found in almost every gulf and on almost every island of that sea, in Malta, Venice, Genoa, Leghorn, Algiers, Tunis, and Marseilles, a rival and an enemy. Hardly could he rely on the shelter of one friendly port. Most of his supplies had to be obtained from England; and there were not more than three or four harbours, Naples, Cagliari, and Trapani, for instance, in which he could obtain a common commodity such as bread, for either love or money.  Foul weather had seriously injured his ships, and the stock of provisions already ran short; but being now within sight from the graceful minarets of the town, it was thought best before retiring, to try the effect of a summons, such as had carried consternation through the palaces of Rome and Florence. An officer was therefore sent on shore with a letter from the Admiral to the Dey, giving an account of the recent seizure by Tunis pirates of the Princess and some other English ships, the names and cargoes of which were duly specified, and concluding with a demand in the name of the Commonwealth of England for their restitution, together with the instant release of all English captives. After several questions and explanations had passed between the two powers, Commissioners were mutually named to consider these demands, and they met on board the flag-ship, the St. George.  The agents of the Dey, professing the utmost readiness to make peace, would undertake to respect the flag of England in all times to come, but they steadily refused to give up the prizes which they had already acquired.  Finding them puffed up with a vain pride in their own strength, the English commander ceased to negotiate, sent some of his frigates forward to block up the entrance of the harbour, whilst he carried the St. George as close as he could under the guns of Porto Ferino, in order to obtain a good view of the coast and its means of defence. A council of officers, after a long debate, advised an attempt to enter the port with their whole squadron, and attack the great ships of the enemy under the very embrasures of the castle; but on consulting the locker, and finding there a scarcity both of bread and liquor,—only five days' drink and fourteen days' bread,—Blake felt that it would not be wise to attempt so perilous a service without better provision. Under these circumstances he left Captain Stayner, one of his most distinguished officers, with the Plymouth and five other ships, to keep guard over the harbour, and if possible prevent the pirate fleet from escaping to sea, while he sailed with the remainder of his force to Cagliari, a friendly station on the south-eastern limb of the Island of Sardinia, to refit and provision.

At Cagliari Blake found the Langport and the other frigates which he had sent from Leghorn to the Balearic Islands, with a new French frigate in prize and 3000 dollars obtained for the wreck of a French cruiser which they had captured and run on shore at Majorca. But Cagliari could not supply bread enough for the wants of the English squadron, and the Sea-General was obliged to send out vessels in all directions in search of this essential article of diet. The Langport and the Diamond were despatched to Majorca and the Spanish coast for bread; the Maidstone and the Hampshire went to Genoa and the ports of Northern Italy for bread; the Hope was permanently stationed on the Sardinian coast to procure bread; two frigates were despatched to Algiers for bread or biscuit. The want of these necessaries delayed his operations some weeks; but on the 8th of March, the St. George was once more under the guns of Porto Ferino, and an English officer was at the

Dey's palace trying to induce him to make reparation
and render up the English captives without bloodshed.
Vain of his strength, and confident that Blake had
sailed away on the former occasion from fear of his
magnificent artillery, the barbarian replied in insolent
terms to every proposal made by this agent. He refused
them the commonest civilities: even permission to take
on board a little fresh water.—"Tell the Dey," said
Blake, curling his whiskers in scorn and anger, "that
God has given the benefit of water to all his creatures;
and for men to deny it to each other is equally insolent
and wicked." — The barbarian replied with defiance.
"Here," he said to Blake's officers, "here are our Castles
of Goletta and Porto Ferino: do your worst; and do
not think to brave us with the sight of your great
fleet."—A short consultation of the English captains
took place, and the commander laid before them his
plan. "We judged it necessary," he afterwards wrote
to Secretary Thurloe, "for the honour of the fleet, our
nation and religion, seeing they would not deal with
us as friends, to make them feel us as enemies,
and it was therefore determined in a council of war
to endeavour the firing of their ships in Porto Ferino."
The artillerymen on shore were at their guns, the
horse was drawn up and the infantry disposed along
the line of the harbour to repel the anticipated attempt
to land, when, to the extreme surprise of the Dey,
the English fleet again drew off, and stood out to
sea without firing a single gun. Gradually the white
sails faded from sight. Night came down, but no
enemy appeared in the offing. Next day all was silent:
the English fleet had vanished from before their eyes
like the mirage of their own deserts. A second day
elapsed, a third, fourth, and fifth, but nothing was seen
of those haughty islanders, of whose courage they had

heard so much in the ports of Italy and Spain. To the spirit of defiance succeeded a feeling of contempt. All Tunis believed they had looked their last on that famous red cross; by degrees a false sense of security crept over the excited corsairs; their watchfulness relaxed, their ardour melted away; and when Blake suddenly returned from Trapani—whither he had sailed for the very purpose of throwing the pirates off their guard—he found them in a less organised and enthusiastic attitude of defence, though their means were still such as an ordinary man would have thought it madness to encounter.

Late in the afternoon of April 3d, 1655, the English flag was once more descried from the towers of Porto Ferino. Soon after break of day on the following morning, without firing a single gun, the whole squadron rode into the harbour before a light gale, and to the amazement of the Turkish janizaries and artillerymen on shore coolly proceeded to drop anchors within half musket-range of the great batteries. The English had prepared themselves for a terrible day. Long before it was yet light they came on deck, and at a signal from the St. George divine service was performed throughout the fleet in an extremely solemn and impressive manner. This pious act completed, orders were given to advance. Captain Cobham, in the Newcastle frigate, was the first to gain the corsair harbour; but he was quickly followed by the Taunton, Foresight, Amity, Mermaid, and Merlin. Close in their wake came the great ships, the St. Andrew, Vice-admiral Badily, first; the Plymouth, Captain Stayner, second; and the St. George, third. These and other war-ships stationed themselves directly in front of the castles and as near to them as they could float. The boldness of this movement awed the stout hearts of the corsairs for a few seconds, but they

soon recovered, and here and there a ready gun
sent its iron contents crashing in amongst the masts
and rigging. The Dey now gave his final instructions, and the first broadsides from the English ships
were answered from the immense park of artillery displayed along the shore—not less than a hundred and
twenty guns of large calibre vomiting out death from
their brazen throats at the first discharge. In a short
time the fire of Porto Ferino was made to bear on the
line of great ships, these fiercely replying with their
tremendous broadsides against its solid masonry; and
for two hours the air was torn and the sky obscured by
the incessant volleys of flame and smoke, dense, hot and
sulphurous. At the onset all the issues of the day
seemed to lie with the artillery. Fortunately, the gale
which in the early morning had carried the English
fleet into the harbour, continued to blow during the
battle, throwing volumes of smoke in the faces of the
corsairs and helping to prevent their cannoneers from
taking aim. On the other side, almost every shot from
the ships told with effect on the castles, batteries and
platform. Some of the guns were silenced and many
parts of the breastwork were cleared by the cannonade;
but the conflict was still undecided when Blake made a
new movement, which had been in his mind from the
first, but was not deemed practicable until that moment.
Drafting a number of picked men from each ship, he
lowered the long boats and sent them, under cover of
the black sky, with instructions to row alongside the
great corsair vessels, and throw into them a quantity of
lighted brands and torches. One of his favourite officers,
John Stoaks—a man who had served with distinction in
the Dutch war, commanding the Dragon in the battle of
Portland, the Laurel in that of the Texel, and who was
at this time captain of the St. George—was selected for

the execution of this important trust; and he achieved his perilous task with such consummate address, that in spite of a galling fire from the musketeers on shore, he succeeded in effecting a lodgment under the ports of the huge pirates, and threw into them his burning brands. The work of destruction was then swift and awful. The whole of the nine great ships-of-war, the naval strength of the Tunisians, were at once clothed in fire. Even the assailants felt cowed at an event so sudden and so terrible, and the battle almost ceased at the instant, as if both parties were entranced by the gorgeous spectacle. The frantic corsairs made many efforts to stop the progress of destruction; but wherever the fire appeared to slacken for an instant, a broadside from one of the English frigates raked its deck, stirred up the burning embers, and scattered the daring fellows who had ventured on board. At last the decks were abandoned by the pirates, and the red glare of the consuming squadron shot up freely and furiously against the sky, tinging with a hot and lurid light a scene which the April sun could scarcely reach through the artificial pall of battle. In four hours from the crash of the first broadside, the work was done. The pirate ships, so long the terror of peaceful traders, were burnt to their very keels. The batteries on shore were completely silenced, and most of the guns planted on the raised platform were either damaged or dismounted. The walls of Goletta and of Porto Ferino had been much shaken; several breaches had been made in them; and both strongholds might have been carried by assault had there existed any reason for their capture. But Blake's ends had been accomplished in the destruction of the fleet. His losses in this celebrated action amounted to no more than twenty-five killed and about forty wounded; the loss of life on shore, though the men fought behind breastworks and other cover, must have been very considerable, though it was of course impossible for the English to obtain an exact account of the casualties.

After reading the pirates this tremendous lesson—to which there was scarcely a parallel in history until Exmouth's splendid bombardment of Algiers in our own time,—the English squadron sailed for Tripoli on the same errand; but the Dey of that place, warned by the fate of Tunis, received them with every demonstration of honour and regard; he acceded with apparent zeal to their demands, and entered into a treaty to respect the Commonwealth flag at all times and in all places. This summary dealing with the dependent powers of Turkey brought the governments of London and Constantinople into connexion and correspondence. Blake himself seems to have had some doubts whether his instructions, vague and ample as they were, would be held to justify him in entering the ports of a power with which his country was not actually at war, and destroying its fleets and fortifications. Had not the Dey's haughty words chafed his spirit, it is not certain that he would have proceeded so far without waiting for fresh instructions; and as soon as the action at Tunis was over, he despatched a full account of the incident to Sir Thomas Bendish, Cromwell's ambassador at Constantinople, which that functionary was desired to lay before the Grand Vizier should any complaints be made on the subject. The Turks were then at war with the Venetian Republic, and the destruction of so large a portion of their fleet by an enemy hitherto unknown in the affairs of the Mediterranean roused their anger to a high degree; but the Grand Vizier hesitated to involve himself with a new and powerful enemy by any hasty expression of his resentment. Tunisian agents went to Constantinople to complain of Blake to the Grand Seigneur. They

attributed their inability to defend their fleet and castles
to the want of heavier guns; and the government immediately ordered six pieces of brass ordnance of the
largest calibre to be despatched to Porto Ferino. Bendish was led to consider the Grand Vizier satisfied with
Blake's explanations; but the incident was nevertheless
a sharp thorn in his master's side; and for several months
the English traders at Smyrna lived in fear of retalia-
tions. Fear or policy, however, prevailed in the divan,
and so long as the formidable Sea-General lived, the
English residents in the Levant continued to pursue
their peaceful enterprises without molestation.

After settling his affairs at Tripoli, Blake ran into
the Adriatic, where the Venetians received him with
such honours as are given to royal visitors. His late
actions had spoken in the most convincing language
to the able and astute rulers of Venice, and they lost
no time in offering friendship to the western Republic.
On his return towards the Straits of Gibraltar, he again
called at Tunis to inquire if the Dey were prepared to
treat of peace. In answer to his first summons, a white
flag was raised at the castle of Porto Ferino; and after
some negotiation of a merely technical nature, a treaty
was signed and ratified in terms equally honourable and
advantageous to England. The humbled corsair even
consented to allow an English consular agent to reside
at his court. A flying visit to the island of Malta
served to teach the proud and unprincipled Templars
some respect for the rights and properties of heretical
Englishmen. These priestly marauders believed themselves a serious power in the Mediterranean; in some
degree they made a pretence of being the guardians and
the arbiters of Catholic Europe. When the expedition
under the Duke of Guise appeared before Valetta, they
haughtily refused to allow it the shelter of their port.

But the unceremonious manner in which Blake had exacted reparation from the princes of Italy, and even laid his hands on Pope Alexander's own coffers, warned them that their clerical character would afford them no protection from the strong arm of English justice, and they restored to the lawful owners the spoils of their warfare against English heretics.

There only remained Algiers. But force was no longer necessary in dealing with the great pirate cities; the blow struck against the system at Tunis had cowed the corsairs from Tripoli to the shores of Fez and Morocco. When the English squadron stood into the Bay of Algiers, boldly as if on a visit of courtesy to a friendly power, and Blake sent his officer, as usual, to demand restitution of property and the liberation of Christian slaves, the Dey received the messenger with great civility, paid a handsome compliment to the English Admiral, and to show his good will sent a present of live cattle to the fleet—an extremely seasonable and politic gift, which at once made him popular with the ill-fed seamen. With regard to the specific demands of the Admiral he answered with great adroitness, that the ships and men captured by his people in times past, whether from the English or from other nations, had become the property of private individuals, most of whom had bought them at full price in open market; that they had been seized during a period of recognised and inveterate war between Islam and Christendom, when no treaties existed, and when therefore none could be broken; that he could not restore the captives without using violence towards his subjects, and creating general discontent, if not rebellion in his dominions. He urged, moreover, that, considering the general prevalence of piracy in Europe as well as in Africa, the English required too much when they demanded the unconditional surrender of his prizes.

Finally, if these objections should seem to the Admiral as clear as they did to himself, he said he would procure the liberation of all English captives then in his country at a moderate ransom per head, and enter for himself and his people into a solemn engagement not to molest English traders for all time to come. The humble tone of the pirate prince recommended his argument; a contract was therefore made for the ransom of all the captives at a fixed price, and the poor wretches were liberated and sent on board the ships of their deliverers. Before the fleet sailed from the harbour a noble and touching incident occurred, adding one more to the long list of illustrations of the English seaman's character. The ships were lying in-shore, not far from the mole-head, when a number of men were observed swimming towards them, pursued by several turbaned Moors in boats; and on coming under the bows of our vessels, the fugitives cried to the sailors in Dutch to save them from their Moslem pursuers. Forgetting that only a few months before we had been at war with the Dutch, regardless of every consideration beyond the humane instincts of the moment, our sailors helped the poor wretches to clamber up, when they discovered that they were runaway slaves, and the men in chase of them their masters. Here, then, was a new difficulty! The Dey claimed the fugitives in virtue of the new treaty, and appealed to the accepted principle of compensation for all restored captives. But the idea of giving back Christian men, even enemies, from the freedom of an English man-of-war into the hands of pirates and infidels was not to be entertained by Puritan sailors. Some one suggested to his fellows a subscription: how much the Admiral himself paid into this fund he has carefully concealed, but every seaman in the fleet generously agreed to give up a dollar of his wages to buy the poor

Hollanders their freedom. A bargain was soon made, the money was paid by the fleet-treasurer, and the liberated men went home to tell their countrymen this story of the magnanimous islanders.

Before the end of April 1655, Blake had brought his extraordinary cruise to an end. In six months he had established himself as a power in that great midland sea from which his countrymen had been politically excluded since the age of the Crusades. He had redressed with a high hand the grievances of many years, and had taught nations to which the very name of Englishman was a strange sound, to respect our honour and our rights. The pirates of Barbary had been chastised as they had never yet been chastised in history. The petty princes of Italy had been made to feel the power of the northern Protestants. The Pope himself had learned to tremble on his seven hills; and the echoes of our guns had startled the Council-chambers of Venice and Constantinople. Blake sent home not less than sixteen ships laden with treasure, received in satisfaction of former injuries, or taken by force from hostile states. Some of the Italian princes sent embassies to London to cultivate the friendship of Cromwell. The representatives of the Grand Duke of Tuscany and the Doge of Venice distinguished themselves in these missions by the splendour of their appointments. The former had orders to solicit the honour of a present of the Protector's portrait, which was painted for his master by Cooper, and hung in the ducal palace among the choicest products of Italian art.

# CHAPTER IX.



THE correspondence between Blake and Cromwell, so far as it related to the affairs of Spain and the course to be pursued by the southern fleet, had been carried on in cipher, and all the instructions sent from London were secret. But the time had come to throw off the mask. During the six months consumed in the bold and successful exploits which had established on both shores of the Mediterranean a salutary awe of English prowess, the object of the expedition under Penn and Venables remained a profound mystery. Penn himself, when he sailed from Portsmouth was unaware of the precise service on which his squadron was to be employed, for his orders were not to open the letter of final instructions until far enough from Europe to prevent any risk of their nature transpiring :—a very necessary precaution as the event proved, for that worldly seaman, already foreseeing the downfall of the Commonwealth, and anxious to secure to himself the gratitude of the royal family by unexpected and splendid services in their cause, no sooner found himself at the head of a large fleet than he entered into communication with the exile court at Cologne, and offered to desert with his entire power from the Commonwealth, and sail into whatever port should be named by Charles and his council. Had he known the errand on which he was about to proceed, he would unquestionably have told the Stuarts, who, in their turn, would have eagerly seized the opportunity of strengthening their interests at Madrid by forwarding such a piece of state intelligence. On the receipt of it, there is no reason to believe that Philip IV. would have refused any longer to grant the use of one of his harbours in the Low Countries for the reception of the revolters. But having no port to receive so large a fleet—nor any means of supporting it, except piracy,—from which he was perhaps warned by the mysterious fate of his cousin Maurice, Charles declined the traitorous offer, and desired the Admiral to reserve his loyalty for some happier season. The expedition therefore sailed on its unknown voyage; and it was not until late in the spring of 1655 that news arrived in Europe from the west relating the particulars of an attack made by Penn and Venables on the great Spanish settlement of Hispaniola.

The idea of a secret expedition to invade an island possessed by a power against which war had not been declared, would be excessively offensive to modern notions of public honour. But in Cromwell's time the peace of Europe was not fixed on certain bases. Commerce and colonies lay almost beyond the pale of law and treaties. No French admiral would have thought it right to plunder Lyme or Sandown; but not one Frenchman in ten would have hesitated to seize the merchants of either of these ports on the high seas. Countries might be at war in one latitude, though not in all—at sea when not on land. The seizure of Vendôme's fleet had not led to a war between France and England. The destruction of Rupert's squadron in the harbours of Carthagena had not interrupted the relations, such as they were, between London and Madrid. Europe, indeed, had never known such a thing as peace on the high seas; from the Northern jarl to the African corsair, the strong arm had always ruled on the highway of nations. Even when England and Spain had seemed to be on the best terms with each other in Europe, envy, jealousy and distrust reigned in the New World, and the elements of discord often broke into open violence and bloodshed. Cromwell affected to believe that war already existed between the two countries in that hemisphere, and that an armament was needed for the protection of English interests in America.

Real causes for a war with Spain were neither few nor remote, though it is probable that the most active of these were such as would exercise little influence over the minds of statesmen in the nineteenth century. The first and gravest was the religious situation. Spain was ultra-Catholic, England ultra-Protestant. The most powerful and warlike of the sects which supported Cromwell sincerely believed that Spain was the devil's stronghold in Europe. The Reformed faith—tolerated in the Holy Roman Empire, in France, and still more recently in Portugal—had never found mercy at Madrid. Racks, wheels, boiling oil, and other yet more delicate means of torture, opposed the spread of new doctrines throughout Spain and the Indies; while frequent burnings and gibbetings kept the masses of the people true to the creed of their fathers. The horror excited in Puritan England by reports of these atrocities was naturally heightened by the fact that foreign residents —even Englishmen—sometimes fell under the frowns of the Holy Office, and suffered, without appeal, judgments given by that secret and terrible tribunal. In fact, the Inquisition was the great obstacle to a solid and durable peace between the two powers. When the Spanish Ambassador first proposed an alliance, Cromwell made this one of his two essential conditions :—that English merchants living in Spain should be allowed to exercise their own religion, have the use of Bibles and such other pious books as they might require, and be free from the control of the Holy Office. The Ambassador refused even to transmit this demand to his master, and the attempt at negotiation failed. Other causes tended to excite the war-feeling. The murder of Ascham had not been forgotten; nor had the favours extended and the shelter afforded to Rupert and his revolted ships at Cadiz and Carthagena been forgiven. Among political reasons, the obstinate refusal to allow foreign traders to visit any of the ports of America and the West India Islands, was the first and strongest. Liberty of trade—freedom from the Holy Office : these were the two conditions on which the Protector offered to treat. " What," exclaimed the Ambassador, " my master has but two eyes, and you ask him to pluck out both at once ! " Unable to make terms with the Catholic court, Cromwell prepared for war.

Though Mazarin, acting on his famous maxim of state, seemed willing to give way on every point before the energetic rulers of the new Commonwealth, the causes of quarrel with France were not yet fully removed. The cruisers of the two countries still carried letters of marque; and daily encounters took place at sea without either accelerating or retarding the long and tedious negotiations of M. Bordeaux. For three years this agent had been in London asking for peace. Crafty diplomatists fancied that Cromwell employed his time in maturely weighing the relative advantages of a French and a Spanish alliance, and the ambassadors of the rival powers intrigued day and night to gain his ear. To the surprise of the old formalists, he at length took a decisive attitude against Spain, without attempting to hurry on the settlement of his differences with France. Fearless of consequences, while Penn and Venables went out to attack Hispaniola, Blake harassed the trade of Marseilles and kept the Toulon fleet locked up in the Mediterranean harbours. Whenever his cruisers found ships at sea sailing to or from French ports, they seized them as lawful prizes. One of his frigates took a Hamburg vessel bound for Marseilles, which he condemned. Another captured two Hamburgers and a Hollander; but as he found by their papers that two of these were not bound for French ports, they were set free; the other, carrying goods to Rouen, was confiscated. Such incidents occurred almost daily. Loud and bitter complaints were made by the men of business in France at the delay of peace; discontent spread to other classes; and Bordeaux was urged by his countrymen to conclude a treaty with the Commonwealth at almost any sacrifice, rather than continue a state of things so wounding to the pride and disastrous to the commerce of France.

Even the pride of Louis XIV. yielded to the interests of his country. He treated on Cromwell's own terms. The point of honour and precedence was waived; Louis consented to banish the Stuart Princes, together with Hyde, Ormonde, and fifteen other of their adherents, from the soil of France; maritime hostilities were at once to cease between the two nations; and the treaty was on the very eve of signature, when news arrived in London of the horrible massacre of the Vaudois by the soldiers of the Duke of Savoy, an intimate friend and ally of the King of France. No event in history had fired the Protestant passions of the English people like the atrocious invasion of those Piedmont valleys. Fasts, prayers, denunciations, offered themselves as vents for the national fervour; collections of money were made for the sufferers in all the churches of London; and some of the bolder spirits proposed to send an army to the Savoy Alps; a project to which the Government was not altogether averse. But for the moment Cromwell trusted to his influence over Mazarin as the best means of obtaining justice for those poor Protestant villagers. He told Bordeaux that he would not make peace with his master until he knew his sentiments on the subject of the massacre and banishment of the Vaudois; and Blake received orders to uphold Protestant interests in the south with all the powers at his command. The presence of an English fleet in the Mediterranean gave force to Cromwell's suggestions. At first the Ambassador of Louis contended that France had nothing to do with the matter,—that the Duke of Savoy was an independent prince,—that the Vaudois were rebels as well as heretics, and had justly incurred chastisement at the hands of their sovereign. Cromwell remained inexorable; and Bordeaux's master was at last compelled to interfere. Under the double pressure of English and French remonstrance, the Duke of Savoy granted a full amnesty to the Vaudois, and confirmed to them their ancient right to exercise their own forms of divine worship by a new decree.

Cromwell's letters informed Blake that, in consequence of the blow about to be struck in the Western Archipelago, his presence with the fleet, if not his more active services, would be required on the Atlantic coast of Spain; and in consequence of these orders he sailed from Algiers towards the Straits of Gibraltar. But as the two countries were still at peace, he called at Malaga for fresh water, when a curious incident occurred. A party of English sailors from his fleet, in rambling about the town, suddenly came upon a procession of priests carrying a Host through the streets,

and instead of falling on their knees before the sacred
symbol, like the pious Spaniards, the Puritan seamen
laughed at and derided those who did so, until one of the
clergy called on the populace to avenge the insult aimed
at their religion. A street fight ensued; and with the
advantage of numbers and local knowledge on their side,
the Malagayans beat the scoffers back to their ships,
whither they carried an English version of the fray to
their commander. Indignation and true policy concurred in inducing Blake to treat the affair gravely.
In Lisbon, Venice and other Catholic ports, mob-law
had been applied to the sailors of English merchant-
vessels on the ground of alleged want of respect for
the forms of foreign worship; and considering the new
relations which the two countries were about to assume,
he judged it due to the honour of his flag and necessary
to the safety of his countrymen, to show the Spaniards
that he could and would redress such wrongs with
promptitude and severity. Half measures, he felt, would
be useless in such a case; so sending a trumpeter into
the town, he demanded, not retaliation on the offending
mob, as was expected, but that the priest who had set
them on should be given up to justice. The Spaniards
were astounded. Give up a Catholic priest to the judgment of heretics! The Governor of Malaga replied that he
had no power over the offender, as in Spain the servants
of the Church were not responsible to the civil power.
" I will not stay to inquire," said the stern Englishman,
" who has the power to send the offender to me; but if
he be not on board the St. George within three hours,
I will burn your city to the ground." And so he dismissed the messenger. No excuse, no protest, was
admitted; and before the three hours had expired the
priest made his appearance in the fleet. Blake then
called accusers and accused together; heard the story

on both sides; and decided that the seamen had behaved
with rudeness and impropriety towards the natives, and
thereby provoked the attack of which they complained.
He told the priest that if he had sent an account of what
had occurred to him, the men should have been severely
punished, as he would not suffer them to affront the
religion of any people at whose ports they touched; but
he expressed his extreme displeasure at the Spaniards
taking the law into their own hands, as he would have
them and all the world know that an Englishman was
not to be judged and punished except by Englishmen.
With this warning for the future, Blake, satisfied with
the priest being given up and being completely at his
mercy, treated him with civility and sent him back
unharmed to his friends.  Cromwell was mightily pleased
with this little incident.  He took the letters referring
to it in his own hand to the Council, read them out
with a smiling face, and when he had finished reading,
declared that by such means they would make the name
of Englishman as great as that of Roman was in Rome's
proudest days.

Early in June the fleet passed the Straits and anchored
once more in the Bay of Cadiz, where they received a
hospitable reception.  By the treaties then existing
between the two states, not more than ten English ships-
of-war could claim to enter any Spanish port at one
time; yet as a mark of extraordinary confidence and
respect, when the Governor of Cadiz sent down a present of bread, flesh and vegetables to the St. George, he
desired it to be intimated to the Admiral, that although
the capitulations declared that "there cannot come in
hither above ten ships-of-war at once, nevertheless his
lordship might come in with all his forces and welcome."
But Blake, expecting every hour to receive intelligence
from London which would compel him to exchange

pacific greetings for acts of vigorous hostility, would have refused the invitation even had he not suspected that a snare might be concealed under this show of extreme courtesy. He excused himself on the plea that he had only touched at Cadiz on his way, and could stay no longer than was required to take fresh water and other necessaries on board. In the city every effort was made to learn what he intended to do next. Whether his fleet was bound for England, Lisbon or the Barbary coast, could not be ascertained even by the agents of the Council of State. Cromwell kept his secret, and Blake kept his secret. But among the best-informed English residents in Cadiz, rumour fixed on Salee, the famous rovers of which still harassed our southern trade, as the scene in which the next grand naval spectacle would be exhibited.

The mystery cleared. Barely had Blake weighed anchor at Cadiz harbour when news arrived from the western Archipelago. Penn, it turned out, had sailed from Barbadoes to Hispaniola. There the regiments were landed and given up to the sole direction of Venables; who, through cowardice, incapacity or treason—for he also, though unknown to Penn, was in correspondence with the Stuarts,—frittered away his most favourable opportunities, and finally led his men into a disastrous situation, from which they were only rescued by the intrepidity of Admiral Goodson and a body of seamen sent from the fleet. The English had retired from the island disgraced and discomfited:—so far the expedition, begun with secret treason, had ended in a signal failure. But after this first overthrow, as the sealed orders required Penn to establish an interest in any part of the Spanish Indies, he sailed for Jamaica, landed his troops, put down a feeble attempt at resistance, and added that fine island to the permanent colonial empire of his country.

When this intelligence reached Madrid, Philip declared war against England—seized the persons of all English residents, merchants, factors and agents connected with the interests of their commerce, and laid an embargo on all their merchandise and properties, amongst others on those of Nicholas Blake, the Admiral's brother. The reported failure of the English at Hispaniola raised the spirits of the court to an extravagant height : the Governor of the island was made a grandee and pensioned ; even the messenger who brought the news to Spain had 1500 ducats a-year settled on him for life. Blake's rapid and effective cruise in the Mediterranean, following in the immediate rear of the brilliant actions of the Dutch war, had caused the maritime powers of Europe, and particularly Spain, from its own experience of the Dutch admirals, to regard with blended interest and alarm what appeared to be the invincible prowess and fortunes of the young Commonwealth. The first signal check to that ascending power was therefore hailed with a delight out of all proportion to its importance. In the safety of Hispaniola, Philip forgot the loss of Jamaica ; in the escape of his Silver Fleets from the English squadron in the West Indies, he overlooked the more resolute and watchful enemy who lay in wait for them under the very guns of Cadiz.

While staying in the Channel before Cadiz, Blake had learned from his scouts that the Silver Fleet was expected from America in four or five weeks, and war being then inevitable, he stood across to Cape Santa Maria, the most southern point of land in Portugal, intending to make the bay or bays lying between that promontory and Cape St. Vincent the bases of his summer operations ; with his frigates and fast sailers ranging the sea in a vast circle as far as wind and weather would permit, in search of the anticipated prize. In the Spanish harbour ten large galleons were being prepared for sea — six of them, it was reported, being intended for service at Hispaniola, the others for the Mediterranean; but Blake, suspecting they were designed as a convoy for the Silver Fleet, endeavoured by absence from the port, by insult and by other provocations to entice them out. But nothing would induce them to stir. Nearly a month the St. George rode before the little town of Lagos. The war-ships kept out at sea, the frigates menaced the coast; still the galleons did not move. At last, in the full belief that Philip would not allow his admirals to risk a battle—a belief founded on information reaching London through various and independent channels — Cromwell desired Blake to send home part of his fleet, so as to reduce the heavy expenses of the war; but before these instructions could be carried into effect, news arrived at Lagos that the merchants of Seville, Cadiz, and San Lucar, seeing the government neglect to provide the necessary protection for their trade, had combined to equip at their private expense a squadron strong enough to put to sea for convoy service, and even give battle in case of need; and under these circumstances he abandoned the idea of sending back any part of his fleet, and as speedily as he was able he got such of his vessels as were sea-worthy, and many that were not sea-worthy, together. On the 4th of July he wrote to Cromwell in reference to the state of his ships :—" Seeing it hath pleased your Highness to command my longer stay in and about these parts with the rest of the ships, I shall make bold to offer one humble desire, which I conceive to be my duty for the service of the Commonwealth and the better effecting the ends proposed,—that your Highness will be pleased to consider the condition of our fleet, especially of the great ships, which are very foul and defective, particularly the ship in which I am—being very leaky and the mainmast unsound." Yet it was in vessels of this character that he had ruined Prince Rupert, cleared the Channel Islands, fought the battle of Portland, and chastised the pirates of Porto Ferino! Early in August the Spanish squadron, consisting of 28 men-of-war, and six fire-ships, with 36 long-boats, and 6000 troops on board, sailed from Cadiz, with the apparent intention of fighting the English.

Towards the middle of the month the two squadrons came in sight off the coast of Portugal, Blake having been southward in search of the Spaniards; but, after dodging each other for some days, they separated without exchanging a single shot, for reasons which are explained at length in the following letter from Blake to the Lord Protector:

MAY IT PLEASE YOUR HIGHNESS,—Your commands of the 30th July I received by the Assurance frigate the 13th instant, with the intelligence of a great fleet prepared to come out of Cadiz and their design from your secretary, which in part we have found to be true, as I shall give your Highness an account.

The 6th inst. I received a letter from Captain Smith (which comes herewith), whereupon we stood away for the coast of Barbary, as far as Mamora, within three leagues; but having no news of the fleet there, we made towards the Bay of Cadiz, sending two frigates before to gain intelligence, who returned to us the 12th instant with this, that the fleet sailed from thence seven days before, and were plying off Cape St. Vincent, to which place we hastened; and the 15th, in the morning, espied them to the windward of us, we being then off the Bay of Lagos, whither we desired to go for water; but they bearing up upon us, with intent (as we thought) to fight us, I called a council of war, which unanimously resolved to engage the first opportunity, being moved thereunto with an eager desire we had to see some end of our tedious expectation, and to prevent that accession of strength mentioned in the secretary's intelligence (whereof we likewise had notice from other hands), and also out of a despair of being able to keep the sea many days longer for want of liquor. But the Spanish fleet forthwith tacked and stood the other way, and we after them all that night. In the morning we were fair by them; but there being little wind (not enough to work our ships) and a great sea, so that we could not make use of our lower tier, and also a thick fog, we did nothing that day; their fleet being then thirty-one in all. The next day we continued in the same resolution, and sent some frigates ahead to gain the wind, and to engage them; but the evening approaching, and a great part of our fleet far astern, we thought it best to desist for that time. These checks of Providence did put us upon second thoughts, and a strict review of the instructions which I had received; the which being all perused and compared together at a council of war, we could not find in them any authority given unto us to attack this party, but rather the contrary; and we had reason also to conceive it was not the intention of your Highness that we should be the first breakers of the peace, seeing your Highness having notice of the coming forth of the Spanish fleet did not give us any new direction at all touching the same in your last order of the 30th of July. Upon these grounds we receded from our first resolution, and took into consideration the state of our fleet, which we found in all things to be extremely defective, but more particularly in want of liquor; some of the ships having not beverage for above four days, and the whole not able to make above eight, and that at short allowance; and no small part both of our beverage and water stinking.  Hereupon it was debated amongst us whether we should return to the Bay of Lagos or go to Lisbon for supplies, there being no other place but those two.  To go to Lagos it was not held good, both because all that country could not afford us one pipe of beverage wine, and to get water there very difficult, and upon the least wind from the south or east almost impossible, and the place a dangerous road for such a fleet to anchor in, which we must have done for getting a quantity of water, beside many other inconveniences.  It was therefore resolved that we should go to Lisbon.  Nevertheless, we kept in sight two days after, and on the 22nd inst. we lay a great part of the day with our sails hauled up, until they were very near us; but perceiving they had no intention to engage us, nor any commission to that purpose, as we thought, and also understood by a small frigate of theirs of twenty-four guns, the captain whereof coming accidentally amongst us, I commanded aboard, who told us the same; and withal that they knew nothing of the expected fleet at all, but only that they were bound to attend the coming of the same.  Hereupon, our liquor growing less, we stood away for Lisbon, where we arrived on the 24th instant, and anchored in the road of Cascaes. . . . How these passages of Providence will be looked upon, or what construction our carriage in this business may receive, I know not (although it hath been with all integrity of heart), but this we know, that our condition is dark and sad, and, without especial mercy, like to be very miserable :—our ships extremely foul, winter drawing on, our victuals expiring, all stores failing, our men falling sick through the badness of drink, and eating their victuals boiled in salt water for two months' space; the coming of a supply uncertain (we received not one word from the Commissioners of the Admiralty and Navy by the last), and though it come timely, yet if beer come not with it, we shall be undone that way. We have no place or friend, our recruits here slow, and our mariners (which I most apprehend) apt to fall into discontents through their long keeping abroad. Our only comfort is that we have a God to lean upon, although we walk in darkness and see no light. I shall not trouble your Highness with any complaints of myself, of the indisposition of my body, or troubles of my mind; my many infirmities will one day, I doubt not, sufficiently plead for me or against me, so that I may be free of so great a burden, consoling myself in the mean time in the Lord, and in the firm purpose of my heart with all faithfulness and sincerity to discharge the trust while reposed in me. . . . . As soon as we have got a sufficient proportion of liquor, which I hope may be in five or six days, we intend (God willing) to sail to the southward cape, and to spend some time thereabouts, so long as we can possibly lengthen out our victuals, so that we may be able to get home, in case the victualling ships do not come in time; which we shall then be forced to do, or must perish in the sea. I have no more at present to trouble your Highness with (this already being I fear too much), but shall ever remain,

Your Highness's most humble

And faithful servant,

ROBERT BLAKE.

Aboard the (St.) George, in Cascaes Road,
    August 30, 1655.

The allusion to his own indisposition of body and trouble of mind, contained in this letter, though brief and by the way, is extremely touching. He had left a sick room to go on board. For nearly a year he had never quitted the " very foul and defective " flag-ship. Want of exercise and sweet food, beer, wine, water, bread and vegetables, had helped to develop scurvy and dropsy; and his sufferings from these diseases were acute and continuous. In fact, his constitution was completely undermined. For three weeks after the date of the letter just quoted, he kept his station in the Spanish waters, when, finding no relief come in, and supposing that the Silver Fleet would now remain in America until spring, he reluctantly turned his bows towards the north, and brought his squadron home to repair and replenish.

But there was no rest for him at home. Arrived in England, he found that in the present posture of affairs his retirement from the service, even for a time, would be extremely detrimental to the country. The Council had no one to take his place. Deane, Penn, Ascue, Lawson, all the men who had served with him in the Dutch war with eminent ability and success, were now either dead or out of employment:—Ascue had been pensioned and dismissed on the alleged ground of his want of success against De Ruiter, but in reality because suspected of a leaning towards the exiles; Penn had been ostensibly broken for the failure on Hispaniola, but more likely because Cromwell had heard of his treacherous offers; Lawson lay under a cloud, and was soon afterwards arrested as a Fifth-monarchy conspirator; Deane was dead; and Monk had neither the genius nor the desire for naval commands. But while the more experienced commanders were thus falling away, the duties and demands of the service were daily increasing. The nation was committed to a war with Spain. The Pope, ill at ease since the fright of the previous spring, was warmly engaged in a project for uniting all the Catholic maritime powers in a league against the formidable heretics; and agents from Venice, Florence, Madrid and some other cities, had already met in Rome. Genoa had taken up a threatening attitude; for as many merchants of that Republic were interested in the safe arrival of the Silver Fleet, they strongly urged the government to join their armada with that of Spain for its protection. Holland was again wavering in her friendship, and report affirmed that the King of Spain had tempted them to declare war against England by the offer of Dunkirk and two other ports in the narrow seas. Nor was peace yet firmly established with the Barbary powers; at the very first reverse of fortune these corsairs would have gladly seized the moment of retaliation and revenge. What perhaps most of all annoyed Cromwell was that John, King of Portugal, who had found means to delay the execution of the treaties entered into twenty months ago—especially the clause which secured to English subjects in his dominions immunity from the Holy Office—now manifested a disposition to withdraw from the compact altogether.

In face of so many perils and uncertainties, Blake's services were indispensable. At such a time, his very name was worth a squadron. Not to speak of the moral strength which his presence would give to any fleet going southward, the occasional sight of his flag would be pretty certain to keep the Barbary corsairs quiet; a sudden visit to the Tagus might bring John of Braganza to reason; and the dread of another call at Leghorn would probably be sufficient to frighten the Pope and the Grand Duke out of the proposed league of Catholic princes. However anxious for repose of mind and body, Blake could not decline the responsibilities of command without a breach of duty to his country; and ill as he was, he lent his days and nights to the duties of his station, visiting the dockyards and arsenals, and urging

the work of repair and replenishment by his presence
and his counsels.  But though he would not refuse the
last pulse of his brain to his country, his age and bodily
sufferings warned him of the fatal consequences which
might result to the service should he fall a victim to any
sudden sickness while in those distant seas, with no
colleague on board to whom in case of need he could
devolve the supreme command; he therefore begged the
Council of State to nominate another Sea-General to
share his responsibilities and assist him with his knowledge.  Whether he actually named Montagu for the
office is uncertain; but true to the plan of their parliamentary predecessors, the Council fixed on this soldier,
a young man of good family, and a confidential friend of
Cromwell, as the new general.  The preparations of the
fleet went on rapidly.  Towards the end of February,
1656, the Generals went on board the Naseby, then in
the Downs with part of the fleet, and they continued in
the Channel, cruising between the river mouth and St.
Helen's road, for the better expedition of affairs.  The
trouble of getting in the necessary provisions was almost
incredible; every naval station on the coast was short of
stores; nor could they be procured in sufficient haste
at any price or favour.  Blake's patience was at length
tired out, and he resolved to sail without them.  "The
expectation of the provisions and fire-ships," he wrote
to Cromwell on the 8th of March, "shall be no cause
of stay: but as soon as ever we can get a supply from
the shore of the things that are essentially requisite,
which we are labouring at, we shall with the help of
God be gone."  At St. Helen's in the Isle of Wight, he
received his final instructions, and while his fleet was
getting under weigh for the south, he wrote his last
letter in England — a very pious and a very touching
farewell:

### *General Blake to Secretary Thurloe.*

SIR,—I have received yours of the 13th instant, together with the enclosed note of the galleons; as also your intelligence touching the end of the war between the Protestant and Popish cantons, and the peace settled there, and likewise the probabilities of a truce for six years betwixt France and Spain; and the being of Charles Stuart with his company in Flanders. These sudden transactions seem to have some great matters in the womb of them; but we know that God is the supreme disposer of all the counsels, designs, and confederations in the world; and we know He is able to order them all for the greater good of His people. And our trust is, that He will do so even for our good also, if we can believe in Him. The Lord help our unbelief, and subdue our hearts to the obedience of His holy will in all things. We are now getting an anchor aboard, making ready to sail, although there be little wind, or none at all. But we shall use our utmost endeavours to get to sea, not losing any opportunity that God shall afford us; as we have hitherto been careful, and hope that his Highness is confident we are and shall continue so, as far as God shall enable us; which is all at present from

Your very affectionate friend and servant,

ROBERT BLAKE.

Aboard the Naseby in St. Helen's Road,
March 15, 1656, (new style).

Two days before the date of this letter he had made his will, writing the whole of it out with his own hand.

This solemn act accomplished, and the final instructions received from the Council of State, orders were given to get the ships under weigh. The squadron coasted as far west as Torbay, and as the white cliffs and verdant slopes of Devonshire faded from his sight, the departing hero saw his last of England. As the Sea-Generals passed down the Portuguese coast, they sent their letters to King John and assurances of support to Mr. Meadows, English envoy at the court of Lisbon, in his demand for a complete recognition of all the clauses of the late treaty. But they never once slackened sail until they were again in the Bay of Cadiz, where their dispositions soon made the inhabitants aware that their daring intention was to remain the entire summer, and to hold the royal harbour in a state of perpetual blockade. By these means the Silver Fleets would be kept at sea in imminent danger, and the usual trade of the Seville and Cadiz merchants would be destroyed. The Spaniards did not, however, dream of fighting with the renovated fleet. Now and then a slight skirmish took place between a couple of stray ketches, shallops, or long-boats; and one morning in the midst of a dead calm, when even the English frigates could not move a point of the compass, the royal galleon and two other ships rowed out and fought at a great advantage with some of Blake's outsiders. But the principal damage done on either side in this encounter was effected by a chance shot from one of the frigates lying close in shore, for this cannon-ball knocked down part of a church and killed two men.

While these affairs were going on, serious news came in hot haste from Lisbon. King John, suffering from stone, and in the hands of his priests, absolutely refused to accept the treaty; and the majesty of England had been insulted in the person of its envoy. Don Pantaleone and his brother, the Conde de Torre, as was generally given out at the time, waylaid and pistolled Mr. Meadows in the streets of the capital,—probably out of revenge for the death of their brother, who had been executed in London for murder. No attempt was made to discover the assassins. The wound did not prove mortal; but Blake remembered the unatoned murders of Ascham and Dorislaus; and this time he was resolved to show the world that England would cause the law of nations to be respected towards her servants. Leaving a few frigates to keep watch over Cadiz, the whole fleet weighed for Lisbon, and in the first week of June anchored in Cascaes road at the Tagus mouth. But fear and dismay travelled faster than the Naseby, and as soon as it was known in Lisbon that Blake's instructions were clear and ample, the people rose against the priest party and compelled the invalid King to make peace with England. John sent for Mr. Meadows; and on receiving a promise that the Sea-Generals would not molest his ships or damage his ports, he consented to accept the treaty substantially as it then stood :—that is, with one or two verbal alterations, which in the opinion of the resident English, would not unfavourably affect their just claims, while, on the other hand, they would have the effect of soothing the King's pride. The right of our nation to have Bibles and other pious books in their houses, without being considered as thereby breaking the laws of the country, was conceded. The proposal of an appeal to the Pope in all disputes about religion, previously insisted on by the Portuguese, was abandoned. The lives and properties of English settlers were placed beyond the reach of the Holy Office. The customs were reduced to twenty-three per cent. And, finally, the King consented to pay down in silver 50,000*l.* sterling, besides 20,000*l.* and some other moneys due to the English for demurrage and freight of ships. A careful perusal of all the correspondence of John and his agents with the English would probably incline the reader to believe that the hasty admission of these various claims, after two years of intrigue and subterfuge, was intended only as a feint to gain time and induce the Generals not to enter the Tagus. But Blake knew the King of old, and he declared his fixed resolution to remain at Cascaes—or in case of need to sail up the river to Lisbon, and there wait the fulfilment of the treaty. Flurried by a message so energetic, the court sent to Mr. Meadows to beg that he would obtain for them some sort of assurance from the Generals that they would not molest their trade, if they, on their part, held fast to the terms of the treaty. Whereupon Blake and Montagu wrote:—"If his majesty of Portugal do perform on his part, and cause the money, which is by the treaty to be forthwith paid to his Highness's use, to be put into our possession, that it may be conveyed to England,—he may confidently assure himself that we shall never so far dishonour his Highness nor prostitute our own reputation, and bring a scandal on the faith and holiness of the religion we profess, as to violate any of the articles of the treaty." John had no resource but to pay the money, which was accordingly put on board and sent to England.

A ludicrous incident served to show the effect of Blake's southern campaigns in the capital of the Catholic world. Pope Alexander VII. had been active in his hostility to England. He had invited Spain, Genoa, Florence, and other maritime states, to make common cause against Puritan intruders into the Mediterranean. He had been the chief abettor of the King of Portugal in his faithless attempt to evade treaties. He had interposed the strongest obstacles to a just settlement of the Protestant question of the Vaudois. His Holiness, therefore, listened with fear and trembling for the renewed echoes of that Puritan cannon which had already left so many records of its presence on the shores

of Spain, Italy, and Barbary. One morning in the middle
of June, while the red cross of the Commonwealth was
still floating in the Tagus, and Blake was occupied in
taking on board the Portuguese dollars, it was suddenly
announced in the streets of Rome that the English fleet
was cannonading Civita Vecchia!   The poor Pope, supposing in his terror that the formidable heretics would
in a few hours be thundering at the gates of the Eternal
City, caused earthworks to be thrown up, and the cannon
of St. Angelo to be dismounted, carried into the streets,
and placed in the most commanding positions for defence.
As no enemy appeared, scouts were sent down to Civita
Vecchia, when it turned out that no damage had been
done—that no English vessel had been seen in that
harbour—and that the firing which had given rise to
the little comedy in Rome proceeded from a couple of
Dutchmen, the crews of which were wasting their powder
in a fit of drink.

The state of affairs remained unchanged before Cadiz.
Cromwell, harassed for funds, was anxious to strike
some sudden and tremendous blow against the great
enemy of his country; and therefore sent out Captain
Loyd, " known to us to be a person of integrity," with
a set of propositions as to how and where such a blow
could be best dealt; " desiring to give no rule to you,"
—Blake and Montagu,—but " rather as queries than
as resolutions:"—a remarkable instance of submission
in a man of Cromwell's imperious character.   The
queries were:—Would it not be possible to burn the
galleons at their moorings in the harbour ?  Could Cadiz
itself be attacked with success ?  Or, failing both these,
might not an attempt be made to carry the town and
Castle of Gibraltar ?   All these were points to be
maturely considered.   Drake had once burnt a fleet in
the Bay of Cadiz.   Essex and Raleigh had once carried

the city by assault. On their way from Cascaes road the
Sea-Generals held many consultations, examined charts
and compared opinions; intending, if the project of
burning the Spanish fleet as it lay in the Carracas
appeared feasible, to fall suddenly and fiercely to the
work of destruction the moment of their arrival. But
not a single pilot could be found willing to undertake
the responsibility of carrying an English war-ship into
that narrow and dangerous harbour. Times had changed
since Drake surprised the Spaniards. The expedition
under Essex had taught them their weakness and their
strength. When he arrived in the Bay, Blake obtained
exact information from spies, and secret agents, as
to the means of defence possessed by the city, from
which it appeared,—that the navigation of the channel
was extremely difficult at all times,—that the Spaniards
had thrown a number of heavy chains across it,—that
large vessels had been placed in convenient positions
ready to be sunk at the first signal of an attempt
to enter 'it by force,—that guns had been planted on
both shores of the passage,—and that the preparations
for defence were altogether of the most complete and
formidable character. It was therefore obvious to the
council of war, that in order to destroy the fleet in
Carracas it would be necessary first to subdue Cadiz.
And this point was considered; but only for a moment.
That the city was strong by nature, and still stronger by
art, was well known to military men; but Cromwell's
spies had led him to believe that it was ill-supplied
with troops, and it was on this circumstance that he
had indulged in his dream of an attack. On the spot
the council of war obtained more exact accounts, when
it appeared that in Cadiz, town and island, Porto Santa
Maria and Rotto, where the Duke of Medina commanded in person, there were about forty thousand

regular troops, some regiments of which vast force enjoyed the well-won reputation of being the finest infantry in the world. Under these circumstances they voted it irrational to think of making any attempt on the mainland, unless a large body of troops could be sent from England to co-operate with the fleet, as had been the case when Essex and Raleigh forced their way into the town. An attack on Gibraltar was declared impracticable for similar reasons; the Spaniards having recently strengthened the works and thrown a powerful garrison into that important stronghold.

On receiving the letters in which these decisions of the war-council were reported, the Protector and his Council wrote to Blake and Montagu:

GENTLEMEN,—We have seen a letter written by you to the Commissioners of the Admiralty, dated 9th May, from Tangier, which arrived here yesterday morning, whereby we understand the posture of the enemy, and that for the several reasons expressed by you in that said letter, it seems to you not rational to attempt the burning of the Spanish fleet in Cadiz; and thereupon apprehending that some of your ships may be spared into the Channel for the better securing of trade, and the blocking up of Dunkirk and Ostend, where the pirates and ships-of-war grow so numerous, that lately eighteen or nineteen of them in a body took twenty of our merchant-ships in two fleets, being under a convoy of a Dutch ship of thirty-six guns; therefore we have resolved to call into these seas part of the fleet now with you; and to that end we desire you, upon the receipt hereof, to give orders to ten ships, under a good officer, to sail with the first opportunity of wind and weather into the Downs, requiring them to give immediate notice unto us of their arrival. We leave it wholly unto you which of the ships you will send, conceiving you to be best able to judge which of them will be fittest for this service and may be best spared by you. Some thoughts we have had that the lesser sort of ships, and especially frigates, will best answer the aforesaid ends here. This we have resolved, not knowing anything of your posture or counsels more than your aforesaid letter represents. But in case you are upon any design, or if aught else hath emerged, either upon our letter and instruction sent by Captain Loyd, or from your own thoughts, with which these orders will not well consist, we leave it to you, notwithstanding what we have herein written, whether you will send these ships or not; our intentions not being to disappoint any thing which may be in your eye or design to be done there by the fleet.

The fleet had barely taken up its position in the Bay of Cadiz before it began to experience some of that extreme weather to which the hopes of the Spaniards seemed now chiefly turned as a means of compelling the English to go home. Several captains of ships were on board the Naseby receiving their instructions to sail for England in compliance with the request of the Council, when a gust of wind suddenly rose in the east and south-east. It increased into a tremendous gale, snapt the anchor-chains, tore the cordage into shreds, and scattered the fleet—seven or eight ships, of which the Naseby was one, excepted—far and wide from Sagres to Tangier, doing serious damage to the entire squadron. The night which followed this terrible day was dark as well as tempestuous. Here and there the lights were hung out all night long as signals of distress, and in every pause of the storm the commanders heard signal-guns booming over the sea from great distances. About one o'clock, the Naseby had a narrow escape of wreck.

The Taunton, her sails torn and rudder unmanageable, came drifting before the gale right on them. Lights were hoisted and orders given for Captain Vallis, her commander, to open a new sail; but the poor fellow seemed to have lost all power over her movements. On she came, stern foremost, against the Naseby, which vessel had hitherto kept at anchor. A few moments and a collision appeared inevitable. Blake ordered his cables to be cut as a last chance, when suddenly, as he says in his letter to Cromwell—"it pleased God in very much mercy that she"—the Taunton—"let slip, and getting a sail open with much ado steered clear off us, else one or both of us, in all likelihood, had immediately gone to the bottom." Nearly all the vessels of his fleet lost their long-boats, and many of them their cables and anchors:—the Resolution had one of her anchors snapt into two pieces, and the other bent almost double. But none were absolutely lost. The Kent and the Taunton were the longest absent from the general gathering; but after a few days of painful suspense, to the infinite joy of their comrades they also returned. In one of his letters Montagu says, "the sea ran mountains high;" and he added suggestively—"Judge you what this sea is to ride in winter time!" Great damage was also done to the Spanish ships lying in harbour; many of the merchant-men being torn from their moorings and driven out to sea.

Six of the English ships, including the Kent, Bristol and Mermaid, were judged to be no longer fit for so rude a service, and were sent home to England. Meantime the Generals did their utmost to exasperate the enemy to come out and fight. But neither insult nor spoliation could sufficiently stir the Hidalgo blood: as the Lisbon agent expressed it in his correspondence, "the Spaniard used his buckler rather than his sword." Hearing that a Sicilian and a Genoese galley had taken part with the Spaniards of Malaga against the English, Blake despatched the Ruby, Nantwich, and Lyon, with the Fox fire-ship, to that port, in search of the offenders, and with orders to infest and alarm the coast on that side from Gibraltar to Valentia. Still the Cadiz galleons would not venture out. Blake then drew off a number of frigates and good sailers for a temporary guard, and with the body of his fleet sailed for the African coast in search of water and provisions; intending also to pay a brief visit to Salee, on the west coast of Africa, and teach the lawless rovers of that city some respect for European commerce and civilisation. Success attended him and his officers. The expedition against Malaga was brilliantly executed. The English ships stood into the harbour at mid-day, with colours and pennons flying, and anchored between the bulwark and the pier-head in three fathoms of water. The people on shore were taken quite aback, fancying the ships were come in to give themselves up to the King of Spain. But they were roused from this dream by a sudden declaration that, if the Genoese galley were not given up to the English, they would proceed to fire every ship that was within the pier. After exchanging signals, the two galleys made an attempt to quit the port, the Genoese covering the Sicilian like a shield, when the frigates poured a broadside into the insolent Genoese, which broke her rudder, killed forty of her crew, and carried off her oars in splinters. The Sicilian slipt away in the confusion, but the Genoese was obliged to put back into the port, where she was grappled by the fire-ship and instantly wrapt in flames. The cannon of the land-works now opened on the English, and in return the ships began to bombard the town. A dozen resolute fellows leapt on shore from a long-boat, and in a few minutes they had spiked eight pieces of heavy ordnance under the very walls of the town. The people were amazed and stunned; many of the gentry fled away; the citizens hid themselves in their wine-casks; and it was thought that a force of 4000 men would have been able to capture and plunder the place, so great was the terror of the people.

Blake and Montagu returned to their Cadiz station, but the Spaniards still remained in port. No Silver Fleets appeared. July and August passed away in glorious but not very profitable cruises, skirmishes and blockades. Winter was drawing near, and every ship in the service required to be careened and refitted. Victuals of every kind ran short. To obtain supplies even of bread and water, it was necessary to seek the ports of a friendly power. Blake, therefore, appointed Captain Richard Stayner, of the Speaker, to watch the bay with a squadron of seven ships, the Speaker, Bridgwater, Providence, Plymouth, and three others; and with the remainder of his power he sailed early in September for the northern part of Portugal. The Generals, however, had not come to an anchor in Aviero Bay before a fortunate accident brought a division of the long-expected Silver Fleet in sight of Stayner's squadron. Four magnificent Spanish galleons and two merchantmen of Indian build, all of them laden with cargoes of gold, silver, pearls and precious stones, hides, indigo, sugar, cochineal, varinas and tobacco, and having the Viceroy of Lima and his family, a general, an admiral, and vice-admiral, together with about two thousand inferior persons on board, had left the Havanna early in June bound for Cadiz, under the impression that their European fleets would be able to protect them against the English, and without touching land at any point, they had made the whole voyage in the short space of fifty-seven days. On their way they picked up a little French barque, laden with hides, and afterwards, among the Western Islands, a Portuguese corn-factor, both of which vessels they made prizes. Either from mistake or from malice, the Portuguese sailors, when their captors inquired from them where the English fleet lay, replied that the Spaniards had beaten Blake a month ago, and driven him away from their coast; they consequently continued their voyage towards Europe in the utmost confidence, instead of running to the Azores for a convoy. In passing San Lucar, they noticed a long-boat in the act of crossing the bar; but by some fatality they proceeded towards Cadiz without staying to inquire how an English long-boat could be entering the river if Blake's squadron had been discomfited and driven home. Even when they observed Stayner's frigates, just at dusk on the 8th of September, some five or six leagues eastward towards Cadiz, they concluded that these must be Spanish guardships lying about the harbour, and therefore did their best to keep close to them all night, putting their own lights on for company, and occasionally firing guns to announce their fortunate arrival. At day-dawn, they discovered their mistake; and, though they had a vast preponderance of force, they separated, and some of them ran ashore as the only means of saving the vast treasures with which they were freighted. A fresh gale, blowing hard from the north-east, had scattered the English squadron, and only the Speaker, the Plymouth, and the Bridgwater were at first sufficiently near the galleons to engage with them. Stayner naturally made for the flag-ship of the Spaniard; but finding that it was one of the weakest in the fleet, and suspecting that the flag was raised on that vessel merely to deceive and draw off an enemy from the gold and silver galleons, he let her go, and she succeeded in making her escape with her Lisbon prize into Cadiz. The battle raged between the other vessels for six hours. From the walls and towers of Cadiz the Spaniards could see every turn of the engagement; two of their galleons were on fire at the same moment; two others of their ships went down to rise no more. After defending his charge with heroic valour, their Vice-admiral was overpowered, his vessel, on fire in several places, was hastily rifled by the conquerors of its gold and silver; the prisoners were removed to the Speaker, and it was then left to fill and sink. In this galleon went down the unfortunate Viceroy of Lima, with his wife and daughter. The Plymouth chased one of the traders to the shore, where she ran aground near Cape Degar; but it appeared by the statement of prisoners taken that she had no silver on board. The galleon of the Rear-admiral was taken, a prize of very great value. "The ship we took," says Stayner in his letter to Blake, "is worth all the rest of the fleet." It was a royal galleon of about 500 tons burthen with 350 men on board when she struck her colours, and contained two million pieces of eight. Two other prizes were afterwards picked up; and of the eight vessels only two escaped capture or destruction. The money lost amounted to nine million pieces of eight. The loss in men on the English side was very slight; but several of the frigates were much damaged, especially the Speaker, which had borne the chief brunt of the battle.

Among the prisoners taken was the young Marquis de Badajoz, son of the Viceroy of Lima, whose melancholy and romantic story at once became a theme for poets and tale-tellers. His father was born a few leagues from Madrid, of a noble but reduced family of pure Hidalgo blood. In early life his royal master made him Governor of Chili, in South America; afterwards he was translated to the Vice-royalty of Lima, which country ho governed fourteen years; but his period of office being completed, his family grown up to youth, his own labours rewarded with wealth and honours, he embarked in the vice-admiral with his lady, his four sons, and his three daughters—two of them affianced brides, one to a son of the great Duke of Medina Cœli, the other to Don Juan de Joyas, Rear-admiral of the fleet, and now Stayner's prisoner. When the flames began to spread in the galleon, the marchioness and one of her daughters swooning with heat and fear fell on their faces and were scorched to death. One of the boys also fell a victim to the fire. The marquis might have escaped unhurt, but seeing the blackened bodies of his companions where they lay, he rushed towards them, threw his arms about his wife, and died in the embrace. The young marquis, his brothers, and sisters, were saved by the English boarders and carried to the Speaker, where they were treated with compassion even by the rude sailors. The eldest boy afterwards became quite a favourite with the two commanders: "He is a most pregnant, ingenious, and learned youth as I ever met with," said Montagu, "and his story is the saddest that ever I heard of or read of to my remembrance." The whole fortune of the family, consisting of 800,000 pieces of eight, was on board the vice-admiral; much of it was plundered by the boarders, and the rest went down with the wreck.

Cromwell had already desired one of the Generals to return home for a short time, to consult with the Board of Admiralty on the state of the fleet and on the general conduct of the war; and he had named Montagu for this purpose, as his absence would be least severely felt. Blake was desired, if the plan met with his approval, to make a selection from the squadron under his command of such good sailers as would be best likely to stand the

wear of a winter campaign, and with these vessels keep
guard before the harbour of Cadiz, and utterly destroy
its commerce. He thereupon removed the red cross of
the Commonwealth to the mast of the Swiftsure; and
collecting all Stayner's prizes with the other ships
intended for home, he took farewell of his colleague,
committing him to the mercies of God and the good-will
of his countrymen. England soon rang with the new
glories of its great seamen. Poems, plaudits and rewards
met the victorious Montagu. A knighthood was reserved
for Stayner. The bullion which he had captured was
landed at Portsmouth, and some eight-and-thirty wagons,
attended by chosen picquets of soldiers carried it triumphantly through the western towns to London, where it
was paraded through the City, and then immediately
carried to the Tower and coined into English money.

# CHAPTER X.

## SANTA CRUZ.

STAYNER's brilliant success against the first division of the Silver Fleets which had fallen in the way of an English squadron, encouraged Blake in the idea that by remaining at sea all winter, he might be able to strike such a blow at the naval power of Spain, as would shake that empire. The Mexican galleons had been disposed of by his lieutenant; those of Peru, known to be still more richly laden with gold, silver, pearls and precious stones, were on their way to Spain. Could he only keep the mouth of the Carracas closed, so as to prevent any caraval going out to warn them of their danger, it was not unlikely that they would follow in the track of the former fleet, and fall into his hands. But this advantage was only to be gained by a winter at sea: and in such a sea, with a fleet in the worst condition, and in his state of increasing bodily infirmity! The best of the great ships had gone home with the Naseby, Cromwell believing from all past naval experience that it would be impossible for them to ride through the storms of December and January on that dangerous coast: what remained as the Cadiz blockading squadron were about twenty frigates, with the Swiftsure, a vessel of 898 tons burden, carrying 380 men and 64 guns, as admiral. Yet the duties were numerous and of different kinds which this fleet of frigates was expected to perform. Simply to keep the seas would have been no easy task; but Blake was expected to hold the whole southern coast of Spain in a state of siege,—to close the Straits of Gibraltar against the enemy,—to intercept the Silver Fleets should they arrive,—to prevent the coming in of oak, hemp, tar, and other materials for ship-building from the north of Europe,—to entice out and then fight with the war-galleons known to be fitting up in Cadiz by the merchants of Seville for the defence of their property,—to cut off all communication over sea between Spain and Flanders,—to harass and destroy the enemy's trade, particularly that of their colonies and settlements in America,—to watch and check the movements of the Barbary corsairs,—and finally, to protect the interests of English commerce with Portugal and the Straits of Gibraltar, then fiercely menaced by Biscayan and other Spanish privateers.

The Commonwealth expected full and daring service from its officers. But however much was hoped in England from the Admiral's genius and good-fortune, the wonders of this winter cruise and the brilliant action with which it closed in the early spring at Santa Cruz surpassed every expectation. For the first few weeks, the Spaniards affected to laugh at a madman who could dream of riding in that tempestuous ocean for a whole winter. Nevertheless, October and November passed away; and though daily storms scattered the squadron, carrying some of the frigates to the African ports, others into the Straits, and now and then an unfortunate vessel as far as Cape St. Vincent, the bay was never free from the enemy: and after a day or two of decent weather, the fleet was found riding in all its strength across the entrance to Cadiz. Opinion then worked gradually round. The citizens began to fear that nature would probably not fight their battle as effectually as they had hoped. If the American fleet was to come in, other means of defence must be considered. Some rich merchants at last offered to fit out a powerful squadron. At their expense eight royal galleons were prepared; guns were put on board twelve traders of heavy burden; and a solemn appeal was made to the chivalry of Spain to go on board the relief squadron as volunteers, and in that capacity make one grand effort to dislodge the enemy from his insulting position. Much was expected from this appeal; several spirited gentlemen offered their services, and the agents talked in heroic measures of their intended feats:—but for some reason not known to the English, the squadron did not venture outside the passage, and Blake continued master at sea. About mid-winter, De Ruiter anchored off the bar of San Lucar with nine or ten Dutch men-of-war; and the opinion current in diplomatic circles in the south of Europe was, that he intended openly to join the Spaniards against England. European diplomacy was probably well acquainted with the secret leanings of the States-General; but it erred in assuming that they would have the courage to declare their preference, and take upon themselves the consequences of their friendship for Spain. They rather chose to work for her in secret. Under false flags and with forged papers they from time to time carried succours to Cadiz and San Lucar; in the name of the Genoese they built and equipped in their dockyards as many frigates and men-of-war as would have formed a powerful fleet; and indeed at that very moment they had six magnificent ships, of from sixty to seventy guns each, on the stocks nearly finished. But De Ruiter carefully abstained from any offence against the red cross. He made a show of the profoundest respect for Blake personally, and sailed away into the Mediterranean, as he pretended on a voyage against the pirates of Algiers and Tripoli.

The English were compelled to rule the Barbary powers with a rod of iron. A few months ago the Admiral had paid his promised visit to Salee, when he summoned the formidable rovers of that port to a consultation; but as the barbarians did not for the space of two days comply with his request, he drove two of their fleetest vessels on the rocks and broke them into fragments, threatening to deal in like manner with their entire fleet if they persisted in their refusal to treat with him according to the usages of nations. The Prince of Salee had already learned by the example of Tunis that Blake never threatened in vain, and on receiving this peremptory intimation he sent an agent to the Naseby. The sudden recal of the fleet towards the Bay of Cadiz, in expectation of the Silver Fleet, had prevented the formal conclusion of a treaty; but the rovers became more guarded from that time in their interference with English merchants. Early in February a violent storm in the Bay of Cadiz drove the blockading fleet towards the Straits, and the heavy gales increasing, Blake ran into Tetuan, a Morocco port just within the Straits, for shelter; and as some questions had arisen between him and the Dey of Algiers, ere he returned to Cadiz, he ran along the coast to that city, paid the Dey a flying visit, and arranged all his difficulties without having to fire a single shot. The affair of Porto Ferino had relieved him from the necessity of any more fighting with the pirates. In passing Tangier, then a settlement of the Portuguese, he found it closely invested by the Moors, and so severely distressed as to be not unlikely to fall into their hands. In the high spirit of Christian chivalry he detached a

part of his fleet to relieve the garrison, break the besiegers' lines and support the interests of the new King
of Portugal, Alphonso VI., on those shores:—a service
which had the happy effect of saving the town and
drawing still closer the bonds of friendship established
by his means between London and Lisbon.

Discontents arose and multiplied in Spain.  The loss
of one Silver Fleet and the long delay of another rendered money scarce, crippling both public and private
means.  New taxes had to be imposed.  Voluntary gifts
and loans were tried,—and many Hidalgo families stript
themselves of part of their ancient wealth to uphold the
glory of their King.  The Church also contributed its
blessing and its money towards the support of a war
against heretics.  But these donations went a short
way towards meeting the enormous expenditure; and
in its hour of need government was compelled to exact
a fifth part of the estates, stock and property of every
merchant in the empire.  Thousands were ruined by
this sweeping measure.  Trade almost ceased.  The
Spanish dollar rose in value; debts were left unpaid;
and many of the most princely residents of Cadiz and
Seville were broken in their fortunes.  In England
the splendour of victory, the humiliation of a haughty
foe, and the sight of wagons filled with captured gold
and silver, helped to sustain the popularity of the war;
but the trading interests suffered severely from the
corsairs of Brest and the Bay of Biscay.  The amount
of money taken from the enemy was slight when compared with the losses of private persons.  Few indeed
gained by the war except the privateers of the two
nations, and that band of lawless adventurers who
plundered peaceful traders under cover of any flag
which it suited them for the moment to unfurl.

Nothing excites more wonder and admiration than

the poverty of means with which this bold watch and guard was maintained. Hardly a single ship was seaworthy. The Fairfax, the Worcester, the Plymouth, the Newcastle, the Foresight, were all seriously damaged. Some were short of a mast, others had no powder; all were in want of spars, canvass, hemp and stores. Worst of all, sickness had carried off the ablest seamen of the fleet; and more than one of the frigates had not sufficient hands for the ordinary working service, much less for war. On the 11th of March, 1657, Blake writes from before Cadiz to the Admiralty:

"Our fleet at present, by reason of a long continuance abroad, are grown so foul, that if a fleet outward bound should design to avoid us, few of our ships would be able to follow them up. I have acquainted you often with my thoughts of keeping out those ships so long, whereby they are not only rendered in a great measure unserviceable, but withal exposed to desperate hazards: wherein, though the Lord hath most wonderfully and mercifully preserved us hitherto, I know no rule to tempt Him, and therefore again mind you of it, that if any such accident should for the future happen to the damage of his Highness and the nation—which God forbid—the blame may not be at our doors, for we account it a great mercy that the Lord hath not given them [the Spaniards] the opportunity to take advantage of these our damages. Truly our fleet is generally in that condition, that it troubles me to think what the consequence may prove if such another storm, as we have had three or four lately, should overtake us before we have time and opportunity a little to repair. Our number of men is lessened through death and sickness, occasioned partly through the badness of victuals and the long continuance of poor men at sea. The captain of the Fairfax tells me, in particular, that they are forced to call all their company on deck whenever they go to tack.  Therefore (I) desire that, if you intend us to stay out this summer, or any considerable part thereof, that you will forthwith send us a sufficient supply of able seamen."

But Cromwell was too busy with his own schemes to think of the brave men who were fighting the battles of their country on a distant station.  No succours were sent out; nothing but apologies and excuses.  The Lords of Admiralty said they were sorry to hear of his illness; sorry also to hear of the wretched state of his ships; but they could not promise him any immediate aid, because the Lord Protector's time was completely taken up with Parliamentary intrigues, the great question of Kingship being then under consideration.  The events of the next few days, however, put an end to the tasks which held the sick Admiral a sort of prisoner in those waters.  Letters of intelligence came to hand announcing that the second Silver Fleet, consisting of six royal galleons and sixteen other great ships, was on its way towards Europe; but that having heard of the former disaster, and learning that the enemy was still in force before the Bay of Cadiz, it had run for safety into harbour in one of the Canary Islands.  At first this news was of a doubtful nature; perhaps an invention of the Spaniards to draw him from his post; certainly it was too vague a report to justify a run with his whole squadron into a latitude so remote; but several hands, unknown to each other, furnished Blake with the same intelligence, and his habitual caution at last admitted that there were grounds for trusting to the general accuracy of his information.  Finding that the fleet already prepared for sea, did not venture forth, he arranged his plans, called in his cruisers, and on the 13th of April set sail with his whole force, now recruited to twenty-five ships and frigates, for those islands.  Don

Diego Diagues, the Spanish Admiral at Santa Cruz, had news of Blake's intended movement, and he made instant preparations to give the assailants a warm reception should they venture to attack his fleet. The port of Santa Cruz was then one of the strongest naval positions in the world. The harbour, shaped like a horseshoe, was defended at the north side of the entrance by a regular castle, mounted with the heaviest ordnance and well garrisoned; along the inner line of the Bay seven powerful forts were disposed; and connecting these forts with each other and with the castle was a line of earthworks, which served to cover the gunners and musketeers from the fire of an enemy. Sufficiently formidable of themselves to appal the stoutest heart, these works were now strengthened by the whole force of the Silver Fleet. The precious metals, pearls, and jewels were carried on shore into the town; but the usual freightage, hides, sugar, spices, and cochineal, remained on board, Don Diego having no fears for their safety. The royal galleons were then stationed on each side the narrow entrance of the Bay; their anchors dropped out, and their broadsides turned towards the sea. The other armed vessels were moored in a semicircle round the inner line, with openings between them so as to allow full play to the batteries on shore in case of necessity. Large bodies of musketeers were placed on the earthworks uniting the more solid fortifications; and in this admirable arrangement of his means of resistance Diagues waited with confidence the appearance of his English assailants.

On the evening of Saturday, April 18th, the foremost of the English frigates sighted what they believed to be the nearest point of land in the Canary Islands; but the weather was extremely thick and hazy, and it was noon on Sunday before they were certain of their exact bearings. This circumstance afforded Diego timely warning of their approach. Next morning, Monday, the red cross of the Commonwealth was descried at daybreak from the royal galleons; the fleet appearing about three leagues distant, under crowded sail and bearing in before a stiff breeze. A Dutch captain, who had seen something of the late war, happened to be lying at that moment in the Santa Cruz roadstead with his vessel; when he saw the Sea-General's pennon floating on the wind, and the frigates in advance making direct for the harbour, he felt they were bent on mischief, and anxious to avoid any portion of the hard knocks likely to be given in the coming fray, he went to the Spanish Admiral and asked permission to retire. Diagues smiled at his fears. Why, his naval force alone was almost equal to the English. The royal galleons were mounted with the finest brass ordnance in the world. Their broadsides would oppose a living wall of fire against assault. With his castles, batteries, and earthworks, his powerful and spirited garrison, his double line of war-ships, he considered, and not unreasonably considered, that his position was impregnable. The Dutchman shook his head: "For all this," he said, "I am very sure that Blake will soon be in among you."—"Well," replied the haughty Spaniard, "go, if you will; and let Blake come if he dare."—The Dutchman returned to his ship, hoisted sail, and escaped the destruction which awaited every vessel afloat within the Bay of Santa Cruz that fatal morning.

As soon as day dawned on the English fleet, a frigate, which had been sent forward in the night for that purpose, signalled to the Swiftsure the welcome intelligence that the whole body of the Silver Fleet lay at anchor within the harbour. Thereupon Blake roused from his sick-bed by the prospect of action, called a council of war, stated the case in a few brief and pregnant words, and ended with a proposal to ride into the port and attack the enemy in his formidable position. The shape of the harbour, the situation of the great castle, and the direction of the wind—then blowing steadily landwards—made it useless to think of bringing off the royal galleons. It only remained therefore to destroy them where they stood, with their threatening broadsides pointing towards the English ships. Many thought this scheme would be equally impossible to carry out; but the captains who had served in the attack on Porto Ferino had no doubt of the bold conception of their general being brilliantly executed. At least it was resolved to make the attempt. Between six and seven o'clock, a solemn prayer was offered to the Disposer of events: no oath, no irreverent ribaldry was ever heard on board that fleet; no rum or brandy was given out on the eve of battle; but every man on those gallant ships knelt down humbly, and in that fervent spirit which was in all trials and temptations the Roundheads' sustaining fire, asked the God of battles to bless His people, and put forth His right arm in support of the good cause. At seven all was ready—the sailors had breakfasted and prayed. A division of the best-equipped and most powerful ships was then drawn off and sent forward under the gallant Stayner to attack the royal galleons and force an entrance into the harbour; Blake reserving to himself the task of silencing the castles and batteries on land. Stayner's old frigate, the Speaker, now bearing his pennon as Vice-admiral, led the van of this attacking squadron right at the entrance, unchecked by the tremendous broadsides of the galleons and regardless of the terrific flanking fire from the castle and batteries. In a space of time almost incredibly short he had passed the outer defences and established himself near the royal galleons, in the centre of a huge semicircle of shot. Blake instantly followed with the remainder of his fleet, and covering Stayner's flank with his frigates, so as to leave him free to fight the great ships without interruption from the batteries on shore, he commenced a furious cannonade on the whole line of defences, and especially against the castle. The Spaniards fought throughout the day with desperate valour, and for some hours the old peak of Teneriffe witnessed a scene which might almost be compared with one of its own stupendous outbursts. The Spanish musketeers kept up a destructive fire from behind the covered way. Yet in spite of the highest courage, unanimity and conduct on the side of the defence, the cannonade along the earthworks gradually slackened. One by one the batteries ceased to answer. Before twelve o'clock Blake was able to leave the completion of this part of his task to a few well-stationed frigates, while he turned with the main body to the assistance of Stayner, engaged for four hours in an unequal contest with galleons of greatly superior force in men and guns. Diagues made heroic efforts to recover his failing ground; but it was now too late to turn the tide of victory. By two o'clock the battle was won. Two of the Spanish ships had gone down, and every other vessel in the harbour, whether royal galleon, ship-of-war, or trader, was in flames. Miles and miles round the scene of action, the lurid and fatal lights could be seen, throbbing and burning against the dull sky. The fire had done its work swiftly and awfully. Not a sail, not a single spar was left above water. The charred keels floated hither and thither. Some of them filled and sank. Others were thrown upon the strand. Here and there the stump of a burnt mast projected from the surface; but not a single ship—not a single cargo—escaped destruction. All went down together in the tremendous calamity.

Their victory complete, the next care of the English was to get away safely from the Bay, as the great guns of the castle at its entrance, supplied with fresh gunners, kept up a deadly fire. Blake's plan, when he stood with a strong breeze into Santa Cruz, seems to have been to fight and destroy the Spanish galleons, first silencing as many of the land-batteries as might be necessary to that end, and then to retire with his fleet from the harbour at the ebb-tide; but just as the devouring flames had got safe hold of the Spaniards' hulls, ensuring the complete destruction of their ships, the wind began to veer a little towards the south-west—a change, as the pious sailors remarked, which had not been known to occur on that coast for many years—and by skilful management the whole squadron came out of the Bay with one slight accident, the striking of a frigate on an unknown rock. But she got off without serious damage; and by seven o'clock in the evening all the ships were out in the Bay beyond gun-range. The loss of the Spaniards was immense. The finest part of their Silver Fleet was utterly annihilated: ships, guns, equipments, cargoes, all were gone. Considering the many disadvantages under which they had fought, the losses of the English were comparatively unimportant. Not a single ship was missing at the muster; but several frigates, particularly the Speaker, were rendered unfit for further service. The slain amounted to no more than 50; the wounded were about 150 in number.

Perhaps no naval action has ever been more warmly admired and more curiously criticised than this attack on Santa Cruz. "Of all the desperate attempts," says royalist Heath, "that were ever made in the world against an enemy by sea, this of the noble Blake's is not inferior to any."—"The whole action," writes Clarendon "was so miraculous, that all men who knew the place concluded that no sober man, with what courage soever endued, would ever undertake it; whilst the Spaniards comforted themselves with the belief that they were devils and not men who had destroyed them in such a manner. And it can hardly be imagined how small loss the English sustained in this unparalleled action; no one ship being left behind, and the killed and wounded not exceeding two hundred men, when the slaughter on board the Spanish ships and on the shore was incredible." On the other side, it has been alleged by Sir Philip Warwick and later writers, that when Blake stood into the Bay of Santa Cruz there was no reasonable probability that the wind would change when the work of destruction was effected; that had it not changed, the squadron would have been wind-bound within reach of the great artillery of the castle for an indefinite period; that, in short, nothing less than the unexpected turn of wind could have saved the fleet which his rashness had placed in such imminent peril.

To these criticisms it would probably be a sufficient answer to say, that during his whole naval career the great Admiral never made a serious mistake: even his unequal and disastrous encounter with Tromp in the Downs was defensible on political and naval grounds. The best proof, however, that he could bring his fleet out of the harbour when its work was done, is the fact that he did bring it out; had it appeared to him desirable for the ships to remain at anchor under the castle-guns there is no reason to believe that they would have been unable to hold their position. Masters of the harbour for twelve hours, it would have been easy to remain masters for twelve days. Nor is it clear that the change of wind took place before the fleet quitted the Bay — as accounts written on the spot represent

that change as occurring after the muster in the offing
—when a speedy return to Spain, not an escape from
Santa Cruz, figures as the great object of providential
interposition.

Intelligence of this great naval exploit reached London
as Cromwell's second Parliament was drawing its first
session to a close. The excitement was extreme. Popular ballads, in which Antichrist and the Inquisition were
treated with disdainful waggery, were sung at every
street-corner under the fantastic and picturesque gables
of old London. The Lord Protector sent his secretary
down to the House with the letter of details; and when
honourable members had heard the whole story from
Blake's own hand, they tendered him the thanks of the
country for his eminent services, and voted five hundred
pounds for the purchase of a jewel to be given him as
a mark of honour and respect. The House partook of
the liberal enthusiasm which filled the cities of London
and Westminster. The representatives gave one hundred pounds to Captain Story, the messenger of such
glorious news. They ordered a letter of thanks to be
written to the officers of the fleet. Finally, they set
apart an early day for a solemn national thanksgiving.

Cromwell himself wrote to the dying General a letter
of thanks and congratulation:

Sir,—I have received yours of the [20th April], and
thereby the account of the good success it hath pleased
God to give you at the Canaries, in your attempt upon
the King of Spain's ships in the Bay of Santa Cruz. The
mercy therein to us and this Commonwealth is very signal, both in the loss the enemy hath received, as also in
the preservation of our ships and men, which indeed was
very wonderful, and according to the wonted goodness
and loving-kindness of the Lord, wherewith His people

hath been followed in all these late revolutions; and call for on our part, that we should fear before Him, and still hope in His mercy. We cannot but take notice also, how eminently it hath pleased God to make use of you in this service, assisting you with wisdom in the conduct, and courage in the execution; and have sent you a small jewel, as a testimony of our own and the Parliament's good acceptance of your carriage in this action. We are also informed that the officers of the fleet and the seamen carried themselves with much honesty and courage, and we are considering of a way to shew our acceptance thereof. In the meantime we desire you to return our hearty thanks and acknowledgments to them. Thus beseeching the Lord to continue His presence with you, I remain your very affectionate friend."

The favourable wind which brought the squadron out of Santa Cruz carried it once more at a steady and rapid pace to the shores of Andalusia; but intelligence of the terrible disaster at the Canaries had already reached the merchants of Cadiz, and new endeavours were made to induce the States-General of Holland to unite with Spain in a league against the proud and victorious islanders. Dutch statesmen, alarmed at the extraordinary growth of English influence at sea, were disposed to entertain the advances made to them by their ancient and mortal enemies; they expedited the preparations of their fleet, and raised it to a force of seventy sail. Cromwell's ministers could obtain no satisfactory explanation of the reasons for this armament or of the service on which it was to be employed; and as soon as the battle of Santa Cruz had disabled Spain for some time, they wrote to inform Blake of their fears and uncertainties, and to beg that he would return with convenient haste to England. Warned of these intrigues with the States-General, the English frigates kept strict watch over the motions of the Dutch squadron in those seas, and soon found that, while declining to commit themselves to the hazards and expenses of another naval war, the officers readily engaged themselves to bring into Cadiz and other ports the gold and silver landed at Santa Cruz, by order of Don Diego Diagues, before the late attack. Aware of the contract, Blake declared these Dutchmen lawful prizes; and instructed the captains of his cruisers to chase, capture or destroy them whenever found with Spanish cargoes on board. By these prompt measures several of their ships and frigates were taken, laden in great part with gold and silver from that island. One of these Dutch vessels was reported to have a million pieces of eight on board. Another of his captures, the Flying Fame of Amsterdam, ran on shore near Suebra, in order to save the cargo; but it was got off again at full tide by the English frigates: it had 448 Spaniards, passengers from the Canaries, on board, besides a very valuable freight. Remonstrances were of course made by the Ambassadors of Holland against this rigorous policy. But Blake had little patience with the wiles and subterfuges of diplomacy. His object in those seas was to destroy the trade, the resources, the fleets of Spain; he considered its gold and silver, its pearls and precious stones, its spices, sugar, hides and cochineal lawful prey; and in whatever bottoms or under whatever flag he found these articles, he believed his right to seize them indisputable. The Dutchmen railed and spouted — but they kept the peace. From Norway to Barbary the echoes of Blake's thunder had been heard. The wavering were confirmed in their friendship for the Commonwealth; States which had so far proudly held aloof evinced the desire to cultivate a closer alliance; false friends suddenly grew eager and demonstrative in their civilities. To use the emphatic words of our agent at Lisbon, the English were "every where held in terror and honour."

But the hero's health was now failing fast. The excitement of Santa Cruz had fearfully augmented his disorders; his friends could see that he was nigh to death. Want of rest, want of fresh food and wholesome wine, strain of heart and of intellect, the fester of an unhealed wound, the wrack and waste of a cruise un-exampled in activity and in success, had done their work even on his vigorous constitution. He had gained his victory, but he had sacrificed his life. He had only to come home and die. Few commanders have ever won so entirely the love, devotion, adoration of their officers and men. It was an article of faith for the captains to believe in his genius and fortune. The common sailors would have leapt into the sea, or rushed into the cannon's mouth, to gain a word of approbation from his lips. But their hearts refused to believe that he who had taught them to fight in fire and in water, who had courted death in plague, in tempest, and in battle, was now dying in the midst of victory. For himself, he knew that his work was nearly finished. And he was most anxious, if God were willing, to go home, and die in his native town. He had his country's express permission to return should he think it useful to the service; but it lay on his conscience to perform one other task before he quitted for ever the seas in which he had kept his glorious watch. He felt bound to pay a second visit to Salee, and compel the Moorish corsairs to restore the Christian captives to their freedom, and enter into a treaty of peace with England. This visit to Salee was his last, and, in the opinion of gentle hearts, his most illustrious action. An accident had formerly defeated his attempt to exact reparation from these formidable pirates for the injuries inflicted by them on English commerce; before he finally quitted the southern waters, he considered it a sacred duty to return to Salee and complete the negociations then suddenly interrupted.

Unlike the pirates of Tunis, Tripoli, and Algiers, who went out to sea in the largest class of war-ships, the Moors of Salee, a town forming part of the dominions of the Emperor of Fez and Morocco, made their excursions in small but well-built and extremely fast-sailing vessels; the bar of the river on which their town was built not affording, even in good weather, more than a depth of ten or twelve feet of water. After a short prevalence of south-west winds, a strong swell of sea always broke on the bar, rendering it impassable for craft of any but the smallest size; so that in winter the pirates were usually compelled to lie still. But with the approach of spring, they would set out in their powerful little frigates, scour the European waters as far as the Bay of Biscay, and the Sardinian sea, rifling unarmed traders, and even making occasional descents on the coasts of Spain and Italy in search of spoil and prisoners. On his second visit to this nest of corsairs, Blake succeeded, without firing a gun, or shedding a drop of blood, in bringing the Moorish Prince to reason:—he had conquered the rovers of Salee at Santa Cruz. The very day on which his frigates appeared off the bar, the Moors accepted his terms; and in less than a week he departed for the north, having taken on board supplies of fresh water, cleared the whole body of Christian captives, and made peace with the pirates.

This crowning act of a virtuous and honourable life accomplished, the dying Admiral turned his thoughts anxiously towards the green hills of his native land. The letter of Cromwell, the thanks of Parliament, the jewelled ring sent to him by an admiring country,—

all reached him together out at sea. These tokens of grateful remembrance caused him a profound emotion. Without after-thought, without selfish impulse, he had served the Commonwealth, day and night, earnestly, anxiously, and with rare devotion. England was grateful to her hero. With the letter of thanks from Cromwell, a new set of instructions arrived, which allowed him to return with part of his fleet, leaving a squadron of some fifteen or twenty frigates to ride before the Bay of Cadiz and intercept its traders; with their usual deference to his judgment and experience, the Protector and Board of Admiralty left the appointment to the command entirely with him; and as his gallant friend Stayner was gone to England, where he received a knighthood and other well-won honours from the Government, he raised Captain Stoaks, the hero of Porto Ferino, and a commander of rare promise, to the responsible position of his Vice-admiral in the Spanish seas.

Hoisting his pennon on his old flag-ship the St. George, Blake saw for the last time the spires and cupolas, the masts and towers, before which he had kept his long and victorious vigils. When he put in for fresh water at Cascaes road he was very weak. "I beseech God to strengthen him," was the fervent prayer of the English Resident at Lisbon, as he departed on the homeward voyage. While the ships rolled through the tempestuous waters of the Bay of Biscay, he grew every day worse and worse. Some gleams of the old spirit broke forth as he approached the latitude of England. He inquired often and anxiously if the white cliffs were yet in sight. He longed to behold once more the swelling downs, the free cities, the goodly churches of his native land. But he was now dying beyond all doubt. Many of his favourite officers silently and mournfully crowded round his bed, anxious to catch the last tones of a voice which had so often called them to glory and victory. Others stood at the poop and forecastle, eagerly examining every speck and line on the horizon, in hope of being first to catch the welcome glimpse of land. Though they were coming home crowned with laurels, gloom and pain were in every face. At last the Lizard was announced. Shortly afterwards the bold cliffs and bare hills of Cornwall loomed out grandly in the distance. But it was now too late for the dying sailor. He had sent for the captains and other great officers of his fleet to bid them farewell; and while they were yet in his cabin, the undulating hills of Devonshire, glowing with the tints of early autumn, came full in view. As the ships rounded Rame Head, the spires and masts of Plymouth, the wooded heights of Mount Edgecombe, the low island of St. Nicholas, the rocky steeps at the Hoe, Mount Batten, the citadel, the many picturesque and familiar features of that magnificent harbour rose one by one to sight. But the eyes which had yearned to behold this scene once more were at that very instant closing in death. Foremost of the victorious squadron, the St. George rode with its precious burden into the Sound; and just as it came within view of the eager thousands crowding the beach, the pier-heads, the walls of the citadel, or darting in countless boats over the smooth waters between St. Nicholas and the docks, ready to catch the first glimpse of the hero of Santa Cruz, and salute him with a true English welcome,—he, in his silent cabin, in the midst of his lion-hearted comrades, now sobbing like little children, yielded up his soul to God.

The mournful news soon spread through the fleet and in the town. The melancholy enthusiasm of the people knew no bounds, and the national love and admiration expressed itself in the solemn splendour of his funeral rites. The day of his death the corpse was left untouched in its cabin, as something sacred; but next morning skilful embalmers were employed to open it; and, in presence of all the great officers of the fleet and port, the bowels were taken out and placed in an urn, to be buried in the great church in Plymouth. The body, embalmed and wrapt in lead, was then put on board again and carried round by sea to Greenwich, where it lay in state several days, on the spot since consecrated to the noblest hospital for seamen in the world. On the 4th of September a solemn procession was formed on the river. The corpse was placed on a state barge, covered with black velvet, and adorned with pencils and escutcheons. Trumpeters in state barges, which bore his pennons, and other barges, carrying the great banners of the Admiralty and the Commonwealth; others again bearing the sword and target, the mantle, crest and helmet, preceded the body. Humphrey and all his other brothers, all the nephews, and other members of his family, together with the secretaries and servants attached to his immediate household, dressed in the deepest mourning, followed. After them came the Protector's Privy Council in their state barge, the Lords of the Admiralty and Navy, the Lord Mayor and Aldermen of the City of London, the Admirals, Vice-admirals and Captains of his fleet, the Field Officers of the army, and a vast procession of civil notables.

In this order they moved slowly up the river from Greenwich to Westminster, where they were received by a military guard and greeted with salvoes of artillery. At the stairs, the heralds re-formed the procession, which then marched slowly through Palace-yard to the venerable Abbey. A new vault had been made for Blake's remains in Henry the Seventh's chapel, and close to that of the great Tudor monarch; and they were lowered into it amidst the tears and prayers of a grateful and admiring nation. Other heroes of the Commonwealth had been already buried within those regal precincts; and on every such occasion loyal tongues had not feared to accuse the new rulers with upstart and indecent pride. But no voice was raised against the interment there of the conqueror of Tromp, the hero of Tunis and Santa Cruz, the liberator of Christian slaves. This illustrious man almost escaped the common lot of greatness; and perhaps no one ever played so conspicuous a part in the drama of history who was followed by less envy, hatred, and other uncharitableness. Personal foes he seems not to have known; and the bitterest enemies of his political creed spoke of what they deemed his errors more in sorrow than in anger. When the imposing ceremonial was closed, a stone slab was laid on the vault,—and they left him in the old Abbey, with no other monument than that of his imperishable renown.

To their eternal infamy, the Stuarts afterwards disturbed the hero's grave. Blake had opposed the King's trial. He had disapproved the usurpation. When he found the sword prevail against law and right, he abandoned politics, like Sydney, Vane, and others of his illustrious compeers, giving up his genius to the service of his country against its foreign enemies. Surely after a life of the most eminent services, the ashes of such a man might have been allowed to rest in peace! The House of Lords, in their zeal for the restored family, gave orders that the bodies of Cromwell, Ireton, and Bradshawe should be dug out of their graves. But even these zealots did not think it decent to molest the remains of Blake. That infamy was reserved for Charles himself. In cold blood, nearly seventeen months after his landing at Dover from the deck of the Naseby, a command was issued by this prince to tear open the unobtrusive vault, drag out the embalmed body, and cast it into a pit in the Abbey yard. Good men looked aghast. But what could the paramour of Lucy Walters, Barbara Palmer, Kate Peg, and Moll Davies, know of the virtues of the illustrious sailor? What sympathy could a royal spendthrift have with the man who, after a life of great employments and the capture of millions, died no richer than he was born? How could the prince who sold Dunkirk and begged a pension from Versailles respect a man who had humbled the pride of Holland, Portugal, and Spain, who had laid the foundations of our influence in the Mediterranean, and in eight years of success had made England the first maritime power in Europe?

A hole was dug near the back door of one of the prebendaries of Westminster:—and the remains of Cromwell's mother, of the gentle Lady Claypole, and of sturdy John Pym, were cast into the same pit with the ashes of Robert Blake.

**THE END.**

1, *Leicester Square, London,*
*October*, 1882.

# BICKERS & SON'S NEW PUBLICATIONS.

*A New Library Edition in 5 volumes, medium 8vo, cloth extra, £3.*

**WRAXALL'S HISTORICAL AND POSTHUMOUS MEMOIRS,** 1722-1784. By Sir NATHANIEL WILLIAM WRAXALL, Bart. With Corrections and Additions from the Author's own MS., and Illustrative Notes by Mrs. PIOZZI and Dr. DORAN. To which are added Reminiscences of Royal and Noble Personages during the last and present centuries, from the Author's unpublished MS. The whole edited and annotated by HENRY B. WHEATLEY, F.S.A. Finely engraved Portraits.

**** The Author left a copy of his "Historical Memoirs of My Own Time" with numerous MS. alterations and corrections, to which were afterwards added Notes by Mrs. Piozzi and Dr. Doran. The present edition is printed from this copy. The Posthumous Memoirs also contain notes by Dr. Doran, and the editor has had the advantage of using a copy of both books, with Notes made by a contemporary of Wraxall, at the time of their original publication. Wraxall left a manuscript containing an additional chapter to his Memoirs, which is now printed for the first time. This edition is completed by the addition of an Index to the two works in one alphabet.

*A New Edition, considerably augmented and carefully revised by the Author,*
*royal 8vo, cloth,* 16s.

**CHAFFER'S HALL MARKS ON GOLD AND SILVER PLATE.** With Tables of Date Letters used in all the Assay Offices of the United Kingdom. Royal 8vo, cloth, 16s.

**** This (6th) edition contains a History of the Goldsmith's Trade in France, with Extracts from the Decrees relating thereto, and engravings of the Standard and other Marks used in that country as well as in other Foreign States. The Provincial Tables of England and Scotland contain many hitherto unpublished marks ; all the recent enactments are quoted. The London Tables (which have never been surpassed for correctness) may now be considered complete. Many valuable hints to Collectors are given, and cases of fraud alluded to, &c.

*Two New Volumes in Illustrated Series of 7s. 6d. Gift Books.*

**NAPOLEON BUONAPARTE, LIFE OF.** By J. G. LOCKHART, with 9 Illustrations by Eminent Artists, reproduced in Permanent Photography and numerous Woodcuts. Demy 8vo, cloth elegant, gilt edges, 7s. 6d.

**WELLINGTON, LIFE OF.** By W. H. MAXWELL. A New Edition, revised, condensed, and completed ; with 12 Illustrations by Eminent Artists, reproduced in Permanent Photography, numerous Woodcuts, and Plan of the Battle of Waterloo. Demy 8vo, cloth elegant, gilt edges, 7s. 6d.

---

**ARNOLD'S (DR. THOMAS) HISTORY OF ROME, AND THE LATER ROMAN COMMONWEALTH.** 5 vols. demy 8vo, cloth, £3.

**** The "History of Rome" cannot be supplied separately.

1, *Leicester Square, London,*

*October,* 1882.

# 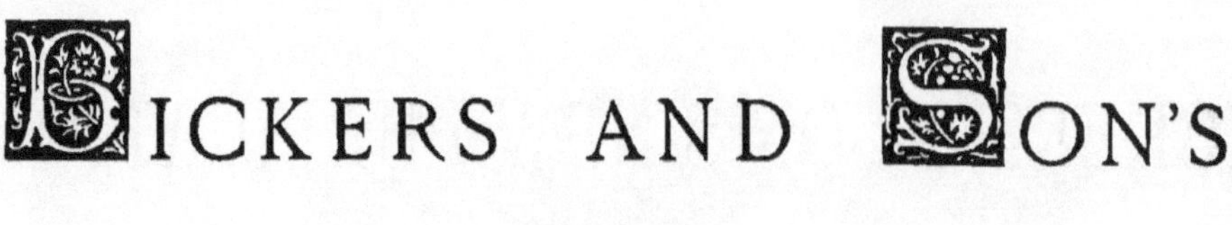 BICKERS AND SON'S

## List

OF

## ILLUSTRATED, STANDARD, AND POPULAR

## Modern Books.

*All new books or new editions are marked thus *.*

---

## *IMPORTANT REMAINDER.*

**BIDA'S ETCHINGS.** The authorized Version of the **FOUR GOSPELS,** with the whole of the magnificent Etchings on Steel (132), after drawings by M. BIDA.

4 vols. folio, appropriately bound in cloth, published at £12 12s., reduced to £4 4s. net.

4 vols. in 2, bound in half-morocco, with gilt edges, £15 15s., reduced to £5 15s. 6d. net.

Or, in best morocco, £18 18s., reduced to £10 10s. net.

*₊* BICKERS AND SON have purchased the entire remaining copies of this superb work, which they offer, for a short time only, on the above exceptional terms. As the stock decreases the prices will be proportionately raised.

---

"An appropriate School Prize."

*A New and Cheaper Edition in One Volume. Imperial 8vo, cloth elegant, gilt edges,* 15s.

**INDIA AND ITS NATIVE PRINCES;** Travels in Central India, and in the Presidencies of Bombay and Bengal. By LOUIS ROUSSELET, carefully revised and edited by Lieut.-Colonel C. BUCKLE. Profusely Illustrated.

*₊* This is not an abridgment, but contains the Complete Text of the superb 4to Edition, with more than half its Illustrations.

# Bickers and Son's Illustrated Series of 7s. 6d. Gift Books.

Demy 8vo, cloth elegant, gilt edges, 7s. 6d.; calf extra, 12s. 6d. each.

*Two New Volumes.*

*NAPOLEON BUONAPARTE, LIFE OF. By J. G. Lockhart, with 9 Illustrations by Eminent Artists, reproduced in Permanent Photography and numerous Woodcuts.

*WELLINGTON, LIFE OF. By W. H. Maxwell. A New Edition, revised, condensed, and completed; with 12 Illustrations by Eminent Artists, reproduced in Permanent Photography, numerous Woodcuts, and Plan of the Battle of Waterloo.

ROBINSON CRUSOE, THE LIFE AND ADVENTURES OF. By Daniel Defoe. With a Memoir of the Author, and Twelve Illustrations by T. Stothard, R.A., in Permanent Photography.

THE PILGRIM'S PROGRESS FROM THIS WORLD TO THAT WHICH IS TO COME. By John Bunyan. With Twelve Illustrations by Thomas Stothard, R.A., reproduced in Permanent Photography.

ROYAL CHARACTERS FROM THE WORKS OF SIR WALTER SCOTT, HISTORICAL AND ROMANTIC. With Twelve Illustrations in Permanent Photography.

THE VICAR OF WAKEFIELD. By Oliver Goldsmith. With Permanent Photographs from Paintings by Mulready, Maclise, and others.

THE GIRLHOOD OF SHAKESPEARE'S HEROINES. A Series of fifteen tales by Mary Cowden Clarke. Rearranged by her sister Sabilla Novello. Illustrated with 9 Photographs from paintings by T. F. Dicksee and W. S. Herrick.

COOK'S VOYAGES ROUND THE WORLD. With an Account of his Life by A. Kippis, D.D. Illustrated with 12 Plates reproduced in exact Facsimile from Drawings made during the Voyages.

DODD'S BEAUTIES OF SHAKESPEARE. By the Rev. William Dodd, LL.D. Elegantly printed on fine paper. Illustrated with 12 Plates, reproduced in Permanent Woodburytype.

GOLDSMITH (OLIVER), THE LIFE AND TIMES OF. By John Forster. Fifth Edition, with 40 Woodcuts.

LAMB'S TALES FROM SHAKESPEARE. By Charles and Mary Lamb. Printed at the Chiswick Press, on superfine paper. Illustrated with 12 Plates from the "Boydell Gallery," reproduced in Permanent Woodburytype.

NELSON, THE LIFE OF. By Robert Southey. Illustrated with 12 Plates by Westall and others, reproduced in Permanent Woodburytype. Facsimiles of Nelson's Handwriting and Plan of Battle of the Nile.

OUR SUMMER MIGRANTS. An Account of the Migratory Birds which pass the Summer in the British Islands. By J. E. Harting, F.L.S., F.Z.S., author of "A Handbook of British Birds," a new edition of White's "Selborne," &c., &c. Illustrated with 30 Illustrations on Wood, from Designs by Thomas Bewick.

**THE NATURAL HISTORY AND ANTIQUITIES OF SELBORNE.** By the Rev. GILBERT WHITE, M.A. Third Edition, with Ten Letters not included in any previous Edition of the Work. The Standard Edition by BENNETT, thoroughly Revised, with Additional Notes, by JAMES EDMUND HARTING, F.L.S., F.Z.S., author of "A Handbook of British Birds," "The Ornithology of Shakespeare," &c. Illustrated with numerous Engravings by THOMAS BEWICK, HARVEY, and others.

---

"THE GEM POCKET EDITION."

**DODD'S BEAUTIES OF SHAKESPEARE.** This exquisite little *bijou* is printed on very fine cream-coloured paper, in the best manner of the Elzevir Press. Cloth extra, 2s.

Or bound in roan, with tuck (like a pocket-book), for travellers, 3s. 6d.

# Lacroix's Works on the Middle Ages and the Eighteenth Century.

*5 Volumes, Imp. 8vo, elegantly bound in Cloth, full gilt sides and leather back, reduced price, £6.*

**THE ARTS IN THE MIDDLE AGES AND AT THE PERIOD OF THE RENAISSANCE,** *New Edition*, including the Chapter on Music. By PAUL LACROIX. 20 Chromo-lithographs and 420 Wood Engravings.

*** This volume can only be supplied with the set.

**MANNERS, CUSTOMS, AND DRESS, DURING THE MIDDLE AGES.** By PAUL LACROIX. Illustrated with 15 Chromo-lithographic Prints and upwards of 400 Engravings on Wood. £1, 11s. 6d. ; reduced to 25s.
Or in calf, super extra, gilt sides and edges, 31s. 6d. *net.*

**MILITARY AND RELIGIOUS LIFE IN THE MIDDLE AGES, AND AT THE PERIOD OF THE RENAISSANCE.** By PAUL LACROIX. 13 Chromo-lithographs and 400 Engravings on Wood. £1, 11s. 6d. ; reduced to 25s.
Or in calf, super extra, gilt sides and edges, 31s. 6d. *net.*

**THE EIGHTEENTH CENTURY.** Its Institutions, Customs, and Costumes. France, 1700-1789. By PAUL LACROIX. Illustrated by 21 Chromo-lithographs and 351 Wood Engravings.

*** This volume can only be supplied with the set.

**SCIENCE AND LITERATURE IN THE MIDDLE AGES AND AT THE PERIOD OF THE RENAISSANCE.** With 13 Chromo-lithographs and 400 Engravings on Wood. £1, 11s. 6d.; reduced to 25s.
Or in calf, super extra, gilt sides and edges, 31s. 6d. *net.*
Sets elegantly bound in the best morocco, super extra, gilt edges, £9, 9s. *net.*

**MUSIC.** A Supplementary Chapter to the Arts of the Middle Ages and paged to follow on that volume. With 21 Illustrations and 1 Chromo-lithograph. Wrapper, 2s. 6d.

# SHAKESPEARE'S WORKS.

### Various Editions.

*A New and Improved Edition, in Ten vols. demy 8vo, cloth extra, price £4, 10s.*

**DYCE'S SHAKESPEARE.** The Complete Works of William Shakespeare. With Notes and Copious Glossary. Edited by the late Rev. ALEXANDER DYCE. With finely engraved Droeshout and Stratford Portraits, and Portrait of the Editor.

" Mr. Dyce's 'Shakespeare' is re-issued in a new and improved form. The importance and value of this work can hardly be overrated. . . . In the edition published by Messrs. Bickers and Son the text is printed as it left Mr. Dyce's hands; but the notes, which hitherto have been placed at the end of the plays, are to be found at the foot of the pages—decidedly an advantageous change."—*Times.*

**SHAKESPEARE'S PLAYS AND POEMS.** Edited, with a Scrupulous Revision of the Text, but without Note or Comment, by CHARLES and MARY COWDEN CLARKE. With an Introductory Essay and Copious Glossary. Four Library 8vo vols. cloth gilt, £1, 11s. 6d.

Or calf extra, £2, 12s. 6d.

*** This splendid edition of Shakespeare's works is copyright, having been carefully revised and amplified by Mr. and Mrs. Cowden Clarke. The Text is selected with great care, and is printed from a new fount of ancient type on toned paper, forming four handsome volumes, bound in cloth extra, calf extra, or in the best morocco.

### 12th Thousand.

**SHAKESPEARE.** The Best One Volume Edition, with Essay and Glossary, by CHARLES and MARY COWDEN CLARKE. Large 8vo, beautifully printed and bound, cloth extra, 9s.

Or calf extra, 15s.

### "The Leicester Square Edition."

*The most charming single volume illustrated edition of Shakespeare ever published.*

**SHAKESPEARE'S COMPLETE WORKS.**—Edited by CHARLES and MARY COWDEN CLARKE. With Portrait and 21 choice Illustrations from the "Boydell Gallery."

Cloth elegant, gilt edges, 15s.

Or calf extra, gilt edges, £1, 8s.

Morocco, blocked, gilt edges, £1, 16s.

**SHAKESPEARE—THE BOYDELL TABLE EDITION.** 2 vols. The above text printed on thick superfine paper, with Sixty-six Illustrations. Cloth elegant, gilt edges, £1, 11s. 6d.

Or, in calf extra, gilt edges, £2, 12s. 6d.

Morocco blocked, gilt edges, £3, 7s. 6d.

*An illustrated Library Edition of Shakespeare, 4 vols. demy 8vo, cloth extra.*

**THE BOYDELL SHAKESPEARE.** The Complete Works of WILLIAM SHAKESPEARE. Edited with a Scrupulous Revision of the Text, by CHARLES and MARY COWDEN CLARKE. With Glossary, &c. Illustrated with 66 Illustrations from the " Boydell Gallery," *price 2 guineas.*

Or, in calf extra, gilt edges, £3, 3s. net.

# 𝔈nglish 𝔊entleman's 𝔏ibrary.

*Demy 8vo, cloth extra (uniform binding), illustrated :—*

**GEORGE SELWYN AND HIS CONTEMPORARIES.** With Memoirs and Notes by JOHN HENEAGE JESSE. With Portraits finely engraved on steel. 4 volumes, demy 8vo, cloth extra, price £2, 2s.

**BOSWELL'S LIFE OF SAMUEL JOHNSON.** With the Tours to Wales and the Hebrides. A reprint of the first quarto edition, the text carefully collated and restored ; all variations marked ; and new notes, embodying the latest information. The whole edited by PERCY FITZGERALD, M.A., F.S.A. 3 vols. demy 8vo, cloth, 27s.

**D'ARBLAY'S (MADAME) DIARY AND LETTERS.** Edited by her Niece, CHARLOTTE BARRET. A New Edition, illustrated by numerous fine Portraits engraved on Steel. 4 vols. 8vo, cloth extra, 36s.

**GOLDSMITH'S (OLIVER) LIFE AND TIMES.** By JOHN FORSTER. The Illustrated Library Edition. 2 vols. demy 8vo, cloth, 15s.; reduced to 10s. 6d. *net.*

**GRAMMONT (COUNT), MEMOIRS OF.** By ANTHONY HAMILTON. A New Edition, with a Biographical Sketch of Count Hamilton, numerous Historical and Illustrative Notes by Sir WALTER SCOTT, and 64 Copper-plate Portraits by EDWARD SCRIVEN. 8vo, cloth extra, 12s.

**MAXWELL'S LIFE OF THE DUKE OF WELLINGTON.** Three vols. 8vo, with numerous highly finished Line and Wood Engravings by Eminent Artists. Cloth extra, 22s. 6d. ; reduced to 15s. *net.*

**MONTAGU'S (LADY MARY WORTLEY) LETTERS AND WORKS.** Edited by LORD WHARNCLIFFE. With important Additions and Corrections, derived from the Original Manuscripts, and a New Memoir. Two vols. 8vo, with fine Steel Portraits, cloth extra, 18s. ; reduced to 12s. *net.*

**ROSCOE'S LIFE OF LORENZO DE MEDICI,** called "THE MAGNIFICENT." A New and much improved Edition. Edited by his Son, THOMAS ROSCOE. Demy 8vo, with Portraits and numerous Plates, cloth extra, 7s. 6d.

**ROSCOE'S LIFE AND PONTIFICATE OF LEO THE TENTH.** Edited by his Son, THOMAS ROSCOE. Two vols. 8vo, with numerous Plates, cloth extra, 15s. ; reduced to 10s. 6d. *net.*

**SAINT-SIMON (MEMOIRS OF THE DUKE OF),** during the Reign of Louis the Fourteenth and the Regency. Translated from the French and edited by BAYLE ST. JOHN. A New Edition. Three vols. 8vo, cloth extra, 27s.

**WALPOLE'S (HORACE) ANECDOTES OF PAINTING IN ENGLAND.** With some Account of the principal English Artists, and incidental Notices of Sculptors, Carvers, Enamellers, Architects, Medallists, Engravers, &c. With Additions by Rev. JAMES DALLAWAY. Edited, with Additional Notes by RALPH N. WORNUM. Three vols. 8vo, with upwards of 150 Portraits and Plates, cloth extra, 27s.

**WALPOLE'S (HORACE) ENTIRE CORRESPONDENCE.** Chronologically arranged, with the Prefaces and Notes of CROKER, Lord DOVER, and others ; the Notes of all previous Editors, and Additional Notes by PETER CUNNINGHAM. Nine vols. 8vo, with numerous fine Portraits engraved on Steel, cloth extra, £4, 1s.

*⁎⁎⁎ The above offered in complete sets, 37 vols. uniformly bound.*

|  | £ | s. | d. |
|---|---|---|---|
| Cloth . . . . . . . . . . . . . . . *net* | 13 | 15 | 0 |
| Half Calf . . . . . . . . . . . . . ,, | 18 | 5 | 0 |
| Calf extra . . . . . . . . . . . . ,, | 21 | 15 | 0 |
| Tree marbled calf . . . . . . . . . ,, | 23 | 0 | 0 |

## Reprints of Standard Authors.

NO HANDSOMER LIBRARY BOOKS HAVE EVER ISSUED FROM THE PRESS.

*Each Work is carefully edited, collated with the early copies, and printed in the best style on superior paper.*

**ARNOLD'S (DR. THOMAS) HISTORY OF ROME, AND THE LATER ROMAN COMMONWEALTH.** 5 vols. demy 8vo, cloth, £3.

*** The "History of Rome" cannot be supplied separately.

*——— **HISTORY OF THE LATER ROMAN COMMONWEALTH.** 2 vols. demy 8vo, cloth, 24s.

**BUNYAN'S PILGRIM'S PROGRESS FROM THIS WORLD TO THAT WHICH IS TO COME.** Edition de luxe, containing the complete set of 16 Designs by T. STOTHARD, R.A., reproduced in Permanent Photography from a fine proof set of the original chalk-stipple engravings. Elegantly bound in half roxburghe style, gilt top, 10s. 6d. ; or in half vellum, with vegetable vellum sides and gilt top, 12s. (For Cheaper Edition see page 3.)

**COLUMBUS (CHRISTOPHER) LIFE AND VOYAGES OF.** Together with the Voyages of his Companions. By WASHINGTON IRVING. 3 vols. demy 8vo, cloth, 22s. 6d. ; reduced to 10s. 6d. net.

*New Edition, uniform with "Pepys' Diary."*

**DIARY OF JOHN EVELYN, Esq., F.R.S.,** to which are added a selection from his familiar letters and the private correspondence between King Charles I. and Sir Edward Nicholas, and between Sir Edward Hyde (afterwards Earl of Clarendon) and Sir Richard Browne. Edited from the original MSS. by WILLIAM BRAY, F.S.A. With a Life of the author by HENRY B. WHEATLEY, F.S.A. With numerous portraits. 4 vols. medium 8vo, cloth extra, £2, 8s. 0d.

*——— **EDITION DE LUXE** of the above, containing, in addition to the Original Illustrations, 100 Selected Engravings. A few copies remain. Only Sixty (each numbered) were printed. 4 vols. imperial 8vo, half-roxburghe, price £7 net.

**FIELDING'S MISCELLANIES AND POEMS,** forming Vol. XI. of his complete Works. Half roxburghe, top edge gilt, 7s. 6d.

These Poems and Miscellanies have never before appeared in a collected edition of his Works, and will range with any library 8vo edition.

**HERBERT'S POEMS AND REMAINS.** With S. T. COLERIDGE's Notes, and Life by IZAAK WALTON. Revised, with Additional Notes, by Mr. J. YEOWELL. 2 vols. Cloth, 21s.

**JONSON'S (BEN) COMPLETE WORKS.** With Notes, Critical and Explanatory, and a Biographical Memoir by W. GIFFORD, Esq. An exact reprint of the now scarce edition, with Introduction and Appendices by Lieut.-Colonel CUNNINGHAM. 9 vols. medium 8vo, cloth, £5, 5s. ; reduced to £3, 3s. net.

**MILTON'S POETICAL WORKS.** Edited by the Rev. J. MITFORD. With Portrait and Twenty-seven Illustrations by R. WESTALL, R.A. 2 vols, 8vo, cloth, 21s.

**MILTON (JOHN), THE POETICAL WORKS OF.** Complete in one volume. Printed in large type, with Life by A. CHALMERS, M.A., F.S.A. Twelve Illustrations by R. WESTALL, R.A., in Permanent Woodburytype. Demy 8vo, cloth elegant, 9s.

**MILTON (JOHN), THE POETICAL WORKS OF.** With a Life of the Author by the Rev. JOHN MITFORD. A fine Library Edition, printed on rich ribbed paper. 2 vols. demy 8vo, cloth, 15s. ; reduced to 10s. net.

This is an exact reprint, *on superior paper*, of the 2 vols. of Poems in the 8 vol. edition of Milton's Complete Works.

**MILTON (JOHN), THE POETICAL WORKS OF.** With a Life of the Author by A. CHALMERS, M.A., F.S.A. 8vo, cloth, 6s.

Or calf extra, 12s. 6d.

N.B.—This is on thinner paper than the 2 vol. edition above, and is printed from the same large and elegant type.

**MOTLEY'S RISE OF THE DUTCH REPUBLIC.** The Library Edition, uniform with the "History of the Netherlands." 3 vols. demy 8vo, cloth, 31s. 6d. (For One Volume Edition see page 9.)

**RELIQUES OF ANCIENT ENGLISH POETRY,** consisting of Old Heroic Ballads, Songs, and other Pieces of our Earlier Poets, together with some few of later date, by THOMAS PERCY, D.D., F.S.A. Edited, with a General Introduction, additional Prefaces, Notes, &c., by HENRY B. WHEATLEY, F.S.A. 3 vols. medium 8vo, cloth, 36s. ; reduced to 21s. *net.*

*** 25 Copies printed on fine large Paper, price, in half roxburghe, 42s. per vol.*

**SHERIDAN (RICHARD BRINSLEY), THE DRAMATIC WORKS OF.** With a Memoir of his Life by J. P. BROWNE, M.D., and Selections from his Life by THOMAS MOORE. 2 vols. demy 8vo, half roxburghe, gilt top, 21s.

—— **"THE POPULAR LARGE TYPE EDITION."** The above text, reprinted on thinner paper, forming one handsome volume, demy 8vo, cloth extra, 7s. 6d.

**SMOLLETT (TOBIAS, M.D.), THE WORKS OF.** With Memoir of his Life. To which is prefixed a view of the Commencement and Progress of Romance, by JOHN MOORE, M.D. A New edition. Edited by J. P. BROWNE, M.D. 8 vols. demy 8vo, half roxburghe, gilt top, £4, 4s.

**SPENSER'S COMPLETE WORKS.** With Life, Notes, and Glossary, by JOHN PAYNE COLLIER, Esq., F.S.A. 5 vols. medium 8vo. Published at £3, 15s. ; £2 7s. 6d. *net.*

**STERNE (LAURENCE), THE WORKS OF.** With a Life of the Author, written by himself. A New Edition, with Appendix, containing several Unpublished Letters, &c. Edited by J. P. BROWNE, M.D. With Portrait of Sterne, Engraved on Steel for this Edition. 4 vols. demy 8vo, half roxburghe, top edge gilt, £2, 2s.

**TAYLOR'S (BISHOP JEREMY) RULE AND EXERCISE OF HOLY LIVING AND DYING.** 2 vols. medium 8vo, 21s.

*The Library Edition of Lane's " Arabian Nights."*

**THE THOUSAND AND ONE NIGHTS**; Commonly called The Arabian Nights' Entertainment. A New Translation from the Arabic, with copious Notes by EDWARD WILLIAM LANE, Author of "The Modern Egyptians." Illustrated with many hundred Engravings on Wood from original designs by WILLIAM HARVEY. A New Edition in 3 vols. demy 8vo, cloth gilt, price £1, 11s. 6d. ; reduced to 22s. 6d. Or calf extra, £1, 15s. *net.*

***WRAXALL'S HISTORICAL AND POSTHUMOUS MEMOIRS,** 1772-1784. By Sir NATHANIEL WILLIAM WRAXALL, Bart. With Corrections and Additions from the Author's own MS., and Illustrative Notes by Mrs. PIOZZI and Dr. DORAN. To which are added Reminiscences of Royal and Noble Personages during the last and present centuries, from the Author's unpublished MS. The whole edited and annotated by HENRY B. WHEATLEY, F.S.A. Finely engraved Portraits. 5 volumes, medium 8vo, cloth extra, £3.

*** The Author left a copy of his " Historical Memoirs of My Own Time" with numerous MS. alterations and corrections, to which were afterwards added Notes by Mrs. Piozzi and Dr. Doran. The present edition is printed from this copy. The Posthumous Memoirs also contain notes by Dr. Doran, and the editor has had the advantage of using a copy of both books, with Notes made by a contemporary of Wraxall, at the time of their original publication. Wraxall left a manuscript containing an additional chapter to his Memoirs, which is now printed for the first time. This edition is completed by the addition of an Index to the two works in one alphabet.*

## "Vickers and Son's Historical Library."

**MOTLEY'S (JOHN LOTHROP) RISE OF THE DUTCH REPUBLIC.**
A New Edition, complete in 1 vol. medium 8vo, cloth, 9s.  *pp.* 920.

**PRESCOTT'S (W. H.) HISTORY OF THE CONQUEST OF MEXICO.**
A New and Revised Edition, with the Author's latest Corrections and Additions.
Edited by JOHN FOSTER KIRK.  1 vol. medium 8vo, cloth extra, 9s.

—— **HISTORY OF THE CONQUEST OF PERU.**  A New and Revised
Edition, with the Author's latest Corrections and Additions.  Edited by JOHN
FOSTER KIRK.  1 vol. medium 8vo, cloth extra, 9s.

—— **HISTORY OF THE REIGN OF FERDINAND AND ISABELLA.**
A New Edition.  Edited by JOHN FOSTER KIRK.  1 vol. medium 8vo, cloth, 9s.
Prices of above, half calf gilt, 10s.
,,     ,,     calf extra, 12s. 6d.

## Books of Reference, etc.

CHAFFERS' (WM.) MARKS AND MONOGRAMS ON POTTERY
AND PORCELAIN of the Renaissance and Modern Periods, with Histori-
cal Notices of each Manufactory.  Preceded by an Introductory Essay on the
Vasa Fictilia of the Greek, Romano-British, and Mediæval Eras, by WILLIAM
CHAFFERS, Author of "Hall Marks on Gold and Silver Plate," "The Keramic Gal-
lery," &c.  Sixth Edition, revised and considerably augmented, with 3,000 Potters'
Marks and Illustrations, and an Appendix containing an Account of Japanese Kera-
mic Manufactures, &c. &c., royal 8vo, cloth, 42s.

8TH THOUSAND.

**CHAFFERS' (WM.) THE COLLECTOR'S HANDBOOK OF MARKS
AND MONOGRAMS ON POTTERY AND PORCELAIN** of the
Renaissance and Modern Periods.  With nearly 3,000 Marks and a most valuable
Index, by WILLIAM CHAFFERS.  Fcap. 8vo, limp cloth, 6s.

**** This handbook will be of great service to those Collectors who in their travels have occasion to
refer momentarily to any work treating on the subject.  A veritable Multum in Parvo.

* —— **HALL MARKS ON GOLD AND SILVER PLATE.**  A New Edition,
considerably augmented and carefully revised by the Author.  With Tables of Date
Letters used in all the Assay Offices of the United Kingdom.  Royal 8vo, cloth,
16s.

**** This (6th) edition contains a History of the Goldsmith's Trade in France, with Extracts from the
Decrees relating thereto, and engravings of the Standard and other Marks used in that country
as well as in other Foreign States.  The Provincial Tables of England and Scotland contain
many hitherto unpublished marks ; all the recent enactments are quoted.  The London Tables
(which have never been surpassed for correctness) may now be considered complete.  Many
valuable hints to Collectors are given, and cases of fraud alluded to, &c.

**CLARKE'S (MRS. COWDEN) COMPLETE CONCORDANCE TO
SHAKESPEARE,** being a verbal Index to all Passages in the Dramatic Works
of the Poet.  New and Revised Edition, super royal 8vo, cloth extra, gilt top, 25s.
Calf extra, or half morocco flexible back, 30s. *net.*

**FAIRBAIRN'S CRESTS OF THE FAMILIES OF GREAT BRITAIN
AND IRELAND.**  Compiled from the best authorities, by JAMES FAIRBAIRN,
and revised by LAWRENCE BUTTERS.  One Volume of Plates, containing nearly
2,000 Crests and Crowns of all Nations, Coronets, Regalia, Chaplets and Helmets,
Flags of all Nations, Scrolls, Monograms, Reversed Initials, Arms of Cities, &c.
Two vols. royal 8vo, cloth, 42s.

**LATHAM (DR. R. G.), A DICTIONARY OF THE ENGLISH LAN-GUAGE,** founded on that of Dr. S. Johnson, as edited by the Rev. H. J. Todd, with numerous Emendations and Additions. Second Edition, 4 vols. 4to, half-bound morocco, flexible, £4, 10s. *net.*

**LITCHFIELD'S POTTERY AND PORCELAIN, A GUIDE TO COL-LECTORS.** By F. LITCHFIELD. Second Edition, with Illustrations and marks. Post 8vo, cloth, 5s.

**SHAKESPEARIAN THOUGHT (INDEX TO):** being a Collection of Allusions, Reflections, Images, Familiar and Descriptive Passages and Sentiments from the Plays and Poems of Shakespeare, alphabetically arranged and classified under appropriate headings, by CECIL ARNOLD. 1 vol. demy 8vo, cloth extra, 7s. 6d. ; reduced to 4s. 6d. *net.*

**THE THEORY AND PRACTICE OF LINEAR PERSPECTIVE**, applied to Landscapes, Interiors, and the Figure. For the Use of Artists, Art Students, &c. By V. PELLEGRIN. With a Sheet of 16 Figures. Cloth, 1s.

"The Author, himself a painter and accustomed to the manipulation of geometrical methods, was particularly qualified for writing this treatise ; and he has been able, by dint of research and ability, to condense into a small number of pages the laws of perspective, and to extract from a confused mass, rules which are very simple and easily applicable to every possible case."

*** The work has been adopted by the French Government, and is now in general use in the public libraries and schools of France.

## Miscellaneous.

**BOOK OF COMMON PRAYER.** With the Psalter, and with finely-executed woodcut borders round every page, exactly copied from "QUEEN ELIZABETH'S PRAYER-BOOK," and comprising Holbein's "Dance of Death," Albert Durer's "Life of Christ," &c. Crown 8vo, cloth uncut, 10s. ; reduced to 6s. *net.*
Ditto, cloth extra, 12s. ; reduced to 7s. *net.*
Ditto, calf antique, 16s. ; reduced to 12s. *net.*

**BULWER'S (DOWAGER LADY) "SHELLS FROM THE SANDS OF TIME."** A Series of Essays, handsomely printed in crown 8vo, cloth extra, 5s.

**BRERETON'S (REV. J. L.) COUNTY EDUCATION.** A Contribution of Experiments, Estimates, and Suggestions, Illustrated with Maps, Plans, &c. 8vo, cloth, 3s. 6d.
Ditto. Cheaper edition. 8vo, paper wrapper, 2s. 6d.

—— **REPORTS OF THE DEVON AND NORFOLK COUNTY SCHOOL ASSOCIATIONS FOR THE YEAR** 1874. 8vo, wrapper, 1s.

—— **THE HIGHER LIFE.** Attempts at the Apostolic Teaching for English Disciples. Crown 8vo, cloth, 3s. 6d.

**CREED OF THE GOSPEL OF S. JOHN (THE).** Crown 8vo, cloth, 3s. 6d.

**CHRISTIAN YEAR (THE).** Thoughts in Verse for the Sundays and Holy days throughout the Year. By JOHN KEBLE. Exquisitely printed on toned paper, with elaborate borders round every page. Printed at the Chiswick Press. Small 4to, cloth extra, with Twenty-four Illustrations by FR. OVERBECK, reproduced in Permanent Photography. 15s. ; reduced to 10s. *net.*
Ditto, antique calf, £1, 10s.
Ditto, morocco elegant, £2, 2s.

**CHRISTIAN YEAR (THE).** Another Edition, in fcap. 8vo, with Twelve Photographic Pictures by FR. OVERBECK, selected from the 4to edition. Cloth gilt, 5s.
Ditto, calf antique, red edges, 12s.
Ditto, morocco extra, 18s.

—— Another Edition, 32mo, with 6 Photographic Pictures, elegantly bound in cloth extra, gilt edges, 2s. 6d.
Ditto, morocco extra, 6s. 6d. *net.*
Ditto, morocco limp, 4s. 6d. *net.*

**CHRISTIAN YEAR (THE.)** Thoughts in Verse for the Sundays and Holy days throughout the Year. By JOHN KEBLE. Exquisitely printed on toned paper, with elaborate borders round every page. Small 4to, cloth extra, 10s. 6d. ; reduced to 7s. net.
———— Another Edition in fcap. 8vo, without the borders, cloth extra, 3s.
———— Another Edition in 32mo, cloth extra, 1s. 6d.

**DARWIN'S THEORY EXAMINED.** Crown 8vo, cloth, 2s. 6d.

**ELLIS'S (WM.) ENGLISH EXERCISES.** Revised and Improved by the Rev. T. K. ARNOLD, M.A. 12mo. 26th Edition, cloth, 3s. 6d.

**FAMILY PRAYER AND BIBLE READINGS.** 12mo, cloth, red edges, 5s.

**GRAY'S POETICAL WORKS.** Illustrated by BIRKET FOSTER, handsomely printed. 18mo, cloth, 3s. 6d.

**HARTING'S OUR SUMMER MIGRANTS.** An Account of the Migratory Birds which pass the Summer in the British Islands. By J. E. HARTING, F.L.S., F.Z.S., author of "A Handbook of British Birds," a new edition of White's "Selborne," &c., &c. Illustrated with 30 Illustrations on Wood, from Designs by THOMAS BEWICK. Fcap. 8vo, cloth elegant, 3s. 6d. (*See page 3 for 8vo. edition.*)

**HERBERT'S (GEORGE) POETICAL WORKS.** New Edition, edited by CHARLES COWDEN CLARKE, with Introduction by JOHN NICHOL, B.A. Oxon, numerous head and tail pieces. Fcap. 8vo, cloth extra, gilt edges, 3s. 6d.
    Ditto.    ditto.    calf antique, red edges, 8s.

**HEROES OF EUROPE.** By H. G. HEWLETT. A Companion Volume to the Heroes of England. 12mo, numerous Illustrations, cloth gilt, 3s. 6d.

**HUNTINGFORD. A PRACTICAL INTERPRETATION OF THE REVELATION OF ST. JOHN THE DIVINE.** A revised Edition of the "Voice of the Last Prophet." By the Rev. EDWARD HUNTINGFORD, D.C.L. Crown 8vo, cloth, 400 pp., 5s.

———— **ADVICE TO SCHOOL-BOYS.** Sermons on their Duties, Trials, and Temptations. By the Rev. EDWARD HUNTINGFORD, D.C.L. 8vo, cloth, 3s. 6d.

———— **THE DIVINE FORECAST OF THE CORRUPTION OF CHRISTIANITY:** a miraculous evidence of its truth. Crown 8vo, cloth, 2s.

**"JAMMED," AND OTHER VERSE.** Crown 8vo, cloth, 5s.

**LECTURES ON ART,** delivered at the Royal Academy, London, by HENRY WEEKES, R.A., Professor of Sculpture. With Portrait, a Short Sketch of the Author's Life, and Eight selected Photographs of his Works. Demy 8vo, cloth elegant, 12s. 6d.

**MAJOR'S LATIN GRAMMAR.** 11th Edition. 12mo, cloth, 2s. 6d.

———— **LATIN READER OF PROFESSOR JACOBS;** with Grammatical References and Notes. 12mo, cloth, 3s.

———— **INITIA GRÆCA.** 12mo, cloth, 4s.

———— **INITIA HOMERICA.** The First and Second Books of the Iliad of Homer, with parallel passages from Virgil, and a Greek and English Lexicon. 12mo, cloth, 3s. 6d.

———— **MILTON'S PARADISE LOST.** With Notes Critical and Explanatory. New Edition, 12mo, cloth, 5s.

———— **MILTON'S PARADISE LOST.** The Last Six Books. With Notes, &c. 12mo, cloth, 3s. 6d.

**MOAB'S PATRIARCHAL STONE**, being an Account of the Moabite Stone, its Story and Teaching. By the Rev. JAMES KING. Crown 8vo, cloth, 3*s.* 6*d.*; reduced to 1*s.* 9*d. net.*

**PEPYS (SAMUEL) AND THE WORLD HE LIVED IN.** By HENRY B. WHEATLEY, F.S.A. Second Edition. Contents :— Pepys before the Diary—Pepys in the Diary—Pepys after the Diary—Tangier—Pepys's Books and Collections—London—Pepys's Relations, Friends, and Acquaintances—The Navy—The Court—Public Characters—Manners—Amusements—Portraits of Pepys—List of Secretaries of the Admiralty, Clerks of the Acts, &c., drawn up by Colonel Pasley, R.E. Crown 8vo, cloth extra, 7*s.* 6*d.*

**PYTHOUSE PAPERS** : Correspondence concerning the Civil War, The Popish Plot, and A Contested Election in 1680. Transcribed from MSS. in the possession of V. F. BENETT STANFORD, Esq., M.P. Edited, and with an introduction by WILLIAM ANSELL DAY. Demy 8vo, half-bound, 10*s.* 6*d.*

**QUITE A GENTLEMAN.** A short School-boy Correspondence. Cloth, 1*s.* 6*d.*

*** "The little volume entitled ' Quite a Gentleman ' embodies a correspondence between a boy at a public school and his father and mother, the purpose of which is to determine the difficult question, What is it that constitutes the gentleman? Whether the correspondence be genuine or not, there is the ring of reality about it ; and the ideas set forth are admirable in themselves and excellently put, with a manliness of tone and an avoidance of the goody-goody element which is truly refreshing."—*Scotsman*, Dec. 27th, 1877.

*In two Parts, demy 12mo, cloth, 1s. 6d. each.*

**ROYAL CHARACTERS FROM THE WORKS OF SIR WALTER SCOTT.** A Series of Readings for the Young, Historical and Romantic. Selected and Arranged by WILLIAM T. DOBSON.

Part I., 1033-1437 ; Part II., 1470-1745.

"Every teacher knows and has contrasted the difference with which a botanical, geological, or other scientific lesson is drawled over with the interest shown in stories and historical sketches . . . . and therefore the striking and picturesque scenes in the far-off past which are here selected from the works of the great novelist, may live in the imagination and take root in the memory when prosaic facts and dryer theories fail to leave any permanent impression."—*Preface.*

**REMINISCENCES OF THE LEWS** ; or, Twenty Years' Wild Sport in the Hebrides. By "SIXTY-ONE." With Portrait and Illustrations. Crown 8vo, cloth, 5*s.*

"A thoroughly genuine account of sport. If any one wants to understand the consuming passion for the sport of Highland life, let him read this book."—*Spectator.*

**SELECTED PICTURES FROM THE GALLERIES AND PRIVATE COLLECTIONS OF GREAT BRITAIN.** A Series of 150 line Engravings from the best Artists, edited by S. C. HALL, Esq., F.S.A., &c. Proofs on India paper, imperial folio, each Plate printed with the greatest care, and accompanied by a descriptive page of letterpress of corresponding size. Four volumes, in four neat portfolios, pub. at £52, 10*s.* ; reduced to £16, 16*s. net.*

Or, bound in Two volumes, half morocco, elegantly gilt ; reduced to £20 *net.*

Or, in whole morocco, super extra ; reduced to £22, 10*s. net.*

A few copies of ARTIST'S PROOFS, atlas folio, also on India paper, and of which only a few copies were printed, Four volumes as above, in four neat portfolios, pub. at £105 ; reduced to £21 *net.*

Or, bound in Two volumes, half morocco, elegantly gilt, £23, 10*s. net.*

**SHORT LESSONS ON THE PARABLES OF OUR LORD.** Specially for Bible Classes. 2nd Edition, 18mo, cloth, 2*s.*

**THE CHRIST OF THE PSALMS** ; or, The Key to the Prophecies of David, concerning the Two Advents of Messiah. By CHRISTIANUS. 2 vols. demy 8vo, cloth, 12*s.*

**THE THREE PHASES OF CREATION.** An Appendix to "The Christ of the Psalms." By CHRISTIANUS. Demy 8vo, wrapper, 1s. 3d.

**TRIP TO NORWAY IN 1873.** By "SIXTY-ONE," Author of "Reminiscences of the Lews; or, Twenty Years' Wild Sport in the Hebrides." With Illustrations by FREDERICK MILBANK, Esq., M.P. Crown 8vo, cloth, 6s.

**VIRGIL. THE FIRST BOOK OF VIRGIL'S ÆNEID.** With Vocabularies. Arranged by W. WELCH, M.A. 12mo, cloth, 1s. 6d.


## "𝔚𝔦𝔱𝔥𝔬𝔲𝔱 𝔞 𝔐𝔞𝔰𝔱𝔢𝔯" 𝔖𝔢𝔯𝔦𝔢𝔰.

**LATIN.** A COURSE OF LESSONS IN THE LATIN LANGUAGE. 1s. 6d.

**FRENCH.** A COURSE OF LESSONS IN THE FRENCH LANGUAGE. 1s. 6d.

**ITALIAN.** A COURSE OF LESSONS IN THE ITALIAN LANGUAGE. 1s. 6d.

**SPANISH.** A COURSE OF LESSONS IN THE SPANISH LANGUAGE. 1s. 6d.

**GERMAN.** A COURSE OF LESSONS IN THE GERMAN LANGUAGE.
Part I.    1s. 6d.
Part II.   1s. 6d.
Part III.  1s. 6d.

**BOOK-KEEPING.** A COURSE OF LESSONS IN BOOK-KEEPING—Single and double Entry. 1s. 6d.

**** These Treatises, as their titles import, are designed chiefly for Persons who either have not the opportunity or the wish to avail themselves of the services of a Teacher; they will nevertheless be found exceedingly useful to those disposed to study Languages in the usual way—by pointing out to the intelligent Student in what the language consists, and by giving a general notion of its construction, and the leading principles of its pronunciation: these Treatises may render a vast deal of preliminary explanation unnecessary, and so save time and spare much annoyance to both Pupil and Teacher.


## 𝔄 𝔏𝔦𝔰𝔱 𝔬𝔣 𝔑𝔢𝔴 𝔎𝔢𝔪𝔞𝔦𝔫𝔡𝔢𝔯𝔰.

*OFFERED AT GREATLY REDUCED NET PRICES.*

**CADORE; OR, TITIAN'S COUNTRY.** By JOSIAH GILBERT, one of the authors of "The Dolomite Mountains," &c. With Map, Illustrative Drawings, and Wood-cuts, large 8vo, cloth, published at £1, 11s. 6d.; reduced to 17s. 6d. net.

**CATLIN'S PORTFOLIO OF ILLUSTRATIONS OF THE MANNERS, CUSTOMS, AND CONDITION OF THE NORTH AMERICAN INDIANS.** 31 spirited Chalk Drawings, lithographed in tints, 23½ in. by 16½ in. Folio, half-bound, published £5, 5s.; reduced to 21s. net.

**DORAN'S LIVES OF THE QUEENS OF ENGLAND OF THE HOUSE OF HANOVER.** By Dr. DORAN, F.S.A. 4th edition, carefully revised and much enlarged. 2 vols. demy 8vo, cloth gilt, published at 25s.; reduced to 10s. 6d. net.

**ESTIMATES OF THE ENGLISH KINGS FROM WILLIAM THE CONQUEROR TO GEORGE III.** By J. LANGTON SANFORD. Crown, cloth, 12s.; reduced to 5s. net.

**EVANS'S THROUGH BOSNIA AND HERZEGOVINA ON FOOT DURING THE INSURRECTION,** with an Historical Review of Bosnia. Second edition, demy 8vo, cloth extra, published at 18*s.*; reduced to 5*s.* 6*d. net.*

**FIGUIER.—REPTILES AND BIRDS.** Best Library Edition, 307 Illustrations, demy 8vo, cloth, 14*s.*; reduced to 5*s.* 6*d. net.*

**FRESHFIELD (DOUGLAS W.), TRAVELS IN THE CENTRAL CAUCASUS AND BASHAN.** 2 Maps. Coloured Illustrations, and Woodcuts by EDWARD WHYMPER. 18*s.*; reduced to 7*s. net.*

**GELL AND GANDY'S POMPEIANA**; or, The Topography, Edifices and Ornaments of Pompeii, with upwards of 100 line Engravings by Goodall, Cooke, Heath, Pye, &c. Demy 8vo, cloth, extra gilt. Pub. at 18*s.*; reduced to 10*s.* 6*d. net.*

**HORATII OPERA.** Cura M. H. MILMAN. 100 Illustrations. Crown 8vo, cloth. Published at 7*s.* 6*d.*; reduced to 3*s.* 6*d. net.*

**LONGFELLOW'S POETICAL WORKS.** Rossetti's Library Edition (Moxon). Cloth, 7*s.* 6*d.*; reduced to 4*s.* 6*d. net.*
Ditto, calf extra; reduced to 9*s. net.*

**MILTON'S ODE ON THE MORNING OF CHRIST'S NATIVITY.** Cloth gilt, 4*s.* 6*d.*; reduced to 3*s. net.*

**MORAL EMBLEMS.** With Aphorisms, Adages, and Proverbs of all Ages and Nations, from JACOB CATS and ROBERT FARLIE. With Illustrations freely rendered from Designs found in their Works by JOHN LEIGHTON, F.S.A. The whole translated and edited, with additions, by RICHARD PIGOT. 242 Illustrations, beautifully engraved on wood. 4to, cloth elegant, 25*s.* (published at 31*s.* 6*d.*)

**PAST DAYS IN INDIA**; or, Sporting Reminiscences of the Valley of the Soane and the Basin of Singrowlee. By a late Customs Officer, N.W. Provinces, India. Post 8vo., cloth, 10*s.* 6*d.*; reduced to 3*s. net.*

**PICKERING'S DIAMOND CLASSICS.**
Tasso, 2 vols. cloth, 12*s.*; reduced to 5*s. net.*
Petrarch          ,,          6*s.*;      ,,          2*s.* 3*d. net.* .
Dante, 2 vols. ,,          12*s.*;      ,,          5*s.*          ,,

**PORTER'S (MAJOR WHITWORTH) HISTORY OF THE KNIGHTS OF MALTA; OR, THE ORDER OF THE HOSPITAL OF ST. JOHN OF JERUSALEM.** 2 vols. 8vo, cloth, £1, 4*s.*; reduced to 21*s. net.*

**RECOLLECTIONS OF PAST LIFE.** By SIR HENRY HOLLAND, Bart., M.D., F.R.S., D.C.L., &c. &c. 10*s.* 6*d.*; reduced to 6*s.* 6*d. net.*

**RIDICULA REDIVIVA.** (Nursery Rhymes). By J. E. ROGERS. Printed in Colours. 7*s.* 6*d.*; reduced to 3*s. net.*

**SCOTT'S BIBLE.** Last Edition, 6 vols. 4to, calf antique, red edges; reduced to £5, 5*s. net.*

**SHAKESPEARE SCENES AND CHARACTERS.** A Series of Illustrations Engraved on Steel, with Explanatory Text, selected and arranged by PROFESSOR E. DOWDEN, LL.D. Royal 8vo, cloth elegant, published at £2, 12*s.* 6*d.*; reduced to 25*s. net*; or in half-rox., 27*s.* 6*d. net.*

**SKERTCHLEY'S (J. A.) DAHOMEY AS IT IS.** Numerous Woodcuts. 8vo, cloth, 16*s.*; reduced to 5*s.* 6*d. net.*

**SOUTH AMERICA, A JOURNEY ACROSS, FROM THE PACIFIC OCEAN TO THE ATLANTIC OCEAN.** By PAUL MARCOY. 600 beautiful Engravings on Wood, drawn by E. RIOU, and Eleven Maps in colours, from drawings by the Author. Large Paper Edition, handsomely printed on wove paper, with very fine impressions of the Illustrations. 4 vols. small folio, elegantly bound in cloth gilt, reduced to £2, 10s. (published at £4, 4s.)

**SUMNER, DR. (BISHOP OF WINCHESTER), LIFE OF.** During a Forty Years' Episcopate. By the Rev. GEORGE HENRY SUMNER, M.A. With a Portrait. Demy 8vo, cloth extra, 14s. ; reduced to 7s. 6d. *net.*

**THORVALDSEN, HIS LIFE AND WORKS.** By EUGENE PLON. 39 Engravings on Steel and Wood, large 8vo, cloth, £1, 5s. ; reduced to 8s. *net.*

**TYROL AND THE TYROLESE:** The People and the Land in their Social, Sporting, and Mountaineering Aspects. By W. A. BAILLIE GROHMAN. With numerous Illustrations. Crown 8vo, cloth extra, published at 6s. ; reduced to 3s. *net.*

**WHEELER'S TRAVELS OF HERODOTUS.** 2 vols. crown 8vo, cloth, 18s. ; reduced to 5s. 6d. *net.*

**WHEELER'S GEOGRAPHY OF HERODOTUS.** 8vo, plates, cloth, 18s. ; reduced to 6s. *net.*

**WHETHAM'S (BODDAM-) WESTERN WANDERINGS:** a Record of Travel in the United States. 12 full page illustrations, 8vo, cloth gilt, 15s. ; reduced to 4s. 9d. *net.*

**WOLF-HUNTING AND WILD SPORT IN LOWER BRITTANY.** By the Author of "Paul Pendril," &c. &c. With illustrations by Colonel H. HOPE CREALOCKE, C.B. 8vo, cloth, 12s. ; reduced to 4s. 6d. *net.*

## Notice.

**** All Books in this List may be had Elegantly Bound in every style of leather binding. Many are offered at greatly reduced "net prices," and are not subject to the usual discount.*

# THE COMPLETE WORKS OF CHARLES DICKENS.

## POCKET VOLUME EDITION.

### PUBLISHED IN THIRTY ELEGANT LITTLE VOLUMES.

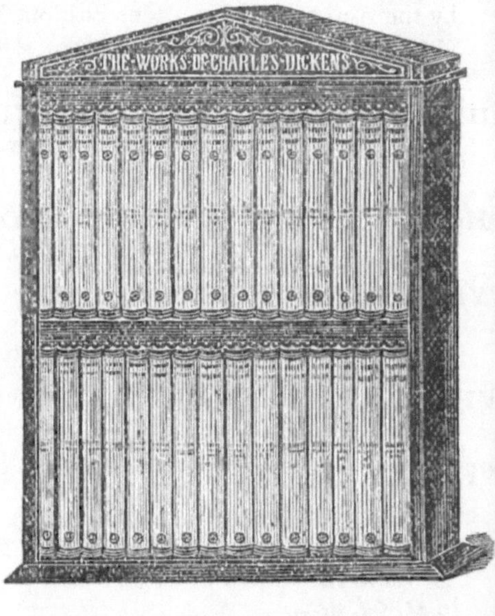


**REDUCED NET PRICES IN CABINET.**

| | £ s. d. |
|---|---|
| Bound in cloth elegant, primrose coloured edges, in handsome cloth cabinet | 1 15 0 |
| „ French morocco, gilt edges, in superior leather cabinet, with lock and key | 5 0 0 |
| „ Best Levant morocco, gilt edges, in elegant leather cabinet, with lock and key | 6 6 0 |

### SIZE OF CABINET.

| | |
|---|---|
| Length | 12¾ inches. |
| Width | 12 „ |
| Depth | 4½ „ |

**REDUCED NET PRICES IN POLISHED EBONISED CASE.**

| | £ s. d. |
|---|---|
| Bound in cloth elegant, primrose coloured edges | 2 0 0 |
| „ Half Anglo-russia, primrose coloured edges | 2 15 0 |

### SIZE OF CASE.

| | |
|---|---|
| Length | 14 inches. |
| Width | 13½ „ |
| Depth | 4½ „ |

The Cabinets and Cases are of the best workmanship, and form elegant drawing-room ornaments. If preferred, they may be placed on ornamental brackets *fixed* to the wall.

*** *This edition may be had in 30 vols. cloth extra, without Case or Cabinet, net price 30s.*

## BICKERS AND SON, 1, LEICESTER SQUARE.

CHISWICK PRESS:—C. WHITTINGHAM AND CO., TOOKS COURT, CHANCERY LANE.